SWIMMING IN DEEP WATER

SWIMMING IN DEEP WATER

A NOVEL OF JOSEPH SMITH

WARREN DRIGGS

Swimming in Deep Water

Published by
Paradise Rim Books
Salt Lake City, UT

ISBN: 978-0-9987795-2-2
eISBN: 978-0-9987795-3-9

Book Design by GKS Creative, Nashville

Library of Congress Information is on file with the Publisher.

AUTHOR'S NOTE

Swimming in Deep Water is a novel. However, while I used the techniques of a novel by embellishing details, inventing dialogue, simplifying complicated events, and dramatizing certain scenes, I have done my best to unfold Joseph's story as it actually happened. This story is based on historical facts and claims, at least with the sober acknowledgement that historical truth is elusive.

All of the central characters are real, with the exception of Ezra Wells, his wife, Rachel, and The Reverend, who are characters of my imagination. While I invented necessary dialogue for the novel, I did not speak for God. Whenever God is speaking through Joseph, I have quoted Him verbatim. However, I found Him to be a bit wordy at times, so I cropped a few of His words.

ALSO BY
WARREN DRIGGS

A Tortoise in the Road

Old Scratch

For Dan

As for the perils which I am called to pass through, they seem but a small thing to me, as the wrath of man has been my common lot all the days of my life. But, nevertheless, deep water is what I swim in; it has always been second nature to me.

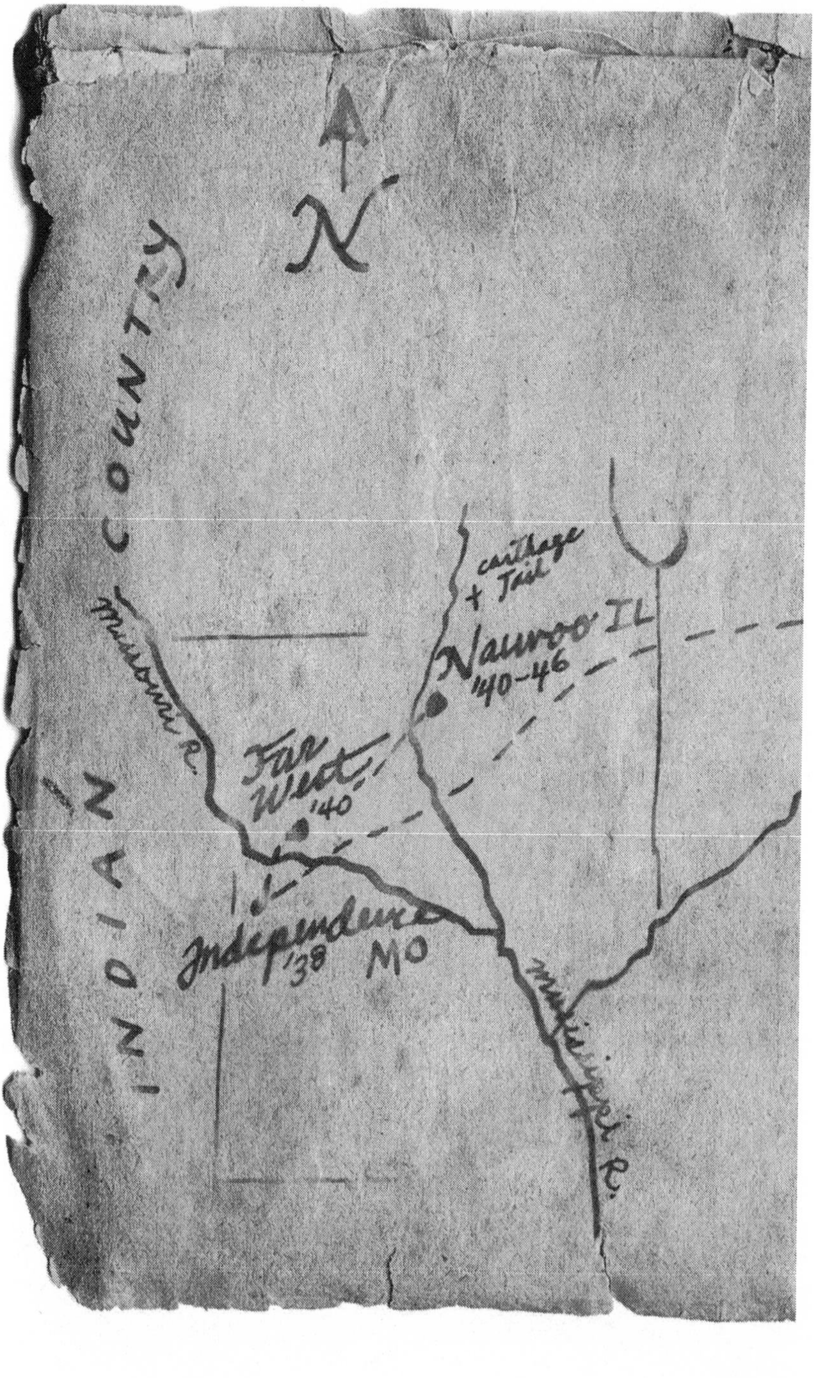
N
INDIAN COUNTRY
Missouri R.
Far West '40
Independence '38
MO
Carthage + Jail
Nauvoo IL '40-46
Mississippi R.

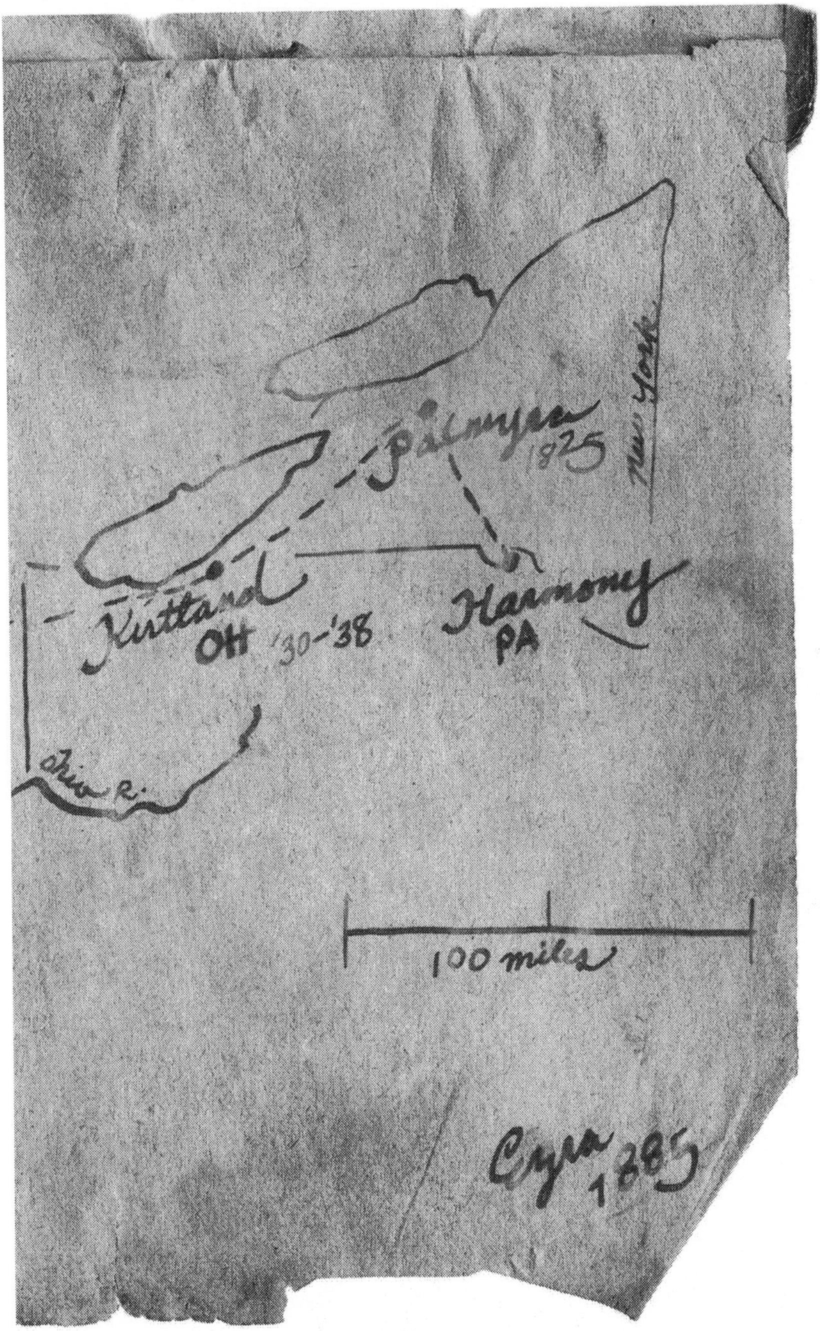

Palmyra 1825
New York
Kirtland
OH '30-'38
Harmony
PA
Ohio R.
100 miles
1885

PROLOGUE

June 1844

"Do you think they'll really kill us?"

Joseph sat on the dirty floor of the cell and stared at his boots. He answered without looking up, "Yeah, I think we're dead men."

Two days earlier, he'd tried to escape by rowing across the choppy Mississippi River in the middle of the night, but Emma told him he was a coward, and the whole town would pay for it. So he rowed back to turn himself over to the law. He would face his enemies who demanded that he be tried for his crimes.

Five of them were crammed into the cell, locked behind a thick wooden door at the top of a narrow staircase on the jail's second floor. There were no bars on the windows. They could have jumped, but they would have landed on the bayonets of the state militia which surrounded the jail. The Governor claimed the soldiers were there to protect them from a lynching, but Joseph and his cellmates knew they'd actually been sent to prevent an escape.

The windows were open because of the summer heat and the militiamen milled about below playing cards, boiling potatoes, and roasting pieces of meat over bonfires. *Shhht, shhht, shhht.* A whetstone slid down the sharp edge of a bayonet. "He's got it comin', you ask me." *Shhht, shhht, shhht.* "Went and got himself an army. Goddamned traitor's what he is." The smell of coffee and bacon wafted up through the windows, but the prisoners couldn't think about their hunger when they were about to be shot.

Ezra hardly slept that first night, and he knew the others didn't either; especially Joseph, who usually kept everyone up with his snoring. But not that night. This was the American frontier, and they knew justice was meted out with swift and capricious irregularity.

The following afternoon they froze when they heard boots on the stairs. There was the jingle of keys and the door opened. The jailer held a bottle of cheap wine and two pipes of tobacco.

"Here, go on and take yourselves some comfort. I figure it's the least I could do for ya."

They sat on the floor and passed the bottle around. The wine had gone bad but they drank it anyway. Willard, Joseph's plump scribe, stood and paced. He was pale and shiny, and there were wet patches under his arms, around his collar, and below his fleshy breasts. He said the wine tasted like vinegar and Joseph reminded them that the Romans shoved a rag of vinegar into Jesus' mouth when he was on the cross. Willard suggested they break the bottle to use as a weapon because all they had was a small pistol which a church member had smuggled into them in the lining of his jacket.

"If I am to be a martyr for the Kingdom, then I will do it willingly," said Joseph as he turned the loaded pistol around in his hands, "like a lamb to the slaughter."

Joseph got up off the floor and lay down on the cot, the only one in the room. He was remarkably handsome, except perhaps for his nose that, in profile, looked like a ship's sail. His golden-brown hair was brushed back from his forehead, and his deep-set eyes were bright blue. He had always been tall and lean, but the excesses of the previous twelve years showed, and now he reclined with his fingers laced together over his paunchy stomach, looking up at the ceiling.

Ezra sat on the floor and watched his best friend. What was he thinking about? Ez wondered. Was he about to have another revelation from God, or was he hatching another plan to escape? Ez marveled at how far they had come, neither of them formally educated, nor the products of privilege. They had grown up surrounded by rocky farmland and grinding poverty. How could Joseph, now only thirty-nine years old, have accomplished all he had if God hadn't chosen him? But then there were the ugly crimes (or the alleged crimes) and the lusty miscalculations. All these thoughts got caught up in the thatch of his brain, roaming around, multiplying and replenishing like rodents, followed by the antidote that exterminated them: the angel and the golden tablets.

"I miss Emma," said Joseph.

No one responded. Hyrum, Joseph's older brother, cracked his knuckles, one at a time, staring at the window but not really seeing it. They all leaned heavy on their thoughts.

"She's a good woman, my Emma. But sometimes I wonder if she ever understood my destiny."

Indeed, she hadn't. She'd wanted to believe him, but maybe her parents had been right all along. Maybe the handsome, charismatic boy she'd eloped with was a ne'er-do-well, or worse, a con man. Oh, but she loved him, even though he'd hurt her with all his philandering. And now she paced the floor of their Nauvoo Mansion, fifteen miles away. More than once, she had promised God that if He would spare her husband one more time, she would never ask for anything else. Now, here she was, again, banging on heaven's door.

Emma's once striking beauty had been eroded by the passage of time, and by God's commandment that she must share her husband with other women. This was a commandment she had been loath to accept in good cheer. It had all been secretive; this sleeping around, and she'd been cursed with the debilitating plague of suspicion, walking through the dusty streets of town wondering which of the women were sleeping with her husband.

The sensibilities of Joseph's nineteenth-century neighbors had been stretched to the point of snapping. It was bad enough that he'd married so many girls, but he'd also secretly married women who already had husbands, something that spawned unhallowed outrage from his enemies.

Joseph also claimed that he would become a god one day. However, he didn't hoard this reward for himself. He promised his flock that if they followed him, they could become gods, too. This God business rubbed people the wrong way. The Mormons, on the other hand, were thrilled to know their suffering would pay off handsomely in the end. Joseph was right, they *were* the Chosen People, and soon Jesus would return and burn their wicked enemies to a crisp. And those enemies would have no one to blame but themselves, because the Mormons had given them every reasonable chance to repent.

The philandering was galling, and there were plenty who wanted to lynch him for it. But that isn't why Joseph and his friends were in jail. The states of Ohio, Missouri, and now Illinois wanted him for more specific crimes, including treason and attempted murder.

In recent weeks, with his enemies marshaling evidence of his flagrant lawlessness, Joseph had felt like a cornered rat. Maybe not a rat, for that would imply that he'd been complicit in this mess, or that he'd erred. No, he felt more like a bull in the ring that had been unfairly tormented, bullied, and wounded, before making its final gallant charge at the cape.

The second night in jail was even longer. It was hot and sticky. The prisoners wore sacred garments underneath their clothes which made it even hotter, but they wore them because they believed the holy garments would provide a shield of protection. They didn't know if the cotton fabric would stop a musket ball, but it might, so they wore them just in case.

Ezra lay on the floor with only a dirty blanket for comfort. He thought about all they'd been through. If they were to be murdered the next day, would it have been worth it? He didn't think so. But did it matter what he thought? Did it matter that they might have done things differently? Maybe it had all been foreordained and they had no choice about any of it. Maybe it was their destiny to be exactly where they were; in that godforsaken jail cell waiting to be shot.

Joseph lay next to him, thinking. Sleep would not come, for he knew history had its eyes on him.

The next day they moved about their cage, straining to hear the sound of their rescue. Then they heard it, the faint hum and quiver of the earth's crust—the sound of horses pounding toward them. Willard bolted to the window and let out a desperate cry, the sound of a wild animal about to be eaten alive. The roiling nausea, and then it came—vomit splashing to the floor.

Two hundred of them, their faces painted black with wet gunpowder, were digging their spurs into the sides of their beasts. It was the enemy. The state militia, which surrounded the jail, did not offer a whiff of protection. Some of the soldiers even began smearing their faces black, too. The prisoners upstairs were frantic. They were trapped with nowhere to hide. The door burst open downstairs and they heard a string of cursing. There was a stampede of boots running up the wooden staircase to their cell. John dropped to his knees in the corner, pleading hysterically for God's mercy. Willard tried to hide under the cot.

"God, help us!" Joseph yelled.

But God remained silent. They were on their own.

PART I

NEW YORK

1820 - 1830

1

The Angel Moroni

A pot-bellied stove in the corner overheated the room and steam rose from the newfangled cast-iron printing press. Cold rain flicked the leaded-glass window, flanked on each side by tools that looked like they belonged in a medieval torture chamber. A fat man with perfect yellow teeth looked out the window. His jowls sagged and his lips were stacked one on top of the other like pillows. He smelled of grease and body odor, and his apron was covered with ink.

"Calm down, Egbert," she said. "He'll come with the money."

"But just look at 'em out there, will ya? They'll skin me alive if I go and print the damned thing."

The woman looked out the window at the horde gathered in the rain, righteous citizens who had formed a committee to boycott the book. The master printer's wife was a large, boneless woman who ordered her husband around the print shop. She had faith the young man would come up with the money, but little faith in anything else, especially the book the handsome lad claimed to have translated from a stack of golden tablets.

She'd read bits and pieces of the book while laying the type, standing on sore feet, organizing approximately twenty words per minute. It was unpleasant work, and she resented her husband for not having made enough money so someone else could do it; a promise he had made to her when the shop opened ten years earlier. And, naturally, he resented her for constantly reminding him of that promise. The book made no sense to her because she read the words in reverse, and because it was written in the form of scripture. And she was normally loath to read scripture.

"I bet he ain't comin'," said the apprentice, a fourteen-year-old boy with a pockmarked face who smelled of piss. His was the unenviable job of tanning hides used to spread the ink in vats of urine, stomping on the hides with his bare feet every morning to soften them up.

"He'll be here, just like he said he would," she said. "Now quit your stallin' and get back to work!"

There was a commotion outside and the door swung open. Joseph shook the rain off like a wet hound and smiled. He was strikingly handsome: tall with blue eyes, golden hair, and noble posture. There was an easy confidence about him, as if he should be welcomed, even admired perhaps, wherever he went.

"Hello, Mr. and Mrs. Grandin! Sorry I'm late. I had a heckuva time getting through the crowd." He smiled good-naturedly and turned toward the window. "See, I told you so. They're already lining up to buy my book!"

"Listen, Joe," the printer said, "you seem like a nice young man, and this here book you went and wrote sounds like one helluva story, but—"

"What he's trying to say," interrupted his wife, "is that we can't finish it, not with everybody up in arms like they are."

"But, you've got to! Here, I have more of the money."

"Look out the window, would ya? They'll run me out of town if I do."

"But we had a deal. You said I could pay the rest when it's done!"

"I know, and I hate to go and renege on it, but . . . ."

"Maybe, Egbert," she faced her husband, "if he pays for the whole thing, up front."

"But I don't have the money yet, and even if I could scare up . . . ."

The printer put out his hand, as if to ward off a verbal blow. "She's right, son. As soon as you got the whole three thousand in hard cash, I'll go and finish it. That's the end of it."

"But—"

"There won't be no 'but.' I've gone and said my piece."

Joseph opened the door to the cold rain that now came at an angle. He hesitated when he saw the angry crowd.

"I'm sorry," the printer said to Joseph's back, which nearly filled the doorway.

Joseph did not turn around. He closed the door behind him and stepped off the wooden sidewalk onto Market Street where ruts from the wagon wheels collected puddles of muddy water. The smell of freshly sawn cedar mixed with the scent of mud. He'd walked the two miles into town and would have to walk back, because the two horses his family owned were needed on the farm.

"So where's your gold Bible!"

"Did the angel go and change his mind on ya? Went and took it back to heaven, did he?"

Joseph was taller than anyone in the crowd of hecklers and stronger, too, having grown hard as stone felling trees and working the small farm with his father and five brothers. He was glad they weren't with him now, because they would have started a riot.

"Repent, young man!"

"Enough of this blasphemy!"

These pious do-gooders knew God would never have sent an angel to the son of Joe Smith, a hard-luck entrepreneur with a weakness for the bottle. So, they'd formed a citizens committee to make sure his Golden Bible never got off the ground.

Joseph looked straight ahead as the crowd made way for him. Because of his height, he had to duck below a sagging, drenched banner strung across the muddy road announcing the upcoming

Palmyra Fair. Needles of rain pierced the back of his neck. He was trim and athletic but walked with a slight limp, the result of typhoid fever as a six-year-old boy. When the infection spread to his leg, his mother had screamed as the country doctor chipped away infected pieces of his shinbone with a chisel. Joseph, it was said, did not even whimper.

Joseph was born into poverty and knew its costs. However, despite their penury, his parents had inoculated this boy, their golden-haired dreamer, with a belief that he was special. This nurture mixed with his nature; the confluence of forces carving the canyon of his character.

His britches were soaked and his hand-me-down boots sucked up the mud with each step as he followed the Big Ditch through Palmyra, a town inhabited by three thousand souls, most of whom were frantic evangelicals looking heavenward with giddy anticipation to the Second Coming of Jesus.

The Big Ditch is what they called the recently built Erie Canal. It ran parallel to the town, and fetched up all the way to New York City, some three hundred miles away. It brought riffraff into town—canallers, dockworkers, and gypsies. Joseph remembered hitching a ride to town on the back of a wagon with his friends during its construction. His mother had warned him about the ladies on Canal Street who painted their faces and dressed immodestly. Ladies of the Night, she'd called them. Joseph smiled when he recalled his confusion because he'd only seen them during the day.

His boots squelched out water as he slogged up the footpath to the small log farmhouse. Daylight showed through cracks where the chinking had sloughed off and rags were wedged into the larger spots to keep the weather out. Handmade furniture reflected their parsimony. In the event of fire, they would save the Bible first, a family heirloom with worn pages that had been dutifully read, cover-to-cover. The Smith boys preferred roughhousing over Bible reading, and it was a wonder their ears weren't deformed from all the twisting during mandatory "scripture time."

Joseph took off his mud-caked boots and dropped them on the porch, then trudged up the stairs to the lone bedroom on the second floor which he shared with his brothers Alvin, Hyrum, William, Sam, and Don Carlos. The brothers were close, and even though they occasionally fought, they knew that having a brother to tease wasn't all bad.

The room was stuffed with thin beds and smelled like dirty socks and teenage hormones. A circular target had been drawn on the wall in chalk, and a pocketknife was stuck in the bull's-eye. A slingshot hung from the blade. Several rusty horseshoes were nailed to the beams in the ceiling, which was low and angled with the A-framed roof, making the center of the room the only place Joseph could stand without smacking his head. He stripped off his wet clothes and tossed them into a mildewy pile, then changed into the only other clothes he owned.

His father hollered up to him when he saw Joseph's boots on the porch. "What did Grandin say? Gettin' it printed up, is he?"

Joseph slumped on the top stair. "He says he won't finish it until I pay it all upfront."

"I thought you had yourselves a deal."

"I know, Pa. He'll still print it; I've just got to finagle a way to pay for it first, that's all."

"But that ain't fair!"

"I guess I'll have to figure out a way. Besides, the angel warned me it wasn't going to be easy."

And indeed, the angel had. It had all started eight years earlier, in 1821, when Joseph was sixteen years old. People in Palmyra had been speculating for years about the piles of human skeletons buried in shallow graves near town, and Joseph's fertile teenage mind had busily explored the possibilities. He regaled the family with tales about the mystery of the mass graves as they sat around the farmhouse, ignoring their chores.

"Those are the skeletons of white men who lived here way before Columbus came over on the ships."

"What happened to them?"

"They got slaughtered by the Indians, that's what."

"The Indians?"

"They were savages, the Indians were, and the white people were scared outta their wits. They thought the Indians would scalp 'em alive."

"Didn't they fight back?"

"Sure they did. But they were outnumbered and the Indians just kept on coming. Finally, the white people made their last stand, right here in Palmyra. Fact, we're standing on the final battlefield right now."

"Really?"

"Yeah, it was a bloody massacre. The Indians didn't take any prisoners; they just slaughtered every single one of them down to the last man. They piled all the dead bodies up because they were too lazy to bury them. Course they tortured 'em first."

"Why'd they do that?"

"They were savages. Why else?"

Joseph said the Indians won the final battle because they were still here when Columbus arrived several centuries later. This made perfect sense.

One day, about a year later, the boys were working in the field when Joseph said he was tired and had to go lie down. Shortly thereafter, his mother breathlessly called everyone in to hear some extraordinary news. They stuck their shovels and picks in the dirt and traipsed over to the farmhouse to see what the fuss was all about.

The family sat on two long benches around the battered table that was splattered with drops of dried candle wax. The boys had carved their initials on it, too, which resulted in double chores for a week. Hyrum tried to blame Alvin, but the prominent H.S. carved into the tabletop with a pocketknife appeared to give him away.

Joseph stood near the hearth with his back to the fire, ready to tell his story.

"Go on," said his mother, who sat over a mending project on her lap. She was a small, wiry woman with graying hair pulled sternly back to a knot at the back of her head. Her face was lined from age and the burden of raising six boys, baking bread, milking goats, and fearing God. "Go on, Joseph. Tell 'em what happened."

"Well," he began, "last night I woke up in the middle of the night because the room got real bright all of a sudden. I looked up and saw an angel standing in our bedroom. He was so bright I could hardly even look at him without hurting my eyes."

"An *angel?* In our *bedroom?*" asked Alvin.

"Uh-huh. He was wearing one of those white robes like angels do and he was floating about a foot off the floor."

"Holy crap!" said Sam.

"Stop it with that language!" said Mother Smith. "I won't stand for that vulgarity in this house!"

"Sorry, Ma."

"Did he say anything?" asked Hyrum.

"Yeah, he said his name was Moroni, and he was an ancient warrior who'd come back from the dead to give me a message."

"What kind of message?"

"He said he used to be a white man whose ancestors sailed over to America from Jerusalem about two thousand years ago. They had special boats with a hole in the top and one in the bottom."

"Wait a second. There were holes in the bottom of the boats? How come they didn't sink?"

"How am I supposed to know? I'm just telling you what the angel said."

"Stop with your interruptin'," said Mother Smith. "Let him finish the story."

"Thanks, Ma," said Joseph. "So, anyway, the angel said when they first got here some of them became wicked, so God cursed them with dark skin. See, that's how they got to be Indians in the first place; it was a curse from God."

"Well, I'll be darned," said Pa Smith. "I didn't know that."

"Me neither," said Sam. "And I didn't know the Injuns used to be white men until they got wicked. But I guess it makes sense when you think on it."

"Why would a ghost wear clothes?" asked William.

The others were stumped for a moment. Since no one volunteered an answer, Joseph continued, leaving the conundrum for future contemplation.

"For the next few centuries the white men and the Indians fought toe-to-toe and their last battle was right here in Palmyra. The angel told me the Indians slaughtered all the white people—wiped them clean off the face of the earth. In fact, he was one of them that got killed and his bones are buried in those mounds by our house."

"So lemme get this straight," said William. "This angel used to be a white warrior and now he's comin' back from the dead to where he got killed?"

"Yeah," said Joseph.

"So, why'd he come back? Is he lookin' for revenge?"

"No. He came back from the dead to tell me there's an ancient book about the history of the people who used to live here. The words are engraved on tablets made out of pure gold. Moroni—remember, that's the angel's name—he said he buried the gold tablets in a hillside during the final battle. He got 'em buried in the nick of time too, because the Indians butchered him right after that. Stabbed him with a sword in the gut and then slit his throat. Luckily, the Indians didn't see the tablets, and they've been buried there ever since."

"So where are they? We oughta go dig 'em up."

"Moroni said he'd show me."

The family was thrilled that an angel had come to their house. But thirteen-year-old William was suspicious.

"If it was so bright and he was talkin' to you, how come nobody else woke up?"

"William!" said Mother Smith. "You hush now and let Joseph finish."

"Yeah, William," said Hyrum, "shut your mouth, or I'll shut it for ya."

"Hyrum H. Smith! I'll not put up with that language either. Not today, I won't. Now, go on, Joseph."

"I don't know why you fellas didn't wake up," said Joseph. "Maybe the angel put a sleeping trance on you or something."

"Tell 'em the rest," said Pa Smith.

"Well, at first I was scared, but then I relaxed and talked to the angel for about a half hour."

"Then what happened?"

"I fell back asleep."

"You fell back asleep after *that?*"

"And you say he was talking for a half hour? That's a pretty long time. I wish I'd woken up," said Alvin.

"Me too," said William.

"Yeah," said Don Carlos, the youngest of the brothers. This simple declaration from Don Carlos caused the others to hesitate because it was so unexpected, as if hearing his voice was worth hesitating over, because he rarely spoke.

"Well," Joseph continued, "the angel came a second time about an hour later. He woke me up again and repeated the exact same thing. I fell asleep again, and a few hours later he woke me up for the third time and repeated everything again, word for word."

"So," said William, "lemme get this straight. You're sayin' this angel came with all that brightness and talkin' three times and none of us in that bedroom ever heard or seen a thing? That just doesn't make a lick of sense."

"William, I won't warn you again! You hear me?" Mother Smith stared hard at him.

"Listen to your mother, William," said Pa Smith. "If the angel said there was gold buried in the mountain, and he'd show Joseph where it was, we oughta be happy, not disbelievin'. Now, go on, Joseph."

"Well, for the rest of the night I did some heavy thinking and that's why I was too tired to finish my chores today, because I didn't get much sleep."

"I can see that," said Pa Smith, nodding to the others.

"And this afternoon I was leaning against the fence post to get some shut eye, when the angel came again."

"Whoa, he came *again?*"

"Uh-huh. He told me the exact same thing, just like the other times. I told him I was worried people wouldn't believe me, but he said I should tell my family and they'd believe me."

"How come the angel didn't bump his head on the ceiling like the rest of us, especially if he was floating in the air?" asked William. "There ain't no room unless he was a midget or something."

"William! I've just about had it with you!" said Mother Smith. "One more word and your father's gonna take out the belt!" She looked at her husband for confirmation.

"Yes, ma'am."

"I didn't want to wake you up," said Joseph, "because you'd be too tired to do your chores today."

"Well, we're not goin' contrary to the angel," said Pa Smith. "Not in this house we won't."

"That's right," confirmed Mother Smith. "We won't spit in the angel's eye. That ain't who we are."

"So when are you gettin' the gold book?" asked Hyrum.

"The angel said I need to prove myself first. He said he'd come back in a year and then he'll decide if I can have it. So, I just have to wait, I guess."

"That's right," said Mother Smith. She lifted the sewing from her lap and bit off the thread. "We just need to be patient with the angel. It makes no sense pushin' him on this."

"She's right, your mother," said Pa Smith, an uneducated man who'd been tormented by sour business deals. When he wasn't working the small family farm, he peddled refreshments from a cart. It seemed the waters had never parted for him. "Course, I hope he'll go and give you the gold book before too long."

2

The Golden Tablets

At roughly the same time Angel Moroni was visiting Joseph, an inquisitive young man of Joseph's age stood on the Plymouth Dock, off the coast of England. He was gangly, with dark brown hair, curly sideburns, and overhanging eyebrows. This young man was serious-minded, the type who sacrificed short-term popularity at school for better grades. He paced the dock, waiting to board the *HMS Beagle* for an historic voyage that would make him famous. His life's work would launch a torpedo through religion's iron hull. But, for now, no one in America had ever heard of young Charles Darwin and religion reigned; especially the fanatical sort that involved speaking in strange tongues, rolling around in spiritual trances, and looking skyward for the Second Coming.

Never was this fanaticism on display more than in Palmyra, New York, an area that had come to be labeled the Burned-Over District, because it had been so heavily evangelized that there was no one left to convert. Preachers competed for souls, ringing God's alarm with frantic enthusiasm lest mankind rot in hell. God was on the lookout for human weakness and when He found it (as surely He would), He'd pounce with righteous fury. Usually it was of Biblical proportion (famine, pestilence, and the like), but sometimes it was as ordinary as mere poverty.

It was against this backdrop that Angel Moroni reappeared to Joseph once a year, on schedule, for four consecutive years. Each time he weighed Joseph's worthiness and found him slightly lacking.

Moroni was deeply proprietary about his gold tablets and refused to hand them over to anyone. In the meantime, Joseph was getting antsy, and so were the skeptical neighbors, who rumored that Joseph was stalling. "He oughta just put up or shut up. That's what he oughta do." His father, hoping to buy time for his son, told them Joseph had tried to get the tablets but there'd been a toad guarding the secret burial spot. The toad once smacked Joseph on the side of the head when he'd tried to touch them. This explanation did not resonate with the neighbors.

On the fourth anniversary of their first meeting, the angel told Joseph he had finally proven himself worthy to take possession of the tablets. The angel insisted, however, that Joseph go alone to fetch them. But when word leaked out that he was going up the hill to get them, he was secretly followed by a gang of treasure hunters. This gang had previously teamed up with Joseph on treasure hunts and claimed they had a gentlemen's agreement to split whatever they found. Regrettably, so far at least, there hadn't been much to split. Joseph had even landed in court for fraudulently collecting money from a gullible, elderly man who believed his land sat on top of a gold mine.

As whimsical teenagers, Joseph and his best friend, Ezra Wells, began their treasure hunting adventures with heady optimism. They found a few arrowheads from the Indian mounds, but the buried gold and silver proved to be elusive. Their hunting did, however, result in the discovery of a magic stone. This magic stone was about the size of a biscuit. Young Joseph swore he could see what was buried in the bowels of the earth by peering into the stone, like a crystal ball. Ez had technically found it, but he couldn't see anything when he looked at it. So Joseph kept it, because it made no sense for a perfectly good magic stone to go to waste.

Ezra was a big farm boy who tended to be slightly pudgy. He was sometimes teased for being dumb when, really, he wasn't. Some described him simply as the big oaf that Joe Smith hung around with, a description that was neither fair nor accurate. He was fiercely loyal and kind, and didn't care what other people thought of him. Where Joseph was handsome and garrulous, Ez was plain and shy. His hair was a tangled reddish mess and his clothes rarely fit him, so his trousers were cinched tight and fell no farther than his ankles.

Ez was five years old when his mother passed away giving birth to his sister. His father married a miserable woman who found every reason to blame her unhappiness on Ez and his baby sister, Lorna. Ez's father had finally been worn down by the nag and, in a fit of uncharitable parentage, allowed his new wife to turn his two children out of the house. Ez had done nothing to deserve this dismissal, save his deliverance from the womb of another woman. He'd been separated from his sister, too, the only person on earth who loved him.

The two siblings were passed around from one home to another when finally Ez met Joseph at school, and the Smith family insisted he stay with them for a time. This generosity, from a poor family that could barely feed its own, was something Ez would never forget.

Ez's sister had been taken in by a family that only pretended to give a hoot about the Almighty. Her stepfather despised organized religion and never lost an opportunity to ridicule himself over his erratic belief. His disbelief infected Lorna, who had come to hate God for taking her mother, foisting a wicked stepmother upon her, and yanking her away from her beloved brother.

Ez only hunted for buried treasure because of the adventure but Joseph was enchanted by fanciful bouts of magic. So, naturally, Joseph was thrilled when the angel told him he could finally remove the gold tablets from their hiding spot on the hillside.

"So did he finally get 'em?" Ez asked Mother Smith later that afternoon.

"Oh, he got 'em alright," she said. She bent over and stabbed the cooking fire with a poker. "And he did it by the skin of his teeth."

"What happened?"

She stood and wiped her hands on her apron. "Well, those scoundrels followed him to the secret spot and walloped him a good one. He's pretty banged up, all right, but he managed to escape and ran all the way home with the gunny sack."

"The gunny sack?"

"He hid the gold tablets in a gunny sack."

"Have you seen them?"

"No, sir. Nobody can see them, not even Pa or me. The angel said if anybody else sees them, why, he'll take them straight back to heaven."

"So nobody can see them at all?"

"The angel made it plain as day that if anybody sees them with their natural eyes they'll be smote dead on the instant. Now, I don't know about you, but you can bet your life I'm not about to risk it."

"Is he going to be okay?" asked Ez. "I mean, on account of the beating he took?"

"You know Joseph. He's retiring now with Emma and doesn't want company. Give him a good night's sleep and he'll be right as rain."

Emma Hale was Joseph's new bride, a natural beauty with large brown eyes and olive skin. She'd been raised in a small town across the Pennsylvania border. One of her neighbors, an elderly man whose wits were the subject of debate, believed that Spanish conquistadors had abandoned a gold mine directly under his property. He said he could feel the gold "just a shinin' right under my boots!" When he learned about Joseph and his magic stone, he hired him to find the treasure. After negotiating a digging price of $3 per day, Joseph and Ez traveled to Pennsylvania with the magic stone in tow.

Emma's family lived next to this elderly man, completely unaware that their neighbor's homestead was sitting atop an abandoned gold mine. When Joseph and Ez arrived to begin digging, they met Emma. Ez fell hard for her and was crushed when he overheard her giggling to a friend a few days later, "That Joseph Smith has the bluest eyes I've ever seen, and his lashes are as long as a broom!" When he told Joseph what he'd overheard, Joseph shrugged his shoulders. "Don't worry about it, Ez. Girls ain't worth it."

Emma had a deliciously wicked sense of humor. The two young men went down to the Susquehanna River for a swim after a long day digging for the gold (another day where, unfortunately, they'd come up empty). When they came back out of the water someone had taken their clothes from the shore, leaving only their work boots. Making matters worse, it was cold, being November of 1825, so they were afraid to come out of the water until the coast was clear. And when they finally did, it was with a boot over their privates.

The next day Emma took them a picnic lunch while they were digging, a peace offering, of sorts.

"Holy smokes, Emma! Whaddya put in these sandwiches?"

"Why, I don't know what you're talking about, Joseph."

"It tastes like fire and brimstone! I've never tasted anything so hot in my life!"

"You surely don't know the first thing about gratitude, Joseph Smith. Why, I thought you'd enjoy it."

"Oh, I do," he said as he pulled a hankie from his back pocket and wiped his forehead.

"So do you like them?" she asked.

"Well, it's just that . . . mine's hotter than a pistol. But it's good," he lied.

"Excellent," she said. "Here, let me get you another one."

Ez's sandwich wasn't hot, and Emma winked at him when Joseph turned to grab a canteen lying beside him in the prairie grass.

Emma's father didn't like Joseph; he thought the young man had come to town to bilk his poor old neighbor out of his money. He'd also heard rumors about angels and gold tablets. This was not the future he had envisioned for his only daughter—marriage to a slick-talking gold digger. He was a renowned game hunter with a face like a grizzly, who spent weeks away hunting bears out in the frontier. While he was out of town, Joseph and Emma eloped, leaving only a note. This did not go over well with her father.

It was nine months later that the angel had given Joseph permission to retrieve the gold tablets. Ez found Joseph in his room getting dressed. He was sitting at the foot of his bed, yanking on his boots. He looked fairly good in spite of having been walloped by the gang of ex-treasure hunters who'd followed him to steal the gold. Joseph told Ez he dug where the angel instructed and discovered the engraved tablets inside a stone box, buried about two feet under the ground.

"I got a crowbar and pried off the stone lid and they were in the bottom of the box. The Urim and Thummin was in the box, too."

"The what?"

"The Urim and Thummin. They're like spectacles and I'm supposed to wear them to translate the tablets into English, because the writing on them is ancient."

"You're going to use *spectacles?*"

"Well, see, they're like two round stones. Each one is about a half inch thick. They're held together by a silver bow, so they look like reading glasses. I'm supposed to wear them like spectacles so the stones cover my eyes, and that way I'll be able to translate the writing into modern-day English."

"The stones would be covering your eyes?"

"Uh-huh."

"Well, then how in tarnation are you supposed to see?"

"They're special stones, so I can see right through them."

"You can see right through the stones? Let me see them."

"Sorry, Ez. I'd show them to you, but the angel said it'd be on pain of instant death. Same thing with the gold tablets. So, I don't have much of a choice."

Ez squinted and cocked his head. "Come on, Joseph. It's me you're talking to."

"Sorry, Ez, I can't."

"But nobody's gonna believe you if you don't show them."

"I think that's the point God's trying to make."

"What point?"

"Well, think about it. If everybody could see them they wouldn't need faith, and God wants people to believe through faith; otherwise it'd be too easy."

"Yeah, and what's so bad about that?"

"If everybody believed, God wouldn't know who was faithful and who wasn't. It's like a test."

"I don't understand why God tries to make it so hard."

"But can't you see why He wants to keep it less obvious—so you'll be forced to rely on faith? God likes it when people have faith."

"Hey, I'm not God, but it seems more complicated than it oughta be. God's smart enough to evaluate people in other ways."

"But then the whole concept of faith would disappear. Nobody would need it."

"Well, it still makes no sense." Ez would concede, however, that the ways of God were mysterious. And surely this was proof of that.

Joseph reached for his coat which hung on a hook behind the door and then leaned over to tie his boots, satisfied that the query was essentially over.

"How big are the tablets anyway?"

"Oh, I'd say they're about seven inches wide. Each one is solid gold but they aren't very thick. I'd say the whole stack is, what, maybe six or seven inches thick on account of all the pages. They're bound together with three rings on the side, like a book. It's a pretty special book, too, because it's the history of the ancient Americans—the white man and their former brothers, the Indians, who got cursed with the dark skin."

"You could sell it for a fortune! A single page would be worth more than the farm!"

"I know I could, but the angel wants me to translate the book to English, and then I have to give it back to him when I'm done. He'd know if some of the tablets were missing."

"You gotta give them back?"

"Yeah."

"So where are they now?"

"Well, I was coming home with them in the gunny sack when the guys ambushed me. I think it was Lyman and his boys who must've followed me. Anyway, they had a club and gave me a good wallop, but I fought them off. I ran home through the woods with those bloodsuckers hot on my tail. I called out to my ma when I got close to the house and she opened the kitchen window and I passed the gunny sack to her through the window. Then we hid them underneath the hearth."

"So your ma held them?"

"Yeah, but she didn't see them because they were in the gunny sack."

"Weren't they heavy as all get out? They must weigh a few hundred pounds if they're solid gold. Plus you had the crowbar and the rock thumbin' thing, too."

"It's called the Urim and Thummin. And, yeah, they're pretty heavy but it wasn't that bad."

"I still can't believe you escaped carrying all that weight. You said they smacked you with a club?"

"I ran for my life, Ez. I wasn't about to let them catch me."

"But what about your leg? You aren't the fastest runner with your limp and all."

"It hurt like the dickens, but I ran faster than I've ever run in my life."

Joseph stood before the cloudy mirror above the bureau. He leaned in for a closer look, then stepped back and tugged at the bottom of his jacket to flatten it.

"They'll probably come back, you know."

"Yeah," Joseph said. "You're probably right. I think I'll hide them better tomorrow."

Joseph was ready to leave, but Ez still sat on a small wooden chair in the corner of the room, processing this story. He wore a puzzled frown.

"But how are you supposed to translate them if they're hidden?"

"Well, they won't always be hidden. Besides, with the magic spectacles, I could do it even if they were tucked away someplace out of danger."

"But if you have the magic spectacles covering your eyeballs, why would you need the tablets in the first place?"

"I might need them sometimes—to get the translation just right."

"It still doesn't make sense."

"That's the way the Lord works, Ez."

"But if you don't let people see them, they're not going to believe you." This candid assessment may have been the richest understatement of the nineteenth century.

The next day, Joseph pulled the gunny sack from underneath the hearth and hauled it over to the copper's shop, staying one step ahead of the thieves. He ripped out a few wood planks in the floor and stuffed the gold tablets down the hole, then hammered the planks back into place. Fortunately, the angel returned to warn Joseph that the thieves planned to search the copper's shop next. So Joseph removed them from under the floor and hid them in a barrel of dried beans.

Later that day the hooligans came and ripped up the floor in the copper's shop, but came up empty.

3

The Magic Spectacles

Martin Harris was not a worldly man, but he was prosperous. His three hundred acres of rich farmland near Palmyra was said to be worth over ten thousand dollars. He was middle-aged, with gray hair and a beard that began at the edge of his jaw, so that his cheeks and chin were clean-shaven, leaving the whiskers to grow below his jaw. It made him look like an African lion.

Martin was a religious man who believed in angels. Indeed, he claimed to have had angelic visions himself. He boasted that he'd seen Jesus who, for some inexplicable reason, had taken the shape of a reindeer. He'd seen the Devil, too, who looked like a jackass with short hair like you'd find on a mouse. The Smiths thought these sightings were unlikely, but they needed money to print the book, and Martin had money.

Martin first became intrigued with the gold tablet project when Ma Smith scouted him out as one of the richest men in Palmyra. He agreed to visit the Smith farmhouse where he found Joseph and his brothers out back, leaning against a picket fence in the shade. Two lazy dogs were sprawled out in the dirt and a weary hog wandered by. Seeing the trough was dry, it kept wandering, worn out by the effort. A horse stood chewing in the field.

"Hello there, Mr. Harris," Joseph said.

"Hello boys. Taking a break, are ya?"

"Got the chores done early."

Martin leaned against the fence, which creaked under the weight of his thick frame. "So tell me, what's all this I hear about a gold book you went and found?"

Joseph gave him a synopsis of the story of the angel and the golden tablets. He told Martin that once he finished the translation he'd need money to get the book published.

Martin accidently dropped the pin he'd been picking his teeth with into a pile of straw near the fence. Martin, who'd heard about Joseph's magic stone, asked Joseph to use it to find the pin. Joseph removed the stone from the front pocket of his trousers and dropped it into the bottom of his hat. He pulled the hat up to his face and studied the stone buried in the darkness of his hat. Martin watched him closely to make sure he didn't peek out of the side of his hat. Joseph lifted a few pieces of straw where Martin had been standing and found the pin.

"You found it! This proves you're telling the truth about the gold tablets!" Armed with such compelling proof, Martin agreed to help finance the book's printing.

***

A few months later, a carriage came to a stop at 120th Street in New York City, and Martin Harris stepped out. He was dressed in his finest suit, a passable English worsted gray pinstripe and a tall black hat. He gave the chauffer a handsome tip, for he was about to confirm the world's greatest discovery and felt an extra token was appropriate for the occasion. The spring wind bit throughout the city's streets and the black cherry trees bravely blossomed as they shivered along Broadway.

He clutched his valise, having checked the contents several times that day. He worked his way across the campus of Columbia College to the Department of Languages and strode confidently up the steps.

He removed his hat, smoothed his hair, and stepped inside. The list of offices directed him to the second floor. He climbed the marble staircase, found the door, and entered the office of Dr. Charles Anthon, Professor of Linguistics.

The small reception area was lined with bookshelves, filled with tomes the great professor had presumably written, or read. Martin was not a reader himself and found no joy in the arts, which seemed to be a waste of time reserved for the genteel class that didn't shoulder the burden of running a farm. The secretary was a bookish man who flattered himself with the second-hand prestige of proximity to the learned professor.

"He'll be with you shortly. He's just finishing up with Edgar Allan Poe," he said. Martin didn't know Edgar Allan Poe from Adam.

The inner door opened and Professor Anthon emerged along with Poe, a smallish young man with narrow shoulders and a receding hairline. They shook hands like old friends and Martin was then escorted into Professor Anthon's office. It was a shrine to literacy, its bookshelves sagging from the sheer weight of books. The smell of musty volumes and the smoke of cherry pipe tobacco hung in the air.

"I understand you have a sampling of ancient Hebrew writing."

"Yes, sir, I do," said Martin.

"Well, let me see it then."

Martin opened his valise and removed a single sheet of paper upon which was written a series of strange symbols. He handed it across the desk to the professor.

"This does not appear to be Hebrew. Where did you get it?"

"I'm considering an investment into an ancient book that contains symbols like this. I would like your professional opinion about them."

"They are odd," the professor said as he peered at them through his bifocals and then lifted a magnifying glass for even closer inspection. "They might be a form of Egyptian, but I can't be certain of it."

"Would you be willing to prepare a certification of their authenticity for me?"

"But, as I said, sir, I am not familiar with this type of hieroglyphics. Tell me again where they came from."

"There is a young man in western New York who found ancient tablets with symbols like these. I've copied them for authentication."

"Where are these so-called tablets," asked the professor, "and how did this young man acquire them?"

"Professor Anthon, I have an amazing story to tell you." Martin told the professor about the angel appearing to Joseph in his bedroom, the buried golden tablets, the magic stone, and the pin in the straw. He explained that they'd assumed the etched writing on the gold was Hebrew because it had been written by Jews who had sailed over to America two thousand years earlier. They'd still be living here today, he said, except their cursed doubles, the American Indians, had wiped them off the face of the earth.

"Mr. Harris, I am appalled! You have been taken for your money."

"But you said they were a form of ancient Egyptian." (This had been close enough for Martin.)

"No, I said I was not familiar with this type of hieroglyphics. I said they *could* have been some form of Egyptian. However, now that I know the source of them, I would not authenticate them even if I could."

"I believe the young man," said Martin.

"Well, then I suppose you will pay him, but I believe that would be a terrible mistake in judgment, sir. Tell me about these tablets. What do they look like?"

"I haven't seen them."

"Why not?"

"Because the angel forbids it."

"I see. The angel, you say. At a minimum, sir, I would demand to see them for myself before giving him any more money."

"He said I could see them if I chose, but that I'd die if I did."

"This is preposterous! How on earth am I, a professional linguist, supposed to read a closed book, one that is hidden from me? Why, the very thought is absurd."

"But, I had hoped . . . ."

"I believe we are finished here," the professor said and got up from behind his massive desk.

Martin retrieved the piece of paper with the strange markings and returned it to his valise. He walked out past the secretary whose face was in a book. The secretary looked up, marking his spot with a letter opener. Martin said nothing to the man, descended the staircase, and left the building.

The sharp breeze that had invigorated him an hour earlier was now raw and depressing. Perhaps he'd been a fool after all. Maybe he'd wanted to believe so much that he'd been blinded by desire, like the holder of a lottery ticket who refused to acknowledge the lopsided odds.

Martin made his way back to Broadway Street. The carriage driver who had delivered him to the college was available.

"May I take you, sir, through Central Park perhaps?"

"No, take me straightaway to my hotel."

Martin slouched in his seat, the near-empty valise on his lap. He thought about his greedy wife, a cynical woman who'd sniffed out his wealth with her predatory snout before marrying him. Martin knew she would enjoy the satisfaction of his gullibility, having warned him that Joe Smith and his so-called "gold tablets" were complete foolishness.

And then he remembered something Joseph had shown him. It was a verse from the Bible: "And the vision of all is become unto you as the words of a book that is sealed, which men deliver to one who is learned, saying, 'Read this, I pray thee; and he saith, I cannot;

for it is sealed.'" Martin sat up in the carriage. That's it! This had all been foretold in the Bible. This was the literal fulfillment of biblical prophecy!

Martin returned to Palmyra with new enthusiasm for the book, convinced that God had used *him* to fulfill the prophecy. Because Martin was Joseph's largest benefactor, he was enlisted as a scribe in the translation process. However, he wasn't allowed to see the tablets, of course, no one was. This included Joseph's wife, Emma, who would later say she never actually saw them, but she'd *felt* them. They'd been hidden beneath a dishtowel and she had scooted them a few inches while dusting Joseph's desk.

Emma wanted to believe Joseph, but she was upset that he wouldn't let her see them.

"But, Joseph, I am your *wife*."

"Don't you believe me?"

"I don't know what to believe."

"I'd hoped at least my own wife would believe me."

"We need to trust each other, Joseph."

"That's why you need to trust me on this."

The tablets were rarely in the room during the translation process because there was the constant threat of theft. And, of course, there was the issue of one's safety. They were largely unnecessary in any event because Joseph had the magic spectacles. He read the backside of the stones, which directly covered his eyes. The stones displayed the original ancient text, then, after a few moments, the original text was replaced by the English translation on the stones. Joseph then dictated the English words to Martin who sat on the other side of a makeshift curtain, quill in hand.

The stone spectacles rested on the bridge of his nose for hours at a time and were uncomfortable. So, on a lark, Joseph experimented with the magic stone that he and Ez had found several years earlier.

Luckily, it appeared to work just as well. Joseph dropped the stone into the bottom of his hat and buried his face into the hat to exclude any light. The stone displayed the ancient phrase first, followed by its proper English translation. It wasn't the hat that was magical, for it was just an ordinary straw hat; it was the stone that had special powers. But it was small, and only a few words fit across it at once, so the process took a lot of time, precious time that allowed Martin's greedy wife, Dolly, to frustrate the work.

"Oh, no you don't, Martin! Not one more dime to that boy! Do you hear me? Not another cent!"

"But, Dolly, I've read the book and it's inspired by God."

"Yes, Martin, I know you've *read* it, but have you *seen* it?"

"No, but the book speaks for itself."

"The book you haven't seen."

"It sounds like ancient scripture to me."

"He puts a magic rock in the bottom of his hat and reads from the rock in the dark! My God, Martin, have you completely lost your mind?"

Dolly would not be mollified, not when the money could be used on a new carriage, or a fancier house. She charged over to Joseph's house and demanded to see the tablets. Emma, who was pregnant with their first child, had neither the strength nor the courage to face down this woman.

"Do you mind, Mrs. Smith, if I take a look around?"

"Well, I'm awfully tired. Perhaps you can call on us another time."

"I'll just be a minute. You lie down. Here, let me get you some nice tea."

"But, I don't care for . . . ."

"Shush now. This will help with your condition. I won't take no for an answer, not when you're with child."

Dolly ransacked the Smiths' house looking for the gold book. She looked in every cupboard and under every bed. The next day she woke early and scoured the property looking for freshly dug dirt, thinking perhaps that Joseph might have put them into another hole. It was driving her mad.

"So," Dolly said, "if they aren't in the house, and they aren't because I've hunted high and low, tell me, Joseph Smith, how you can translate them? Go on, tell me; I'm all ears."

Joseph smiled in the face of the cold woman. He might have thrown her out on her ear, but he was both a kind person and one who needed Martin's money.

"I am sorry this upsets you, but it's been necessary to keep the tablets hidden. I know you don't understand, but please be good enough to let my wife sleep."

"So you can't answer my question, can you?"

"I don't need to have the tablets in front of me because I have the Urim and Thummin. So you might as well stop looking because you aren't going to find them."

"Well, I don't care if you've got the Burnin' and Dumbin' or not! That right there's the dumbest thing I've ever heard. And I'll look for them as long as I danged well please! 'Course, I'm not likely to find them because they don't exist. Golden book, schmolden book. It's all a bunch of hogwash, and you know it!"

Martin put an arm around his unhappy wife, who was like a stalk of a thistle. She pulled away from him.

"Don't you see, Martin?" She grabbed his arm and shook it as though to make him agree. "You agree with me, Martin, don't you?" She gave it another shake. "Tell me you see through this nonsense. Tell me!"

Martin made an equivocal promise that he wouldn't pursue it any further if she would only stop her yammering. It was a promise he didn't intend to keep. He justified his lie with the sad realization that she'd kept virtually none of the promises *she'd* made to him on their wedding day.

It would not do to have Martin continue to be the principal scribe, not with a wife who was constantly trying to undermine God's effort to restore the true Church. So Oliver Cowdery, a young man who'd been boarding with the Smiths, replaced him. Oliver was quiet, the type of boy who'd rather read a book than ride a steer. He tried to grow a beard in a futile effort to look older, but it only made him look younger.

Joseph didn't care about Oliver's incipient beard, only that he could write well, having been trained as a schoolteacher.

"Oliver, how would you like to be my scribe?"

"What would I be transcribing?"

Joseph looked him in the eye, not as a challenge but as an invitation. This concentrated look of his was intoxicating.

"You, Oliver, would be transcribing the very word of God."

***

Emma was twenty-three years old when she finally became pregnant with her first child. She had listened to other women wax on about the joy of motherhood for years. They dispensed advice and homespun remedies (there was the popular ginger tea and brandy, and the less popular turkey rhubarb tea). They reminded her that it would be painful, for that was God's way—Eve's curse for having eaten the apple.

Emma was thrilled to become pregnant, and then wondered what she'd been so thrilled about. Her romantic illusions of motherhood caused her to question, and then revolt against, the ways of nature. There was the nausea, swollen veins, lethargy, tender breasts, and the urgency to use the smelly outhouse every ten minutes. And her emotions were completely out of whack. She lumbered around as if she had a watermelon strapped to her belly, and dreamt about delivering a litter of puppies.

"Joseph, hurry, put your hand right here," she said. "There! Did you feel it?"

"It moves like a boy."

"We'll love it whatever it is, won't we?"

"Of course we will," he said, and leaned down to kiss her, his hand still resting on her belly.

They called for the midwife when Emma started bleeding. The midwife came out of the bedroom on occasion to boil more water over the fireplace and mumbled to Joseph that he was in the way, even though he'd tried to angle his way into the corner, next to the mop. When he offered to help she'd only tutted, as if he'd already done plenty. He put his ear to the door but dared not open it because this was the exclusive province of women.

There was one long extended scream, the climactic finish, he assumed. He waited for the wail of an infant. Nothing. The only sound was the tick of the clock. Finally the midwife, a stout woman who didn't fuss with small talk, came out of the room. She held both of his arms with her strong hands and looked at him without saying a word. And then he knew. He hung there between her hands.

"I'm sorry, but poor Emma needs your help now more than ever."

He sank from her grip to the floor.

She pulled him up by his sleeve and directed him to the bedroom where Emma lay sobbing. The bed sheets were covered in blood. He knelt on the braided rug beside the bed and buried his face in the blanket.

They named their dead son Alvin.

4

The Book of Mormon

Ezra was an apprentice of the local wheelwright, a mammoth of a man with no tolerance for sloth. So it was unfortunate that on the day his boss was out fishing, The Reverend came to collect his carriage. Reverend Townsend was the most popular preacher in Palmyra, and he had the finest carriage, too. His lack of humility was strikingly out of step with his service to the Son of Man, whose Second Coming was nigh, and had been so nigh for as long as anyone in town could remember.

The Reverend was a proud man, incapable of envy, because he believed there was nothing to envy in anyone else, and certainly not in the small hamlet of Palmyra, New York. He whaled away for hours at a time, bringing down God's wrath on anyone who drifted off during one of his sermons. He sized them up as godless heathens with sweeping certainty, strolling through town with a stern face lined with deep furrows on account of his piety. Those furrows had been trained to slope downward, as if his face was melting, even while holding forth about Jesus. The great tidings of comfort and joy were nowhere to be seen on his countenance, replaced by the look of a man constantly on the prowl to root out the noxious stain of sin.

"Is my carriage properly repaired? I'll not have shoddy workmanship where the Lord's work is concerned."

"Yessir," said Ez. "We got 'er all finished."

"You *have* finished it."

"Yessir, that's what I said. Got 'er all done."

Ez told him he owed three dollars for the work. The Reverend demanded that he should only be charged two dollars, because that particular carriage took him on errands for the Lord. Ez didn't know what to do. His boss had gone fishing, and The Reverend was scowling as if Ez was cheating the Lord out of His money. He was also distracted by The Reverend's daughter, a perky girl with red hair, freckles, and a white smile. Ez didn't want to disappoint her, and he didn't want to go to hell, so he agreed to the two dollars. He hooked the fancy carriage to their horse and stood in the yard, gazing at her as they rode off. When she turned around and smiled, Ez would have given the repairs for free.

The following Sunday he dressed in his "polished up" clothes and dragged a brush across his head. He sat on the back pew of the chapel, a fine tribute to the Savior with the required complement of stained glass and ornate crosses. The crosses were handsomely carved, some with a desperately pained Jesus, and others unoccupied (but there was the definite implication that He'd once been nailed to a replica). Ez squirmed on the bench through a needless recitation of how sinners, including everyone in the congregation, might be burned to death when Jesus returned for the Second Coming. This unhappy announcement somehow inspired the citizenry, for they returned each week to be admonished again and again, treading onward from their sins like rats on a wheel. The Reverend warned them, as he did every Sunday, that this was no time to hoard their money when they should be donating it to the Church instead. Ez had no money to hoard, so he assumed he was in the clear.

She saw him standing at the back of the chapel (which hardly needed another remodel as The Reverend insisted), and approached him, offering her hand.

"Hi, I'm Rachel."

Ez somehow mumbled his name. Her hand was soft and white, and his was hard and dirty, despite all the scrubbing he'd done in the well that morning behind the wheelwright's shop.

"And who is this young man?" It was The Reverend.

"Oh, this is Ezra, Father. Remember we met him at the wheelwright's shop."

"Yes, of course. Did you enjoy my sermon?"

"Uh, yessir. Very much, sir."

"The Lord needs your contributions, young man. He'll not be sitting idly by whilst you squander your money on frivolous pleasures of the flesh."

"Oh, I know, Reverend."

"Come, Rachel. Your mother has prepared a pot roast to celebrate the sermon I've given."

Within a month, The Reverend could smell the presence of another man on his daughter, so he tried to stuff as much of the Bible into Ez that he could. Ez, who'd been admonished about the Second Coming for six consecutive Sundays, had finally been invited to his first Sunday pot roast.

He walked up to the front door of The Reverend's house, an arrogant dwelling that seemed to be as full of itself as The Reverend. Even the flower bed in front was inconceivably prideful, as was the sign on the front door that read, "Enter All Those Who Fear the Lord." Rachel took his worn coat and hung it on a rack by the door, which was adorned with a crucifix, and led him past portraits of stern-looking ancestors and into the dining room. The room was washed in the shadows of the late afternoon. Ez could smell the pot roast getting cold while The Reverend said grace for ten minutes, admonishing all those at the table, and the Good Lord, too.

"Tell us about yourself, Ezra," said Rachel's mother.

"He's a wheelwright, Elizabeth," said The Reverend. "His mother has passed away, God rest her soul. And his father has been lost to a weakness for the bottle."

"Father," said Rachel, "I believe mother was directing her comments to Ezra."

"Fine, then, Elizabeth. If you insist on leading the discussion you may do so. But first I see we are missing the salt."

"No, it's all right, I best be getting the salt," said Rachel's mother as she slunk into the kitchen.

Rachel was a spitfire. Unlike her mother, she didn't keep her opinions to herself; nor did she simply fetch things like a well-trained hound. But Rachel's mother had accepted her own role as the salt-fetcher, and salt-fetchers eventually lose their voices.

In contrast to the tall, strong Ez, Rachel was thin and short. She buzzed with energy, even when she sat, her knee bouncing under the table as she ate. Her father forbade her to paint her face; he said it made her look like a prostitute. Instead, she pinched her cheeks. This annoyed her father who could find no prohibition in the Bible for cheek pinching.

"What's this nonsense about Joe Smith and his gold book?" asked The Reverend between bites of well-salted pot roast. "Just because he's memorized a few verses from the Bible doesn't qualify him to declare that God has sent an angel to him. Why, it's the most blasphemous thing I've ever heard."

"Well," said Ez, "Joseph has seen the angel lots of times now and he has the golden tablets. In fact, he's translating them into English now."

"He is now, is he? And have you seen these so-called golden tablets of his?"

"No. He'd show them to me but I'd be struck dead if I saw them with my natural eyes."

"And why on earth would anyone believe such nonsense?"

"But Father," said Rachel, "You believe in angels, too, don't you?"

"Certainly I do. But this is totally different and you know it! I believe in real ones, not this Myrondi, or whatever his name is. This is preposterous. Joe Smith is not even trained in the gospel. Why, the whole thing is . . . well, it's laughable."

"There are plenty of people who believe him," said Rachel.

"Perhaps they are the same people he has swindled. I'm told he was convicted of fraud for taking an old man's money with the promise that he would use a magic stone to find a buried gold mine. It would be humorous were it not so evil."

"Well, that trial wasn't totally fair," said Ez. "Joseph had witnesses who said he didn't defraud the old man out of a nickel."

It had been over two years since Joseph had been hired by the elderly man to find the gold mine left by the Spanish conquistadors, employment that did not end well. A criminal charge had been brought against Joseph by the man's nephew when he learned that his uncle, who was senile, had been swindled out of several hundred dollars. The result was a fraud conviction, a blemish that Joseph preferred not to dwell on. This entire ordeal had occurred during the four-year "testing period" imposed by Angel Moroni. (It would be mere speculation to assume this fraud conviction had contributed to the angel's initial reluctance to show Joseph where he'd buried the gold tablets.)

"So," said The Reverend, "this Joe Smith claims he'd been meeting with his angel for over two years at the time of this fraud trial."

"Yessir."

"Well, young man, don't you find that to be an odd time to be convicted of fraud?"

"I don't know."

"And he claims the angel kept coming for another two years after that, as if angels commonly associate with convicted frauds."

"I don't think that was it at all."

"No?"

"It looks worse than it really was. I know Joseph and he's honest as the day is long."

"And what is the nature of his so-called golden book?"

"The nature?"

"Yes, what is it about?"

"I think it's sort of like the Bible, but I haven't read it yet. That's just what Joseph told me."

"Young man, I need not remind you that you are supping in my home!" He banged his fist on the table and his wife jumped, along with the salt-and-pepper shakers. "The Bible is the single word of God! Because of your youth and naiveté, I will assume you are confused. Otherwise I order you from my property at once for this heresy!"

There was silence as The Reverend stood at the head of the table, fuming with God's steam. No one even chewed. Rachel reached over and touched Ez's arm.

"I'm sorry, sir," Ez said. "I know the Bible's the word of God. Heck, everybody knows that."

"Then what possible worth is this fraudulent gold bible?"

"It's a story of the Americans who lived here two thousand years ago."

The Reverend sat back down. "So it's not a religious book?"

"Well, sort of. See, they had prophets back then, too, and one of them was named Mormon. That's how the book got its name. Anyways, the book is about how Jesus came to America."

"How Jesus came to America?"

"Yessir."

"Have you lost your mind?" He stared at Rachel, making it quite clear that she was not to have anything further to do with this foolish boy who had fallen off his rocker.

"Jesus came to see the people here, too. They needed to hear what was in the Bible and stuff just like the people in Egypt and places like that."

"And when, pray tell, did He do that?"

"When He was in the tomb."

"Excuse me?"

"Yessir. Joseph said Jesus didn't just sit in the tomb twiddling His thumbs for three days. He used that time to come over here to visit."

This was more than the God-fearing Reverend could reasonably bear. He shoved his chair back from the table again and stood, glaring at Ez as if it had been he, not Joseph, who had perpetrated such blasphemy. Ez wisely took his cue and left immediately after thanking Rachel's mother for the dinner. Her head was down, however, and she said nothing in return so as not to earn another scolding from her self-righteous husband.

It is a wonder that Ez and Rachel were ever married, believing as he did in his best friend, Joseph. But Rachel refused to eat until her father allowed it. When The Reverend finally agreed, after exacting a promise that neither of them would speak of the golden book again, he pulled Ez aside to warn him that he was not to enjoy the sinful power of the flesh for anything but holy procreation.

The small room they took at the Palmyra Inn on their wedding night was furnished with only a bed and dresser. It was dimly lit and smelled of rosemary oil hair tonic and candle wax. Rachel stood patiently in the soft light, as if she was being fitted for a gown, while Ez worked the delicate buttons on her dress with the exploratory paws of a grizzly.

She shook out her hair and turned again to face him. She looked even smaller to Ez than she had with clothes on. She removed his shirt and trousers, his excitement now categorically evident, and blew out the candle on the nightstand.

***

God gave Joseph permission to show the golden tablets to three people. Ordinarily this would have been a death sentence, but these three witnesses were given temporary immunity.

"So, now can I see them?" asked Emma.

"I think I should pick men who have helped with the translation."

"I would have helped."

"But I'll need these men to swear an oath that they've seen them. If the oath is a woman's, and especially my wife's, it wouldn't be as persuasive."

He selected Martin Harris, Oliver Cowdery, and David Whitmer, a lifelong friend of Oliver's.

David Whitmer was an unimaginative-looking man with a mouth that drooped at the corners. He was of German descent and spoke with an accent, so when he testified that, "zee Book of Mormon is zee truth," he did so with "zee conviction of zee Lord."

It was a summer day in 1829 when the four of them walked into the woods near Joseph's home. Red oak and sugar maple trees had surrendered to patches of rich farmland, one felled tree at a time. But adjacent to the Smiths' home there were still untamed groves and the summer sun streaked through them like rays from heaven.

They were gone for over an hour. The small group of believers back at the farmhouse paced and fretted. Why was it taking so long?

"Don't worry, the angel's gonna come," said Joseph's mother as she gave the kitchen table the scrubbing of its life. Then she attacked the cupboards.

Meanwhile, nothing was happening out in the woods.

"I think it's me," said Martin. "I must not have enough faith. The spirit will be stronger if I leave."

"It's up to you," said Oliver who'd begun to think it'd been his own sinning, but allowed for the probability that it'd been Martin's fault all along.

"I'll be praying over there," Martin said, pointing to a grove one hundred yards away. "Holler if you see anything."

The angel came shortly after Martin left, hovering about a foot off the ground. He introduced himself and produced the tablets, presenting them out to Oliver and David like a gift. Fortunately, neither man appeared to have suffered bodily harm from the exposure.

Martin was despondent. "Why didn't you call me?"

"We didn't want to scare him away. Maybe he didn't want you to see him."

This made Martin feel even worse. He didn't want to be the odd man out, so Joseph agreed to stay with him while the other two ran back through the woods to the farmhouse to report the good news. Martin and Joseph lagged behind, praying earnestly (especially Martin who was quickly repenting for his sins). When Moroni appeared again, Martin jumped up and shouted: "Tis enough! Mine eyes have beheld!"

There were eight others who were also allowed to see the tablets (but not the angel). Joseph's father and two of his brothers, along with the Whitmer family, assembled in a room with Joseph. An empty wooden box, slightly larger than a shoebox, sat on a table at the front of the room. The men prayed with all their might for two straight hours. Then they stood, one by one, and looked into the box. And there they were, just as Joseph said they'd be.

"Ez," said Joseph, "I'm sorry you didn't get to see them. It was mostly family."

"Well, I wish I could've been there."

"I know most people don't believe me. I understand. These are miraculous times and I've even doubted myself from time to time."

"Really?"

"Of course. But it all comes down to faith. Without faith we wouldn't believe that Jesus walked on water, or that He came back from the dead. But our fiercest critics believe in miracles too, and that's what I don't understand. Why are their angels so believable but ours isn't?"

"It beats me."

"Maybe it's because our rational brains don't control what's in our hearts. It would be too gullible to rely on faith all the time, but what's so bad about relying on it some of the time?"

"Well, there's nothing wrong with that, I suppose."

"I guess there's always bound to be those stubborn mules that wouldn't see the hand of God if it slapped them in the face."

***

The Reverend stood beneath the faded *Grandin's Print Shop* sign. He checked his pocket watch which hung from a gold chain fastened to his breast pocket. He did so out of habit, and perhaps to impress, for it was a fine piece of plated gold, given to him by the Church. The conflict did not bother him, which was rich, for he *was* the Church and controlled its purse.

The shop was scheduled to open at eight in the morning, and it was a few minutes after the hour. This irked The Reverend because sloth was the Devil's tool. The apprentice finally arrived to open the shop, smelling like the vat of urine he'd been stomping in.

"Good God, young man! You smell foul!"

"Sorry, mister. I was just out back tannin' the hides."

"Where is your employer?"

"He was here real late last night, so I bet he ain't comin' in 'til later. He was workin' on Joe Smith's book, and I think he finished 'er up."

"Are you certain of this?"

"Well, I ain't no liar."

"You are not a liar."

"I know, mister. That's what I said."

Why were people so inferior? The Reverend wondered. These uncouth heathens were the very ones he was trying to save, the ones who were likely to fall for this Joe Smith malarkey. Sometimes he wondered why he even bothered. But then he realized like a punch to the stomach that this was his flock, a flock he might very well lose to the chicanery of the handsome and charismatic Joseph Smith. And without a flock, he could not remain a well-kept shepherd. He checked his pocket watch again.

Grandin had been reluctant to meet with The Reverend, the de-facto chair of the committee to boycott the book, because he'd promised to print it if Joseph could come up with the money. This act of courage did not rival the Crossing of the Delaware, or Paul Revere's ride, but he knew he would share the blame for allowing all that blasphemy to run amok in their fair city. And at a time when the Second Coming was nigh at hand, no less.

"You cannot allow this vile book to see the light of day," The Reverend said.

"But I promised the lad."

"The community will not appreciate this betrayal, Mr. Grandin."

In the meantime, Joseph had been busy lining up his financing. Surely no bank would help him, for he had no collateral. He could've used the gold tablets as collateral, but they'd already been taken back to heaven. That left only Martin Harris, the hen-pecked, credulous landowner.

"But I have no more money, Joseph."

"You could mortgage your farm."

"That's all I've got left."

"God will bless you, Martin. You know that."

By this time, God had begun speaking to twenty-three-year-old Joseph, personally dictating His words on things from the mundane to the extraordinary. Joseph dutifully wrote down each revelation, word for word, and collected them in the new Book of Commandments. Obviously, this was not a book to be trifled with.

The Word of God, in simple manuscript form, ought not to have languished in the stench-filled print shop, so God had plenty to say on the financing of its printing. The Almighty aimed His remarks squarely at poor Martin: "I am the Lord your God! I direct you, Martin Harris, to repent lest I smite you! I command that thou shalt not covet thine own property, but give it freely to the printing of the Book of Mormon instead. And misery thou shalt receive if you do not obey this commandment; yea, even your own destruction. Pay the printers debt! Thus saith the Lord. Amen."

Martin dared not risk his destruction, especially when God had laid out the stakes so clearly. He sold his farm and gave the money to Joseph. The next day Joseph walked back to Grandin's print shop, clutching the money in his hand as he made his way through the crowd of protestors who shouted obscenities at him. When at last he made it to the front door of the shop, he turned around and offered a warm smile to his neighbors. He then turned his back on them and opened the door.

5

The Prophet

When Joseph was only fifteen years old, two years before he ever met the Angel Moroni, Joseph witnessed the most glorious event in human history. Never before had it happened. This event was more miraculous than the booming voice of God in the Garden of Eden, or His finger spelling out the Ten Commandments on Mount Sinai. God and Jesus Christ came down from the heavens, together, and personally paid a visit to Joseph, face-to-face. The remarkable event was not well publicized at the time. Joseph only told his parents and a few of his siblings, and when he did the details were sketchy.

Joseph reported that the Heavenly Beings hovered in the customary fashion about a foot off the ground. They didn't say much, only that the *true* Church—the one Jesus established when He was on the earth—disappeared once all the original apostles died off. This, regrettably, left nothing but untrue Churches scattered across the face of the earth. It was time to restore the truth, and They wanted Joseph to head the effort.

Years later, the neighbors were not amused when word leaked out that Joseph claimed he'd seen God and Jesus in the flesh when he was a teenager. The angel business had been difficult enough for them to stomach. "That Joe Smith's a damned liar, 'cause ya can't look at the face of God and live to tell about it. You'd burn up. Everybody knows that." The Reverend nearly suffered a stroke when he heard that Joseph now claimed he saw God several years earlier but hadn't mentioned it much. Joseph had no religious training and was prone to mischief, so why would God appear to *him?* It made no sense at all. But what was done was done, and Joseph was now obliged to rebuild the Church of Jesus Christ, from scratch.

The naysayers became even more indignant when Joseph revealed the identity of his *next* heavenly messenger.

Shortly after the Book of Mormon was printed, Joseph went to the woods to pray for direction on how to go about starting a true Church. While he was deep in prayer, John the Baptist appeared. This came as something of a shock. However, it made sense. After all, baptism had always been a key ingredient to salvation, and no one knew more about baptisms than John the Baptist.

Ez was familiar with the story in the Bible about King Herod's daughter and her nasty wish.

"Joseph, I thought John the Baptist got his head chopped off and it was served to Herod's daughter on a silver platter."

"That's what the Bible says."

"So, when you saw him did he have his head, or not?"

"Of course he did. He'd been resurrected to a perfect state."

This was no small comfort to Ez. Rachel, however, was dubious. "Ez, you really believe him?"

"Joseph isn't perfect. We've had our share of mischief, but he's changed since we were kids. He wouldn't lie to me."

In the meantime, Oliver found his own magic stone and began having revelations, too. This would not do. Oliver could not be allowed to ambush Joseph's sacred calling in such brazen fashion. Fortunately, God's next revelation to Joseph cleared it up: "Behold, only my servant, Joseph Smith, shall receive commandments. Those things written from Oliver's peep-stone are not from me, but from Satan instead. Thus saith the Lord. Amen."

The church was off and running with a handful of members, but Emma was not among them. She loved Joseph with all her heart, but her father's criticism of Joseph stung. "Is it not enough that he elopes with you? Is it not enough that he's a treasure hunter who bilked my neighbor out of his money? Is it not enough that he has no job, no career, no ambition, other than to continue to play this ruse, this nonsense? And now he claims to have been visited by God and Jesus, and angels, and John the Baptist? My God, Emma, this must stop!"

And yet, Emma knew there was something special about Joseph. He *was* a good man. His critics didn't know him. They said he was a lazy profiteer, but she saw the times he came home with dirty trousers, having anonymously weeded the widow's garden. They said he was greedy, but she saw the times he gave away whatever food they had to hungry people who needed it more. They said he was unkind, but she saw him stay awake with the sick, mangy stray hound, laying down with it and stroking its hair until it had taken its final breath. They said he was petty, but she heard him speak in private, and never heard him say an unkind thing about someone behind their back. And they said he was unrighteous, but she saw the countless hours he spent on his knees in prayer.

Perhaps that's why she finally agreed to be baptized six weeks later. Of course, it may have also been Joseph's next revelation. This time the Lord spoke directly to Emma, and He didn't mince His words: "Hearken unto the voice of the Lord while I speak unto you, Emma Smith. Murmur not because of the things that thou hast not seen. Thy calling shall be for a comfort to my servant, Joseph Smith, thy husband. Let thy soul delight in him. And except you do this, you cannot come where I am. Thus saith the Lord. Amen."

"Alright, Joseph, I'll do it," she said. "But I want you to tell me again. Are you one hundred percent sure about this?"

"Of course I'm sure. Do you honestly think I could have written that book? I can barely even write a proper letter!"

This was compelling, she knew. Her husband had the uncommon gift of imaginative gab, but he wasn't a writer.

It was Rachel's baptism; however, that really stirred the pot. Reverend Townsend's daughter had joined Joe Smith's church! In fact, over fifty souls from The Reverend's flock had hearkened to Joseph's magnetic personality and joined, too. Many joined because they knew he couldn't have written the Book of Mormon all by himself—that the golden tablets must have existed after all.

It was late when Ez came in from the wheelwright's shop covered in axle grease and sweat. He dunked his shirt into a bucket of water and wrung it out, then hung it on a nail by the door. Rachel was stirring something on the stove.

"Ez," said Rachel, "I've been thinking. Didn't Joseph say Moroni was an angel, like a spirit?"

"Yeah, so?"

"Then how could he lift the tablets and haul them around? They must've weighed a ton and his hands would've gone right them."

"I'm not sure how that worked. What's for dinner?"

"No, Ez. Listen to me. How could he have done that?"

"Angels can do things we can't. How did Jonah live in the belly of a whale? It just happened and we can't explain it."

She was quiet for a minute. "What's the angel going to do with them in heaven, anyway? Put them on a shelf?"

"How am I supposed to know?" he said. He leaned down to untie his boots. "What's in the pot? Smells good."

"Maybe Joseph just went and made it all up."

"The book is five hundred pages long! Joseph's smart, but he's not *that* smart."

"Okay then," asked Rachel, "if Joseph didn't write it then who did?"

"I guess it would've been the ancient Americans who actually did the writing."

"I thought they were supposed to be bloodthirsty savages?"

"Not all of them."

"They were pretty backwards. They didn't even have paper."

"It comes down to faith, Rachel. Do you believe Jesus walked on water, or don't you? See what I mean? You need faith; that's all there is to it."

"Maybe you're right." She dipped a large wooden spoon into the pot she'd been stirring, blew on it, and then sipped it. "There's something else that doesn't make sense. My father says Joseph copied a lot from the Bible and put it in the Book of Mormon, word for word."

"What's so bad about that? Your father doesn't believe in the Bible now?"

"Well, he says if Joseph translated directly from the ancient tablets, how come the words are exactly the same as the ones from the King James Version that wasn't even written until 1620? See what I mean? It doesn't make sense."

"Look at me, Rach. I'm no preacher from some highfalutin' college, okay? I'm just a wheelwright, so I don't know all that technical stuff. If I really thought about it, maybe I could stump your pa with a thing or two. Like, how does he explain how Jesus came back from the dead? Huh?"

"I don't know."

"See, that's what I'm talking about. So I'm not going to get into it with your pa or anybody else. But I'm telling you, Rachel, this here thing's the truth or my name isn't Ezra Wells. And I want you to join me, as my wife."

"And my father?"

"You're not married to your father. Course, it's got to be your decision. But if you read the Book of Mormon, you'll know there's no way Joseph just went and made it all up."

Rachel's decision to join the new Church was complicated. She'd read the Book of Mormon, hiding it in a biscuit tin or under the bed in case her father stopped by. She believed on some level, but her faith was incomplete. Would God penalize her for having a wobbly belief? And just how wobbly could it be? Was there a threshold for wobbliness?

The Reverend was apoplectic when he heard Rachel had been baptized. He told her, spittle flying, that she was disowned for the betrayal. She would never again be allowed in his home or his Church (he assumed the Church was his).

"Ezra, you have taken my daughter and delivered her to the buffetings of Satan! How could you possibly believe Christ would 'restore' his Church to a convicted fraud? Joe Smith is an ignorant ploughboy!"

When Ez reminded him that Jesus once entrusted His Church to a gang of illiterate fisherman, The Reverend screamed, "How dare you twist things for your own perverted purposes! Those fishermen were men of God!"

"Not at first, they weren't."

"I'll not discuss this with you! You will leave my home this instant!"

Rachel's mother was devastated. She tried to talk her husband out of the banishment, but he dismissed her with an angry glare.

"I shouldn't have been baptized, Ez," said Rachel. She stood with her hands clamped in her armpits. "It wasn't worth it. Look what's happened."

"But, Rach, maybe they'll come around and see that the Book of Mormon's true."

"You can't be serious."

"But you believe it, don't you?"

"Honestly, Ez? All these different angels and gold tablets?"

"So if you don't believe it, why'd you get baptized?"

"I did it for you."

***

"Brothers and Sisters," Joseph began. "Thank you for coming to the first official meeting of the Church. Now, I've never done much preaching before, so I hope you'll forgive me if I don't throw in enough 'Thus Saiths' and 'Behold Thees,' but what I will tell you comes straight from my heart."

No one crammed into his small house that day faulted him for his ineloquence. In fact, they loved him for it. He stood so tall and handsome in his navy wool trousers and a cleanly pressed white shirt. The natural light came through the window and caused his blue eyes to appear indigo. He was clean-shaven, as he always was, and his golden hair was swept back from his forehead. A woman in the audience ran her thumb and finger along the crease of her dress, sharpening it. She leaned toward him as if toward the lips of God. His chosen-ness was on him like a scent and his followers could smell it, intoxicated by the aroma.

Joseph initially had the ordinary suspicion people have when told they're special. After a while, however, he believed those people were right; maybe he really had been touched by the Almighty.

"I have often wondered why God chose me. Jesus was a humble man, too, and the preachers scorned Him because He wasn't one of them. Now all these preachers talk about fire, brimstone, and hell. Me, I don't understand that. I believe God loves us and wants us to be happy. He promises that if we forgive one another, if we give to the poor, if we are kind and compassionate, one day we'll live with Him again, despite our imperfections. Why would any loving father cast his children into the pit of hell? It makes no sense. We should shout for joy and not cower in fear of Him."

They saw an ordinary young man without all the accoutrements of the ministry. His sermons didn't lecture them, or frighten them with the probability of their damnation. Life was hard enough. Joseph promised hope and prosperity. His sermons soared with inspiring rhetoric about the love of God, not the fear. Joseph's God didn't focus on all the reasons they should burn in hell.

How could they ever listen to the likes of The Reverend again, to the incessant badgering that beat them down to their miserable and wretched pulps? How could they be inspired by a tyrannical God who hunted down each and every sin and then threw a fit when He found them? There was no hope in that. Joseph was a different kind of preacher who gave away salvation for free. He'd become a student of the scriptures and could have quoted them from memory if he'd wanted to, but he knew that was superficial, something anyone could do. They loved Joseph because of the way he made them *feel*, and no ordinary preacher could do that.

PART II

KIRTLAND

1831 - 1838

6

Sidney and the United Order

Joseph and his small band of Mormons left New York on a frigid winter night in January 1831, having been run out of town by the righteous citizens of Palmyra. Perhaps if Joseph had shown less outward certainty of his chosen-ness, the community wouldn't have been so touchy. Or maybe if Joseph had acknowledged that The Reverend also spoke the truth, the townsfolk might have doused their torches and returned their pitchforks to the barn.

God commanded Joseph to build the *New* Jerusalem city, and He hinted that it ought to be built out west where land was cheaper. It was forecast that Jesus would come to this new city for the Second Coming, so they had to establish it quickly, for time was running out. Joseph commissioned Oliver to go find the ideal spot. Oliver was a brave young man, but there were Indians out west and he didn't dare go alone, so Parley Pratt went with him.

Parley was an emotional man who'd been born with missionary zeal, a genetic disposition that inspired him to leave his small farm in the wilderness of western New York to preach the gospel. One day while out preaching, he came upon a copy of the recently printed Book of Mormon and walked fifty miles on blistered feet to meet its author. He was so taken by Joseph that he demanded to be baptized, posthaste, for the promise of eternal life was mouthwatering.

Oliver and Parley journeyed west, pulled by the spirit like the undertow of the sea. They finally found the perfect spot in Missouri, one thousand miles to the west where the grass, it was said, grew greener. A few hundred miles into their journey, however, they passed through a small village in Ohio called Kirtland. Kirtland had a burgeoning population of two hundred souls, and nearly every one of them looked impatiently heavenward for the Second Coming. Oliver and Parley were introduced to the preacher there, a man named Sidney Rigdon.

Sidney was a big fish in the puddle of Kirtland. He told his flock that an angel appeared to him and instructed them to join ranks with the Mormons. So they did. Even though the angel hadn't left his name, they assumed it must have been Moroni, based on Sidney's description.

"Ez," said Joseph, "I think we ought to move to Kirtland."

"When?"

"As soon as possible."

"You mean, just pack up and go?"

"God is calling us to Kirtland."

"But what about our houses? And there's my wheelwright job. I'm being groomed to take over the whole operation!"

"How can we stay here in New York where everyone persecutes us? Your wife's own family has turned her away, and so has Emma's. Why not move out west where we can live in peace?"

"Rachel won't leave; not right now anyway. Besides, I thought Oliver and Parley found the New Jerusalem in Missouri, not Ohio."

"Well, maybe Ohio could be the eastern boundary of it. It has to be pretty big for everyone to fit."

"That doesn't make sense, Joseph. We only have a hundred members."

"The Church will grow, believe me. The local preacher out there named Sidney Rigdon has already joined up, and so has his entire congregation. This is the hand of God at work, Ez. Can't you see?"

Joseph announced that everyone should pack up for a move to Ohio. This was not met with enthusiasm.

"Ez, I'm putting my foot down on this one!" Rachel said. She didn't particularly like Joseph. She'd never come right out and said it, but Ez could tell by the way she refused to fawn over him like the others did.

"Come on, Rach. Be reasonable."

"*Me* be reasonable? Good night, Ez, we can't just leave. This is where we grew up."

"Your father won't even speak to you."

She stood with her hands in her armpits like she did, staring at him. "Tell me," she said, "are you one hundred percent sure on this?"

"Nobody can be a hundred percent on anything. But I'm telling you, Rach, I'm sure enough. But we need to be together on this."

This was what Rachel loved about Ez. He didn't treat her like chattel like so many other men. And he wasn't a know-it-all, which caused her to trust him more than those who claimed to know everything. Her love for Ezra was so fierce, so uncompromising, that she would leave family and home for him, and convince herself, if need be, that she believed.

Sister Gilmore was an elderly woman who collected cats. She nearly had a heart attack when she couldn't take her piano. Her arthritic hands hadn't touched the instrument in years. "But I worked all my life for this piano! It's a Bosendorfer!" Joseph pulled over a footstool and sat across from her, beneath a discolored square on the wall where a picture had been. Three cats swarmed around them, combing their ankles. He could have reminded her to consider the lilies of the field, but instead he took both of her gnarled hands in his and looked at her with compassion, making her feel like the most important person in the world, a feeling she hadn't had for many difficult years. To a passerby he looked like a handsome grandson.

"I know how much that piano means to you, and I'm sure that when you play it is the loveliest sound on earth." He assured her that she could buy a new one in Ohio, and if not, God would reward her with ten pianos in heaven. He wrapped his muscular arms around her bony frame and said, "I need you, Sister."

"Then I must take my cats."

Ez cobbled together enough rusty wagons and sleighs to make the three-hundred-mile trip. But before leaving, he wanted to pay one last visit to his father who hadn't responded to Ez's letters, presumably too ashamed to face the son he abandoned, and too frightened of his second wife. Ez dressed in every stitch of clothing he owned and walked the ten miles out to his father's small homestead. He chose to walk because he wanted to be alone, and needed time to think.

A square piece of wood was nailed to a post announcing his destination. Someone had driven nails partway into the wood and bent them down flat to spell the letters WELLS. He knocked on the door and a shadow passed behind the curtain. His stepmother finally answered the door.

"I'm leaving soon and wanted to see my father."

"He isn't home."

"May I come in?"

"There's no room for you here, Ezra. Besides, I'm battling a bug and I wouldn't want you to catch it." This pathetic woman had drained the meager kitty on every potion, but the remedial effect was wasted on her chronic need to feel symptoms of one terrible illness or another, and then describe them to others.

"But I'm sure he'd want to see me and maybe we could . . . ."

"I'm sorry, Ezra, but this isn't a convenient time. I've been down sick and the rest of us haven't felt well at all. I'm sorry."

Ez waited outside for a few more minutes, hoping his father had seen him and would come out. He didn't. Ez walked back in tears. He cried for the ten-year-old boy who'd been abandoned, and for the twenty-five-year-old fatherless man he'd become. He cried for his sister, Lorna, and for his dead mother. He even cried for his father. He followed the icy wagon ruts when a carriage stopped to give him a ride. He waved them off because he wanted to wallow in self-pity. The walk was cathartic, though, and it felt good. By the time he arrived home, Ez was ready to leave the state. There was nothing left for him in New York.

The only person who saw them off that freezing night in January was Rachel's mother, the salt fetcher. She'd told The Reverend that she was going out to visit a sick friend while he stayed home to prepare his next sermon on Christ's wrath. She removed a locket from around her neck and placed it around Rachel's. Her fingers were cold. It was the only piece of jewelry she owned. This woman who had endured a life sentence of emotional famine from her husband spoke not a word.

The Mormons climbed aboard the sleighs that were weighed down with the few possessions they could carry. Rachel's mother stood to the side as the sleighs pulled away, her hands to her face as her small body shook. Rachel watched her standing in the snow, refusing to move until the sleigh was out of sight.

The children were bundled up on the floor of the sleighs like rolled up rugs, excited for the adventure, while the adults sat hunched against the cold. They stared into the icy black wind, determined to believe they were on God's mission.

Joseph had assured them that Kirtland was the land of milk and honey. No one publically expressed their disappointment when they arrived to see only a small scattering of cabins and frozen farmland.

Sidney Rigdon was a wordy orator who liked to hear his own voice, so he listened to it for hours on end. Whereas Joseph was young and energetic, always optimistic and unafraid, Sidney was older, stern, and pessimistic; his eyes constantly darting about as if he expected trouble from an unknown source. He was sickly looking and had premature liver spots on his delicate hands. Joseph, however, took a genuine liking to him, because Joseph liked everyone. And even though Sidney was reluctant to share the small puddle with Joseph, he couldn't resist the handsome lad and his infectious youthfulness.

Sidney bore a close resemblance to New York preachers, the ones who scared the dickens out of their flocks. He was the Kirtland Ringmaster, directing every step in his circus tent, while his frightened parishioners balanced on the high wire, the flames of hell licking just below them.

The Mormons from New York arrived just in time to be treated to one of Sidney's long sermons. He held a Bible that was hardbound and black, as Bibles always are, for there must be something malevolent about a colorful one. It was swollen to nearly twice its thickness, as if it had been left out in the rain. When the sermon mercifully ended in a crescendo for God to save them from the fiery finish, the Kirtland members fell to the ground, rolling around like dizzy seals. After a few minutes, they took their unusual worship outside, to the snow, and rolled some more. The New Yorkers looked at each other with amusement at this alien breed of worship. And when the Kirtland members then stood upon a nearby tree stump and began preaching to invisible congregations, Joseph shook his head. This was not his type of Church.

"What do you think?" Emma whispered that night as they lay in Sidney's small guest bedroom. It was so cold that Joseph had thrown the bed-side rug on top of the blanket as an extra layer.

"I hope we've done the right thing."

"They are odd, aren't they?"

"I didn't dare look at you when they started rolling around like that. I thought I'd break out laughing."

"Me, too."

Ten minutes later, when the only sound they heard was the pop of the fire from the hearth outside their door, Emma whispered, "I still can't believe that man on the tree stump. My father would have us committed!"

"Yeah, we must be crazy."

"And what on earth were they *saying?*"

"I wish I knew."

They laughed into their pillows, and when they thought they'd laughed it out, Emma whispered, "They're odd, but they probably aren't sleeping under a rug," and they started again.

A few minutes later, Joseph rolled over to Emma. "Thanks for coming. I know this has been hard on you. But it'll work out, I know it will. God has a plan for us."

Emma stared into his face in the darkness. There was only the ticking of the fire as it cooled, otherwise the house was quiet. She kissed him.

***

The New York Mormons began building their cabins as quickly as they could. Friendship developed among the Saints, an honorific they'd begun using to describe each other. This wasn't necessarily meant to reflect on their worthiness, but rather as mere identification as a fellow member of the tribe. However, with all the "Saint" talk, it was difficult for the most pious among them to stay grounded. "After all," said Parley, "we *are* the Chosen People."

Emma was relieved to live in a community where her husband was revered, not ridiculed. She stood, once the Pride of Pennsylvania, with a mouthful of nails and a bucket of chinking mud hanging from her fist. There was a hammer in her other hand. She teased Joseph over the twelve-inch-diameter window he'd designed. "What kind of prophet can't even measure a window?" He threw a snowball at her, which quickly mushroomed into a town snowball fight, at least among the New Yorkers. Rachel said the kids squealed "like the first pig off the ark." The Kirtlanders stood on the sidelines, glancing at Sidney, who didn't cotton to the fun. After all, these were the last days.

The Kirtlanders soon came to see that Joseph didn't just casually sip from the cup of life, he chugged. Their new Prophet didn't demonstrate his piety with a scowl, and they liked it. He laughed, wrestled, and told jokes. And where in the Good Book did it demand the absence of joy, they asked? The females, in particular, were eager to give the handsome young Prophet the benefit of the doubt, some of them willing to postpone the Second Coming indefinitely.

After the tumult of New York, Ez and Rachel settled down to the new place, naively assuming all the turmoil has passed. "Life will be normal now," they said, forgetting that "normal" is really a state of continual tumultuousness.

Sidney was dead set on implementing a program he called the United Order. This program required the Mormons to give everything they had to the Church, which then doled it out based upon need. Sidney insisted this was the structural theme of heaven, the long pole in the tent. He said it was something Jesus had meant to do when He was on the earth, but He'd run out of time. It soon became apparent, however, that the level of maturity necessary to effectively live that lifestyle was simply too high, even for the Chosen People. It could have been the foundation for an Aesop fable, because the wealthier Saints wanted to share less and the poorer ones wanted them to share more.

They lived on the frontier and most of them didn't know which fork to use, or whether to pour a cabernet or a chardonnay, but they weren't so simpleminded that they couldn't smell mischief.

"Joseph," said Brother Peterson, "I'll be damned if I'm about to give Brother Crandall another hen when he won't lift a finger to help!" And Brother Crandall, who was poorer, said, "I'll be damned if Brother Peterson won't share his corn, and especially when my Martha's been down with the flu. He goes and takes all his luck for granite."

Even Ez had had enough. "Joseph, this is more trouble than it's worth."

"I know it's a challenge, but the United Order is God's will."

"Well, geez, how long is God going to make us share every cotton pickin' little thing? Rachel isn't happy making bread just to give it away."

"I'll tell you what," said Joseph. "You tell Rachel to come see me and we'll get her stocked up. Emma and I have a little extra we could spare."

"I don't want it from you, Joseph. I want it from the slackers!"

Sidney knew the flock was antsy over his pet project, nearly on the verge of revolt. He stood to speak at the next church meeting and his written notes shook in his delicate hands. His face was flushed.

"Brothers and Sisters," he began, "the Devil came to me three times last night. He told me of his wicked plan to stop the United Order. I yelled at the filthy serpent, but he got mad and dragged me from bed by my heels. I was afraid he'd drag me all the way to the pit of hell!"

Ez thought the whole business of being dragged out of bed by his heels was rather farfetched. Joseph was suspicious, too, but he wanted to give the United Order one more chance. So they did for a while, with sputtering starts, stops, givers, and takers until it eventually petered out. Those who had opposed the program discovered with immense relief that the sky hadn't fallen.

Joseph and Emma's house was taking longer to build than expected, so they moved in with the Johnson family on the outskirts of town. The Johnsons were happy to take the Prophet in, because a few months earlier Joseph had cured Sister Johnson's lame arm. He'd taken her wrinkled limb and set it straight as an arrow through the power of prayer.

Having a place to stay was a godsend because Emma was pregnant again and could barely walk. Her legs throbbed and her stomach bore the vertical line of fertility; all the down payments for the reward of delivering a child through a canal that seemed poorly designed for such a task.

The young parents-to-be weren't overly superstitious, but they were mindful of their previous loss and did all they could not to jinx it. Emma soaked in herbal baths, took slow walks around the house, drank moderate amounts of wine, and even wore a corset much of the time—all of the well-known things that should have produced a healthy child.

She delivered twins, both of whom died within hours of their birth.

Joseph's face was puffy and his eyes were red and empty. Was this a test—the refiner's fire for God's chosen servant? Emma looked at him with a blank expression, and then, as if she were blaming him for God's role in the cruelty, she said, "If you're the Prophet and can heal the sick, why can't you heal our own children?"

Joseph had no words, no parable that would turn their dead children into a lesson on the Glory of God. There was no way to bully the Almighty. He kissed her clammy forehead and promised that God would make it up to them somehow.

Another set of twins was born the very next day in the nearby town of Orange. Their mother had died in childbirth, leaving the destitute father with five other children. He offered the newborn twins to Emma and the Prophet, which left them no time to wallow in grief, for there were diapers to rinse.

They thanked God, who had come through for them, if only a little.

7

Tarred and Feathered

Trouble started when the Johnsons' teenage son, Eli, accused Joseph of spying on his sister while she was bathing. The Smiths were staying in a spare bedroom in the Johnsons' house while they waited for their new house to be built. The bedroom was next to the bathroom and Eli swore he caught Joseph ogling his rather plain-looking sister, who had large breasts. Joseph vehemently denied this accusation; the house was small and there were only so many directions one's eyes could look.

"Look me in the eye, Joseph, and tell me this isn't true," Emma hissed when they were finally alone in their bedroom.

"Of course it isn't. It's a simple misunderstanding, but I'll take responsibility for it if it'll help. But, no, I didn't spy on her. Of course I didn't."

Emma stared at him hard for a few more seconds then picked up her basket of laundry.

This was only part of the problem, however. Eli's best friend was a no-account named Symonds who accused Joseph of playing favorites when divvying up the land (Symonds basically wanted more than he'd been given). Joseph was the de-facto Benevolent Dictator, and sometimes his benevolence resulted in uncommon business practices. Joseph thought the problem had been solved when he received a revelation awarding Symonds an additional parcel of land (it was a lousy parcel, but still God had given it to him at no additional cost). This charitable act backfired because, regrettably, Joseph misspelled

Symonds' name in the revelation. Joseph thought this was petty, but Symonds didn't.

"Just who in the hell does he think he is?" Symonds complained to Eli.

"Doesn't sound like much of a prophet to me," said Eli. "Can't even spell your name right."

"How am I supposed to believe in some prophet who can't even spell? Everybody knows you spell my name with a 'y' and not an 'i' and now it's written up permanent in the Book of Commandments. He can have the damned land far as I'm concerned. It ain't worth a nickel, anyways."

"Yeah, he buys it cheap and turns around and sells it to us for a big profit."

"He's makin' a bundle on us, alright."

"That's nuthin' compared to what he did to my sister. Spying on her like he done. He needs to be taught a lesson, that's what he needs. He's a swindler *and* a pervert!"

Over the next few days, Eli took every opportunity to confront Joseph. He'd walk by him in the small house and bump him with his shoulder, or stand in his way so Joseph had to walk around him. If Joseph looked at him, Eli would say, "What're you starin' at?"

Joseph wasn't afraid of these two; indeed, he wanted to knock their blocks off. But he was the prophet and it wouldn't do to have him engage in a bloody fistfight. A few days later he was out in the yard feeding the horses when Eli and Symonds approached him.

"Listen, fellas, I don't want any trouble," said Joseph.

"Well, you got it now!" said Eli, and spit in Joseph's direction. A dollop of saliva dripped to Eli's shirt, which was permanently stained under his arms and around the collar. There were drops of dried tobacco chew near his belly.

Ez happened to be riding by on his horse. "Something the matter here, boys?"

"It's none of your damned business," said Eli.

"Yeah," said Symonds, "You heard him, it ain't nuthin' to nobody."

"It's okay, Ez," said Joseph. "We were just having a little chat."

Ez got off his horse and the beast seemed to sigh with relief.

"We don't want any trouble," Joseph said, and then mumbled something under his breath that sounded an awful lot like, "Jackass."

"What'd you say?"

"I didn't say anything," said Joseph.

"Bullshit!" said Eli and took a step in Joseph's direction.

Ez stepped forward and Eli took a step back, for Ez was imposing and had no fear of this dirty teenager and his ignorant friend.

"This ain't over! Come on, Symonds, let's get outta here." They walked away, but Eli turned and walked backwards for a few steps. "Next time your buddy here's not gonna be around to save ya."

The following day was the first official Church conference and Joseph had promised to reveal the answer to a three-thousand-year-old mystery: the location of the Lost Ten Tribes of Israel. The congregation was conversant with the Bible, and knew all about the ancient prophet Jacob, who'd been given the nickname "Israel" for some reason. Israel had twelve sons who were leaders of their respective tribes. Unfortunately, their evil enemies conquered all twelve of the tribes and ran them off their land. Ten of the tribes disappeared completely, and people had been looking for them ever since.

Joseph dressed with unusual deliberation for the conference. He wore a linen shirt with French cuffs and a cream-colored cravat, which Emma had taught him to tie. She was amused by all his fussing. He wore a gold vest over his shirt and a navy blue blazer. Tan wool trousers and polished boots completed the ensemble.

He stood before his flock of two hundred sheep; tall, handsome, and confident. He didn't regret spending money on the fine clothes, money his followers tithed to the Church. He was the Prophet, after all, and should look the part.

"After they were scattered," began Joseph, "the Lost Ten Tribes of Israel wandered around trying to evade capture. They kept walking until they finally found a home where no one would find them and they could live their lives in peace."

"Where'd they go?"

"They lived in a land near the North Pole. That's why they were never found."

"They were in the North Pole? *That's* where they've been all this time?"

"Yes."

Ez and others with a rudimentary grasp of geography wondered how they wound up in the North Pole when they'd most recently been spotted in Egypt.

During the conference, Joseph appointed a few men to be High Priests in the new Church. This was no trivial honor and one of the appointees jumped onto the table with his arms outstretched, looking up at the ceiling. "I can see God! And, wait, hold it, yep, there's Jesus, too!" The rest of them looked up, but if they saw anything, they kept it to themselves.

Joseph also became carried away in the moment. He saw an elderly man sitting to the side with his deformed hand that curled inward at the wrist. Joseph took hold of it. A hush fell over the gathering while everyone waited for a miracle. "I command you, Brother, in the name of Jesus Christ, to straighten your hand!"

This man, who had an advanced case of rheumatoid arthritis, tried gallantly to straighten it, but it wouldn't budge. Joseph tugged at it again, but still nothing. Joseph spotted another man who was lame and couldn't walk. He commanded him to stand and take some steps. The man only mustered one clumsy half-step before he fell and strained his hip.

When Brother Cole left to retrieve his dead baby, Joseph knew he was in trouble. The baby had died the day before, but Brother Cole refused to bury it until after the conference because he'd hoped for a miracle. Joseph had no choice; he needed to bring the child back from the dead. This was clearly an unreasonable expectation, but Joseph did his best. He prayed frantically but the dead baby didn't whimper. Brother Cole blamed Joseph for the failure.

"What did they expect?" Ez asked Joseph following the conference. "You're not Jesus, for crying out loud."

"I got carried away and now the Saints have lost faith in me."

Indeed, there was rumbling among the Saints when the healings had so publically backfired. Joseph said the healings failed because they weren't technically living in the *real* Promised Land, which was farther west, out in Missouri. He said miracles of that magnitude would only occur in Missouri, and not in Ohio where the land hadn't been properly consecrated.

The next day, God commanded Joseph to visit the Saints in Missouri, where Oliver and Parley had been waiting. The timing of this revelation was fortuitous, because Joseph needed to get out of town until the hubbub over the Peeping Tom accusations and failed healings had blown over.

Eli and Symonds were gathered around the livery stable with a few other scoundrels who drank too much and rarely bathed.

"I heard he's fixin' to leave."

"He's a chickenshit and knows what he's got comin'."

"I figure it's gonna take four or five men, at least."

"I'll get 'em. Doc Dennison and his boys'll help, and so will Mason."

That night in March of 1832 was clear and cold. They gathered early to prepare the pine tar. It was black and thick, so thick it had to be heated to a near boil so it could be poured. They took turns stirring it with a stick as it bubbled in the cast-iron pot over a fire behind the neighbor's barn. A bottle of rotgut made its way around as they convinced each other that Joseph had it coming.

Joseph was sleeping in a trundle bed, next to one of the adopted twins who had the measles. They burst into the house and dragged him out, still in his bedclothes. Joseph fought back; swinging, kicking, scratching, and biting. Picture frames were knocked off their nails and fell to the floor. A table in the entryway was kicked over. There was screaming and cursing. A kerosene lamp crashed to the floor. They reached the front porch and Joseph liberated a bare foot. He kicked Eli in the groin, dropping him like an empty pair of trousers. He curled in a ball, his mouth opening and closing like a goldfish out of water.

They took the sick infant too, and Emma came screaming into the melee. She yanked the child from one of the men whose hands were full with Joseph. Symonds grabbed her.

"Take your filthy hands off me, you pig!" she screamed with God's rage. Symonds knew he was no match for this woman who would have gouged his eyes out and bitten him to the bone. He turned and ran to catch up with the others who'd dragged Joseph to the neighbor's barn.

Two gray mules stood witness in the cold night, uninterested in the brutal beating. A few chickens stirred in a nearby coop. Otherwise they were alone. Four men pinned Joseph down and tore away his shirt. Eli, whose testicles still bore the imprint of Joseph's foot, was enraged. He and Symonds lifted the pot of boiling tar and poured it over Joseph. He screamed.

Tar splashed onto Symonds' feet and he dropped his side of the pot and hopped away, cursing.

"Let's castrate him!"

"I beg you," pled Joseph. "I'll die."

"He's right," said Doc Dennison. "We castrate him and he'll go and bleed to death. I don't want my hands on it. This here's plenty of punishment."

Eli grabbed a bottle of poison and shoved it at Joseph's mouth. Joseph clenched his teeth and shook his head from side to side. The bottle chipped his front tooth and the acid burned his lips. Symonds ripped a feather pillow apart and shook it above Joseph. The tar was still hot and steam rose from where he was pinned down in the dirt.

"Let's get out of here!"

Ezra was in bed when he heard hooves pounding toward his house. Ethan Lange, a neighbor, yelled Ez's name before he got off his horse. He banged on the door.

"It's Joseph! Hurry! They got him!"

"Slow down," said Ez as he put on his britches and boots. "And close the door so the young'uns' don't catch the measles!" Ethan stood in the dark just inside the log house. His hair stuck up like the whiskered seeds of a dandelion. Ez lit the lantern and re-hung it on the nail in the kitchen.

"Ez!" whispered Rachel loudly, "What's going on?" She'd pulled the blanket up to her neck so Ethan wouldn't see her nightdress. She whispered because she didn't want to wake the children, who were sitting up in bed, wide awake.

"It's Joseph," whispered Ethan at full volume. "The Johnson boys dragged him outta bed and they're tarrin' him!"

Ez was on his horse before either the man or beast was fully awake. "Where is he?" he yelled as they approached the Johnson's house where Emma stood beneath a lantern on the sagging front porch. She was hysterical.

"They took him down the road and . . . . " Ez kicked his horse and hooves threw up chunks of frozen mud.

Joseph was bent in half, stumbling back toward the house, like a drunkard.

"Joseph!"

"Sorry, Ez," he moaned. He was stripped to the waist and covered in black tar and feathers. The tar was still warm.

The neighbors heard the commotion and came out in their nightclothes, holding their lanterns at arm's length and squinting into the darkness. They carried Joseph into the house where everyone could see the full extent of his condition. His face was puffy and blotchy, his mouth was bloody, and one eye was swollen shut.

Emma cut the tar from his hair while others scraped it from his body. His skin was raw and blistered. He didn't say much, only that he was sorry for all the trouble. He lisped slightly, and they saw that his front tooth was chipped.

"What happened to your tooth?"

"They tried to shove a bottle of poison down my throat," he whispered, the chipped tooth turning it into a whistle. "It must have chipped my tooth."

"My God," cried Emma, and put a tar-covered hand to her mouth.

His head rested on the sticky black pillow and he turned toward her with the trace of a smile, taking a portion of the pillow with him. "So, Emma, do you still think I'm handsome?" He winked, but his eyelid stuck closed from the tar.

They kept asking him who'd done it, but Joseph said he wasn't sure. But Ez knew, and so did Sister Johnson, Eli's mother, who kept her head down, working extra hard on the tar as a demonstration of her remorse.

It was five o'clock in the morning by the time he'd been scraped and cleaned well enough that he wouldn't stick to the sheets.

The next day was Sunday and the Saints dragged themselves to church. They assumed Joseph wouldn't be able to make it.

And then he walked in. His face looked like it'd been kicked by a mule, and his hair stood up in clumps, like it'd been cut with a dull hay sickle. Emma walked in behind him and shrugged her shoulders, as if she'd tried to keep him home but it'd been no use.

Joseph walked to the front. "Brothers and Sisters," he said, "it's good to be with you today." He spoke with a new whistle, a slight but unmistakable reminder of the torture he had suffered that would stay with him for the rest of his life. "Maybe you've heard I had a little tussle last night. From the looks of it, I guess they got the best of me! But I'll be back to my old self soon enough. What I've been through is nothing compared to the Savior's suffering. And what did He do? He turned the other cheek. So that's what I did, and now both my cheeks are sore!" Joseph laughed in that easy way of his.

And his legend grew.

8

Brigham Young

In the fall of 1832, there came to Kirtland a traveling carpenter from Vermont named Brigham Young. This no-nonsense thirty-year-old had been a Methodist until he read the Book of Mormon. He was baptized and became a zealot for the One and Only True Church. Brigham was an organizational genius, a born leader with a stubborn willingness to fight. He led with strength, dispatching his enemies by the force of his iron will. He complemented Joseph, who focused on the esoteric and led through persuasion.

"I want you all to meet our newest member," said Joseph. "This is Brigham Young." Fifty people were packed into Joseph and Emma's new home. It wasn't quite finished but they'd moved in early because they couldn't keep living at the Johnsons, where Eli loitered without apology. Rags were stuffed into cracks around the window frames to keep the cold out. The window glass was thick and wavy, and had bubbles in it. There were extra logs in the fireplace. The room smelled of kerosene, hair oil, and wet wool.

"I've asked Brother Brigham to say the opening prayer," said Joseph.

Brigham was shorter than Joseph—almost everyone was. He was stocky with an oversized chest. He stood near the hearth and blew his nose loudly into his handkerchief. His prayer began as an ordinary one, complete with the requisite number of "Thees" and "Thous." But the volume gradually rose, becoming so loud that he seemed to be shouting all the way to heaven. Rachel, whose head was bowed, kicked Ez in the shin. And when Brigham started praying in jumbled tongues she kicked him again. Ez peeked at Joseph who was scanning the room through half-opened slits in his eyes. He saw Ez and shrugged his shoulders.

When the prayer ended, Joseph said, "Brother Brigham was praying in the true Adamic language. That is the way Adam spoke when he was living in the Garden of Eden."

Rachel looked at Ez and cocked an eyebrow. Ez shot Joseph a look that Joseph pretended not to see. Ez was amazed at the ease and effortlessness of this lie. Joseph told him afterward that he didn't want to upset Brigham, a new member, and maybe Adam really did speak that way for all he knew.

The Smiths' adopted baby, the one with the measles who'd been yanked from his bed the night Joseph was tortured, died a week later. This was their fourth child to die. Emma felt totally powerless. Other mothers allowed their children to climb onto the hearth, pull the dog's tail, or eat food that'd fallen to the floor. So why did her children die and not theirs?

Brigham believed the baby died because it'd been exposed to cold weather the night Joseph was tarred, and he wanted revenge. "We can't let those bastards get away with this," he said.

"This is Joseph's fight," said Ez. "And he doesn't think it'll do any good to retaliate. And it won't bring the baby back."

"So help me, they give me any excuse and I'll knock their heads off."

"Don't go borrowing trouble, Brigham. What's done is done."

Brigham built a small coffin for the child. Joseph's voice cracked during the graveside service. He still bore the wounds of the beating and the terrible haircut. His swollen eye had gone from livid blue to dirty yellow. Those in attendance wondered, again, why he and Emma had been cursed with the loss of yet another child.

***

God had previously commanded Joseph to visit the Saints in Missouri, and now that he'd healed, it was time to go. Thirty men agreed to go with him. Rachel didn't want Ez to go, but relented when it was clear he was going anyway.

"I'll bring you back something nice from St. Louey."

"With what? You planning to rob a bank or something?"

"Are you sure it's okay if I go?"

"Just promise me you'll stay out of trouble," and she slugged him on his arm.

He turned to leave.

"Excuse me, Ezra William Wells. Aren't you forgetting something?"

She stood on her tippy toes and he kissed her. "There's no city girl who loves you like I do, and don't you forget it, Buster. Now you best get moving."

The thirty men took a steamboat down the Mississippi. They chugged into the St. Louis pier where the water was ugly brown and dirty foam floated away in bands to the slow moving current. Ez carried a cardboard suitcase wrapped shut with twine. Inside was a change of clothes, his shaving kit, and a well-worn copy of the Book of Mormon. A bedroll and canteen were strapped to his back. He made his way like a pickpocket through the crowd of real estate tycoons, fur trappers, and bankers with newspapers tucked under their arms. He apologized to everyone he bumped into, but his courtesy was ignored as the scrum made its way, carrying shopping bags, rifles, and baskets of produce.

The smell of rotting garbage and coal smoke made him want to vomit. There was a bazaar underway just off the pier and women were gathered over a table of colorful scarves, their heads bobbing up and down like hens pecking at grain. Beggars and hookers lined the streets and hotel rooms cost a dollar. They stopped in a saloon where a roughneck bartender set down dirty glasses of whiskey that tasted like turpentine. The outline of a pistol showed beneath his apron.

They pressed on to the Promised Land, which was located in Independence, Missouri, a two hundred mile walk. They endured harsh weather, blisters, and mosquitoes, knowing the Promised Land would be special. But Independence was a disappointment. It was a crude frontier town surrounded by Indians. Shawnees and Kickapoos traipsed through town all hours of the day and night. They erected their teepees in Indian Territory, just to the west of the Promised Land, and the old Missouri settlers built houses just to the east. So the Mormons were squeezed tight between the two, neither of which appeared to care a lick about the truth that was sitting right in front of their noses.

President Andrew Jackson, who had recently signed the Indian Removal Act, had sent the Indians there. Unfortunately for the Indians, Old Hickory hadn't read the Book of Mormon, so he didn't know these so-called savages were formerly white Jews. His naiveté on this issue cost the Indians dearly. After the government took all their property, they were ordered to move west, to the other side of the Mississippi River. This was justified because, among other things, they didn't have proper title to the land.

Most of the Mormons in Missouri had never met Joseph personally, and they took an immediate liking to him. "He's so tall and handsome," some of the sisters whispered. "I can really feel his spirit," others gushed.

Joseph told them he couldn't stay long. "But Joseph," said Oliver, "you just got here! This is the Promised Land."

"I know. But I can't abandon the Saints up in Kirtland."

"So you'll just abandon us instead?"

"What would you have me do? I can't be in both places."

"Why can't the Saints in Kirtland come down here? This is where we belong."

"The New Jerusalem isn't properly built up yet."

"That's exactly why we need them! We've been working our tails off getting it ready for the Second Coming, but we need your help."

"Keep up the good work and we'll unite the Saints later."

Oliver turned around to face the wilderness and threw his gloves to the ground. "And when's that going to be?" he asked without turning around.

"Soon."

As they were leaving, an uncommonly faithful man came to Joseph and told him that his wife had come down with consumption. Joseph followed him to his small cabin where the woman lay in damp sheets, sweating with fever. Her fingers were clubbed like drumsticks, a dire telltale sign. Joseph wanted to help the woman, of course he did, but he worried the healing power might not work again, even though they were well within the undisputed geographical boundaries of the Promised Land. So he didn't go out on a limb with any promises, for he knew God would not be hog-tied in this way. The poor woman succumbed before they could get out of town.

Joseph's spirits dragged on the long walk back to Kirtland. His thumbs were tucked under the straps of his backpack and his canteen swung in rhythm with each stride. Little grasshoppers flew up wherever they stepped.

"Don't be so hard on yourself, Joseph."

"You know what hurts the most?" He put his head down and walked a few more steps on the dusty road, kicking at a few rocks with his boots. "It's that they still believe in me and I've let them down."

"You can only do your best. And if that's not enough, well, God will have to step in."

"That's what I'm counting on."

The strain on the charismatic twenty-seven-year-old Prophet was demanding. His fledging Church was split in two places, separated by eight hundred miles of bad roads and Indians. They needed him in both places, but Kirtland needed him more because they were on the verge of bankruptcy. And Joseph knew the true Church had no business going bankrupt.

No matter how many jars of pickled beets and sacks of Brussels sprouts were donated to the Lord, it seemed the Church was always short on cash. At least theirs was a holy poverty, for they knew they were the Chosen People, but it didn't appear the meek were about to inherit anything. Joseph had borrowed as much as he could against real estate the Church owned. This infusion of cash did not produce an encore to the loaves and fishes, but it did allow him to buy a nicer home on one hundred acres in Kirtland.

"Ez," asked Rachel, "why does Emma get the nicest house in town? You and the rest of the men work your tails off."

"He'll pay it back."

"I should certainly hope so! I swear, every time I see her she has a new set of clothes."

The Smith's newfound affluence showed itself in his suits—beautiful black tailcoats with velvet trim and knotted cravats. Emma, too, had inched her way up the ladder to silk and twill, but she'd done so reluctantly because she was sensitive to the talk around town. Joseph had begun to enjoy the finer things in life at the expense of the widow's mite, but he was also charitable.

Emma asked him, "Whatever happened to the pig we got from Brother Whitmer?"

"I gave it to Sister Hemstrom, the old widow."

"I don't mean to be selfish, really I don't, but why do you give everything away when we're barely getting by ourselves?"

"She needs it more than we do, Emma."

Joseph was careful in his generosity. Not calculating, for that implies everything he did had an unrighteous motive, which is inaccurate. However, he was publicly generous in a way that made the people in his little church love him for his bigheartedness. Emma began to believe that he might crave their love and attention more than he craved love and attention from her.

***

God commanded Joseph to build a temple. This was to be a glitzy affair, one fancy enough for Jesus, because the Saints didn't want to offend Him with something that wasn't top-of-the-line. Fortunately, the Lord was quite specific about the type of temple He wanted, so they were spared the anxiety of second-guessing His tastes. He ordered it to be three stories high with a foundation that was to be precisely fifty-five feet by sixty-five feet. God didn't elaborate on His reasons for ordering these particular dimensions, but the Saints assumed He must've had a perfectly valid reason.

The men cut blocks of sandstone quarried from Gildersleeve Mountain and loaded them to rickety wagons. They were all engaged in following the Almighty's blueprint, so it was mostly harmonious. However, there were the occasional rifts. Once, an overzealous Canadian convert began praying over a piece of sandstone, beseeching God to help him dislodge the stone so loudly that his former neighbors in Quebec could've heard him. Joseph galloped down on his horse in a cloud of dust to see what the fuss was all about.

"What's the matter with you? You're braying so loud you sound just like a jackass!"

The other men at the job site shoveled faster, pretending not to be listening. On his way out of town, the former Saint muttered, "I'll be goddamned if I'm gonna let some foul-mouthed prophet talk to *me* like that!"

"What got into *him*?" asked Brigham as the convert rode off.

"I was too hard on him," said Joseph. "He was just doing his best, and here I go and chastise him for praying."

"That wasn't praying," said Ez.

"No, it sure wasn't," said Brigham.

Ez threw another block of sandstone to the wagon bed where it landed with an explosion of dust. "They sure didn't pray like that in the Bible."

"No," said Joseph. "But the Bible is not completely accurate. In fact, I've decided to re-translate it."

"Why?" Ez figured the Bible was the Bible, and didn't need tinkering.

"See, the Book of Mormon is the most accurate book on earth because I translated it directly from the golden tablets by divine revelation. But the Bible isn't as accurate because it's been translated so many times. So I'm going to re-translate it one final time, because it ought to be 100% exactly right."

Joseph began his re-write with the first section, which he titled the Book of Moses. He said it should have been included in the Bible from the beginning, but wasn't for some reason.

"This will be the Inspired Version of the Bible, and it will replace the King James Version." Joseph was careful to emphasize that the Bible was still the word of God, and wasn't wholly deficient—only that it needed some shoring up in parts.

"So what are some of the new parts?" asked Brigham a few weeks into the edit.

"The Bible has never been entirely clear on who created the world. God has now told me that both He *and* Jesus created it, so I think it's important that I put that back in. And the Bible was missing the part where we all lived as spirits in heaven before we were born, so I included that, too."

"We did?"

"Yes. We all lived with God as spirits and voted to come down from heaven to get our bodies."

"We voted?"

"Yes, and those who voted in Jesus' favor were allowed to come down to earth and get a body."

"I'll be darned," said Ez. "What happened to people who voted for somebody else?"

"They weren't born. They're just evil spirits under Satan's command."

"Well, I agree *that* oughta be put back in there."

"Actually, God created millions of worlds, not just the planet we're living on."

"I didn't know that either."

But the most exciting thing in the new Inspired Version of the Bible was further proof that Joseph was the Chosen Prophet. Apparently, three thousand years earlier, Moses had actually prophesied that Joseph would become the modern prophet. However, for some reason that prophecy had been edited out along the way. So Joseph put it back in where it belonged. Joseph's new translation of the Bible now correctly reads: "A seer would arise in the latter days and would be called Joseph, after the name of his father." This seer would be "highly esteemed and would be great like unto Moses."

Naturally, the Saints were thrilled to have this corroborating piece of evidence that Joseph was indeed the Prophet for the Last Days, just as Moses predicted he would be. Joseph's father was also named Joseph, so the Saints were hard-pressed to figure who *else* the Bible would've been referring to.

A preacher from Cleveland rode through Kirtland after Joseph completed the first round of editing. He wore a tall black hat and expensive coat over a fine twill shirt with mother-of-pearl buttons. He was in the tavern when someone brought up the new Bible.

"My God, it is pure blasphemy to translate the Bible!"

"But it's been done many times, has it not?" said Brigham.

"Not in hundreds of years. And what's this nonsense I've heard about him inserting his own name into the Holy Bible? Why, the arrogance of it stinks to high heaven!"

"But this is the *Inspired Version* of the Bible, so it's more accurate."

"Oh, please," the preacher said. "If you could do that, everybody would do it."

"Well, I don't remember seeing *your* name in it."

"And that is precisely because I am a minister of God and do not have the audacity to do such a thing." He took another drink and shook his head. "Inserting your own name into the Bible—why, it's the most preposterous thing I've ever heard! Where is this Joseph Smith anyway?"

"He's working on the temple. Wanna meet him?"

"I certainly would! I'd like to see with my own eyes a young man who has the unmitigated gall to insert his own name into the Holy Bible."

The men escorted the preacher to the quarry at the base of Gildersleeve Mountain where Joseph was directing the cutting of stone. He was filthy.

"*That* is your prophet?"

"Indeed it is. Come on, we'll introduce you."

The preacher tiptoed through the chips of stone and mud to where Joseph stood holding a shovel. He was eating an apple.

"Joseph, this here's a preacher from Cleveland."

Joseph threw the apple core to the side and wiped his hand on the seam of his trousers, then extended it to the preacher. "It's a pleasure to meet you, sir."

The preacher reluctantly held out his hand and winced when Joseph took it. He pulled a handkerchief from his pocket and wiped his hand of the dirt and shame at having shaken the hand of a blasphemous tyrant.

"So, if you're the prophet, why don't you show me a miracle?"

"Okay, I can do that sure enough," said Joseph.

"You can?" asked the preacher.

"Sure I can. Now, let's see, would you like me to make you blind or crippled? Maybe make your hand withered? You tell me. Go ahead and take your pick and it shall be done."

"Well, now," said the preacher, "of course I want no such thing."

"In that case, I guess I can't help you, because I surely don't want to bring trouble on anyone else just to convince you. That wouldn't be fair now, would it?"

The rest of the Saints laughed, and the preacher left in a huff. Oh, how the Saints loved their unorthodox Prophet.

These were heady times in Kirtland where everything seemed to be directed by the calculating hand of Providence. So when Brother Hyde fell to the ground from a thirty-foot scaffold while whitewashing the temple walls, the Saints saw additional evidence of God's mercy because Brother Hyde didn't die, he only fractured his skull.

Their belief was real to them, but without definitive form. So when the disbeliever reached for tangible proof, there wasn't much to grab.

9

The Mummy

They had lain peacefully for 2,000 years in the catacombs of Thebes, the ancient Egyptian city on the bank of the Nile. No one disturbed their slumber until 1820, when the temptation to dig for antiquity and the enticement to plunder became too great. The catacombs were not off-limits; just about anyone could roam around inside. Goats, dogs, and rats patrolled them, competing for space with the impoverished Arabian families living there. The floors were strewn with broken bones and human dust, for the corpses had been there for two millennia. These were the mummies, and there were hundreds of them.

The stench in the dark tombs was eye-watering. Peasants used coffins for firewood, and the smell of roasting dogs, rats, or skinny goats combined to make the tombs uninhabitable. But it was in this humble place that the world's greatest discovery was made. And the man who made it had no idea what he'd found.

Antonio Lebolo was an enterprising Italian with a predisposition to greed. He'd heard about the archeological digs and smelled profit, so he packed his bags and headed to Egypt. He found it easy to outwit the Arabian peasants by pretending to be fluent in hieroglyphics. When he saw obelisks that were covered with ancient writing, presumably of some consequence (because who builds an obelisk to print the mundane?), he told the peasants the writing was that of his ancestors, so they belonged to him. The peasants didn't make a fuss because the obelisks couldn't be eaten, or burned.

Lebolo spent his time in the catacombs, looting the burial sites. He justified the pillage as a contribution to the Arabian economy because he paid ten shillings a piece for the mummies (and re-sold them for a handsome profit). An English traveler bought one of the mummies on his way to Cairo. He'd hoped it'd been wrapped with a gold coin inside—a bribe for the gatekeeper in Paradise. When he didn't find gold on the poor mummified Egyptian, he threw it into the Nile. Lebolo, who had mummies to spare, sold him another one from his stock at a nice discount. Unfortunately, this mummy wound up in the Nile, too.

The Arabian peasants allowed the profiteers' access to the catacombs, unaware of the bounty they held, for who among them had use for a decayed mummy? One of the looters noted in his journal the following:

> *Upon entering the catacomb through a passage, I sought a resting-place and sat; but when my weight bore upon the body of an Egyptian, it crushed like a bandbox. I used my hands to sustain my weight, but they found no better support; so I sank amid the broken mummies with a crash of bones, which raised such a cloud of dust that I had to sit motionless for half an hour, waiting for it to subside. I was finally able to move about, but with every step I took I crushed a mummy in some part or another. It was choked with mummies, and I couldn't pass without putting my face in contact with that of some decayed Egyptian; bones, legs, arms, and heads rolled from above. Thus, I proceeded from one cave to another, all full of mummies piled up; some standing, some lying, and some on their heads.*

Lebolo found eleven mummies in one cave that were preserved enough to be removed without falling to pieces. He kept those, along with the individual scrolls that were buried alongside each of them.

These scrolls were called breathing permits, like an obituary or calling card, which allowed the mummies safe passage to the next world. Lebolo died soon thereafter, but not before bequeathing the eleven mummies to his nephew, who lived in New York City.

Michael Chandler had been pleasantly surprised by his uncle's bequest. The Lebolos were enthusiastic capitalists, and Chandler was anxious to profit from the unfortunate passing of these Egyptians. So he toured the eastern United States with the eleven mummies in the back of his covered wagon, displaying and selling them off to the highest bidders.

By the time he reached Kirtland in the summer of 1835, he only had four mummies left. The mummies lay side by side in the covered wagon like sacks of flour wrapped in bandages. The curious Kirtlanders lined up to see them for a penny per look. Chandler described the scrolls that lay next to them as Egyptian papyrus, but he didn't know what was written on them. Indeed, no one did. The Rosetta Stone had been discovered thirty years earlier, but the ability to read Egyptian was still rather spotty.

There were illustrations on the papyrus, too, along with the writing. There was the drawing of a man lying on an altar, while another man stood above him with a knife in his hand. The man holding the knife was dressed in an elaborate loincloth and his head was the shape of a cobra. There were strange drawings of vases, columns, knives, and exotic birds in the background. This was a story told with pictures and unintelligible letters or symbols. But what did it mean?

"Hey," one of the Mormons said, "we know somebody who can translate these scrolls. It's our prophet, Joseph Smith."

Chandler leaned against the covered wagon and folded his arms. "Yeah, I think I've heard of him," he said. "Didn't he write a gold Bible?"

"Well, actually it's the Book of Mormon. The ancient Americans wrote their history on a stack of gold tablets. An angel told Joseph where the tablets were buried and he dug them up."

"What did the writing on them look like?" asked Chandler.

"We're not sure because we didn't see it."

"What do you mean you didn't see it? Then how'd you know it was ancient writing?"

"Joseph told us."

"So how'd he figure out what the writing said?"

"He used the Urim and Thummin."

"The what?"

"The Urim and Thummin. They're basically magic eyeglasses."

"Eyeglasses you say?"

"Yeah, they were like spectacles, but we weren't allowed to see them, either." The Mormons who were standing next to the wagon looked at each other, slightly sheepishly.

"So you think this Joe Smith fella can use the magic spectacles to read these scrolls?"

"Yeah, but he doesn't have the spectacles anymore."

"What happened to them?"

"They got taken back up into heaven along with the golden tablets."

"They did?"

"Uh-huh."

"Who took them back to heaven?"

"The angel did. But maybe he can use his peepstone."

Chandler didn't know what a peepstone was either, so they had to explain the magic stone that Joseph put in the bottom of his hat.

"Mind if we take the scrolls for a while so Joseph can read them?"

Chandler was no dummy, and he insisted they buy the mummies first. "I'd really hate to sell them," he lied, "but for the right price I suppose I could let them go."

"How much is that going to cost?"

"Course, I couldn't let the scrolls go without including the mummies, too. It's gotta be a package deal. And all told, for the four of them, let's see..." Chandler stood looking up at the sky with his finger to his lower lip. "Okay, I figure it'd be $2,400. Give me another two hundred and I'll throw in the wagon, too."

"That's an awful lot of money for a bunch of old mummies."

"Yes," said Chandler. "But these are special mummies. That writing's probably important. But there's no guarantee."

The Saints huddled with Joseph, who said he could probably translate the scrolls, but they didn't have the money. This was a terrible dilemma because they itched to know what was written on the scrolls. Was this God's mysterious way of delivering them to Joseph so he could tell the world what they said, just as He'd done with the golden tablets? Why else would Egyptian mummies pop up in the frontier of Ohio? So they sold off enough possessions to buy the four mummies and scrolls.

Joseph was thrilled to have the mummy scrolls. They were tangible possessions that he could keep, unlike the gold tablets. The proper translation of these scrolls would prove, once and for all, that he was the Prophet. So he barricaded himself in his room to begin the arduous task of translating them.

Ez was in his shop several days later, laboring over a stubborn spoke, when Joseph came in.

"You're not going to believe it!" Joseph paced back and forth on the shop's floor that had once been ordinary dirt, but was now rock-hardened clay from spilled oil, grease, sweat, and the excrement of a stray mutt that had wandered in a few years earlier and refused to leave.

"What am I not going to believe?"

"The scrolls."

"Yeah, what about them?"

"Are you ready for this?"

"For what?"

"One of those mummies was the prophet Abraham!"

"Hold on. You mean the *real* Abraham? From the Bible? He's one of the mummies from the back of the wagon?"

"Yes! And one of the scrolls is in his own handwriting!"

"Seriously?"

"And another one of the mummies is Joseph who was sold as a slave into Egypt, and became the Pharaoh's right hand man!"

"Abraham and Joseph of Egypt both? *Holy Mother of Jesus!*" He sat down on a dirty sawhorse, flabbergasted at the news.

"God sent us those mummies, Ez. That's all there is to it. That Chandler fella was just a puppet in God's hands to deliver them to me."

"Can you tell what he looked like?"

"No, there's been way too much decay."

"Who were the other ones? Could they be Noah or someone?"

"I don't know who they were." This admission lent credibility to the identity of the other two somehow.

"Did Abraham give us a special message on his scroll?"

"I'll say he did. The Lord has opened up the mysteries of heaven."

"Like what?"

"Well, for starters, now we know where God lives."

"We do?"

"He lives on Kolob."

"What's Kolob?"

"That's the name of the orb where God lives. There's an order to the universe. There's the Earth and the Moon; we all know that. But what we didn't know until now is the moon's correct name."

"It's not just called the moon?"

"No. Its real name is Olea."

"Olea?"

"Yes, and the correct name of the sun is Shinehah."

"Well, I'll be damned."

"And going up higher, there are the stars, but technically they should be called kokaubeams. And Kolob, where God lives, is the greatest kokaubeam of all. There are millions of worlds out there, and they all have their own Gods, there isn't just one."

"There isn't just one God?"

"No, there are lots of Gods. The God for our planet is Elohim. But other galaxies have their own separate Gods."

"That's what Abraham wrote on the scrolls?"

"Uh-huh."

"And it's in his own handwriting?"

"Well, he might have dictated it to a scribe, I'm not sure. But they're definitely his words. So this is the oldest writing in history!"

Ez, never a student of arithmetic, paused to calculate. "Let's see, the earth is 6,000 years old, so . . . ," he looked up at the ceiling from the sawhorse to concentrate. "Those scrolls are practically half as old as the earth!"

"God is opening the secrets of heaven to us."

"This is the greatest discovery in history!"

Joseph named his translation of the mummy scrolls the Book of Abraham. It immediately became a sacred text of Mormonism, standing next to the Bible and the Book of Mormon as Holy Scripture.

The Saints, now numbering nearly two thousand, were gathered in a large field fanning themselves in the sun. The dry summer weeds were out and grasshoppers jumped around them. The partially completed Kirtland temple provided an inspiring backdrop for the rollout of Mormonism's newest scripture. Joseph stood before the Saints in his Sunday best. In one hand, he held a bound copy of the Book of Mormon, and in the other, a manuscript of the Book of Abraham, both of them having been delivered to him in spectacular fashion.

"Brothers and Sisters." He had to shout to be heard. "God continues to shower the truth upon us. He gave us the Book of Mormon," and he held the book high above his head. "And now He has given us the scroll of Abraham, preserved with his mummified body in the catacombs of Egypt for three thousand years." He held the manuscript above his head with his other hand. "This proves we are the Chosen People, and this is His only true church."

A seventeen-year-old girl stood in the middle of the crowd. Her hair was the color of wheat and she had deep-set green eyes. Most knew her only as Fanny, the Smith's house servant. Was it his stirring sermon that aroused her soul like the sensual touch of warm fingers, or was it the man? Was he looking for her now as his blue eyes swept the audience, or was it just her imagination? Was his voice heating her soul, or only her body, a body that longed for him? She knew it was both, and the thought caused her to blush.

"God has shown me the mysteries of heaven. We were sent to this earth to obtain physical bodies so we can be more like God and Jesus, because they, too, have bodies of flesh and blood."

He found her in the audience and their eyes met. He left them there to caress her for two, three, four long seconds before moving on. It had happened behind the barn, a month after Fanny began working for them. They'd hardly spoken to each other, except through their eyes, and then they'd both been drawn to the nearest privacy with the urgent pull of longing. It had been reckless. It had been hurried, and desperate.

"There was a great war in heaven between those who fought for Jesus and those who fought for Lucifer. Those of us who fought for Jesus were allowed to come to this earth and obtain bodies, and those who fought with Lucifer were cast off to become everlasting demons of darkness."

She had to be careful around Emma—they both did. She pretended not to feel his gaze, but when she was alone with her thoughts, he consumed them.

"God has promised us that we can become Gods, too." He paused to let the significance of this new doctrine sink in. "Now, I know our Christian friends find fault in this eternal truth. But we know through divine revelation that each of us will progress eternally until, one day, we can also become perfected beings. And when that time comes, each of us will be given our own planet."

There was murmuring in the crowd. This was a bombshell. They would be given their own planets one day. The Saints looked at each other with awe.

"Yes," Joseph continued, "we will live as Gods and Goddesses on our own planets and reign over our posterity, just as our Heavenly Father reigns over us."

Could it really be, Fanny wondered? Would she share a heavenly kingdom with Joseph one day, just as he'd promised her? Would it be like the constellation of stars that conspired to spell his name whenever she looked up at night, or would her hopes drop like falling stars, the empty promise of illusion? Was he God's chosen Prophet, or a master magician? Would God punish her for loving him like she did? Perhaps. But if he was the chosen Prophet, how could it be a sin to have slept with him? And if he was the Prophet and she denied him, would her punishment be even greater? The questions were left dangling in her mind when she noticed that he was looking directly at her. Yes, she was certain of it. She touched her hair. She felt like the first time he'd touched her, a knowing brush of her arm that made her shiver.

"When Jesus comes again, he will come to us, in this, the Promised Land. And the earth will be cleansed with fire and the wicked will be burned. The earth will turn into a crystal ball and Jesus will reign as God in this, His Kingdom."

Joseph genuinely loved his people, and they loved him. They needed someone to believe in, and he needed them to believe in him, too. He inspired them with the promise of eternal life as Gods and Goddesses—not just mere admission to heaven, but to become Gods and rule over their own planet. Now, *that* was motivating. It could only come about, however, through membership in the Church, the very one that God had blessed with overwhelming evidence of authenticity—the Book of Mormon, the Book of Abraham, and the Prophet.

Joseph had learned that motivating his followers was fairly easy. He wasn't crass enough to suggest this was a charade, or a scheme to defraud them. To the contrary, he sold them hope and a promise that no mere preacher or politician could do. The carrot was eternal life as a God, and the stick was everlasting damnation. Become a God with your own planet, or roast on a spit in the pit of hell?

The sell was fairly straightforward.

10

Fanny and the Sexual Feast

The whispers started cropping up before the temple was even finished. Could it really be true that Joseph was carrying on with Fanny Alger, the pretty seventeen-year-old maid? Ez, who was one of the few who could talk to Joseph without dancing around a point, came right out and asked him.

"Joseph, what in tarnation is going on with Fanny?"

"Fanny who?"

"Don't give me that 'Fanny who' business."

"Oh, you mean the Fanny who's living with us?"

"That's exactly who I mean. There're some ugly rumors floating around."

"That is ridiculous. Satan uses my enemies to spread lies. I'm surprised there aren't even more crooked tales about me."

"So, it isn't true?"

"Now why would I go around doing something like that?"

"So you didn't?"

"Ez, if I did something like that everyone would have my head on a skillet. Fanny's a nice girl and I don't want her reputation tarnished."

"So it's a lie?"

"If you were Satan, what would you do to stop God's work? You'd get the Saints to disbelieve me, right? And what better way to do that than to start some ugly rumor like this and watch it spread."

"So it's Satan, and you and Fanny aren't . . . ."

"I try to be friendly to everyone and especially those in my employ. I suppose that generosity has been misinterpreted by some."

"So you've just been friendly, but nothing more than just a . . . ."

"If some people are going to denounce the Prophet, I guess that's their business now, isn't it?"

Fanny was very beautiful, but not according to Rachel. She told Ez that Fanny was too skinny. Ez wisely agreed with her that Fanny was indeed too skinny. In fact, he emphatically insisted that he hated all skinny girls. Then he realized Rachel was skinny too, so he said he liked her being skinny but she was the only skinny one he liked. Rachel just shook her head.

Emma was mortified and threw poor Fanny out. The Saints agreed that it must have been Fanny's fault for being such a hussy, because they couldn't believe the Prophet was having an affair with the teenage maid. Fanny would only say that what happened between them was no one else's business. "It's between Joseph and me." This defense lacked a punch. Fanny must have been a tramp, if for nothing more than refusing to defend the Prophet with more conviction.

Emma wanted to believe her husband's denials, but there was a lot of smoke, so she assumed there was fire. She was too embarrassed to share her shame with anyone but Rachel.

"How am I supposed to compete with her? She's half my age."

"Emma, you are beautiful and strong, and Joseph loves you."

"Does he?"

"Of course he does."

"Rachel, let's be honest. I'm in my thirties and this . . . this *girl*, is young and beautiful."

"But you are smart and strong. And beautiful."

"It doesn't seem like Joseph wants smart and strong, now does it?"

"You don't even know the rumors are true."

"Well, what do *you* think, Rachel? I'm not stupid. She won't even deny it."

Rachel was angry at all men, or so it seemed. That night Ez (who was a man) got a grilling.

"Spit it out, Ez. Did he do it?"

"Nah, he wouldn't do a thing like that."

"Does he deny it?"

"Mostly."

"*Mostly?*"

"Listen, Rach, Joseph's doing the Lord's work and Satan will do whatever he can to confuse people."

Rachel stared at him, having learned that if she let the quiet linger, Ez would eventually confess to fill up the silence. Ez, however, had learned to keep his mouth shut.

Rachel finally blinked. "I don't know. Poor Emma's fit to be tied. If you ever . . . why, so help me Ezra . . . ."

"Rach, come here."

She didn't move. She would not be so easily mollified—she was still mad at all men. Ez stood with his arms outstretched and cocked his head. She reluctantly went to him, satisfied that Ez wasn't like all other men. He was so large and soft that he completely enveloped her, like a child being wrapped in her mother's fur coat.

A week or two later, Joseph caught up to Ez at the temple construction site. "Ez, you got a minute?"

"Sure. What's up?"

"I've been thinking about how the Lord allowed the prophets in the Bible to have multiple wives. They all had them, you know, including Abraham."

"So?"

"Well, what would you think about that?"

"About what?" He took another shovel full of dirt and threw it to a pile.

"What if the Lord brought back the commandment about multiple wives?"

Ez stuck the shovel in the ground. "You mean *now*?"

"Uh-huh."

"Well, that isn't going to happen. And you'd have a helluva time convincing the women to go along with it. Emma's already up in arms."

"But God doesn't change. If the ancient prophets had multiple wives, maybe modern prophets should have them, too. Just to be consistent."

"So you're saying you'd just go out and marry a bunch of other women? Have you completely lost your mind?"

"No, of course not. I'd only do it if God commanded it."

"Well, come on, Joseph. Get serious. That isn't going to happen."

A few days later Joseph rode his horse over to Ez's house. "Can we go for a walk? There's something I want to show you."

"What is it?" asked Ez when Rachel was out of earshot (she'd had the sudden urge to take a rag to the front door, which had never been cleaned so thoroughly, or with such force).

"Listen to this," said Joseph. "It's something I just read from a preacher up in New York." He pulled a crumpled newspaper clipping from his vest pocket and read: "The marriage supper of the Christ is a feast at which every dish is free to every guest. In a holy community, sexual intercourse shouldn't be restrained by law any more than eating and drinking should be. The guests of the marriage supper may each have his favorite dish, each a dish of his own choosing, and without the jealousy of exclusiveness."

Joseph folded the paper and put it back in his pocket. "So what do you think?"

"I'll tell you what I think. That preacher has a hankering for other women. And all that supper talk is just plain crazy."

"Yeah, you're probably right. I just thought it was interesting."

Ez would later regret that he hadn't done more to stop the "sexual dish" business then and there.

***

Emma became pregnant again and Joseph was especially attentive to her. Emma didn't dare dream about the child growing old, and she and Joseph hardly discussed names, for fear they might curse it.

When the midwife came, Rachel came with her so that Emma didn't have to suffer alone. Emma suffered all right, and not in silence, but this time it was worth it.

They named him Joseph III.

***

It was about this time that another beautiful woman arrived in Kirtland: Ez's twenty-five-year-old sister, Lorna. She had been separated from her older brother for more than twenty years, ever since their father, in an astonishing display of poor judgment, abandoned them for his second wife.

The Reed family in Palmyra had taken Lorna in. They hadn't joined Joseph's church because they thought he was a fraud and their opinion had rubbed off on Lorna.

One day, Mr. Reed accidentally shot himself in the head. He'd been climbing over a fence, and set his musket against a picket. He tripped on it somehow, and it fired, quite by chance, into his skull. They found him bent over the fence like a sheet left to dry on the line.

Without her husband, Mrs. Reed couldn't afford to keep fifteen-year-old Lorna, so the girl was taken in by the Bensons. The Bensons wanted her to marry and settle down with a forty-year-old shut-in at the end of the street. But Lorna would not settle like the dust that coated the unused bridle and tack in this man's shed.

The Bensons hoped to polish up her faith (they were Mormons and wanted to save her). It might have worked if not for their sixteen-year-old son, Jacob, who acted like a Billy goat with three peckers. And Lorna, presumably because she hadn't been going to church, acted like a mare that'd backed into the fence. One day Brother Benson—a man with an unblemished record of church attendance—heard some giggling coming from the hayloft. He climbed the ladder and saw a bare foot sticking out of the hay.

"Who's in there?" he hollered.

It was the only time that Jacob hadn't felt amorous toward Lorna. Instead, at least for the moment, he wished she'd never been born.

"I'll give you one more chance and then I'm gonna take a pitchfork to that pile of hay!"

Jacob sat up wearing nothing but hay on his head.

"What in tarnation! Who's in there with ya?" Brother Benson was not an educated man, but he knew Jacob would not be giggling under a pile of hay for no reason, and he knew the smaller foot belonged to someone else.

Finally, Lorna poked her head out, too.

"As God is my witness!"

"Sorry, Pa. We weren't—it ain't what it looks like. She was just . . . ."

"I'll not have you drag my son to hell." He knew Lorna must have beguiled his son because they were churchgoers. "We took you in as any good Christian family would, and this is how you repay us. With this . . . this *filth!*"

"I'm sorry, Brother Benson. I was just—"

"Why, you no-good whore! Seducing our Jacob right under our noses."

"But me and him—we were just—"

"Shut that wicked mouth." Oh, the spittle flew.

"But, if you'll just—"

"I said shut it! Now get up and get out of my house."

"But I'm not dressed and—"

Brother Benson made a move for the pitchfork. Lorna jumped up and tried to cover herself with the dress she held, but he stood in front of the ladder and wouldn't move out of the way. She finally squeezed her way around him and climbed down the ladder while his eyes devoured her. The colt in the barn didn't even bother to look at her bare backside, just switched its tail as she ran past.

Word quickly spread that the Wells girl, Satan's lecherous pawn, was seducing all the boys in town. Lorna was beautiful and had a sinful figure, so, naturally, all the women in town hated her. And the righteous men pretended to as well. "Yeah, she's trouble, that one."

Ez and Rachel would have taken her in, but they were struggling newlyweds and had no room. Besides, The Reverend would've called in the Cavalry of Piety, presumably having forgotten what Jesus had to say about these situations. Joseph's mother considered taking her in but they had no room, either. She also knew that, William, her son (the one who claimed Joseph had invented the story of the angel), would've chased Lorna around the farmhouse like water dripping off the paddles of a steamboat until he caught her (or vice versa).

So Lorna moved in with the Winchell family. Mr. Winchell had a houseful of daughters and a wife, but none of them looked like Lorna. Lorna was fine-boned, with an ample bosom. These features inspired Mr. Winchell to insist that they did, indeed, have room for her. Mrs. Winchell complained to her charitable husband that they didn't, but Mr. Winchell said that, as Christians, it was their duty to make room for her. This led to an argument when she reminded him that he'd refused to take in her own mother on the grounds they had no room. But he stamped his foot in a fit of self-righteousness and said, "Quit your yammerin' now, Bernice. She's stayin'. It's the Christian thing to do."

Mrs. Winchell treated Lorna poorly when Mr. Winchell wasn't around. She didn't give a hoot what the Good Book said about these things. Lorna sneaked out whenever she could to secretly meet up with Jacob Benson, who had promised his parents he would never see her again. They wanted to get married, but Jacob's father wouldn't hear of it. He wouldn't allow his son to marry a tramp that ran around his barn naked. He wanted to see her, of course, even ogle her, but he didn't want his son to marry her.

Jacob's parents were mortified when Lorna became pregnant. "We taught you better!" Jason's father thundered. "We told you she was nothing but a whore, dammit, and now look what you've done!"

Some said Lorna's miscarriage a few months later was God's punishment for their premarital sin. And when Jacob's horse threw him after it'd scared up a snake a few weeks later, and Jacob landed with his head on a rock and died, they said that was God's punishment, too.

That was when Ez insisted that his widowed sister move to Kirtland. The Saints welcomed her, up to a point. However, Lorna didn't believe in God. This confused the Saints. How could anyone not believe in God? Lorna ignored all the signs that should've caused her to reach for God's mercy, but she couldn't reconcile a loving God with such tragedy and hatred. The very people who claimed devotion to His teachings allowed so little of it to seep in.

11

The Curse

It was March of 1836, and Davy Crockett was fighting for his life. Santa Anna's Mexican troops outnumbered Crockett and his fellow Texans seven to one. The Texans were holed up in a Catholic mission that was only lightly fortified against attack (having been built to fight sin, not bullets). The mission was called The Alamo.

The Texans bravely repelled the larger Mexican force twice, but they were routed on the third assault. The Mexicans swarmed through the main doors and scaled the stucco walls like ants, showing no mercy to the trapped defenders. Two hundred Texans were shot to death at point blank range, including Davy Crockett and Jim Bowie, who fought valiantly to the bitter end.

Eight hundred miles to the northeast, another battle was underway in Missouri. It, too, was fought over boundaries and territory. Their battleground was the Promised Land.

The Mormons were not well liked. This puzzled them, because they were honest, hard-working folks who wanted to get along. The frontiersmen they mingled with were a crude bunch who roamed the area with smelly clothes, vulgar sensibilities, and foul mouths. The Mormons didn't want to hoard the truth for themselves, so they told these Missourians if they didn't repent of their wicked ways, they'd go to hell. "Only the righteous can go to heaven, you know." This was a difficult thing for the frontier settlers to hear, because no one wants to know ahead of time that they're headed for the brimstone.

According to letters that filtered back to Kirtland from the Saints in Missouri, the situation there was a tinderbox. The Missourians believed the Mormons aimed to take over the state and make their Church the *only* Church.

"And what would be so doggone bad about that anyway?" Ez wondered out loud to Rachel over dinner back in Kirtland. "We've only told them about the truth for their own damned good." The Mormons tried not to be boastful, but they had the irritating habit of reminding their neighbors that the Last Days had arrived and they were about to be burned crisp if they didn't join their church. "So I don't know why they get their hackles up like they do."

Rachel finished stirring her tea, and tapped her spoon on the brim of the cup. "But we ought to be less preachy about it."

"Sometimes the truth hurts."

She lifted the cup with both hands to her face and blew on her tea. "You know, Ez, they'd probably say the same thing to us."

The Mormons were a homogenous group, so it made perfect sense to them to do business exclusively with other Mormons. This annoyed their neighbors. But it was their political naiveté that turned the tide against them. The Mormons were Northerners, and Northerners didn't own slaves.

Most of the Missouri frontiersmen had come from Tennessee and Kentucky, both slave states. When Missouri had applied for statehood fifteen years earlier, the question of whether it would be a free or slave state sparked impassioned debate. When Joseph said there was even talk they might secede from the Union, Brother Gunderson said "Well, they ought to succeed at *something*."

The impasse was resolved by the Missouri Compromise, which made Missouri a slave state so as not to upset the balance of free vs. slave states. The Mormons didn't have strong opinions on the subject of slavery. They were mostly from the free states of New York and

Ohio and were thrown into the Missouri mess at exactly the wrong time.

Even though Mormons didn't own slaves, they knew their white skin made them holier. God had told them so in their new Holy Scripture. Abraham's scroll, the one buried next to his mummified corpse, made it quite clear that Negroes had been cursed with dark skin because of their wickedness, so they had nobody to blame but themselves. The golden tablets also confirmed this curse, for God didn't cotton to wickedness and used the skin curse freely. And when Joseph re-translated the Bible, he learned that the Negroes had it coming because their ancestors had been lax in keeping the commandments. All three of Mormonism's sacred texts confirmed that people of color were inferior, and had some repenting to do.

"And don't forget about Ham," reminded Brigham. "His seed is cursed with the dark skin because of what he did to Noah." The Biblical story is a long one, but the gist of it, explained Brigham, was that Noah got drunk after the flood and was lying down outside his tent, naked. Two of his sons wanted to cover him up, but his son, Ham, just laughed and let his father lie there naked and drunk. God was so upset that he cursed Ham, and all his posterity, with a dark skin.

The U.S. Constitution had been written fifty years earlier; so the enlightened Framers hadn't been influenced by the gold tablets or the mummy scroll. However, those who had eloquently declared that all men were created equal didn't really mean it. To be precise (precision was important in this delicate matter), the original Constitution declared slaves to be 3/5 of a person for purposes of apportioning delegates to Congress based on state population.

It was in this setting that the church published an article entitled "Free People of Color" in its church newspaper. The article invited Negroes to come to Missouri to join the true church. The Mormons believed this was a charitable invitation to those whose ancestors had so badly misbehaved. But, regrettably, it was politically naive.

The Missouri townsfolk vociferously objected. The mere thought that black people would be allowed to roam freely in their fair community was repugnant. The local newspaper screamed, "You want a bunch of free niggers coming to Missouri? Because that's what the Mormons want! These fanatics want to take over the whole territory. And they fancy doing it with the help of a bunch of niggers! If they get their way, their niggers will team up with our slaves, the very ones we legally own, and there'll be an uprising the likes of which you've never seen! It'll be full rebellion!"

An emergency town meeting was called.

"Them damned Mormons think they can waltz in here and have themselves a bunch of free niggers. This is Missouri, goddammit, and the Good Lord won't put up with it."

"You bet your last dollar He won't. This here's *our* state!"

"You give them niggers an inch and next thing you know they'll wanna vote. Mark my words."

"Just who in the hell do these Mormons think they are? We live in a free country, goddammit, and we oughta have the right to decide who lives here. And I'll be damned if I wanna live next to a bunch of nigger-lovers."

"I propose we draw up a manifesto saying they gotta go. Do I have a second?"

"I'll second it."

"Me too."

The manifesto declared the Mormons must go. The Mormons tried to set things straight in the next issue of their newspaper. Joseph wrote from Kirtland, "Having learned with extreme regret that an article in the last issue has been misunderstood, we feel duty bound to state that our intention was to *stop* Negroes from emigrating to this state, and *prevent* them from being admitted as members of the Church."

The retraction in the newspaper was a bust. The Mormons could have published an entire issue on how much they hated Negroes and it would've made no difference, for the damage had been done. This business with the Negroes was the final straw. Was it not enough that the Mormons told them their churches were wicked and they would burn in hell? Was it not enough that the Mormons were arrogant do-gooders who only did business with each other, and drove the original settlers from their land? Was it not enough that they proclaimed themselves to be future Gods?

A few nights after Joseph's retraction in the newspaper, a mob carrying torches and sledgehammers rode up to the house where the Mormon printing press was kept. This vanguard of moral decency was so overcome with the Christian spirit that they smashed the press to bits and fired their muskets into the air. A horse kicked over its traces and ran away wild with fear.

The Mormons didn't know what to do. Communication with Joseph was slow, and the stakes were high. They might have considered leaving voluntarily, but Missouri was the Promised Land, and God had promised it to *them*.

The Mormon bishop in Independence was a convivial man whose job was to dole out extra food from the bishop's storehouse to the sick and poor. He and his family went without much of the time so other church members could eat. When he saw the mob smash the printing press, he begged them to stop. They knocked him to the ground and kicked him—a simple farmer who didn't even own a musket. The mob stripped him bare in front of the Saints and poured scalding pine tar over him. "Now you look like a proper nigger," they said.

Three nights later, the mob came again. The Mormon men stood on their porches with their lanterns while the women and children huddled behind them. This time the mob issued a cruel warning: if the Mormons didn't leave immediately, their crops would be burned and the men would be given one hundred lashes. Did the mob really expect them to just get up and leave the Promised Land? Didn't they know this is where Jesus was set to return, and would do so at any time? Didn't they care?

If they abandoned the Promised Land, then what? There was no place for them to go. They were surrounded by wilderness with no earthly possessions. They did have one crucial asset though: the truth. It sustained them as much as food and shelter, for they knew God would provide. In the meantime, however, most of the Mormons hoped Jesus would come quickly and smite the sons-of-bitches.

***

Oliver climbed upon his horse in Missouri for a long ride. His destination was Kirtland, Ohio, where he could talk to Joseph face-to-face about the "Missouri problem." The horse was a brown mare, and sturdy. It had to be, for the saddlebags were full.

"I will miss you, my dear," he said to his bride of one year. He leaned down and kissed his newborn daughter's forehead. He looked too young to be a father. He looked instead like the thin, bookish schoolteacher that he had been a few years earlier.

The journey was long. He ate his jerky and biscuits with deliberate slowness to pass the time and had one-way conversations with his horse, marveling at the vastness of the unrelieved sky. He passed through scattered towns where small homesteads were carved from the brush. A child sat outside an unpainted shack sucking its thumb. A swayed-back mule, long in tooth, was tied to a tree. The child stared at Oliver without fear or interest. A dog lay next to him like a worn out rug. A few hens pecked in the spare yard. The door opened and a woman appeared and threw a pan of water onto the dirt. She looked at Oliver tiredly and went back into the house, letting the screen door bang.

Oliver stopped along the way to tell people about the angel and the Book of Mormon that he kept in his saddlebag. They politely listened to this sincere young man, but they didn't believe him, convinced as they were that angels only appeared to prophets of old. This seemed perfectly believable to them, whereas angels appearing in modern times seemed patently absurd.

"But why not now?" asked Oliver. "Why would God close the heavens in these latter days?"

"It's just the way it is," one man said, glancing over Oliver's shoulder at his wife for reinforcement against this odd young man and his miraculous tale. "God already told us all we need to know. Says so right in the Bible. So that's that."

Oliver lay in his bedroll at night smelling the sage and hickory. He heard a coyote at a distance and the ticking of his small fire as it cooled. He looked at the heavens and wondered if he might not be looking at Kolob, or other inhabited planets where children of other Gods were wondering the same thing. His thoughts drifted to his wife at home whose skin became softer and her breasts more supple with each passing mile.

When he finally arrived in Kirtland, he was surprised at its growth; he'd been absent two years. He found Joseph and several other men at the temple construction site. They brushed the dust from their trousers and splashed water on their faces from a bucket, then gathered round to hear about the tribulations in the Promised Land. Oliver told them of the threat to expel the Mormons by fire and bayonet. There was no need to embellish.

Joseph sat on a sandstone block that had been cut for the temple. He removed his gloves with deliberation, one finger at a time, and laid them to the side. He was only twenty-nine years old, facing his first major crisis. He ran his hands through his hair.

The men around him wondered if the Promised Land was worth it. "Just a bunch of mosquitoes and Indians, you ask me," some said. They privately thought there'd been a mistake. The Promised Land ought to have been better.

They waited to hear what Joseph would say, but he'd folded like a pocketknife with his head down and didn't say a word. He watched an ant traverse the dirt at his feet. The ant carried a twig twice its size. Did the ant appreciate the enormity of its burden? The men nudged Ez and Brigham with their nods to bring Joseph back from his thoughts.

"Joseph?" They waited.

"Brothers," he finally said, still directing his comments to the ant, "we must be patient and turn the other cheek." He lifted his head and slowly stood. "Independence, Missouri is the Promised Land. It was promised to us by God himself."

No one spoke until it became clear that Joseph had no more to say.

"So what are we supposed to do?" asked Oliver. "Do we leave?"

"You'll stay, just as the Lord has commanded you."

"But they've threatened to lash our men and burn our homes and crops. You don't understand. These heathens mean business!"

"Tell the Saints we must turn the other cheek."

"But you're our leader. We need you there."

"If I go to Missouri it will only inflame our enemies. I must stay here and complete the Lord's temple."

"So, should I tell them . . . ?"

"You tell them I would confine the Negro to its own species. Maybe that will help the situation."

"But what if. . . ."

"Oliver, God will provide. Now go and tell the Saints that I am with them in spirit."

"But, what about the threat to—"

"I am the Lord's mouthpiece on earth, and I have spoken. Now, go and deliver the Lord's message." With measured deliberation, he picked up his gloves and put them on. He turned his back to the men, picked up a stone, and hoisted it into a wheelbarrow, pushing it toward the temple wall, which now rose eight feet high. He didn't look back, putting a seal on everything that had been said.

12

The Battle for the Promised Land

It was early in 1837, and Rachel's mother sat at the writing table in her husband's den, a shrine dedicated to The Reverend, the man of God who normally sat there. There were community plaques, certificates, and mementos from frightened souls who'd paid handsomely for their salvation. She wanted to believe in God, but her husband's grotesque impiety made it difficult. It'd been six miserable years since he'd banished their daughter.

Before her on the writing desk was the one thing she'd dreamed about since her daughter's exile. It was a letter from Rachel, postmarked from a town in Ohio called Kirtland, a town she had never heard of. *Dearest Mother*, she'd written,

> *I write with a heart filled with longing. We are well and your adorable grandson Thomas is now a precocious five-year-old who follows Ezra around the wheelwright shop with a hammer. He looks like his father and has the sweetest temperament. I had another child, a beautiful baby girl whom we named Elizabeth in your honor. She is as delicate as a porcelain doll. Ezra insists she looks like you. My heart is blessed with my beautiful little family and our belief in the church. I do not wish to preach; I only wish for you to know that we are happy. I long to see you. Perhaps one day Father will see that our decision to join the Mormons was motivated by our sincere belief and not out of spite. I pray that God will soften his heart and allow*

us to reunite as family. Until then, please know that I love you. God bless you, mother.

Rachel

Elizabeth read it again, this the seventh time. She took a piece of writing paper from a tray on the desk and took a quill in her trembling hand. *My Dearest Rachel,* she wrote, *how your letter warmed my heart! How I have longed to hear from you and to know that you are well. I am eternally sorry that—*

She did not hear his approaching footsteps, or the turn of the knob, so immersed was she in thoughts of her daughter.

"What is this?" The Reverend said as he came behind her and snatched the letter from the desk. "You are posting a letter to Rachel behind my back? How dare you disobey me! I am your husband, and I made myself clear on this subject."

"But she is our *daughter*."

"A daughter who has shamed me. A daughter who has run off with devil worshippers."

"I can no longer do this, Husband."

"You must." He took the letter and ripped it in pieces. "Now, I see it is past supper time."

***

Joseph received an urgent letter from the bishop in Missouri pleading for help. For all its promise, turning the other cheek had been an unmitigated disaster.

"What am I supposed to do, Emma? Call forth an army? Order Jesus to come sooner?"

Emma shrugged. The rumors about Fanny Alger had been crushing. "You're the prophet, not me."

The rag-tag mobs in Missouri came again at night. They ordered the Mormons from their homes and whipped the men in front of their families. "Maybe this'll teach you not to butt in. Go on back where you belong." A boy with no shoes and threadbare trousers broke away and grabbed the whip from one of the drunkards. The man knocked him down and his mother ran to him in only her nightclothes and shawl. "Please, he's just a child." The boy crawled to his knees and threw a rock at the thug. "You little shit," he said, then kicked the boy in the head.

Thirteen burning houses painted the night sky a hateful shade of orange. The men ran to fill buckets of water from a nearby stream while others watched in horrified silence, their mouths hanging open like whole cod on ice at the fish market. One child, dressed only in a thin cotton nightgown, held a pillow to her chest. A roof collapsed sending sparks thirty feet in the air. The mob returned the next night, sending the women and children shrieking into the nearby cornfields while their husbands pleaded with the nightriders to spare the town.

Church members took in families whose homes had been destroyed. The refugees slept on floors and huddled in smoky kitchens, telling stories about the suffering of the Jews, God's previously handpicked Chosen People. This made them feel better—their suffering had purpose. And the bond between them grew, forged by suffering, and a common enemy.

Despite it all, the Mormons' belief in the goodness and mercy of God remained, unchallenged, like the children who only got a pair of underwear for Christmas but still believed in Santa Claus.

Even though the Mormons were prepared to carry the cross of the Chosen People, they realized that conventional Christ-like pacifism had shown itself to be wholly inadequate. So they organized a resistance—they would go toe-to-toe with the godless mobsters. Satan was obviously obsessed with destroying the only true church.

They *must* have the truth; why else would Satan have bothered with them?

The Mormons were ready when the mob returned at night to sack the bishop's storehouse. A whistle sounded and the Cavalry of Saints came on horseback, catching a miscreant who'd thrown a brick at the storehouse window. They hauled him directly to the judge who lived on the other side of town.

It took three Mormons to hold their prisoner as he jerked and pulled. He bit one of them on the forearm so hard his teeth scraped the bone. While the Mormon screamed in pain, another man clobbered the criminal on the head with his lantern. They knocked on the judge's door. He came down in his nightclothes.

"This couldn't have waited until morning?" he yelled at them. "Can't you see it's nearly midnight? What the hell is wrong with you Mormons?" The door slammed shut.

They locked their prisoner in a broom closet for the night, and the next morning hauled him to court where the judge was only slightly more accommodating. "Now, tell me what couldn't wait, and make it quick. Can't you see I'm busy?" The villain claimed his innocence in a diabolical rant, his Adam's apple bobbing with each lie. His Mormon captors were arrested on the spot for kidnapping.

"But, Judge, we caught him red-handed! We have forty witnesses! They broke into the storehouse and burned our homes to the ground."

"Then you'll only spend one night in jail. And there will be no mercy the next time. Have I made myself clear?"

Joseph's response to this injustice was another revelation, one that was sure to inflame his flock down in Missouri. Ez tried to talk him out of it.

"Joseph, think this through. You shouldn't blame the Saints in Missouri for their own suffering."

"It's the Lord's rebuke, not mine."

The following revelation was sent immediately to Missouri: "I, the Lord God, have caused the affliction to come upon the Saints in Missouri because of their transgressions. Behold, there was envying, and lustful and covetous desires among them. Therefore, they have polluted their inheritance. But, notwithstanding their sins, my bowels are filled with compassion toward them. Amen."

"I think Joseph got this one wrong," Ez said to Brigham. "I don't know what they might've been coveting down there in Missouri, other than a house that wasn't burned to the ground."

Brigham's voice was hard. "They only have themselves to blame, just like the Lord said. Only the righteous can enjoy the bounties of the Promised Land."

"What bounties?"

"Ez, this is no time for sarcasm."

"But to have their inheritances polluted?"

"It's not our place to second-guess God. When He speaks through the Prophet, all thinking must stop and strict obedience is required."

"I don't know. It just doesn't feel right to me."

"You must doubt your doubts, Ezra."

"Huh?"

"You heard me. I don't want to discuss this any further, and I suggest you leave it alone."

The Missouri Saints were surprisingly contrite when they received God's rebuke. Perhaps they *had* been too lustful. However, notwithstanding God's instructions that they should meekly suffer the ravages of fire and hunger, the Saints in Missouri were itching for a fight. They got one a few days later when a Missourian brazenly threw a torch into a Mormon's barn. Mormon vigilantes rode out to confront him.

The Mormons would claim later that the Missourians fired the first shots. One musket ball hit a Mormon in the chest, knocking him from his horse. He'd recently converted to the church and had moved his family down from Canada to live in the Promised Land, where his blood lay pooled on the frozen November mud.

Another one of the nightriders edged his way around the burning barn, aiming to shoot one of God's chosen people in the back. A Mormon sharpshooter fired from behind a stack of logs. The Missourian caught a slug in the neck.

The next day the Missourians held a war council. "Them goddamned Mormons went and killed Lamont in cold blood. We got to get us some revenge!"

The sheriff arrested two Mormons involved in the shootings and stuck them in the local jail, a ramshackle affair that looked more like a barn than a reputable penal institution. This was the Wild West (or, technically, the Wild Mid-West) and frontier justice was meted out with arbitrary and capricious irregularity. The Fourth and Fifth Amendments had been ratified, and the citizenry should've been obliged to honor them, but they didn't.

The Mormons—now two thousand strong—were convinced their jailed brethren were about to be lynched, so they gathered in force at the outskirts of town with whatever weapons they could find: rusty shovels, pitchforks, slingshots, and muskets. If their brethren were hanged, the Mormons would cross their own Rubicon and attack with God's vengeance.

Lilburn Boggs, the Lt. Governor of Missouri, also wanted a fight. Boggs was a craven, fussy little man with a perpetual pout and suspicious scruples. He believed the Mormons had devised a plan to take over his state (he appeared to claim Missouri as his very own).

Boggs knew the Mormons were growing in numbers. New converts dripped steadily in from the north as if there was a leaky gasket at the border. He knew his political career was doomed if this state of affairs continued for much longer. Mormons voted exclusively for other Mormons, and he wasn't about to convert. Boggs declared that he "owed it to the people" to respond to this Mormon takeover.

So he called out the state militia.

A roughneck named Thomas Pitcher was appointed to lead the militia. It was said that Pitcher would drive a bayonet through you and leave it there, just to make a point. A knife fight had left a scar in the shape of an X on his weathered cheek, so his face looked like a wrinkled treasure map. His eyes were bloodshot from drink, and he wore an untamed beard stained with chewing tobacco. He smelled of whiskey and rot.

Boggs, immaculately dressed, rode his horse up to the Mormons standing guard in front of their gutted houses, a picture of genteel snobbery in the frontier where it didn't belong. He brushed dust from the pant leg of his fine suit.

"My name is Lilburn Boggs, and this is Tom Pitcher," he said and jerked a thumb toward his companion. Pitcher offered a baleful grin that exposed a few remaining yellow teeth. "If you refuse to disarm, you will be given no further protection and will be driven from the state by force."

"So what are we supposed to do?"

"That, my friends, is completely up to you. But I assure you the State of Missouri will no longer tolerate your outrages."

It was an unholy proposition, but the Mormons were left with no other options. The Bible said that God knew when a single sparrow fell, so surely He was keenly aware of the Chosen Peoples' current predicament. They surrendered their weapons.

That very night the mob led by Tom Pitcher (who all Mormons pray will rot in hell), rode through the outskirts of the Mormon towns and burned down the remaining houses and barns with impunity. The Mormons heard the wild, desperate shriek of a horse that hadn't escaped a barn in time. Then they could smell it.

The defenseless men, women, and children ran for the woods, or to the banks of the Blue River. God's chosen people squeezed around campfires that night, stamping their feet to keep them from freezing. Huddled together for warmth, they looked to the heavens. Had God forgotten them? Or was He up there, on the orb of Kolob, looking down upon their suffering with a twinkle in His eye, knowing they would triumph in the end?

And then the stars fell.

It was the greatest meteor shower in more than a century. A hailstorm of thunderbolt iron rained down on the terrified Missourians like an artillery barrage. They frantically crossed themselves and ran for cover. But not the Saints. They knew the Second Coming had finally arrived and Jesus was en route. Soon the mob would be reduced to a pile of evil ashes and the Saints would be given their just rewards. They held cold hands and waited.

They awoke to a numb, gray dawn, still waiting on Jesus. They were wretched, cold, and hungry.

***

Word of the banishment from Missouri reached Joseph by courier a few weeks later. He was ambitious for himself and for his people. But now there had come shooting, bleeding, and dying for his sake. His small church had become a violent lightning rod, and it was flashing out of control.

The national newspapers ran stories of the "Mormon mistreatment." This was not headline news, at least not on par with the attempt on President Jackson's life by a deranged assassin, or the Great Fire of New York. Nor did it compete for ink with the Panic of 1837, or the death of William Clark who, along with his friend,

Meriwether Lewis, had made history thirty years earlier. But at least it was something, and it temporarily put a check on the militia.

13

Zion's Camp

The clerk, a simpering, pretentious little man, entered the Office of the President of the United States. It was the middle of winter, but Congress had recently appropriated enough money to install central heat into the White House. Andrew Jackson, not one to engage in idle chitchat, looked up from his desk.

"What is it?"

"Mr. President, we have received an unusual letter and I thought you might like to see it."

"Well, what is it?"

"It is a letter from Joseph Smith."

"And who, in God's name, is he?" asked Jackson irritably.

"He is the leader of a small sect of Christians in Missouri, or perhaps it is Ohio."

"And how does this concern me? Can't you see I am busy?"

"I apologize, Mr. President, but this is a most unusual letter."

"Fine, let me see it."

Jackson adjusted his reading glasses and leaned back in his chair. It was a petition for redress of grievances suffered by the Mormons in Missouri. The letter itself was unremarkable, save its demand, but the accompanying attachment captured the clerk's attention. It was a revelation aimed at President Jackson personally, coming directly as it had from God. The Almighty was unhappy:

> *Let the Saints importune at the feet of the President. And if the President heeds them not, then I, the Lord, will arise and come out of my hiding place, and in my fury I will vex the nation. And in my hot displeasure, and fierce anger, will I cut off those wicked and unjust stewards, and cast them into outer darkness where there is weeping and wailing and gnashing of teeth. Thus saith I, the Lord your God, Amen.*

The President set the letter down and removed his glasses. "These are the ravings of a madman."

"Shall I prepare a response over your signature?"

"Of course not."

Unfortunately, the revelation did not have the desired effect on the President, but it made the Saints feel better. Just knowing Old Hickory must have been shaking in his boots was enough. Brigham told the owner of the local hardware shop, "Well, I think Jackson had it coming, I really do. He has nobody to blame but himself."

The travails in Missouri caused a heavenly shift. God saw fit to issue a new commandment, one that trumped His earlier instruction to turn the other cheek. The times called for a different strategy: "Behold, the redemption of Zion must come by power! For ye must be let out of bondage by power! Thus saith I, the Lord your God. Amen."

Joseph told his clerk, "Get the church newspaper to print an urgent notice. We need everyone to pitch in with whatever weapons they can find—old muskets, swords, rusty butcher knives—whatever we can get."

"Will do, Brother Joseph."

"And we'll need volunteers. I'd like five hundred men if we can get them."

A week later, Sidney stood gallantly in the town square and promised a great victory for the two hundred volunteers as they bid farewell to their families for the eight-hundred-mile march to liberate the Missouri Saints. They called themselves "Zion's Camp."

"You are Christian martyrs, travelling as Mohammed did to liberate the Chosen People!" Sidney had forgotten the Chosen People had actually been Jews, not Muslims. But he appreciated the symbolism of the Prophet Mohammed. And, after all, it was time for a jihad of sorts.

The Promised Land hung in the balance. Canvas packs were strapped to their backs and dented kettles tied to their sword belts with twine. Tomahawks and hatchets swung from supply wagons filled with food and ammunition. There were shooting contests and wrestling matches along the way to ward off boredom. Joseph won them all because of his incredible will to win and the physical specimen that he'd become. When Ez beat him arm wrestling, Joseph blamed it on a sore bicep from lifting a can of milk. Ez let it go.

They passed through a small town and bought a pig, then sat around, poking it on a homemade spit over the fire, its four stiff legs flung out in a cry for help. The march was a companionable time, at first. They knew they were on God's mission, and believed that God took the side of the sufferers against those who persecuted them.

Joseph owned a bulldog named Bear. The dog was so vicious it had to be tied up. It paced back and forth at the end of its rope, staring at the men with contempt. Everyone hated the dog, except Joseph. One of the men muttered under his breath, "Next thing you know, he'll wanna baptize the damned thing."

One day it got loose and chased a man named Sylvester up a tree. When it had been restrained, the man climbed down, furious. "So help me, I'll shoot that damned dog."

"You'll not lay a finger on that dog," Joseph said levelly. "If you do, God will strike you dead, and the dog will eat the flesh off your bones."

"Not if I kill the damn thing first, it won't."

Ez leaned over to Brigham. "If you think you're a fella of some importance, try ordering someone else's dog around."

Several of the men jumped to Sylvester's defense. They thought it unfair to be struck down for complaining about an uncontrollable dog.

Joseph was surprised by the insurrection. "This was a test. I was just trying to show you how base and ignoble your attitude has become."

Ez knew that Joseph was imperfect. The man he knew was kind and generous, and gifted by God with a magnetic personality, but he could be arrogant and prone to unpredictable fits of anger. Sometimes this was rash and unexpected, a surge of anger he couldn't control. But that was rare, for almost everything he did was deliberate. He didn't beat his flock over the head, not when he could persuade them with the mere touch of his fingertip. Brute force was obvious, but subtle influence more effective. Joseph understood the difference.

All summer long they walked. The land was so hot the cooking pots scorched their fingers and the dirt burned the soles of their feet. The leaves hung straight down, and even the rabbits moved slowly. It was dry, too; so dry the men said the bushes would start following the dogs around. Bear panted in the shade of the wagons, and the men marched without their shirts. Sleep was difficult because of the heat and their sticky bodies. They lay on their bedrolls, hoping for a breeze, even a warm one. There was only the sound of crickets.

Martin Harris, at fifty the oldest man on the march, was not physically commanding. He had a certain swagger, however, because he'd once been rich (before he gave it all to Joseph to finance the Book of Mormon). He'd also been allowed to see the golden tablets out in the woods. He boasted that God would protect him from harm. When he saw a black snake on the dusty road he decided it was time to prove it.

The men surrounded the snake. Martin sat on a rock and took off his boot, whistling a tune with confidence. His dirty sock had holes and his feet smelled like spoiled meat. The other men egged him on.

"I will now prove that I have the spirit of the Lord," Martin said, and walked up to the snake. He stuck his bare toe in front of its head. The snake appeared to consider the toe, perhaps took a whiff, then turned and slid away.

The men were disappointed.

"See, I said God would protect me."

Martin saw another snake a few days later and tried it again. Perhaps it was a different kind of snake, or maybe the snake didn't realize how special Martin was, because this time it bit him, leaving two small dots, like quotation marks, above his ankle. The men fell to the ground with laughter, rolling in the hot dirt, howling, while Martin jumped up and down on his good foot. "This ain't funny! I could die. Hurry, somebody suck the venom out!"

Joseph, who'd been lagging behind, came upon the scene. "Martin, you are mocking God's spirit."

"But, dammit, I just got bit by a snake!"

"God ordered the snake to bite you because of your arrogance."

The men quit laughing and pretended to be upset with Martin and his showboating, too. But they didn't dare look at each other or they'd burst out laughing again, so they kept their heads down and kicked at the dirt as if they were disappointed in Martin's spiritual recklessness.

Martin's gullibility was a reliable source of entertainment for the bored men. He lost considerable sums of money at craps and card games because he was willfully blind to the fact that the other men were conspiring to make a fool of him. He desperately wanted to be accepted, but he knew, deep down, that the younger men teased him. So he tried harder to gain their acceptance (he jumped into a puddle of muddy water on a bet, and walked into a camp of Indians wearing a feather). Martin was otherwise well liked, a generous do-gooder with an aptitude for misguided charity at the expense of his pocketbook. When he'd lose, he'd say: "Doggone it, fellas, I've gone and done it again, haven't I?"

A few days later, they came upon an Indian mound on the bank of the Illinois River. They dug until they discovered the remains of a buried skeleton.

Joseph was on his hands and knees, scraping the last layer of dirt away with a dinner plate. He finished and put his hands on his thighs. "This man was a white Indian. His name was Zelf."

"Zelf? A white Indian?"

"Uh-huh. He was a warrior under the great chief Onandagus. The curse of red skin was removed because he was such a steadfast warrior."

None of them had ever heard of Onandagus, or Zelf. Joseph picked up the thighbone and used it to point to an arrowhead still stuck in poor Zelf's ribcage. He then drew out the configuration of the battlefield in the dirt with the bone. He told the men that the arrow to the heart had been Zelf's lethal blow, but his leg had also been shattered by a rock, thrown at full force by a slingshot. Indeed, Zelf's final moments appeared to have been dreadful.

"How do we know you didn't just go and make all this up?" asked Sylvester.

"Quit ruining the spirit," the men said.

Joseph walked over to Sylvester and put his arm around his shoulder. "If I didn't know better, I probably wouldn't believe it either."

Sylvester grunted and threw his shovel to the back of wagon. "Whatever you say, Joseph."

The trek resumed. Exhausted from the heat, the men prayed again and again for rain. Finally their prayers were answered with rain that rinsed the sky. It fell hard, dimpling the dirt like bullets and bouncing off the canvas of their covered wagons. Wheels stuck in the mud, and the men's boots threatened to come off with each step. And when it finally stopped, the mosquitoes came out in droves, biting the men so many times that their heads and necks puffed up like banana squashes. The men realized that Missouri had untold ways of getting under their skin. They hung their wet clothes over the fire to steam and stink on sticks angled into the dirt.

***

Pitcher and his boys had heard rumors about the Mormon Army headed their way, and they issued the clarion call: "The Mormons are coming to kill us!"

"I need more men," Pitcher told Lt. Governor Boggs. "We can't let them take our state."

"Count on it. They've assembled an Army to attack Missouri, and we'll defend her!"

All of the remaining Mormon homes in Missouri were burned. The Promised Land had now effectively been torched. The irony was cruel, for it wasn't the wretched heathens that had been scorched in the Last Days, it was the Mormons.

Joseph and his warriors tried to hurry, but cholera had infected their camp. The men soaked the sick ones in cold water and fed them whiskey thickened with flour. Soon they ran out of flour and whiskey. They vomited until there was nothing left but acid flavored strings of spit, and they had diarrhea the color of milk. Joseph's vicious dog also got sick. "Let's give Bear a blessing," one of the men said in an awkward attempt to gain Joseph's favor. When it died, the men pretended to mourn.

They drifted off to sleep and Joseph wandered to the side of the camp, searching the heavens with his arms outstretched, begging God to help them. The fire popped and snapped as it collapsed. Exhausted men snored. But the heavens were quiet. Fourteen men died and were buried using rusty shovels in the cursed earth of Missouri.

The scouts they'd sent ahead reported the Missouri state militia was dug in on the other side of the Missouri River.

"We'll camp here, out in the open," said Joseph.

"That," said Sylvester "is about as dumb as a Missouri whore. I'm going down by the river where I can at least get me some fresh water."

Joseph removed his hat. His hair was damp and clung to his forehead. "If we're in the woods by the river they'll ambush us. Out here in the prairie we can see them coming."

"You can stay here all you like, but I'm going to the river."

"We stay here, and that is an order!"

"You won't let us speak freely anymore!" Sylvester yelled, spittle flecking his lips. "You won't even let us think for ourselves! I don't even know why I came on this goddamned march."

Joseph picked up the bugle that he used to call the men to prayer, and threw it at Sylvester. The bugle flew past his head and crashed against a rock. The men looked down and kicked their boots, as if they'd suddenly become concerned about the dust on them.

That night Ez sat on a rock near the campfire cleaning his fingernails with a pocketknife, listening to Sylvester drone on about the inequity of it all. When he'd finally heard enough, he walked over to Sylvester and stood in front of him.

"What're you lookin' at?" asked Sylvester.

Ez just glared at him.

"Fine, then. I'm going to catch me some shut eye," Sylvester finally said and walked away, his bootlaces trailing.

The next day they crept close to the river when they spotted a boatload of militia rowing across for a surprise attack. Some of Joseph's men believed he could have walked across the river and smacked their enemies upside the head. Others would just as soon have seen him sink. Halfway across the river, the militiamen's boat took on water and went under. Some of them drowned.

"Men," said Joseph, "that was Jehovah's doing."

Ez wondered if that was the sort of thing Jehovah would do, stooping to capsize a boat. Another group rowed across and began firing their muskets at the Mormons. Jehovah must have known this second boat wasn't a serious threat and didn't need capsizing, because their musket balls landed two hundred yards short. A sudden storm blew up and soaked the enemy's gunpowder. Joseph told his men the rain had been the work of Jehovah, too. Ez nodded. That sounded more like something He would have done.

Late that night, Joseph and a handful of men sneaked across the river to visit the Mormon settlement, which was under siege. He stayed up all night, blessing the sick and praying with his people. At dawn he woke his mates and they rowed back across the river, leaving the Saints in Missouri with only the hope that they'd be rewarded in heaven. And their enemies? Joseph promised they would rot in hell. This, perhaps as much as the promise that they would become Gods, pleased them to no end.

Joseph arrived back at Zion's Camp while the men were gathered around the fire, cooking breakfast. They sat at makeshift tables, knees pressed to knees, eating watered-down hominy.

"It's time we turned around." He knew the church, and his legacy, would not have survived a massacre.

"You mean to tell me," Sylvester said, "that we come all this way and now we're gonna put our tails between our legs like a bunch of sissies?"

"There's been enough bloodshed, and the cholera has taken our strength. God wants us to save our energy for the retaking of Zion."

"And when's that gonna be?"

"Within two years. And when we do, there won't be a dog left to open its mouth against us. You have my word."

14

Words of Wisdom

The Kirtland temple was nearing completion. It promised to be a grand affair: tall, white, and majestic, sitting on a rise of land that made it look like a fairy tale castle. During its construction, however, the church leaders had been forced to meet at Joseph's house to do their business, traipsing in with their cigars and muddy boots.

Emma had long been sensitive to smoke. She stayed away from Joseph's study, where the church leaders met to discuss Church policy over whiskey and cigars. It helped a bit, but the smell carried through the house. One day, she snapped.

She walked into the study with the light of battle in her eye.

"Now listen up," Emma said to the men who were pinned to their chairs by a thick fog of smoky, rancid air. "We can hardly breathe around here. You waltz in here and light your cigars and spit tobacco all over the floor. Good Lord, I think I could hit a spittoon better than you. Especially you, Ez. You ought to practice your aim so Rachel doesn't have to scrub the floor all day and night, the poor thing."

"Yeah, Ez," said Parley.

Emma wheeled around and faced him. "Well, listen to you, Parley P. Pratt. You've got a lot of nerve. You drink so much I'm afraid you'll knock over my spinning wheel."

The men laughed. Parley, who'd just taken the cork out of his flask for another pull, re-corked it quickly.

"She has a point, Brethren," Joseph said.

"Thank you, Joseph. I'm glad someone here has a lick of sense."

Joseph smiled. "I suppose you'd like us to form our own temperance society."

"The sisters would surely welcome that," she said. "We might even be more affectionate if we didn't have to smell that nasty stuff. Now, I'll leave you all to discuss whatever it is you discuss." A moment later she stuck her head back into the room. "The mop's in the closet behind you."

Brigham took a drag from his cigar and held it at arm's length, inspecting it, before dropping it into the spittoon, where it landed with a hiss.

Several weeks later (long enough for the brethren to partially forget that Emma had prodded him with the idea), Joseph came to a decision.

"Brethren, I've been thinking. The Eastern newspapers say there are now over five thousand groups who've pledged total abstinence from alcohol."

"I hope you're not suggesting we oughta do the same," said Parley. "Because if you are, let's send that bottle around again."

"I've asked the Lord to give me some guidance," said Joseph. "We'll follow His word."

Brigham wiped tobacco spit off his chin with his sleeve. "Just don't tell me we'll be giving up the chew."

A week later God spoke loud and clear. The Word of Wisdom was the result. The gist was that God forbade the use of alcohol and tobacco. He also forbade coffee and tea (for reasons He didn't make entirely clear). Joseph made the announcement at the next service, reading from the text that God had dictated to him. Emma shrugged her shoulders when she caught Ez looking at her on the front pew, as if she'd been just as surprised as anyone else that the Almighty had come to His senses. He noticed her wink in Rachel's direction.

"What was that all about?" he asked Rachel.

"I don't know what you're talking about. Now shush, they're about to say the prayer."

There remained one liquor store in town, but it closed early and wasn't open on weekends. This was a terrible burden for Brother Poulson, the town drunk, who arrived at the liquor store exactly one minute before closing one snowy Friday evening. He purchased a pint, slid it into the back pocket of his trousers, and left the store. The clerk locked the door behind him and closed the blinds. Two steps later, Brother Poulson slipped on the icy boardwalk, landing squarely on his bottom. He reached back and felt the seat of his pants was wet. "Goddammit," he said, "that had better be blood!"

***

Joseph knew that the true church ought to have twelve apostles. This only made sense. "Ez, I think you'd make an excellent apostle."

"Me?"

"You love the Lord and understand the nature of revelation."

"But, jeez, an *apostle*? I don't know the scriptures like you do. That's for men like Peter and James and Luke."

Most of the men wanted to be selected because that would've put them in very select company. However, it would've been unseemly to actually lobby for the position, something that neither Matthew nor Luke presumably did. Joseph ultimately decided to allow the Three Witnesses to select the Twelve Apostles (but they couldn't pick themselves).

Martin, Oliver, and David met behind closed doors. "What about Brother Clawson?"

"I zeepose, but he has zee nasty temper," said David.

"Okay, then, what about Brother Gilbert?"

"I could live with him," said Martin, "but it'd probably go to his head."

Round and round they went. The last one they selected was Phineas Young, Brigham's younger brother.

"Well, that's a fine how-do-you-do," said Joseph's mother when the selections were announced. "What's wrong with your own brothers? I've got nothing against Phineas, and I'm sure he's a good boy, but for Pete's sake."

Joseph didn't want to displease his mother, so he trumped the Three Witnesses and chose his brother, William, instead. Most of the Saints (aside from Phineas) agreed Joseph should have had the prerogative to do this. But *William*? He was the rascal who'd run around saying Joseph had concocted the story about the golden tablets. This was not the sort of thing that ordinarily makes for a good apostle.

"I think Joseph overstepped his bounds on that one," said a man who'd been passed over.

"Well, sometimes they don't work out. I mean, look at Jesus. He picked Judas and that didn't work out so well, either."

Joseph's decision to appoint William was controversial because William didn't even attend church, and called the golden tablets "a bunch of hogwash." Joseph had only wanted to put a burr under William's saddle and cause him to start believing, which was a Christian thing to do. Eventually he hoped William would become a good apostle—perhaps not as good as Peter, James, or John—but good. Regrettably, the burr hadn't been prickly enough.

The rumors started when William made eyes at the prettiest fifteen-year-old girl in Kirtland. William denied any impropriety, as any good apostle would. He was incensed to learn that Joseph believed the rumors, so he promptly resigned his apostleship and paraded through town telling anyone who would listen that Joseph was a fraud.

"Mother, you need to talk to him. He won't listen to me."

"Now, Joseph, you've got to be patient with him. He's just blowing off steam."

"Blowing off steam? He's telling everyone I'm a fraud! And he's an apostle!"

"He's just sensitive about that nasty rumor with the girl. He's a good boy."

It came to a head soon enough. Joseph found William at the livery stable and ordered him to publicly recant his denunciations. But William wouldn't back down.

Joseph had had enough. He stepped back, spat on his hands, and cracked William in the mouth. Fists flew. Shirts ripped. Dust swirled. Joseph threw a hard right-cross that split his brother's lip and rattled every tooth in his jaw. In return, William, who'd settled many scores with his fists, feinted left, jinked right, and caught Joseph's nose with a roundhouse. Stunned, Joseph shook his head to clear it. William charged, throwing Joseph to the ground. The men rolled in the dirt raining punches.

Hyrum finally pulled William off Joseph, who was laying flat on his back. Blood poured from his nose and spilled onto his torn white shirt. They both stood, heaving, pretending to want more of it, their nostrils wide like bulls tuckered out from mounting. A crowd had gathered, for there was always a crowd wherever Joseph went. The owner of the stable ran out, yelling at the two hoodlums to take their mischief elsewhere. When he saw the pugilists were the Smith boys he was at a complete loss for words, especially when he saw the Prophet had been given the worst of it.

The entire family was embarrassed about the fistfight; the Prophet shouldn't get into a fistfight with anyone, and certainly not with an Ex-Apostle. Lyman said it best: "You sure didn't see Jesus givin' Judas Iscariot a whuppin'."

Hyrum commanded everyone to go home and not talk about it. So they went home and talked about it. The whole thing was officially forgotten and remembered for months. "You shoulda seen it! They were beatin' merry hell out of one another!" Then the storyteller would lower his voice. "And the prophet got showed up pretty good, you ask me."

No one breathed a word of it when Joseph was around.

The same thing happened after the scuffle between Joseph and his brother-in-law, Calvin Stoddard. Calvin believed in the truth with vim and vigor. He'd become upset, however, when Joseph asked him to return some water rights that Joseph had previously given him. This had become a recurring problem around town—Joseph giving and taking property at his whim (or at the whim of the Lord, as it were).

"Joseph's an Indian giver. He gave me that land and now he's trying to take it back for himself. Of all the dirty, low down—"

"But, Cal," said Brigham, "why make a big fuss when he gave you the shares to begin with?"

"He bought them shares with the church's money and now he acts like they're his, that's why! It's our money. We're the ones who donated it in the first place. So who's he to say who gets what?"

Ez found Rachel stirring a pot of stew when he came home. A dishtowel was draped over her shoulder and strands of hair spilled loose around her face from the auburn pile pinned back on her head. She swiped at them with the back of her hand.

Just then a mouse ran past and ducked into the nearest crack in the floorboard just as Rachel, broom in hand, took a swing at it.

"I've never seen so many of the little buggers," she said. "Got three today." Ez smiled. It was clear that Rachel actually enjoyed hunting mice. She constantly bragged about her daily body count.

Ez lowered his bulk into a chair. "Now it's Calvin who's up in arms. Why get all bottled up about it?" he asked. "They're only measly water shares."

"I think it's the principle of the thing," said Rachel, keeping an eye on the crack in the wall the mouse had used for its escape.

"But we should be talking about spiritual things, not water shares."

"I think that's the point. Joseph should focus on religion and not on buying and selling land, especially when he's making a profit off the Saints."

"But I don't think he's being—"

"There it is!" She took two quick steps toward the corner and swung the broom. "Got him!"

They sat for dinner: Ez, Rachel, and their son Thomas, a toddler now. Rachel was not a good cook and Thomas was throwing whatever it was onto the floor where the dog ate it without even sniffing. Rachel was fastidious about blessing the food, and Ez was grateful for the protection it might provide. She prayed with such elegant simplicity it seemed wasted on her stew.

Ez was quiet during dinner. After the dishes had been cleaned and put away, he looked at his wife. "You think he's doing that on purpose?"

"Doing what on purpose?"

"Trying to make a profit off the Saints."

"I have no idea."

***

Joseph was still smarting over the fight with William. He knew he needed to re-establish his authority. Ez tried to reason with him. "Just let it go, Joseph. Calvin isn't worth it. Don't make it worse."

"If I let some upstart think he can get the better of me, there's no telling what may come of it. It's not righteous to be a push-over."

Calvin was leaning against a small woodshed next to his house when Joseph rode up. When he saw the look on Joseph's face, he knew the Prophet hadn't come to pray over their toddler who had the flu. Joseph's sister looked out the window, alarmed.

What happened next was too one-sided to be called a fight. Joseph hit Calvin so hard that witnesses said he would have landed in Indiana if a picket fence hadn't stopped him. Upon regaining consciousness, Calvin concluded that the water shares had been vastly overrated. Joseph waited patiently until Calvin opened his eyes. He reached down and pulled Calvin up, dusted him off, and embraced him. Then he got on his horse and rode away.

Within a week, both William and Calvin repented for bad-mouthing the prophet. William said he'd been "buffaloed by evil spirits" and Calvin said there'd been a "simple misunderstanding." William was immediately re-instated as one of the Twelve Apostles, which was a relief, because it felt wrong having just the eleven.

***

The grand opening of the temple was spectacular. The women had made the curtains and sewn the new special underwear that Mormons wore from that time forward. They were Joseph's design and looked like a one-piece union suit with a button flap in the back. Only the Saints who were initiated into the secret ceremonies of the temple were allowed to wear them. Joseph said the sacred underwear would protect them from harm, and would be a reminder that they were the Chosen People, and ought to act like it.

"Do we really have to wear these things?" complained Rachel.

"They're sacred, Rach. We *get* to wear them."

"But they're hot as Hades. And they're ugly."

"Rachel, these undergarments are holy."

"Fine, I'll wear them and sweat to death if everyone insists. I just hope they're necessary."

"I don't know what I'm going to do with you sometimes."

"Well, you can start by stacking some of this wood. That is, unless you're too hot wearing those ugly things."

"Rach?"

"What now?" she said, feigning exasperation.

"I love you."

"You're a fine one, Ezra Wells, and I love you, too. But the wood still needs to be stacked. Because I'll tell you something right now, mister: that holy underwear won't protect you from that."

The temple ceremony was to be so hush-hush that temple-goers had to solemnly swear never to reveal its rituals, accepting death as punishment if they did. Top-secret handshakes and passwords were whispered in the ceremony. These secret codes would be required to enter heaven. Without them there could be no entrance. No exceptions. The secrets had to be so well protected that a guard was permanently stationed at the temple door in case an unworthy sinner tried to sneak in and learn the secret passwords.

The interior of the temple was elegant for the Ohio frontier. There were elaborately carved gilded scrollwork, ornate pulpits, and chandeliers—all the necessary staples for a worthy house of worship. The mummies were there, too, displayed behind theatre rope on the main floor, next to a small gift shop.

Unlike Rachel, Ez hadn't strategized for weeks about what he'd wear to the grand opening.

"Ezra, you look like a wheelwright in those trousers."

"But I am a wheelwright."

"Well, today you're not. I don't want you looking like you came straight from the shop. Not today I won't. Now, what about this dress?" She held it up in front of her and pulled the bottom hem to the side, like she was demonstrating a curtsy.

"It looks good."

"Ezra, pay attention! You're not even looking!"

Rachel yanked on his necktie, cinching it even tighter. She spit on her palm to wet his hair in a futile effort to get it to lay flat while Ez stood patiently as she fussed over him.

There were two thousand Mormons living in Kirtland and nearly all of them were in attendance. They milled about the temple grounds in their Sunday best, admiring the three-story structure built precisely to the dimensions God had ordered. Parley's suit fit him like a corset, and Brigham had shaved twice.

Joseph and Emma rode up in a brand new carriage befitting the grand occasion. He looked like he'd come directly from the House of Lords, and she modeled a gown she'd been sewing for months. Emma was still a beautiful woman, but five births, infant deaths, and the haunting suspicion of her husband's infidelities had all exacted a toll. She felt increasingly like soft fruit about to spoil.

Joseph helped her out of the carriage that'd stopped in front on Joseph Street. They walked up to the door. People slapped him on the back. "She's a beauty." "It's so gorgeous." "Jesus has to be pleased." The temple was Joseph's creation and his feelings for it were intensely proprietary. Not many men but thirty years of age could boast of such an achievement.

The services lasted three days straight, but the women were only allowed on the first day. All day and night the men prayed, drank, ate, and spoke in incoherent tongues. On the third day, the sound of rushing wind filled the temple. "That's the sound of angels swooping in," Joseph said. The others didn't actually see the angels, per se, but a few said they may have felt a breeze as they flew by.

On the final night, after fasting and praying, Joseph and Oliver stepped up to the pulpit. A satin veil was lowered around them so they were hidden from the others. Aides pulled a rope on a pulley a few minutes later to lift the veil. Joseph and Oliver stood, arm in arm, looking up to the ceiling.

"We have seen Jesus," said Joseph. "He was standing here on this pulpit on a slab of pure gold. His eyes were like fire, and his hair was white as snow. He said: 'I am He who was slain. Behold, your sins are forgiven.'"

Some of the men reported later that they thought they heard muffled voices that sounded like Jesus behind the curtain, but these reports were equivocal at best, because they admitted they didn't know exactly what Jesus' voice sounded like. "But it sounded an awful lot like it could've been Him."

Joseph said, almost as an afterthought (because Jesus took second fiddle to no one), "Moses appeared before us, too. And so did the Biblical prophet, Elijah, who told us that the Second Coming is nigh, even at the door."

The show at the temple was an inspiring manifestation of the truth. But there were private mutterings that Jesus only came when the drapes were drawn.

15

Boom and Bust

It was 1837, and people were racing west to buy land. This was evidence of their Manifest Destiny, the notion that white Americans had the right, even the destiny, to claim the continent that had been ordained for them. They came on horses and in wagons, alone and in pairs. Many of them stopped in Kirtland, devout souls who'd heard about Joseph Smith and wanted to join the church.

Joseph considered himself to be a sensible businessman. He mortgaged the temple and used the money to buy more land, parlaying the widow's mite with God's house hanging in the balance. Using the Lord's address as collateral made perfect sense, and banks were happy to gouge the Lord, if necessary. Unfortunately, foresight was a blessing that even the Prophet did not possess.

Joseph encouraged Ez to buy real estate, too. Ez agreed this was a wise investment opportunity. He insisted that Rachel did, also. But when they lost their money, Rachel accused Ez of making a "bone-headed investment," forgetting that she'd given her tacit approval.

"Look here, Rachel," Ez said at the time. "How much did we buy our land for?"

"Didn't we pay fifty dollars for it?"

"That's exactly right. And how much do you think it's worth now?"

"I haven't the foggiest idea."

"Well, then, I'll tell you. LaMar's property just sold for $2,000 and it's the same size lot as we have."

"Well," she said, "it is a little closer to the temple."

"Okay, fine. But even if we sold for half that much we'd still make a bundle. That's why we need to buy more lots now."

"But you just said they cost $2,000!"

"I know. That's why we should buy. In two years they'll be double that."

"But we don't have $2,000, Ezra Wells, now do we."

"Rach, haven't you been listening to a thing I said? We can *borrow* it. We just go to the bank and use our house as collateral."

"So you're telling me the bank is just going to give us $2,000 for nothing?"

"Of course not. We've got to pay them back."

"And how are we supposed to do that?"

"When we sell the new lots." He tried to be patient with Rachel who didn't know the first thing about high finance. "That's what I keep trying to tell you."

"I don't know, Ez. Some people back east say this is just a land boom. If it goes bust we'd be in it up to our ears."

"Those people back east don't know what they're talking about. Land in Ohio is worth a heckuva lot more than in New York. It'll probably always be that way."

"Well, if you say so. But it doesn't make a lot of sense to me. That's all I'm saying."

The inevitable bust came soon thereafter.

"I told you so," Rachel said.

"But you said you agreed with it."

"No, I was very careful not to say that."

"Well, it sure sounded that way to me."

Most everyone in town agreed that it was actually Andrew Jackson's fault. By 1836, the United States Treasury was flooded with paper money and speculative notes. President Jackson issued an executive order requiring buyers of government land to pay in gold or silver coins. People frantically tried to exchange their paper notes for hard currency, but the local banks couldn't meet the demand. The result was the Panic of 1837 and a deep national depression, which stopped land speculation in its tracks. Overnight the Mormons' lands were next to worthless. So it was quite clear to Joseph, Ezra, and all the others who sought to make an overnight fortune in real estate, that their losses were President Jackson's fault.

LaMar, who'd strutted around, boasting about his collection of $2,000 lots, walked around town mumbling to himself about the good old days.

"If it wasn't for Joseph," he complained, "I wouldn't be broke like I am. He should've known better."

"It isn't Joseph's fault," said Ez.

"The hell it ain't! He said I ought to invest, so I did. What good is a prophet if he doesn't even know what a good investment is?"

"Well, he can't know everything."

"But he should've known this. Either that or he should've kept his big mouth shut. Now me and the wife don't know what we're gonna do. And I'm not the only one."

Indeed, he wasn't. But, really, LaMar had no one to blame but himself. A few weeks before President Jackson ruined everything, Ez had tried to buy a lot from LaMar for $2,000. LaMar said he'd prayed about it and couldn't let it go for less than $2,500. So, Ez didn't buy it.

Ez told Rachel, "Some people have all the nerve. LaMar got greedy and now he blames Joseph. If he isn't going to blame Jackson, like he should, he ought to blame the Good Lord, because he prayed about it and got the wrong answer."

"He should've listened to me. That's what he should've done," said Rachel. "But what do I know? I'm just a woman."

"Now, don't start up with that again."

"Start up with what?" she asked innocently.

"This whole business about going belly up, that's what."

"Now, Ezra, dear, I'm not about to say I told you so." She turned to Thomas, making a great show for Ez's benefit. "Goodness gracious, son. Look at this ratty old coat of yours. I'd love to buy you a new one, but we can't now that your father got too big for his britches."

***

The real estate bust prompted the treasure hunt in Massachusetts. A few months before, Joseph had read in the newspaper about a cache of gold and silver buried under a house in Salem, Massachusetts. He was convinced God had placed the story in the newspaper for the Saints' benefit. But Joseph also believed God wouldn't just hand over the gold and silver, for that would've made it too easy. God wanted the Saints to earn it, lest they become soft. God detested soft Saints.

A new convert named Burgess had lived in Massachusetts. He claimed to know the whereabouts of the particular house that sat atop the treasure and agreed to lead the expedition. While Ez was packing for the trip, Rachel asked, "If this man knows where this so-called treasure is buried, why didn't he dig it up already?"

"He said he didn't have time."

"Ez, be serious. What about your wheelwright shop?"

"I won't be gone long. Besides, Edward can hold down the fort." Edward, Ezra's apprentice, struggled with the basics of his trade, but Ez wanted to help him because Edward was born with a "brain condition." Around town, Edward was mostly known as That Mongoloid.

Rachel was incredulous. "You're going to let Edward run the shop?" She loved Ez for his generosity but believed Edward was incapable of anything but sweeping the floor.

"He'll do just fine."

"Please reconsider, Ezra." Ez knew that whenever Rachel called him by his full name it was the result of anger, frustration, or impatience.

"Joseph had a revelation about this, Rach." Rachel knew that when Ez used something *less* than her full name, he was as irritated as she.

"I thought this was supposed to be a missionary expedition," said Rachel.

"Well, that's what Joseph wants people to think because it might look bad if the Prophet and Apostles go all the way to Massachusetts to dig for buried treasure under a house."

"You think?"

"Now, Rach, there's no need for that."

"I'm sorry, Ezra, really I am. I just don't remember Peter, James, and John leaving their families to go treasure hunting."

To mask the real purpose of the trip (and to provide heavenly cover), Joseph published God's next revelation in the Book of Commandments: "I, the Lord God, am not displeased with your coming on this journey. I have much treasure in this city for you. They shall not discover your secret parts, and its wealth pertaining to gold and silver shall be yours. Concern not yourselves about your debts, for I will give you the power to pay them. Thus saith the Lord. Amen."

They roamed the neighborhoods of Salem looking for the house. Brother Burgess, who at one point in the journey had been the most admired man alive, was losing support by the hour. Brigham complained, "That Burgess fella must be half off his rocker, traipsing around like a dog in heat sniffing for the gold." They tracked down one lead after another until they finally found the house, but it was occupied and the tenant wouldn't leave. So they prayed for the Good Lord to nudge him, perhaps with an infestation of termites, or a leaky roof. But the tenant didn't budge.

Joseph said the failure was caused by someone in their group who wasn't keeping the commandments. They thought it was probably Burgess. They didn't know this as a fact, but just felt some mischief out of him somehow. Eventually they gave up and returned to Kirtland, broke.

16

The Anti-Bank

The Saints were long on Jesus, but short on cash. The springs of charity had dried up, not for want of generosity, but from a lack of funds. Joseph had to do something to avoid a financial catastrophe, and he had to do it fast.

So he started his own bank.

It seemed easy enough—just print notes and exchange them for hard cash. Complicating things, however, was an uptick in counterfeiting. Even the Chosen People weren't above a little mischief—the lure of easy money was intoxicating. Take Brother Midgley, for example. He had a sturdy belief in Jesus but he was also a swindler (his loyal wife would later say he was an "honest swindler"). Midgley bought an old jug from Brother Olson with a counterfeit half-dollar note. Olson tilted the jug and there was the gentle slosh of kerosene. "Comes with it," he said. Olson was happy with the bargain because he knew there was a tiny hole in his old jug. He took the half-dollar note to Clyde's Hardware Store to buy a new jug, walked up to the counter with the new jug, and handed the clerk the phony note.

"Hold your horses," the clerk said. "This note's a counterfeit. You're trying to cheat me!"

"No I'm not!" said Brother Olson. "I've never cheated anybody in my life."

Just then Brother Midgley came into the store looking for Brother Olson. "There you are, you low-down cheat! That jug you sold me has a hole in it, and you knew it. I lost half a gallon of kerosene. Leaked right out."

"See!" the clerk said, "You're a cheat and now we have proof. You can't pass fake money off to me. Not in my store, you can't. And I don't give a hoot if you're a member of the church or not!"

"Now hold on, both of ya," said Brother Olson. "I got that phony note from *you*, Brother Midgley! You're the snake in this deal, not me!"

Hyrum walked into the store just in time to stop a fistfight. Brother Midgley swore he didn't know the note had been a counterfeit (even though he'd produced it in his shed), and Brother Olson said he didn't know the jug had a hole (even though he did). Hyrum persuaded both men to apologize and shake hands. They left the store, each one smug in knowing he'd been the bigger man.

There was only one snag to Joseph's bank. State law required it to have valid security before it could open. This regulation annoyed him.

"The Ohio legislature won't let us incorporate the bank," said Joseph.

"Why not?" asked Ez.

"They're persecuting us because we're Mormons."

"What about the Constitution? Haven't they ever heard of that?"

"They keep coming up with one frivolous excuse after another. It's persecution, pure and simple."

"That isn't right."

"No it's not. But they say you've got to have collateral if you're going to be a bank."

"Why don't we just open the bank anyway?"

"They'd just close us down," said Joseph. "We can't call ourselves a bank without their permission."

"Then we won't call it a bank," said Ez. "We'll just call it 'not a bank' or something."

"But I've already incorporated it. We planned to call it the Kirtland Safety Society Bank. The notes are already printed."

They both stood, heads down, contemplating the injustice. "Hey, I just thought of something," said Ez. "If they're going to be so picky about it, why don't we just form an anti-bank."

"I'm listening."

"Yeah, we could just call it the Kirtland Safety Society *ANTI*-Bank. That way we aren't technically calling it a bank."

"That might work."

And so they did. They squeezed the word "ANTI" in front of the word "Bank" on all their pre-printed notes and opened up for business. Business was booming, too. They distributed $40,000 worth of notes within a few weeks. This creative solution might have saved the day, but for the cruel and capricious nature of finance.

Joseph's secretary, Warren Parrish, was an honest man who looked like he had aged twenty years since the bank opened. Ez found him poring over a ledger on his desk. The pigeonholes behind him, small wooden boxes mounted to the wall like cells in a honeycomb, were stuffed with papers, envelopes, and other accoutrements of high finance. All around him filing cabinets and ledgers lay strewn about, as if a desperate accountant was searching for one inexplicably missing digit.

"I'm worried, Ez," he said.

"What's the matter?"

"Do you know how much money we have in the bank?"

"What exactly do you mean by 'money'?"

"Listen, Ez." Warren massaged his neck and looked around furtively. He practically jumped when he heard a squeak in the floor. "We only have about $6,000 cash in the vault," he said.

"That doesn't sound like much."

"It's not. But I've heard Joseph telling people we have a lot more than that. In fact, the other day I overheard him say we had $60,000 cash on hand and another $600,000 at our command. That just isn't true, Ez, and I don't know who else I can talk to. I've tried to talk to him but he won't listen."

"Are you sure you're counting all the—"

"Ez, listen to me! This is serious. If there's a run on the bank we're in big trouble. We don't have more than a few pennies on the dollar to all our notes out there."

Like the carelessly dropped match that sets a forest alight, someone said something to someone else. Within hours, people were stampeding to the ANTI-Bank to redeem the notes. But Warren had counted correctly. They ran out of money within a few minutes and had to close the doors. People all over town frantically tried to exchange the notes but they were next to worthless and nobody wanted them. The anti-bank's customers were furious. Brother Midgley (the honest swindler) advanced on a teller, screeching, "I don't give a damn if he's the Prophet or not. I've been cheated and I want my money!"

Non-Mormon creditors had Joseph arrested. The Saints came up with just enough to bail him out of jail. Joseph was accustomed to others disbelieving him, but not the Saints. And now his admirers, who were reeling from the inevitable scars of the marketplace, were saying things like, "A true prophet has no business carrying on like he did with my money. No business at all. He's a downright liar and a thief."

***

Parley Pratt tossed all night. His wife lay beside him in a mobcap. She could tolerate the scratching of the rodents in the walls, but this rolling around was intolerable. Finally, Parley got up and fixed a cup of catnip tea, which he insisted cured insomnia, when really it didn't. He returned to bed and began snoring within minutes. She poked him, which caused the racket to stop, but only temporarily. The irony that he'd woken her and resumed his slumber in such an obnoxious way annoyed her. She got up and fixed her own cup of catnip tea.

The next morning Parley sat in his writing studio and picked up his pen. He believed Joseph had betrayed him. Parley was devout, a lion of the church, impervious to ridicule, and tireless in his defense of Joseph. The events of the past few months had come as a terrible blow. He knew what he was about to do would irreparably harm his relationship with the Prophet, but his dire financial situation required nothing less. He wrote:

> *Dear Joseph,*
>
> *If you are still determined to pursue this wicked course until you and the church sink into hell, at least have mercy on me and my family for those three real estate lots which you sold to me at the extraordinary price of $2,000, which never cost you more than $100.*

He looked at the few nice furnishings he and his wife had accumulated—the silver coffee service, the Oriental rug, and the china hutch; trappings that would be lost to his creditors. He'd shielded their financial affairs from her delicate sensibilities, but soon she would learn they were penniless. She would never look at him quite the same way, with the same admiration for his wisdom and business acumen.

> *If you do not pay me I shall be under the painful necessity of bringing charges against you for extortion, and taking advantage of your brother by undue religious influence, such as saying it was the "will of God" that I should have to pay $2,000 per lot.*

Parley suspected Joseph might lash out impulsively, like a cornered animal gone mad with fear, for Joseph had become angrier and prone to unpredictable rages.

Joseph sat in his home office when the letter arrived, hunkered down trying to avert the financial disaster, dashing off missives to loyal government officials, which alternately scolded and praised them into action on his behalf. He read Parley's letter and slammed his fist on the writing table. Emma, who had learned to tiptoe around the house so as not to make him angry, opened the door.

"What is it?"

"Parley's threatening to sue me!"

"Oh dear," she said and backed out, quietly closing the door.

Joseph ruminated about all that had gone wrong. It wasn't his nature to first look inward, but here he tried. He loved Parley, and knew he was not a vindictive man, complaining without reason. And it was this thought that tore at his gut.

Joseph had stood before his flock many times to confess his weaknesses, a strategy that made them love him even more, for he understood that everyone loved a repentant sinner. But no, he thought, it wasn't a *strategy*, for that would imply it had been manipulative. He had no money to repay Parley, and even if he did, it would set a precedent requiring him to repay others, too. That wouldn't be fair—he hadn't guaranteed anything. If Parley had made a bundle would he have given it back? No, he would have kept every penny. So, yes, it had gone poorly, as investments are wont to do. But, no, he would not be made to take the blame.

He pulled a piece of stationary from his pile.

Brother Parley P. Pratt,

Please be advised that you are hereby ordered to stand trial before a church tribunal on the charge of threatening the Prophet of the Lord. You are hereby advised that the charges brought against you are serious and will be met with excommunication from the church if the tribunal finds evidence against you.

Parley knew his excommunication was likely, making his salvation a genuine long shot. He also knew the money was long gone and suing Joseph wouldn't bring it back. So he apologized to Joseph and agreed not to sue him. Joseph concluded that, with the apology, there was no need to excommunicate Parley from the only true church.

Unfortunately, several other apostles were in the same fix. They nursed their grudges and met in secret to conspire against Joseph. His enemies were circling, like sharks, their fins revealing themselves before silently slipping into the murky water around him. He knew they were there, seen and unseen, waiting to strike.

Rachel opened her door to find Emma in tears. "I don't know what's going on, but I'm sick about this whole business," she said. "Just sick about it." She dabbed at the corner of her eyes with a handkerchief. "I can barely even show my face."

"How's Joseph taking it?"

"He feels terrible. Of course he does. He doesn't care about the money as much as you think. We have a nice house, but, my goodness, he's always giving away whatever we have." She wiped her nose and tucked the handkerchief back into her dress pocket. "People expect him to be perfect, but he's not. I'm sorry, but he's just not."

"It'll be all right, you'll see," said Rachel. She hugged Emma, looking over her shoulder at Ez with a grimace.

Emma pulled away. "There's Martin, too. And Oliver," she said. "Joseph is a complete mess."

Martin's faith in Joseph had become watered down, a drop at a time, so that eventually the embers of his belief had been doused. He had recently fallen under the spell of a young woman who swore she could read the future by using a black peep-stone. Oliver and David had also fallen for her. So, the Three Witnesses had all been smitten. This enticing Prophetess danced and twirled around before falling to the ground in a state of complete exhaustion. That's when she prophesied using the black peep-stone. Indeed, some of her best prophesying occurred when she was flat on her back. Joseph said the black peep-stone business was preposterous, for who could rely on a faulty stone to decipher the truth?

Joseph said to him, "Martin, you know better than to fall for that hogwash."

"But she has a gift."

"No she doesn't. Don't believe that nonsense."

"But her peep-stone looks just like yours."

"Martin," he said patiently, "the Lord hasn't blessed it—so it's just a black rock."

Martin didn't buy this explanation. Then he began receiving his own revelations. For example, he claimed God had revealed to him that Palmyra, New York would be wiped off the face of the earth within three months because its citizens were wicked. Martin was so certain of this exclusive scoop that he agreed to have his head chopped off if it didn't come true. It was unlikely, of course, that anyone would actually chop his head off, even if he was wrong.

Joseph excommunicated Martin, because it was untenable for one of the Three Witnesses to believe in the absurdity of a black peep-stone. Martin didn't care. He was a man of immense faith, and he knew that faith needed a vessel. So he joined the Shakers.

The Shakers were fanatics who didn't engage in sexual intercourse. Every member took a pledge of complete abstinence. The leader of the Shakers was a woman who thought sex was an ordeal, and too messy. So instead of having sexual intercourse, the Shakers danced, wiggled, squirmed, and shouted in strange tongues—things people presumably did when they weren't having sexual intercourse.

Martin eventually quit the Shakers (some speculated he wanted out of the pledge). He then joined the Strangites. James Strang, a former Mormon, claimed to have found his *own* stack of tablets buried in a hillside. Strang said the tablets *he* dug up were the writings of the ancient Indians too, just like the Book of Mormon. The main character in Strang's book was a fellow named Rajah Manchu of Vorito. Joseph said this was utter nonsense.

"I'm with Joseph," Brigham said. "That doesn't even sound like an ancient Indian name."

"Sounds to me like he just made it up," said Hyrum. "Who's going to believe there were ancient records buried in a hillside written by Rajah Manchu of Vorito? The whole thing is ridiculous."

It may indeed have been ridiculous, but Joseph's younger brother, Apostle William, didn't think so. He believed it and eventually joined the Strangites, too, and so did a few other apostles.

Rachel was upset when Martin left the Mormon fold. "Ez, it makes no sense. Martin saw the Angel Moroni, face to face. And he saw the golden tablets. So why on earth would he go and join a different church?"

Ez reminded her that even though Martin left the church, and said Joseph was a fraud, he never denied seeing the tablets.

"But," said Rachel, "it's hard to believe he saw the golden tablets when he then goes and leaves the church."

"I think it makes it even *more* believable."

"Why?"

"Think about it. If he thought Joseph was a false prophet, he'd probably say he was just kidding about seeing the angel and the tablets. Right?"

"But Martin says he only saw them with his *spiritual* eyes, not his real eyes."

"Rach, sometimes when you see something in a vision, or a trance, it's even more powerful than if you see it with your real eyes. Martin says he saw them in his mind's eye, and that's good enough for me."

"I still think it waters it down," she said.

Oliver's criticism stung Joseph even more than Martin's. Oliver's previous conviction had publically sprung a leak. He'd been rocked by the rumors of sexual impropriety between Joseph and Fanny Alger. He hadn't wanted to spy on Joseph, but he was upset about a host of things, including the banking fiasco, and he needed confirmation. So he had Joseph followed, and found out that, indeed, Joseph had been carrying on with Fanny, the teenage maid.

"Ez," asked Joseph, "what am I going to do with Oliver?"

"Well, are the rumors true?"

"We've already been over this."

"So they aren't?"

"I've already told you that's what Satan does—he tries to tarnish the reputation of the Prophet."

"Well, if the rumors aren't true, you ought to just say—"

"I don't want to dignify these accusations."

"Why don't you have a meeting with Oliver to clear the air? What could it hurt?"

So, there was a meeting, a showdown of sorts. Joseph begged Oliver to recant the heresies and denounce the rumors. But Oliver wouldn't back down. "Not when I've got the solid proof, I won't," he said.

Joseph denied the affair (as any sensible Prophet would do). However, Oliver was outraged that Joseph wouldn't take responsibility for the tryst. He wrote an ostensibly private letter to his brother, which somehow became public and quickly circulated through Kirtland. The letter set forth the evidence and stated: "What I had said in the meeting was strictly true. The dirty, nasty, filthy affair of his and Fanny Alger's was talked over at length, and I strictly declared that I had never deserted from the truth in the matter."

Having the Prophet's affair with the teenage girl so publically exposed humiliated Emma. His close friendship with Joseph made Rachel suspicious of Ezra, too.

"So, Ez, did he?"

"Rachel, we've already been over this. He's the Prophet. He wouldn't do a thing like that."

"I don't know, Ez," she said. "It just doesn't smell right."

"Listen, Rach, Satan will do whatever he can to stop the Lord's work. Fanny probably has a fancy for Joseph because he's the Prophet, and he's been attentive to her because she's had a difficult life."

"That's it?" Rachel stared at him, hoping he might volunteer something heftier.

***

No one wanted to see a fistfight in the temple. Joseph had gone out of town on a preaching tour to allow time for people to simmer down over the bank's collapse and the revelation of his affair with Fanny, so he wasn't there when it happened.

"We've lost our money and it's Joseph's fault," shouted a temple-goer from the second pew. "He's a fraud!"

"The hell he is!" yelled Hyrum.

"He's gotta go. It's either him or me."

"Then go!" Brigham shouted from the podium, "And take your friends with you."

They argued for a week over who'd thrown the first punch. But it took only a few seconds before fists flew. Sixteen temple-goers were arrested for disturbing the peace, but the charges were dismissed because Brethren on both sides had drawn blood.

Joseph, though publically disappointed that his followers would desecrate the temple with a fistfight, had other fish to fry. His enemies had sworn out a warrant against him for banking fraud, so he called an emergency meeting at the temple. He stood at the podium to speak, but the dissenters booed and catcalled from the pews.

That evening he ran into Ez. It was January, 1838, and Joseph was bundled up from the cold. "I'm finished here. I'm leaving."

"Where are you going?"

"I'm leaving for Missouri. I hope you'll come."

"Well, I suppose Rachel and I'll join up with the Saints down there eventually. You thinking you'll leave in the spring?"

"I'm leaving tonight."

"Tonight?"

"Yes, but please don't tell anyone. I fear for my safety."

Emma went about her work in a trance. It made it easier for her to think about nothing. She was pumping water from the spigot into an empty wooden tub for the children's baths when Joseph intercepted her on the icy, well-trodden path.

"Emma, we need to talk."

"I'm bathing the children."

"The bath can wait."

"No, Joseph, it can't! The children need to be fed, the wash needs to be tended to, the garden needs to be weeded, and the children need a bath. So, no, Joseph, I don't have the luxury of just running away."

"So what would you have me do?"

"You'll do whatever you want."

"If I don't leave they'll run me out of town."

"So I guess you'll go, and I'll manage as I always have. I don't know how, but I will."

"Please, Emma. I'm sorry. I know how hard this has been on you."

"Do you?"

"Yes, I think I do. I know you cringe whenever the neighbors walk by. I know you're embarrassed. I know I've hurt you."

She stared at the dirty ice and snow along the path without seeing it.

"I love you, Emma."

She stepped toward the well with the tub still in her arms. He took it from her gloved hands and set it down in the snow. She didn't want to look at him. He took each of her arms and faced her. "I love you, Emma. You know that. I'll make arrangements for you and the children to join me. This will be a new beginning. It will be better in Missouri. I promise."

"I suppose I'll do whatever you say." But there was no conviction in it.

Joseph picked up the tub and filled it with water, hauled it inside to heat the water over the hearth, and then bathed the children. That night, when Emma thought he had fallen asleep, she heard him weeping.

"I'm sorry, Emma. For everything."

And then he began to sob. Emma knew Joseph had an emotional side, and cried from time to time. But not like this. This was a shoulder-racking, snot-running, sob.

Three nights after Joseph left under cover of darkness, the building that held the Kirtland Printing Press burned to the ground, the obvious result of arson. Joseph's enemies would have printed negative things about him. So, a few loyal Saints burned it down, to protect the Prophet's good name.

PART III

MISSOURI

1838 - 1839

17

The Garden of Eden

They slid the rowboat into the Grand River on the outskirts of Independence and hopped in. On board was the brass of the Mormon Church: Joseph, Orson, Brigham, and Sidney. The water lapped against the side of the boat in easy rhythmic ripples as they paddled north. Along the riverbank there was a concerto of robins, warblers, and bluebirds. It was a spring day out of a fairy tale. It stood to reason that this would be a perfectly good day to rediscover the Garden of Eden.

They paddled to a quiet cove on the eastern bank, less than a mile from town. Brigham rolled his trousers to his knees and stepped out, then tied the boat to the base of a tree and the others disembarked. They followed an overgrown path through elderberry bushes and cattails, still heavy with dew. Their pant legs were wet by the time they came to a bluff overlooking the area. Orson wandered off to explore.

"Hey," Orson hollered to the others. "Come look at this!"

They found him standing next to a pile of stones stacked into what appeared to be the remains of a chimney, or perhaps an altar of some kind. They speculated about who'd built it, and why. Joseph was unusually quiet, contemplative. He finally spoke.

"This is the Valley of God where Adam lived. And this was his altar."

"Wait a minute," said Brigham, "I thought Adam lived in the Garden of Eden."

"Yes, I know," said Joseph. "And this is where it was."

"This is where what was?"

"The Garden of Eden."

"Are you saying this area, right here where we're standing, was the Garden of Eden?"

"No, technically the Garden of Eden was over there, maybe a half-mile or so," he said, pointing to the east. "But this spot here is where they lived after Eve ate the apple and they were expelled from the Garden. Its proper name is Adam-ondi-Ahman. And right over there," he pointed to a bare patch, "is the spot where Cain killed Abel."

"That's amazing!" said Orson. "For some reason I'd always thought Adam and Eve lived over by Egypt. I had no idea the Garden of Eden used to be right here in Missouri."

"God has revealed it to me," said Joseph.

"Are you sure?" Orson was a credulous man, but this stretched his easy belief.

"Yes, I'm sure. This was consecrated as the Promised Land since the beginning of time."

They lingered in the Garden of Eden. They couldn't find the apple tree, and didn't spend a lot of time looking for it. They assumed it wouldn't have survived for so long. But they did imagine where Adam and Eve had slept and how it would have looked. An hour later they filed down the path to the rowboat, treading softly on the ground where the first man once stood.

***

Ez and Rachel took a carriage to St. Louis on their way to consolidate with the Saints in Missouri. He quickly realized that taking Rachel to the big city had been a blunder. She insisted on a bonnet that wrapped around the sides of her head like horse blinders. And he counted eighteen lace holes on the boots she had to have. "If you knew anything about fashion, Ezra, you'd know that all the women wear these now."

There were over two thousand Saints in Far West, the result of an aggressive missionary program led by Joseph himself. He was comfortable on a soapbox in the town square, his golden brown hair brushed back to expose his handsome face and blue eyes. As always, his audiences were mesmerized by his captivating personality. When they'd walk away, the men would mutter to their wives that he wasn't all that smart. The wives would nod their heads and wish they were still listening to Joseph Smith instead of their arrogant husbands, who didn't know the first thing about charm.

Joseph was inspired to save the world, knowing full well that the Mormons shouldn't hoard the truth for themselves. So he sent missionaries to England following a revelation instructing him to take the truth to every nook and cranny. Joseph knew humble people lived in those nooks, unlike the fortunate rich (who thought they were smarter than God).

Joseph asked Ez to go to England to preach, but Rachel wouldn't hear of it.

"Why on God's green earth would you go all the way to England? If you have such a hankering to preach, you can do it here."

The church was growing quickly, but it was losing long-time members. It had already lost Martin Harris and was now on the verge of losing Oliver and David, the other two of the Three Witnesses.

"Ez," asked Oliver, "why do you always turn a blind eye to Joseph's antics?"

"What antics?"

"Look at his affair with Fanny. And there's the banking scandal."

"There are two sides to every story, Oliver."

"For crying' out loud, Ez, I've got proof!"

"Do you believe God called him to be the Prophet, or not?"

"In some ways, yes, I still do."

"In some ways? You saw the angel and the golden tablets with your own eyes! Geez, what more do you want."

"But would a true prophet commit adultery right under Emma's nose?"

"Now, you don't know that as a fact."

"Ez, wake up! I had spies! Even Fanny won't deny it."

Joseph had had enough of Oliver's criticism, so he excommunicated him. If Oliver cared, he didn't show it.

David shared the boat with Oliver, and it was leaking the spirit. He said, "If you believe my testimony in zee Book of Mormon, zen I will tell you zat God spoke to me by His own voice from zee heavens. He told me to separate myself from zee Mormons and Joseph Smith. And I'll swear it on my life."

This baffled the Saints. Why would God go and switch him up like that—telling him one thing, and then another? Somebody wasn't telling the truth. Ez caught up with David at his farm. He was standing with a shovel in one hand and the reins of a horse in the other.

"So, David, why would God tell you to join one church, and a few years later turn around and tell you to leave it? It doesn't make a lick of sense."

"Because zee church isn't true, zat's why."

"Which church isn't true?"

"Zee one you're in. Zee one Joseph's in charge of."

"But that's not what you've been saying the last few years."

"Well, zat was before God spoke to me zee second time and told me to leave."

"But you saw the angel and the golden tablets with your own eyes!"

"I see zem sure enough. Of course, I didn't see zem with my normal eyes."

"What do you mean you 'didn't see them with your normal eyes'?"

"You can't see zee angel with your normal eyes. You'd die. Everybody knows zis. I saw zem with my *spiritual* eyes just as clear as I see you standing here in zee field."

All Three Witnesses had left the church. Of the eight others who swore they'd seen the golden tablets, only three were left: Joseph's father and his two brothers. This did not look good.

The erosion of leadership was unfortunate, coming at a time when persecution of Mormons in Missouri was at an all-time high. The Saints had begun to refer to outsiders as Gentiles, and it was a genuine burden for the Chosen People to share the Promised Land with them. So they formed a band of vigilantes called the Danites.

The Danites were clandestine, with the usual complement of secret oaths and handshakes ordinarily reserved for Masons, Greek fraternities, and the Illuminati. Joseph didn't want his fingerprints to be on the Danites, and didn't want them to be part of the church, per se. After all, it would be unseemly for the true church to sponsor a gang of avengers who retaliated by stealing pigs and burning barns.

Joseph appointed Sampson Avard to lead this hush-hush Gang of Retaliation. Avard was as mean as the enemy, a fact that Joseph hoped would show the Gentiles that the Mormons meant business. The Danites' retaliatory operations had the de-facto endorsement of the Almighty, who had finally come to understand that the Kingdom ought to be built by robbing and plundering non-Mormons. This, some thought, was an odd way to prepare for the Second Coming. But, alas, the ways of God were mysterious.

It was July 4, 1838 when the Mormons threw a parade. This was a patriotic affair, replete with a marching band (an ensemble of men blowing rusty horns and kids banging kerosene cans with sticks). They were Mormons first, Americans second, and Missourians if there was anything left over. They gathered on the outskirts of town and marched to the spot where they planned to build another temple. Sidney stood on a soapbox, fanning himself with his hat. He kick-started the parade with a bombastic rant: "We will exterminate our enemies if need be!" This did nothing to reduce the neighbors' anxieties.

On Election Day four months later, Brother Quigley stepped forward to vote. He planned to cast his ballot for fellow Mormons. He was the church clerk, a frail man who could barely lift a pencil. Two Missouri roughnecks blocked his way.

"Where do you think you're goin', old man?"

"I'm just trying to vote," said Brother Quigley in his high-pitched voice. "Don't want no trouble."

"We'll you found it! Didn't he, Horace?"

This Missourian did not appear to have his wits about him. His eyes were out of alignment and it looked like he cut his own hair.

"Lookee here," he said. "In Jackson County, we don't let niggers or Mormons vote. Ain't that right, Horace?"

"That's right, Raymond. No niggers or Mormons." Horace looked like he might have been dropped on his head, too.

It frustrated the Mormons that they were always lumped in with the Negroes. Joseph tried to quell the resentment by insisting that Negroes shouldn't be allowed to run wild. He said the anti-slavery position would "lay waste to the fair states of the South, and let loose upon the world a people who might overrun our society, and violate the most sacred principles of human society, chastity and virtue." What more could he have said to assuage the neighbors?

An undercover Danite member stood nearby. When the dimwitted Missourians made a stink about the Mormons' voting, he gave the covert hand signal. The Danites galloped up, itching to settle a score. A fence was being built next to the voting booth and there was a pile of cedar fence posts stacked next to it. The Danites grabbed the posts and gave Raymond and Horace some of God's vinegar. Brother Quigley, the fragile clerk who had never swatted a gnat, swung a post wildly at Horace, striking him, against all odds, in his groin. Horace fell to the dirt like a sack of grain. Brother Quigley dropped the post and admired his handiwork. He had never felt the rush of battle before.

In the first battle for Missouri, the Mormons had beaten the Gentiles to a bloody pulp.

After the parade, Joseph stood on a plank of wood in the center of town. He was a commanding figure, tall, young, and handsome, with broad shoulders and an easy smile. The Saints were flush with victory. Brother Quigley stood slightly taller. "You should have seen him today," they told his wife. She looked admiringly at him, surprised that the man she'd married had been so brave. "They had it coming," was all he said.

"We have suffered enough," Joseph began. The cold November wind burned their faces. They could see the steam from Joseph's breath, and it was hot. "We have appealed to judges, magistrates, governors, and the President without success. They tell us to fight our own battles. And that's exactly what we'll do! If the people leave us alone, we will preach the gospel in peace. But if they come to molest us, we will establish our religion by the sword. We'll trample our enemies and make it a gore of blood from the Rocky Mountains to the Atlantic Ocean!"

The explosion of cheers could be heard all the way to St. Louis. This potential smorgasbord of blood, they believed, was in keeping with their commitment to Jesus. It was the acknowledgment that He was worth fighting for. So they'd do it for their lives, liberty, and their pursuit of Jesus. They rode out, infused with religious fervor, and re-confiscated all their horses, pigs, and cows. They may have gone a bit overboard, swiping cows with Gentile brands, and setting a few fires of their own, too.

Ez came in late the next night, cold and tired. He'd tried to justify the looting, but he knew in his heart that it was wrong, because Jesus would never steal a pig, or burn a barn. It seemed incongruent to him that the mastermind of this new policy was the author of the Sermon on the Mount.

"He tried to wait up for you," said Rachel, looking at their son, Thomas, who was laying on the only bed they had. Thomas didn't like going to sleep, and every night Rachel had to talk him into it all over again. But that night he'd fallen asleep still wearing his boots and coat. The bed sagged in the middle and Ez remembered that the ropes needed to be tightened. Thomas lay innocently dreaming of adventure. A hand-me-down musket was propped against the wall. His hair was tangled, and his hands and face were covered with dirt. He smelled like a little boy.

Ez dropped his head. "I'm sorry, Rach. Maybe we shouldn't have come. Maybe we should—"

"No," Rachel said. She took his hand. "We're here and we're sticking with the Saints. God will provide."

"But, the kids . . . ." The emotion of so many trials caught him off guard, coming to the surface quickly. Every muscle in his face was engaged trying to tamp back the tears. "I just don't know if I . . . ."

She reached up and took his chin in her hand. He hadn't shaved that day, and his beard was rough. "We have each other. We'll make it. You hear me? We'll make it, Ez."

Years later, Ez would close his eyes and remember her that night, strong and confident in her small body, fiercely protective of him and their two children. Her red hair was lit by the glow of the fireplace. Her blue eyes danced around his face, searching for a similar resolve from him.

They fell asleep in each other's arms with the two kids curled up next to them. And while they slept, the Missourians burned more cabins.

18

Luke

Ezra's sister, Lorna, had also been driven out of Kirtland, but for entirely different reasons. She'd been found shamelessly naked in the barn, and dared become pregnant outside of wedlock. The pious women there would not tolerate a seducer in their midst. Their God-loving husbands agreed she was trouble, but they did so with private regret, for she had a figure made for sin.

She begged the fare to St. Louis from a man who wanted to please her. She bought a roll of fabric and then took the coach up to Far West, sitting next to a chubby man and wife who held crates of chickens on their laps, and two men who gossiped about her in a Scandinavian language. When she arrived, she rented a room from an elderly man with milky eyes and whose hands were all skin and knuckles. He could not be seduced.

Lorna had learned to sew early in her life, and word spread that she could make and mend clothes. The women didn't want her anywhere near their husband's torn trousers, but the men in town suddenly needed stitches put in places where they hadn't needed them before. Even the Missourians, who rarely did business with the Saints, found britches with loose thread.

***

Luke Carlisle was a twenty-year-old Missourian who worked at his father's blacksmith shop in town. Rachel saw him standing over the forge with his shirt off, his upper body slick with sweat from the fire's heat. When he turned to hoist a piece of iron and his muscles flexed, Rachel found a sudden interest in blacksmithing.

"I didn't know you needed to be so strong to be a blacksmith," she said that evening to Ez, out of the blue.

Despite her momentary carnal desire for Luke, Rachel loved Ezra and his softness as much as any woman has loved a man. Nevertheless, her devotion to Ez (and, it should be fairly noted, her secondary devotion to Jesus) would still permit the wandering thought over a man as desirable as Luke. Ez knew this because she'd never shown interest in blacksmiths before, and she wouldn't have mentioned Luke's missing shirt over supper that evening if he'd been fat.

Luke had his shirt mended by Lorna (so he had one), and the two of them began courting. Some in town thought it patently unfair that God would bless these two Gentiles with such attractiveness when their own spouses looked better with their shirts on.

Lorna gushed, "Luke, he's so this," and "Luke, he's so that." Rachel's only comment was, "I understand he's a blacksmith, is he?"

Ez was concerned because Luke was a Gentile. He thought Rachel ought to be concerned, too, but she didn't act like it. In fact, she invited the lovebirds for supper a few days later. She primped more than she normally did, but did so nonchalantly, hoping Ez wouldn't notice (but he did). He assumed Rachel was disappointed when Luke showed up in a shirt (which she was).

After supper, Luke asked to speak to Ez in private. The two of them retired to the bedroom. Lorna stood outside the door, straining to hear. She frowned and shook her head when Rachel made noise with the dishes.

"Ezra, I know Lorna doesn't have a father, so I thought maybe it'd be suitable if I asked you instead. See, me and Lorna are thinkin' about gettin' married proper."

"It's awfully quick to be talking marriage, isn't it?"

"But me and Lorna are different. We're in love."

"I don't know, Luke. You know we're Mormons."

"I ain't got nuthin' against the Mormons."

"What about your parents?"

"My pa went and give me his blessing 'cause Lorna, she ain't a Mormon either. He don't like the Mormons—said they're gonna cost him the blacksmith shop."

"We don't mean to cause your pa any harm."

"He says ever since the Mormons moved here, all his business went and dried up. Says none of the Mormons'll do business with him on account of they only do their blacksmithin' with other Mormons."

"Well, it's true—we stick together."

"And some of his old customers are now doin' business with that Finstrom fella—the Mormon. I'm not sayin' Finstrom's blacksmithin' ain't good, but he's takin' my pa to the poor house."

"Brother Finstrom doesn't mean any harm."

Ez got up and threw another log on the fire. He poked it a few times with the poker until it settled into the coals and sparks jumped.

"My pa says the Mormons are gonna bring in a bunch of Negroes, too, and have 'em join up with your church. He ain't happy about that either. Course, I suspect you'd understand that, bein' Christian and all."

"We aren't trying to cause any trouble here, Luke. You tell your pa that."

"Accordin' to my pa, the Mormons are plannin' to take over the whole town and vote in their own Sherriff."

"We're peaceful folks and don't want to upset anyone."

"And my ma says the Mormons think they're so damned special, if you'll forgive my cussin', 'cause they think they have the only true church, and all us other folks are goin' straight to hell. But, see, the thing is, we already got us a good church."

"We aren't going to force anyone to join the church. I'm sure your church has some truth in it—course it does. It just doesn't have the complete truth like ours."

When Luke left, Lorna demanded to know every detail about the chat, and she wanted it word for word.

"So what did he say?"

"He said he wanted to get married."

"How *exactly* did he say it?"

"Pretty much just like that."

"Come on, Ez, think!"

"That pretty much sums it up."

"Please tell me you didn't say anything stupid."

"I told him he ought to think hard on it, that's all."

"Why'd you say that? It's not your business anyway!"

"But, Lorna, he isn't one of us."

"And what's that supposed to mean?"

"You know darned good and well what I mean. He's not a Mormon. Missourians hate Mormons—you know that."

"But Luke's different. Besides, I'm not a Mormon either."

"Maybe you aren't a Mormon, per se, but you've got plenty of Mormon in your soul."

"You're not my father, and you don't know what you're talking about. Luke's not like the rest of them."

Luke and Lorna were married two days later. Rachel dragged Ez to the wedding, but Luke's parents boycotted the affair.

***

The ridicule and persecution continued for the Mormons, but they endured it because they knew the church was true. They figured the angel wouldn't give the golden tablets to just anyone and then waltz back up to heaven. They also believed there was honor in suffering. This modest delusion allowed them to believe the church *had* to be true. After all, why would the Missourians persecute them if Satan hadn't been directing the attack? And why would Satan do such a thing if their church wasn't the truest one? So they put up with it, and God let them.

They stuck together. When one of their barns collapsed into a pile of burned pine, they'd have a community barn-raising. They'd be covered in soot and smelled like ash trays by the time they'd hauled away the charred remains. Then they'd go for a swim in the nearby river, change clothes, and rebuild. The Missourians watched from a distance, amazed how they'd all pitch in, singing hymns all the while. "What the hell's the matter with them people," they'd say. "They're crazy, that's what they are." And when there was nothing left to rebuild, a hoedown would erupt. The women lifted their dresses to their knees, pirouetting and dosie do'ing while the men gaped with unbridled pleasure, temporarily forgetting all about Satan and his evil shenanigans. Joseph danced too, and not just with the pretty ones either. Sidney fretted on the sidelines, glancing heavenward with the paranoia of a field mouse with ten hawks circling above it.

Emma was happier to be out of Kirtland, because Fanny, the teenage vamp who'd enticed her husband, hadn't followed him to Missouri, thank God. This spared her friends from offering disingenuous comfort like, "Don't worry, it probably didn't amount to much."

The Saints knew that not every Gentile was a godless sinner. Confused and slightly misguided perhaps, but not irredeemable—some of them tried to understand the Mormons rather than taking a match to their barns.

Town was neutral ground—both Saints and Gentiles did business there. Brother Lyman, a devout Mormon, was at Ez's wheelwright shop when a Gentile came by to have his wagon fixed.

"So what is it about you Mormons anyway?" the Gentile asked. "What's all this talk about golden bibles and such?"

"It's true," said Ez. "Our Prophet wrote the Book of Mormon, which was originally written on golden tablets."

"Wait a minute," Lyman interrupted him. "Technically it wasn't our Prophet who wrote it, he just translated it from another language."

"Anyway," continued Ez, "we believe that book contains sacred scripture and is a perfect book just like the Bible and—"

"Well," Lyman interrupted again, "the Bible isn't technically perfect because it's been rewritten too many times. I just wanted to be clear on that."

"So, anyway," Ez began again, "we believe God picked Joseph Smith to be the one to translate the—"

"If you want to be completely accurate here, Ez, you should tell him it was actually the Angel Moroni who picked him. But, go on."

"Good Lord, Lyman!" said Ez. "Why don't you just tell him since you know so much about it?"

So Lyman did, because he couldn't keep his mouth shut. He was uncomfortable with not knowing, so he tended to make it up as he went along. This, inexplicably, made him feel better.

"Like Ezra was saying, Joseph Smith is the Prophet. But we ought to start with the simple facts."

"Alrighty," said the Missourian as he looked for an excuse to leave, "but I don't have a lot of time right now. See, the missus is expectin'—"

"Fact number one: There's a God; everybody knows that, and he has a son named Jesus. So there's no argument there. Fact number two: There wasn't a true church on the earth until a few years ago."

"You don't know that as a fact," said the Gentile. "We already got us a good church and it seems pretty true to me. And what about all the other churches in the world?"

"I'm just talking about the ones in America, because those are the only ones I know about. Besides, for all we know they might not even have churches in China and places like that. They don't even speak English."

"Well, Lyman," Ez said, "I'm not sure Jesus did either, just to be totally fair."

"You might be right on that," Lyman reluctantly conceded, "but He probably would have if He'd lived in modern times. Anyway, what I was saying is there weren't any true churches on the earth until a few years ago, because why else would God have come down from heaven to tell Joseph Smith to start a true church if one already existed? Am I making sense here?"

"I'd agree with that, but only if I knew Joe Smith really saw—"

"So if you agree, why are you settlers around here so cotton pickin' bullheaded?"

"We just have different churches, that's all."

"If you'd read the danged Book of Mormon, you'd see for yourself."

"I don't read too good, but I'll think on it."

"You do that now," said Lyman.

"Well, I best be goin'. You Mormons seem all right to me, but maybe you shouldn't force it on other folks quite so much."

After the man left, Ez told Lyman this man's advice had been sensible, but Lyman just shrugged his shoulders and said, "As long as they're gonna be so doggone stubborn about it, I don't think that leaves us much of a choice, now does it?"

It was two weeks after Lorna's wedding when Ez found her in the tailor shop with a mouthful of pins. There were two dressmakers dummies impaled on poles near the window. Lorna turned away when the door opened and Ez walked in, but too late; he saw the purple mark just under her eye.

"Good Lord! You've got a shiner. What happened?"

"It's Luke," she said and started to cry. "But it's my fault."

"Now, what in the hell is that supposed to mean?"

"Last night he came in real late, and I could smell it on him."

"He'd been drinking?"

"No, it wasn't that."

"Then what was it?"

"It was nothing."

"Of course it was something, and you're going to tell me."

"What I smelled wasn't the drink. I wish it was."

"Well then, what was it?"

"It was kerosene."

Ez's face was a mask. He turned to leave.

"Wait, Ez! You don't understand!"

"Oh, I understand plenty."

"I'm not sure he had anything to do with it. I just asked him where he'd been and he said it was none of my business. He went to leave again and I tried to stop him, and that's when he pushed me out of the way, and I must've bumped my face. So it wasn't completely his fault. Maybe he didn't do anything. I got no proof."

Ez headed for the door. His blood pumped through the cavities of his heart with righteous purpose, down through every capillary. He punched the first thing he saw and a headless mannequin flew against the wall.

"Ez, please! I beg you! It'll be okay. You'll see. Luke's a good man. He's a good man."

19

The Battle of Crooked River

It was late September, 1838. The Reverend sat alone in his den, staring at the unopened letter. It had sat on his writing desk for three days, untouched, while he contemplated what to do with it. The seal on the envelope was his only daughter's, and it bore the return address of Independence, Missouri, a thousand miles away.

Finally, he picked up a gold letter opener given to him by an appreciative sinner, and slit the seal. As a young man, he could have done card tricks with his hands, had he not been so averse to sin. Now, he was an old man, and his hands trembled.

He removed the letter, taking care not to damage the return address, *Dearest Mother*, it began,

> *I hope this letter finds you well. Not a day passes that I do not think fondly of you. I know Father is still insistent on our lack of communication, but I do hope you received my last post, even though I did not receive a most desired reply.*
>
> *Thomas is eleven. He looks like Father. And Elizabeth, oh, Mother, Elizabeth is so precious. Whenever I speak her name I think of you. She has your delicate hands and beautiful auburn hair. She is so sweet. How I wish you could see her!*
>
> *Ezra and I are well. The church has grown so much! We are happily trying to live the gospel out here in Missouri, where we have all congregated. We have a choir, and it is a joyous occasion when they sing in unison to praise God and our Savior.*

My heart is filled with longing and I pray for our glorious reunion. My greatest desire is that it will speedily come. Until then, I am, fondly yours,

Rachel

He set the letter down and looked out the window. It was winter, and the trees had shed their leaves. Perhaps this would be his last season, he thought with exaggerated melancholy, for he wasn't ill, only tired. The thought of dying frightened him; he believed the ultimate tally of his life might well yield the very result he'd warned others about for decades. Now, in the winter of his own life, he wondered if he'd made a terrible mistake. Had the time finally come to commute the lifetime sentence he'd stubbornly imposed on his only child?

He picked up his writing pen and slid a piece of fine stationary from its box. *Daughter*, he wrote,

It is with a heavy heart that I inform you of your mother's passing six months ago. I am lonely now, my tenure as a minister having come to an end. Too few members of my congregation remain. I am content to hear your little ones are well.

Father

Rachel was thrilled to receive a post from Palmyra, and ripped it open. But the words were incomprehensively wrong. She fell to her knees and wept. Her long-suffering mother, whose voice had been silenced all those years, was dead. If only Rachel could have known that the letter she'd written four years earlier lay on her mother's bedside table, having been read each day until the very day she passed away. Indeed, if only she could have known that the last thought her mother had was of her, perhaps she might have felt some small measure of comfort.

Her emotions swung between anger, pity, and guilt. The anger was directed at her father, and at God. The pity was reserved for her mother. The guilt she bore alone.

The last time she'd seen her, her mother had been wrapped in a shawl on a freezing January night. She'd been hiding from her self-righteous husband as the sleighs and wagons pulled away from Palmyra with a handful of Mormons on board. Her mother had been the only one to see them off, and she'd done so with a broken heart. How Rachel wished she had demanded that her mother come with her. How she wished she could tell her she loved her, and that she was sorry for leaving.

***

A group of Mormons lived in the small town of DeWitt, a mile from the main body of Saints. The Missouri state militia had surrounded the town and refused to let them join the others in Far West. After midnight, Joseph sneaked across the enemy line on foot to see how they were holding up, and then slipped back to Far West to provide a somber report.

"What have we done to deserve this?" Joseph asked Ez. "None of this would have happened except they believed me. And now they need a miracle, and I can't give them one."

"Look at the Chosen People in the Bible. Same thing happened to them. God must want His people to suffer more than everybody else. Why, I don't know."

"And God gave them Moses," said Joseph.

"That's exactly right."

"Maybe I'm like Moses. Or Mohammed." Joseph pondered his own statement before continuing. "Yes, like Mohammed. He knew if you kept giving in to your enemies they'd eventually destroy you, so he finally said "the Koran or the Sword!"

Ez tried to be supportive. "That's right," he said, even though he'd never heard of Mohammed, or the Koran.

"Maybe that's the way it's got to be now: 'Joseph Smith or the Sword!'

"That sounds good," said Ez.

"God has raised me up to be a Prophet, and the people must heed my call!"

"Well, we need to do something." It was true. The Saints were tired of being too Christ-like about the whole affair.

Joseph ordered one hundred men to arm themselves and ride into Dewitt. The squadron of state militia was badly outnumbered and scattered like billiard balls at the break. The Mormons followed them back to their town, burned down their general store, and took a full wagonload of supplies.

Lilburn Boggs, the rat who had terrorized the Saints as Lt. Governor, had since become the Governor of Missouri. He ordered a hard case named Captain Bogart to counter attack. Bogart's heart was as ugly as the stone of a peach. His squad kidnapped three Mormon men and took them down to a marsh near the Crooked River.

Brother Patten was one of the Twelve Apostles. He grew his beard long to compensate for the hair that was missing on top. He was humble, too—not arrogant enough to compare himself to one of the original apostles (not even the less popular ones like Phillip, or Bartholomew). While he had a good heart, he could be rude and aggressive, and he swore like a sailor. Rather than politely asking for assistance, in the manner of more orthodox apostles, he might say, "Get off your sonofabitchin' arse and help poor Sister So-and-So cut that goddamned hay or I'll take this goddamned shovel and stick it up your arse!" He was always helping someone bring in their crops or birth a calf, whether they wanted him to or not.

When word came that the three Mormons were being held captive down by the river, Brother Patten rode his horse through town like he was the Second Coming of Paul Revere, demanding "every sonofabitchin' God-fearin' man" to get off their arse and help free them.

"Ez, please don't go," said Rachel.

"Can I come, Pa?" asked Thomas.

"Absolutely not!" said Rachel.

"But, Pa!"

"You need to be the man of the house while I'm gone."

"Ok, I'll stand guard here," he said and walked away to retrieve his hand-me-down musket. He was growing fast—his pants hung well above his ankles.

Rachel pulled Ez aside. "I don't like the sound of this. I don't like it at all."

Ez lifted his musket off the shelf and opened the door to leave. She took his arm and looked up at him. Her eyes darted across his face, desperately trying to find some purchase, some peg to hang on to. She begged him not to go, but knew he had no choice. He was an honorable man, and she knew it. It made her love him even more.

Sixty men rode off before first light to save their brethren held captive by the bastard Captain Bogart. Joseph, the Modern Mohammed, stayed back with the rest of the Saints. The Chosen People would no longer be peaceful dolts who allowed the Gentiles to wipe their boots on them, because God didn't want doormats in His Kingdom. Some privately thought the Promised Land shouldn't be won with the sword, but not Lyman. He explained that Jesus could have brought down angels from heaven to kill the Roman soldiers that nailed him to the cross, but He made a conscious choice—it wasn't due to weakness. "And that's the main difference, right there," a difference that befuddled Ezra who tried to unravel the logic in it, but gave up.

Caleb Stone was a rugged young man whose faith was not well grounded in study, for he didn't know how to read. He had black hair with a pronounced cowlick. The only imperfection in his handsome face was a nose that listed to one side, the result of a disagreement with his older brother. Caleb volunteered for the adventure because he was naïve, and failed to understand how dangerous life could be, in the way young people are.

"We'll dig in here, by the river," Captain Bogart told his militia in the pre-dawn darkness. "That way we can ambush them when they come ridin' over that hill," he said, pointing to a small rise in the landscape two hundred yards away. The distance between them was the killing field. "The Mormons are gonna be armed to the teeth, so don't shoot 'til they're close. There'll be no time to reload."

They dug in and waited. The Mormons crested the rise as the sun came up and dropped into the field, now only one hundred yards away. Captain Bogart looked down the line at his men and held up his hand, signaling for them to wait. The Mormons rode closer. Bogart's hand stayed up. The Mormons advanced, warily. When they came within sixty yards, Bogart dropped his arm.

Fifty muskets fired at once. A tree full of songbirds scattered in all directions. Two Mormons dropped from their horses. With Patten in the lead, they charged with God's rage. By the time Bogart's men reloaded their ball and powder, the Mormons were nearly upon them, but they got off one more volley before scattering. Brother Patten fell from his mount. His horse, wild with fear, took off in the other direction.

Ez leapt from his horse and ran to Patten. The ball had caught him squarely in the chest. He lay in the dirt as his beard soaked up the blood from the gaping hole like a mop. Even through his pain, his face was strangely peaceful. Perhaps he knew that he had died in the service of the Lord. Perhaps because he was going into shock.

"Ez," he whispered, almost in a gurgle. "I'm sorry I couldn't . . . ."

"You'll be alright, Brother. Please, dear God," Ez begged.

"I promised Mag . . . and my boys . . . ."

"They'll be taken care of, I give you my word."

"Tell them . . . love . . . promise . . . ."

"I swear it."

Patten smiled and closed his eyes. There was a final exhalation of breath, and he was gone.

Ez collapsed onto Patten's chest.

"We got us one!" yelled a Mormon, standing over a dead Missourian.

"Leave him to the buzzards!" someone else shouted.

"No!" Ez stood. His chest was covered with Patten's blood. The other men thought that he'd been shot, too.

Ez took a deep breath. "We're better than that," he said quietly.

They dug a shallow grave for their enemy. It looked like a place where someone had smothered a fire. They draped the bodies of their three friends over their saddles for the long walk back to Far West.

As they were leaving, Ez noticed something out of the corner of his eye. There was movement down by the river, no more than one hundred yards away. He stole another look. Yes, a few militiamen were crouched, advancing.

Ez could have retreated. He could have waved Brother Patten's blood stained shirt. He could have done any number of things to de-escalate the situation. But he wasn't thinking rationally. These bastards had murdered his friends, and even now they clamored for more bloodshed. He picked up his gun, climbed upon his horse, then screamed at the top of his lungs and charged.

Caleb and others followed within seconds. Their muskets were already loaded—they hadn't yet fired a shot. Four militiamen had crawled into position, their guns pointed at the Mormons. Their eyes widened with terror as they were about to be overrun by the pounding hooves of God's Army. They fired wildly at the charging beasts.

There was the briefest delay between the flash of gunpowder and the lead balls that tore through his body, like the delay between the lightning and thunder. And in that moment, Ez looked down the smoking barrel of the musket and saw his sister's new husband—the Missourian, Luke Carlisle.

He felt no pain, despite the lead ball that'd lodged in his stomach and the other one in his thigh. So this is what it feels like to die, he thought. He thought, inexplicably, about the squeaky door that he'd promised Rachel that he'd fix. There was shooting and yelling all around him, the panic evident in their voices.

He blacked out.

20

The Massacre at Haun's Hill

He saw the white light as he approached his Savior, a light so bright it stabbed his eyes. There was the sensation of floating, and then he heard his name spoken. *Was this the voice of Jesus*, he wondered? The words were urgent and insistent, and unaccompanied by a chorus of harps. Now the brightness hurt his eyes, and his hip hurt.

"Ez! Ez! Stay with us! Caleb, gimme your shirt!"

He lay on his back, staring up to the sun. Now the pain in his hip was excruciating.

"Get me a horse. Now!"

He realized he'd been shot. He tried to replay the events in his mind but the pain in his hip did not allow for reverie. They were stuffing a wet rag into his stomach, and he couldn't understand why they weren't tending to his hip. Three men lifted him onto the back of his horse. When the horse began to trot, he passed out from the pain.

He awoke in his own bed. A woman was speaking to him soothingly. Her accent was British. She put a damp cloth to his forehead. There was commotion in the next room. He heard Rachel's voice, beseeching God and the doctor both to save him.

The doctor entered the room with a leather bag. "Give him some whiskey," he said. "I haven't got much morphine."

The woman with the angelic voice leaned in close. "Brother Wells, would you like some liquor? It will help with the pain."

Ez nodded and Patty, the English midwife-cum-nurse, lifted a cup to his lips. It smelled like turpentine. He drank.

The doctor put his bag on the nightstand. "Hold him still," he said dispassionately. Ez's friends held him while the doctor scooped the lead ball from his hip as if he were digging the pit from an avocado. Ez passed out again.

He hovered over the room, looking down at himself in the bed. Rachel was sitting by his side. Was he dreaming? Or was his spirit about to leave him for good? Suddenly he was back in bed. His eyes focused on the wooden beams of the ceiling, which were slightly crooked. He wished he'd set them straighter.

Rachel was beside him when he woke. Her eyes were puffy. A strand of hair had fallen from her collection of pins and tickled him when she bent to kiss his clammy cheek.

"Can you hear me, sweetheart?" She lifted her head and looked at the doctor. "Can he hear me?" She leaned down to him again. "You're going to make it, Ez. You're so strong, and you, you . . . ."

He drifted, vaguely aware of his desperate predicament. His belly was wrapped in a girdle of gauze. It hurt now.

"It's me. Joseph." Joseph was distraught over the loss of three fine men, but he was nearly inconsolable at the thought that his best friend might die.

It was dark out, and the room smelled like blood and candle wax. There was also the whiff of iodine and urine from the bedpan. Ez was propped up on a damp pillow. He lifted his arm at the elbow without opening his eyes and took Joseph's hand.

"Maybe he's cold," said Rachel. "Somebody get me another blanket." Ez was too tired, too drugged, to complain. They had waged a marital battle over temperature for years. It was a battle he knew he would lose, as he always did—grudgingly throwing another log on the fire, tolerating extra blankets on the bed, and allowing her icy feet on his legs while they were trying to sleep.

"Let me bless you," said Joseph.

Ez nodded. Joseph cupped his hands over Ezra's tangled mess of hair and bowed his head in prayer. Everyone else in the room knelt down to silently pray as well.

"Brother Ezra Wells, I bless your fragile body with the strength to withstand your wounds, to repel infection and recover your good health. The Lord is mindful of your suffering and He grants you the gift of recovery as a reward for your valiant defense of His Gospel. You will run and not be weary, walk and not be faint. For this is the solemn promise of God, delivered to you through the holy priesthood of His servant. This I promise you in the name of Jesus Christ, Amen."

They lifted their heads. No one expected an immediate recovery, for they assumed the blessing might take time to kick in. But they knew God would intervene as Joseph promised. Their certainty came from Joseph's power to make such promises, a power that had been given to him in spectacular fashion.

The miraculous event occurred shortly after John the Baptist's visit eight years earlier. Joseph had been out in the woods prayerfully seeking further instructions concerning the establishment of the new church. Sunlight dappled through the trees that shielded his privacy. Without warning, three heavenly beings descended from the sky and hovered in front of him. They wore matching white robes and floated above the ground, just like the other angels. They introduced themselves as Peter, James, and John, three of the original apostles. They told Joseph that the holy priesthood disappeared from the earth when they died. Now that Joseph was restoring the original church, it was imperative that he have the priesthood. Presumably, this transfer of authority to act in God's name was required to be done, person-to-person.

Now, eight years later, Joseph left Ez's room, passing the doctor, who had come to bleed him. The doctor wrapped a tourniquet around Ez's arm and placed a wooden bucket on the floor at the side of the bed, just below Ez's elbow, to capture the blood from the cut. Ez gripped a wooden baton as the blood drained from his arm. The room smelled of rusty iron.

Ez got better slowly but steadily. His family and friends fervently believed his recovery was made possible by Joseph's blessing. They acknowledged the role of the doctor and the bloodletting, but they knew Ez's recovery hinged on the blessing.

***

Word of the battle reached Governor Boggs who was enraged that the Mormons had murdered two of his men. This could not stand. Boggs was a man of dubious integrity, and he hastily reacted by issuing what would go down in historical infamy as the Extermination Order. It read: "The Mormons must be treated as enemies and must be exterminated or driven from the state. Their outrages are beyond all description."

The Mormons braced for more hardship. It was late October, 1838. The weather was cool, and the leaves on the trees blazed like torches in the sunlight. Joseph walked through the town, encouraging frightened church members to be strong.

He came upon a group of his soldiers sitting around a small fire, rubbing their hands to stay warm.

"You've got to stay active, boys!" He grabbed a stick and scratched a large circle in the dirt, then stood in the center and tossed the stick to the side. "Come on, who'll wrestle with me?" The men looked around nervously. If they wrestled the Prophet and beat him there would be repercussions. But they would be disobeying a direct order from him if they didn't. So, one by one, they entered the ring and Joseph threw them out.

Sidney, who detested frivolity, heard the commotion and rushed to the circle. He would not tolerate this irreverence, especially on the Sabbath. He made to draw the sword on his hip and flourish it gallantly in the air. Regrettably, the sword stuck in its scabbard, which fell off his belt. He picked it back up and unsheathed it dramatically.

"You are breaking the Sabbath Day!" he shouted, jabbing at the cloudy sky with his sword. "Wrestling on the Sabbath is a sin!"

"But, see, uh, the Prophet's the one who started it," one of the younger boys said.

The others braced themselves. It was entirely possible Joseph didn't want to be ratted out.

"We were just having a little fun, Brother Sidney," said Joseph. "We don't give a hoot if it's the Sabbath Day or not, do we boys?"

The men glance at each other, for they didn't know if this was a trick, or a test. They looked down at their feet and mumbled agreement.

"I think it's time you left us alone, Sidney. Either that, or get in the ring!"

"I will do no such thing!"

"Then go and prepare a sermon on the Sabbath Day, or something equally useful."

The only man who could humiliate Sidney was Joseph, and he'd done it. It was a testament to Sidney's faith that he tolerated Joseph's lightheartedness at all. Sidney walked away and Joseph sneaked up behind him, knocking the sword out of his hands. The troops laughed nervously. Sidney just looked at his sword on the ground. He knew his place in this transaction.

Joseph realized he'd been unkind and picked up the sword. "I'm sorry," he said with an apologetic smile. "We were only trying to have some fun." Then he turned to the group. "You know, Brother Sidney was probably right. I'm sorry I got carried away."

***

In the early evening on October 30, 1838, the Saints saw a lone horseman approach the town of Far West, which was guarded by eight hundred Mormon men. The horseman was slumped over his saddle, barely able to hold on to the horn. He was covered in blood.

"Where's Joseph?" It was barely a whisper.

Joseph ran to him. "Oh, dear God!"

"I've come from the gristmill," he said through clenched teeth. "It's bad, Brother Joseph—too bad to say."

He slid off the saddle, unable to catch his fall. It was incredible that a man could lose so much blood and still be alive, let alone sit upright on a horse. They carried him into the nearest house, where the sisters, those who could stand the sight and smell of so much blood, began to clean and bandage him. The metallic smell of blood, like the barrel of a gun, was heavy in the room. They put a cup of water to his lips but he pushed it away. He took a breath and told his stunned neighbors what had happened.

Brother Jacob Haun owned a gristmill about two miles from town. The Saints living near the mill had heard about the Extermination Order and erected barricades from timber, old tables, stools, buckets, and rusty tools from the mill. It wasn't a barricade that would inspire a disciplined army to retreat, but it might slow its advance. Twenty-eight Mormon men and boys hid behind the makeshift barricade in case of an attack. They waited all day, plugging holes in the barricade with sticks and discarded wagon wheels.

At four o'clock in the afternoon they saw the riders, led by the county sheriff. Brother Evans stood from behind the barricade, removed his hat, and waved it in the air. He then walked out to meet the militia, armed with only a white bed sheet that he waved in surrender. When he got within a few paces of the militia, the Saints watched in horror as the sheriff lifted his pistol and shot Brother Evans in the face.

The women and children screamed and ran into the woods, where they hid behind low bushes and hickory trees. Mothers clamped their hands over their children's mouths.

The militia left Brother Evans' body in the mud. They galloped to the barricade, dismounted, and opened fire on the men crouched behind it. The Mormons knew the barricade wouldn't hold, so they ran into the blacksmith shop next to the mill for cover. The blacksmith shop was a simple log house that had yet to be chinked—it offered little protection. The militia, some two hundred strong, surrounded the shop. The order to open fire was given and the militia began shooting at the blacksmith shop with half-inch lead balls, practicing their aim by shooting unarmed men and boys through the cracks in the logs. Splinters of wood, like shrapnel, bounced off the log house. Boys trapped inside screamed. Men tried to find cover, any cover. The children bawled in horror as they were hit.

The militiamen walked closer to the shop, close enough to peer through the uneven cracks and see the twenty-eight men and boys huddling in corners, or on the ground, begging for mercy. They stuck their rifles through the logs and fired again and again. Hollow thuds, tissue, bones, and blood, exploded inside the logged tomb. The militiamen went inside and found some of them still alive, writhing in terror and pain. An elderly man dropped his musket and begged for his life. He backed up against the inside wall with his hands out in front of him, turning his head to the side as if to brace himself from the firing squad. His loaded musket was used against him at close range. The militiamen then mutilated his body with a corn knife.

Sardius Smith was only ten years old. He hid behind the bellows, petrified with fear, crouching next to the body of his little brother, who'd been shot in the neck. A militiaman, a monster in human shape, gripped Sardius' small arm, and hauled him out of his hiding place. The man slipped on the bloody floor and cursed.

"Don't shoot him, Reynolds!" one of the militiamen hollered. "He's just a boy, for God's sake!"

"Nits will make lice," said Reynolds. "If he lives he'll become a Mormon." He put his gun to the side of Sardius's ten-year-old head, and pulled the trigger.

The women and children crept back from the bushes when they were sure the militia had gone. There were no survivors. Husbands, sons, and brothers had all been slaughtered.

The messenger had been gut-shot. The murderers had seen him fall and assumed he was dead. Lying on the floor, breathing as lightly as he could, he had witnessed it all. He crawled through the blood of his loved ones as soon as the militiamen galloped away. A few of his friends were still screaming and moaning in pain. They would all die within the hour. He found a horse, the only one the murderers hadn't stolen. He climbed upon it and rode two miles to Far West to report the butchery.

Joseph sat on the edge of the bed with his head in his hands. His shoulders shook. Emma knelt in front of him. "It's not your fault. It's not your fault. It's not your fault."

He stood haltingly, like a puppet being pulled up by a string, then dragged his sleeve across his eyes and nose. This was their thirty-three-year-old Prophet in his moment of greatest despair. He would have done anything to repair it, to take it back. But could he have changed the course of history, he wondered? Or had it all been preordained?

"Bring me my horse," he said softly. And then to Lyman, "Will you go with me?"

"Of course I will."

They rode out in silence, just the two of them. The sun hung low on the horizon, seemingly reluctant to surrender its witness to the atrocity. It would be a clear, cold night, and the militia had dispersed. Behind them in Far West was the Army of Israel, which was too numb yet to clamor for revenge. It was dark by the time they arrived. They saw the glow of a fire in the distance; the militia had burned the mill as a sadistic parting gift.

The smoke drifted above the mill like a gray ghost. The women and children were huddled around a smaller fire just outside the blacksmith shop.

A woman lay on the ground next to her two murdered sons. She put all the blankets she could find over their bullet-ridden bodies and dragged them toward the fire to keep them warm. Joseph dismounted and lay down next to her and her dead boys. Another woman was sobbing over her husband's body. She kept spitting onto her hands and wiping the blood from his face. She took the skirt of her dress and wiped him clean as she could. Her knees were bleeding from kneeling in the frozen mud.

Children clung to their mothers, who stared blankly into the fire. A dead horse had started to bloat. Lyman asked the men who had happened upon the carnage to help him with the bodies. There was a partially dug well next to the mill. He picked up the body of a teenage boy and carried it to the well. His shirt was soaked with the blood of this boy and his hands were sticky with it.

"Don't take him," the dead boy's mother whispered. "Please."

Lyman tried to console her, but she turned her back and howled at the night sky. "*Noooooo!* Please, *noooooo!*" then she crumpled to the ground like she had been shot, too.

A girl dressed only in a dirty gingham dress looked up at her mother numbly. The woman rocked silently back and forth, her hands over her face. She paid no attention to her daughter. Joseph came over and put his hands on her shoulders to comfort her. He said nothing. When she came out of her grief and realized who it was, she screamed into his face. "I hate you! I hate you! I hate you!" She hit him with her balled up fists on his chest and face. "Look what you've done!" She kept hitting him and Lyman rushed over to pull her away. "No," Joseph said in the saddest voice he had ever spoken. "Let her be." When she had exhausted herself, she collapsed into his strong arms. He held her while she wept.

He never said a word.

They collected the bodies and put as many as would fit into the unfinished well. They dug a shallow trench and covered their brothers and fathers with dirt and straw. It would do until they could have a proper burial.

Sister Evans stood stock still in the middle of the mass grave. She pointed wordlessly into the field. "What is it, Sister?" She only pointed. Lyman then saw the white bed sheet fifty yards away and the body of her husband. He carried him to the others and went down to the river to wash the blood from his hands. When he returned, he saw Joseph kneeling in prayer next to the well. It was silent, save the plaintive wail of a lonely dog. The only light came from the fire a few yards away. Joseph was clenching fistfuls of dirt in his hands, like he was trying to squeeze the life back into the dead.

"Dear God, where are you?"

There was no answer.

21

The Firing Squad

Ez was sitting up in bed when Lorna came in. It had been three weeks, and the community was still reeling from the atrocity at Haun's mill.

She stroked his arm. "I'm so sorry, Ez. I don't know what to say."

"There's nothing to say, Sis."

She sat on the bed, gingerly, with one hip, careful not to bump him. They sat in companionable silence.

"By the way," she said, "Luke has been so good to me lately. I was wrong to accuse him. He wouldn't hurt a flea. That's just not Luke."

"There is something . . . ."

The doctor came into the room. "I must change the dressings. Please, I must ask you to leave."

"We're so happy you're feeling better," said Lorna. "Luke and I will keep you in our prayers. Now get some rest."

Lorna left, satisfied in knowing Luke was not the monster she'd suspected. Her suspicion that he'd been part of the mob, and the blow to her face, had been a terrible misunderstanding.

"Come with me to visit him," she'd said to Luke. "It would mean a lot to him."

"I can't, what with the blacksmith shop and all. But let me know how he's doing, and if he says anything."

"Says anything? About what?"

"I don't know—just about how it happened, or whatever."

Luke had replayed the events in his mind over and over again. He and his three friends had escaped to the river as soon as they'd fired on Ez. They'd run up the shallow riverbed to hide their tracks, and then concealed themselves behind some bushes near the shore until they were sure they wouldn't be pursued. As the days passed, he'd dared to relax. If Ez had identified him, Luke would've known by then.

Luke had nothing against Ez, personally. However, there was an ugly part of him that wished Ez had died, because he was the only eyewitness to the crime. Nevertheless, as long as he hadn't been seen, Luke was satisfied that Ez had survived.

Two days later Lorna visited again, and this time she'd dragged Luke with her. Luke studied Ez's face for any sign that he knew. He saw nothing. They chatted for a few moments about superficial things when Ez told Lorna that Rachel needed help with the supper. As Lorna and Luke got up to leave, Ez asked Luke to stay. Lorna was pleased that they would have more time to bond as brothers-in-law.

"Will you please close the door, Sis? I can feel the draft."

She left the two of them alone.

"So, Ezra, how are you getting along?"

"Luke, there's something I want you to know."

"What is it?"

"The only reason I haven't killed you is because it would break my sister's heart."

"What are you talking—"

"Shut up, and listen very carefully."

"You don't know what you're—"

"If you raise your hand to her again, I swear I will kill you with my bare hands."

"But what have I—"

"Do not doubt me, Lucas. I will kill you."

"But—"

"One misstep, one unkind word, and you're a dead man."

"You can't just threaten me like—"

"If it weren't for her, I would break your neck and feed you to the dogs. Never forget that."

Lorna opened the door. "I can't find Rachel anywhere."

Ez smiled and touched her arm. "She must have stepped out. But if you two will forgive me, I need to get some rest now."

***

The Missouri state militia wasn't finished with the Chosen People. They demanded that Joseph surrender himself to stand trial for treason, an unusual demand because he had yet to perform a treasonous act. Joseph knew this meant a hanging, or firing squad, for frontier justice generally ignored the protections of the Fourth, Fifth, Sixth, and Eighth Amendments. The militia also demanded the Mormons surrender all their weapons (they didn't think much of the Second Amendment, either). Finally, they demanded the Saints leave the state altogether, an abject failure to recognize virtually *any* portion of the Framers' intent.

Joseph called an emergency meeting with Hyrum, Sidney, Lyman, and Caleb.

"What am I going to do?" asked Joseph.

"I don't know, Joseph." Sidney looked out the window at the damp November day because he couldn't bear to look him in the eye.

"Maybe I should run. You could tell them you can't find me."

"Is that what God told you to do?"

"God wants me to decide," said Joseph. "I thought maybe if I left in the middle of the night . . . ."

"You really think they're going to believe that?"

"They might."

"But what if they don't? What if they take it out on the Saints?"

"I don't think you have much of a choice," said Sidney. "Maybe God will strike down the judge, or you'll get a fair trial."

None of them knew what to say. Joseph ran his hands through his hair, leaned back and sighed. "So," he said, "there's something I didn't tell you."

"What?"

"It's not just me they want. They want the three of you, too."

The other men stared back at him, comprehending, but not yet embracing the probability that they would swing from a noose, too.

"No," Sidney said, "please God, no."

"And they want you, too, Caleb."

Caleb thought he was going to faint. He sat down on the back of a wagon. His head felt like a boulder and he wanted to lay it down, like the moose he once saw bracing its heavy winter antlers in the branches of a tree.

Lyman looked down at his boots and noted that they needed new soles. The thought of his execution hadn't taken root.

"Maybe the five of us could escape," Joseph said hopefully. "We could scatter."

"No, Joseph." Lyman looked at the caked dirt on his boots. "I can't do that."

"Why not?"

His mouth was dry as sawdust. "Because they'll kill my wife and kids if we do."

The next morning Joseph stood on a stump in front of the dry goods store. None of them had slept the night before. Lyman was shaking. His wife dug her fingernails into the sleeve of his coat, but he didn't appear to notice. Caleb's eyes watered from the stiff breeze. His mother stood by his side, resolute in the face of God's test. Some in the crowd wondered why Joseph hadn't already summoned an angel to rescue them forthwith. The sober realization that Joseph could not order God around frightened them.

"You have stood by me to the end." There was a slight whistle to his voice, a legacy from the beating he had survived years ago. "But it is enough. I shall now offer myself up as a sacrifice to save you. Be of good cheer. I bless you all in the name of Jesus Christ."

Sidney was sore that Joseph had only announced his martyrdom, as if he was the only one being offered up to save the Saints. The men bid their farewells and climbed onto their horses. Emma clung to Joseph's leg as they started off through the crowd. Caleb looked like he would be sick, but he was trying to be brave for his mother. "God will protect you, son," she said. When he turned toward the waiting enemy, she collapsed.

Hyrum pulled a square of white cloth from his coat and held it above his head as they high stepped through the muddy field toward the militia gathered several hundred yards away under the command of Major Lucas, a blasphemous tyrant who was in cahoots with Governor Boggs.

"Well, butter my biscuit if it ain't Joe Smith!"

"We gotcha now! Don't we got 'em, fellas?"

Their horses were confiscated and they were taken behind the militia's line and thrown into a pigpen. Drunken guards surrounded the sty where the mud mixed with pig shit. Hogs might have been content to roll in the mess with no conscious fear that their throats were about to be cut, but these men had the intellect to appreciate their predicament. When night fell they lay in the freezing mud and tried to sleep without success. Around midnight, Major Lucas called Hyrum over to the side of the pen.

"You are hereby sentenced to be shot tomorrow morning at eight o'clock," he said, scarcely trying to hide his pleasure. "Maybe we'll do it in the public square in front of your, how do you call them, your 'Saints' is it?"

Hyrum towered over the smaller major, who backed up. Hyrum leaned over the split-wood fence rail, and spit in his face. "Shoot us and be damned, you coward!"

The major thrust his bayonet to Hyrum's face. Hyrum took a step back. "You'll be shot first, you swine," he said.

By dawn, the five of them were curled on the ground, stippled with goose bumps. There were a few honorable men in the militia who had given the condemned men dirty horse blankets, an incongruent act of kindness when they were about to be shot.

A soldier climbed the fence and kicked at them with his muddy boots.

"Time's up you filthy pigs! Line up!"

He prodded them into line with the end of his bayonet. Hyrum turned to look at his brother, who stood next to him, tall and defiant. Joseph reached over and put his muddy arm on Hyrum's shoulder.

"Please, I'm begging you!" Caleb sobbed. "For the love of God." He half stood at the end of the line.

"You!" the soldier yelled at Caleb. "Get on your knees and beg like a dog."

Caleb dropped to his knees. He wiped his face with a filthy sleeve. Mud, snot, and tears smeared. "Please, I have a mother and—"

The soldier kicked him and he fell over. "Get up!"

Caleb whimpered like a dog. Only those who have stood before a firing squad know a terror so real that one doesn't even notice that he has soiled himself.

Lieutenant Doniphan had been ordered to carry out the execution. Doniphan stepped into the pen. He was a small, dignified man who radiated confidence despite his stature. Unbeknownst to Joseph and his friends, he was familiar with the facts of their case. He walked the line, looking up to each of the men, his back to the muskets behind him. Joseph looked him in the eye, and Doniphan did not flinch. He got to the end of the line where Caleb was still on all fours. His head hung over a puddle of vomit.

"Stand up, young man."

Doniphan turned to face the firing squad. "I am aware of the circumstances of the crime these men stand accused of. I will have none of it. This is not an execution. This is murder in cold blood. Squad, pack up. We're leaving this wretched camp." He turned to the troops under Lucas' command. "The first man who fires on those men, I will personally see that he is hanged, as God is my witness."

Lucas waited until he was sure Doniphan was gone before strutting back into the camp. "Doniphan's a coward," he said. "We can execute them tomorrow."

The five men were forced into the back of an open wagon at the point of a bayonet. They bounced across the bumpy ruts to Far West where the terrified Saints waited. The smell of human excrement hung heavy in the air. They were paraded through the town like unwashed circus animals.

Joseph heard Emma scream from the middle of the crowd and looked over to see one of the militiamen slap her. Eyes wild, he made a move to jump from the wagon, but a Missourian stuck the barrel of his musket to Joseph's chest in warning.

Some of the Mormon men shoved their way through the crowd to the wagon, but most of them slipped silently back, their shame of doing nothing a permanent badge of regret. The throng parted to make way for the wagon. The Saints could not understand why God allowed their Prophet to be spit upon like an animal. The sky opened on cue and spit down rain, as if heaven had turned its back on them, too.

"Hand over them gold tablets and maybe we'll let ya go!"

"Where's your angel now?"

Many of the Saints privately wondered the same thing. However, to voice it would be tantamount to apostasy. So they publically expressed the opposite of doubt, providing dubious testimony that they were *doubly* sure they possessed the truth. This reassured them.

The prisoners were taken to Richmond for a pre-trial hearing where the judge bound them over for trial on charges of murder, treason, arson, burglary, robbery, larceny, and perjury. They were then taken thirty miles to the town of Liberty to await trial.

Joseph had been driven by blood from a town called Independence, and hauled off to be shot in a town called Liberty.

22

Liberty Jail

The diggers had dug the hole in an open field under less than ideal circumstances. They had been told they would be gutted and left to die if they shirked their task. The diggers were horse thieves, Indian Givers, Negroes, a bewildered ninety-pound Chinaman who had simply been in the wrong place at the wrong time, and the former sheriff, who had narrowly escaped the noose after he'd been caught in the broom closet with the mayor's wife.

The ground was hard and rocky, and the work was back breaking. The men were allowed to finally stop digging when the hole was two hundred and fifty feet square and eight feet deep. They lined the foundation with large stones and heavy oak timbers and built a wooden lid to cover the hole. A trap door was cut from the middle of the lid, which would be the only way to get in or out. A second story was built on top of that.

The basement room had two small windows for ventilation and light, located near the ceiling of the room and approximately one foot above the outside ground. Iron bars covered the windows. When the men finished digging their prison, they were cast into it through the trap door.

This inhospitable dungeon was the Liberty Jail, where Joseph and his mates were taken to await trial. Two jailers lived in the room above them, toothless rascals who were given free room and board to care for the prisoners. What little food the prisoners were given was dropped to them through the trap door. The ungracious hosts called it "Mormon beef," because it'd come from their stolen cattle. It was rancid, but they ate it anyway.

There was a wooden bucket in the corner of the room they used for a toilet. They kept it as far away as they could, but the room was small. Every morning the jailers lowered a rope with a hook on the end. The prisoners dragged the bucket to the center of the room, careful to keep it from sloshing, and attached the hook to the handle. For the first few days the guards dumped the bucket outside the barred basement windows, but finally decided that this was crueler than was necessary.

The jailers told their prisoners that the Mormons' livestock had been confiscated and their homes burned. Then they'd beaten the men. Their desire for vengeance gave them something to live for. They lay in their cold cell inventing imaginary scenarios of what they would do to the degenerate villains if they could only escape.

Joseph tried to rise above the empty energy of retribution. "Vengeance is a lazy form of grief," he said. "You'll just grieve more if you're bitter for revenge."

"I can't do it, Joseph," said Lyman. "I'm sorry, but I can't."

Brigham Young visited them in jail as often as he dared, fearful they might throw him in with his friends. He told Joseph that he had a plan to relocate the Saints across the Mississippi River and into Illinois.

"Excellent," said Joseph.

"I've sent advance teams to plant crops along the way. They can be harvested by the time we pass through."

"Well done, Brother."

"But we need to stall until spring." He paused. "God is watching over us," he said, without a trace of irony.

"Indeed He is."

"I'm negotiating to buy a parcel of land," said Brigham. "It's a Half-Breed Tract, but we haven't much of a choice." The federal government, mindful of the increasing number of half-breeds (some white men had an insatiable desire for the occasional squaw), set aside a few undesirable strips of land for the offspring of these interracial couplings. Mormons didn't have the same ugly bias toward the red man, because they knew the Indians were direct ancestors of Jews from the Holy Land.

The cell was cold. Hyrum said it was so cold that "if a dog pissed on a fence, he'd be there 'til spring." There was no fireplace, so the men crowded around a lantern that hung on a nail in the corner, stomping their feet and blowing on their hands. Tiny moths flitted about the lanterns flame. The jailers walked above them and dust trickled down from the ceiling boards. Each man had been given a lice-ridden blanket and a filthy mattress. Rats skittered about unmolested.

"My back ails me," said Sidney. This was only one of his complaints. He had complained of intestinal worms, gout, headaches, chills, ingrown toenails, insomnia, and a host of rashes. He felt aggrieved because his cellmates failed to recognize his suffering. There were a few desultory comments, but he knew this half-hearted sympathy was insincere. Their indifference to his ailments irritated him, which caused the additional symptom of depression.

When no one responded to his latest discomfort from bed bugs, he exasperatedly said, "The Savior's suffering didn't compare to what I'm going through."

Lyman spun around and grabbed his shirtfront. "How dare you compare your suffering to the Savior's!"

Sidney backpedaled as fast as he could. "Perhaps I have overstated the extent of my serious maladies, even though they are many." Lyman glared at Sidney for another moment and then released him. The confrontation was overdue (even though Sidney didn't recall Jesus suffering a case of intestinal worms from *his* reading of the Bible). Sidney was released from jail a month later on a legal technicality; the others were relieved to see him go.

Porter Rockwell also visited them. He was a mangy, crude, foul-smelling butterball who followed Joseph around like a stray dog. He joined the church in order to keep Joseph's attention, not because of a yearning to live the precepts of the Sermon on the Mount. He'd sit outside the jail chatting with the jailers, a dirty towel draped across his lap and a musket resting against his thigh. A can of gun oil would teeter next to him on the ground while he'd swap stories with the jailers.

Emma visited, too. She crouched down and slipped a loaf of bread through the bars of the window. Inside the loaf was an ice pick. Joseph grinned. They wolfed down the bread like they were shoveling hay into a barn, then took turns with the pick, chipping away at the mortar until the handle finally broke off. Two weeks later she brought another loaf and pick. The men were able to pry two stones from the foundation, but the guards caught them trying to escape and confiscated the tool. Joseph said, "Well, boys, if nothing else, at least we cost the county a fair sum for the repairs!"

While the prisoners were chipping away at the mortar, the body of Saints was trudging across frozen dirt roads to what they hoped would be greener pastures in Illinois.

The state of Illinois welcomed them; politicians on both sides of the aisle drooled over the potential Mormon vote. The Whigs (who would become the Republican Party) reminded the Saints that it'd been the slave-loving Democrats who'd mistreated them in Missouri. The Democrats, on the other hand, reassured Brigham that they actually loved the Mormons, indeed practically worshipped them, and there had simply been a misunderstanding. Brigham flirted with both sides, a political miscalculation he would come to regret.

The *St. Louis Daily Union* reported on the massacre at Haun's Mill. The law-abiding citizenry of St. Louis was outraged. This was not the sort of publicity the "Show Me" state wanted, especially with westbound settlers looking for a peaceful place to live. Governor Boggs labeled it the "Mormon War" and claimed the Mormons had started the whole thing. However, there was his ugly Extermination Order for all to see. So the State of Missouri gave the Mormons a stingy restitution payment that allowed them to purchase land in Illinois.

In the meantime, Joseph and his friends languished in jail. Joseph wrote long letters, beseeching the government for reparations. He also received revelations from God in which He came down pretty hard on their enemies. The threats from God were standard fare for what He'd do to those who persecuted His Chosen People: He would burn them, crush them, drown them, smash them, and otherwise smite them. This gave the Saints no small amount of satisfaction.

Joseph educated himself. He read voraciously, subscribing to as many newspapers as he could. He devoured books on history, politics, languages, and religion. His letters developed a literary flavor, if not a bit dramatic. He wrote from jail that, "Hell may pour forth its rage like the burning lava of Mount Vesuvius, or of Etna, or of the most terrible of the burning mountains; and yet Mormonism shall stand! Water, fire, truth, and God are all realities. Truth is Mormonism. God is the author of it!"

After four months the prisoners were moved to a different county. But when it came time for trial they couldn't find enough unbiased jurors, so another change of venue was ordered. The county sheriff who transported them to the new county for trial was a notorious drunk. This would prove to be a condition rich with opportunity for Joseph and his friends.

Hyrum didn't have Joseph's gift of gab, but he was resourceful. While the court was in session, he insisted that he be allowed to use either the outhouse or a mop and bucket. The judge ordered a recess. Hyrum, who'd used diarrhea as a ruse, persuaded a loafer to buy him a jug of whiskey and leave it in a mulberry bush outside the courthouse.

During the transport to the next county, the prisoners offered the sheriff eight hundred dollars and the jug of whiskey if he'd let them go. The sheriff initially refused, but the jug called to him. Soon the barrel of his rifle wove through the air as if he was taking aim at a bumblebee. By nightfall, the sheriff had passed out, snoring into his bedroll. The prisoners pretended to be asleep until they heard his inebriated snore. They led the horses quietly away and high-tailed it for the Mississippi River. They rowed a boat across the river to Illinois where they reunited with the Saints at approximately the same time the sheriff awoke with a blinding hangover.

PART IV

NAUVOO

1839 - 1844

23

The White House

The fine carriage pulled up to the east portico of the White House and Joseph stepped out. He wore a black twill suit and top hat; he completed his natty outfit with an ebony cane because he thought it gave him a fashionable look, and there were few places on earth where high fashion was in more demand than at the east portico of the White House. Senator Henry Clay stepped out of the carriage after him.

"Welcome to the White House," said Senator Clay, as if he were its current occupant, and not the resident he hoped to be. Clay badly wanted the presidency, and he knew Mormons voted in a bloc. Joseph's role was to hand over the Mormon vote to the powerful Senator from Kentucky in exchange for certain considerations.

Joseph believed he should be there at the seat of power, indeed he assumed his status *required* him to be there, for Joseph believed God had even bigger things in store for him. His audience with the President seemed to validate it. There were times of private doubt, but Joseph lived in a bubble, surrounded by people who bestowed hero status upon him. This fawning usually caused his doubts to vanish.

President Van Buren had been briefed for the meeting, one that held little political significance (and was, therefore, largely unimportant). He'd been told that Joseph Smith and his group of ten thousand followers (who called themselves Mormons) had suffered injustice out in the relatively unpopulated area of Missouri. Smith had written a golden Bible, or maybe it had been a new Bible, Van Buren couldn't remember which.

The President stood from behind his massive desk and walked over to greet his guests. His round head was completely bald on top but he'd coaxed the gray hair on the sides to stick out, so his head looked like a fat bird in flight.

"Henry, it's good to see you again. And you, sir, must be Joseph Smith," he said and shook their hands. "I have heard a lot about you."

"It is good to meet you, Mr. President." Joseph stood a full head taller than Van Buren.

"Welcome, Henry, Mr. Smith. Please, sit. May I get you something to drink?"

"No, thank you."

Joseph admired the view of Washington from the windows of the President's office. Portraits of his predecessors hung on the walls. A globe three feet in diameter stood in the corner next to an American flag. There was a bronze bust of George Washington on a bureau, and a ring-necked duck encased in a glass box sat atop the fireplace mantle, courtesy of Lewis and Clark. Van Buren noticed his handsome young guest looked quite comfortable, as if he might put his feet up, or plop onto the sofa to recline with his hands behind his head.

"So, Mr. Smith, I have been told that you and your followers have suffered religious persecution. In Missouri, I believe it was. That is terrible, just terrible."

"Thank you, Mr. President. We have been the victims of severe and unrelenting persecution."

"I see."

"They have burned our homes and driven us from the state."

"So I hear."

"We believe, Mr. President, sir, that we are due financial restitution."

"From the federal government?"

"Yes, sir."

"And why is that?"

"Well, it was the Governor who issued the Extermination Order. Without that, we might have been able to resolve our differences."

"In that case, it appears your remedy is with the State of Missouri, not with me."

"But that is useless. They won't even speak to us. They had me arrested for treason, for something I didn't even do. If I go back, they'll hang me."

"That is most unfortunate. However, I'm afraid my hands are tied. If I intervene the entire state of Missouri will be up in arms."

"But we are citizens."

"I understand, and I am sorry for your misfortune. I am informed that you and your people are honest and hardworking. I wish the best for you, Mr. Smith, and I hope I can count on your votes in the future."

"But, Mr. President, won't you initiate some action on our behalf? You said so yourself that we—"

"I believe your cause may be just, sir, but I am afraid I can do nothing for you. Now, if you will excuse me, I have another appointment."

Joseph walked out of the mansion, seething. Why had he allowed himself to be intimidated by a spineless weasel like Martin Van Buren? So what if he was the President? Joseph had conferred with bigger fish than that, including Jesus and John the Baptist. And his grand vision extended far beyond the votes of a few ignorant Missourians, who could rot in hell for all he cared.

"I used to think those big fellas were smarter than I was," Joseph said to Emma when he returned to Missouri. "But they're nothing special."

***

No matter how many real estate lots they sold, the Mormons went deeper into debt. So Joseph declared bankruptcy. He believed he had no choice, for he didn't *want* to go bankrupt. He blamed the financial collapse on his enemies, who had made it virtually impossible for their economy to prosper. Most of his followers wholeheartedly agreed. There were a few, however, who scratched their heads. "Why is God's mouthpiece letting us go bankrupt? I thought he heard direct from God on things, and here he is goin' belly up again." Their hero had faltered. For some, this was the last straw. For others, the disappointment was temporary until he did something magnanimous, or reported having seen something spectacular.

The Mormons' new community was on the Illinois side of the Mississippi River. There was a bluff near a bend in the river and the land that fell away from it was green and lush. Joseph declared the town should be called Nauvoo, which was Hebrew for "beautiful plantation." And so it was.

Rachel's pain that came from the news of her mother's death had diminished some, and so had the anger toward her father. She realized he was also in pain, if for no other reason than his wife wasn't around to fix his supper. *Dear Father*, she wrote,

> *I was devastated to learn of Mother's passing. I have little doubt you miss her steady hand.*
>
> *We have moved to a beautiful town in western Illinois, just off the Mississippi River. We have named the town Nauvoo. There is much industry in clearing the brush and building our homes, something that is done with cooperation and good cheer. Our church has grown to over ten thousand. These, Father, are good people who have strong faith in Jesus. Our streets are safe from crime and vagrancy. We are truly brothers and sisters.*

Ezra was shot by a gang of outlaws when we lived in Missouri for a time. He was severely wounded but, fortunately, the loving face of God looked down upon us and now he is well. He and Thomas are building a new wheelwright shop in town. I, too, am busy with Thomas and Elizabeth. They are so beautiful. I do so wish you could see them.

Would you consider moving to Nauvoo? I assure you that the community of Saints would welcome you. Please consider this request, as you must be lonely in the home without Mother.

Please do let me know.

As always, your loving daughter,

Rachel

She sealed the envelope and walked with six-year-old Elizabeth down the dirt road to post it. She hadn't discussed this with Ezra, but she knew he wouldn't mind. It was unlikely her father would accept the offer anyway.

The Reverend once again allowed the envelope to sit on his writing desk for two days. He did this for reasons that even he did not understand. Perhaps, he thought, if it bore bad news he might be spared of it for a bit. He was overcome with emotion when he finally opened it. The daughter he'd banished had shown more Christian spirit than he had. He was ashamed. And yet he could not resist the compelling urge to luxuriate in the past and embellish it to suit his satisfaction. The pews had been full and his sermons had been inspiring. He had been important!

It had all begun to unravel, not by mere coincidence, he believed, but because of a young man named Joseph Smith. The charismatic charlatan hadn't merely challenged him; he'd destroyed him. As his life had slowly crumbled, he saw each crumb as evidence of

Joseph's malfeasance. Joseph had taken his daughter, he had taken his grandson, he had taken his parishioners, and he had taken his power.

And now his daughter asked him to join them. This he could not do. Or could he? He looked around his house, once a tribute to the life of a great man, and saw with remorse that it was nothing now. No one cared for his opinion. No one sought him out. The Second Coming had not come, and he was lonely.

He got up from his desk and walked outside. His garden, which had always been lush and lovingly tended, was now overgrown. The house needed a coat of paint and the shutters were closed. He had barricaded himself inside to commiserate over the collapse of his life, where his intellect drained into a pious drivel and his desire for engagement had evaporated like the droplets of wine he'd spilled on the kitchen floor and never bothered to wipe. And now the overgrown foliage looked like it would eventually swallow the house whole, with him inside.

He opened the screen door, whose hinges needed oiling and stepped inside. He hadn't noticed how stale the air was. He settled down at his desk. *Dearest Daughter*, he wrote,

How you have made your father happy. I accept your invitation with a warm and loving heart. I have erred, and for that failure I offer my deepest apology. My hope is that one day perhaps you might forgive me.

I have obligations to attend to here in Palmyra, but I will consider leaving for your home later in the spring. I will write when my plans become clear. In the meantime, I thank you again for your kind and generous offer.

Father

***

The Chosen People's hopes rose with the spring. But typhoid fever came that summer and spread quickly, like a sack of germs left open to spill over. Joseph and Emma surrendered their home to the sick and lived in a small tent on the bluff where the temple would be built. They sat at their friends' bedsides, offering prayer and comfort. When the sick became delusional, muttering nonsense, they knew their friends were lost.

Joseph blessed the sick, resting only a few hours a day, going without food, and begging God to help. Sometimes the blessings worked, and sometimes they didn't. When the Saints recovered, they knew it was because of Joseph's intercession. When they died, they knew it was God's will, that He wouldn't be so easily cornered.

Rachel was perplexed. "Ez, why did Brother Murphy live and Brother Kimball die? They both had the same sickness and Joseph blessed them both, almost word for word."

"It's God's will."

"Well, if it's up to God, why bother with the blessings in the first place?"

Ez knew there had to be a good answer to this, but he didn't know what it was. So he said, "Rach, God will only heal them if we ask with the spirit."

"But, what about Mr. Harding? He isn't even a member of the church and he recovered without a single prayer. He doesn't even believe in God."

Ez had no good answer to the first question, and surely didn't have one for the second. So he said, "God works in mysterious ways, Rach. Everybody knows that."

"I still don't understand. Why even bother if God is just going to do what He wants anyway?"

"Because you should do all you can, just in case."

"Just in case of what?"

"Just in case it makes a difference, that's what. And if we question that, well, we aren't true Saints. So I don't want to talk about it anymore. It's between God and the afflicted."

"Well I'll be darned then, Ezra; maybe Mr. Harding, who doesn't even believe in God, has more faith than we thought." She turned and walked away.

Rachel was a walking contradiction. One day she had enough faith to move a mountain, and the next day she might cross-examine God as if she had Him squirming on the witness stand, not satisfied until she had Him in check-mate. Rachel *did* have faith, and she *did* believe, but she held God accountable for his caprice. And, unlike most Mormon women, she wasn't afraid to voice her suspicions.

***

The heavens had been quiet, apart from the occasional chastisement from God directed squarely at the Gentiles. As such, the Saints were eagerly awaiting the Almighty's next revelation. When it came, it was a surprise, for it wasn't an audacious new spiritual concept, or clarification on how to become a God. It was a series of detailed instructions on how to build a hotel.

The hotel was to be called the Nauvoo Mansion, and God was quite specific on how it would be financed—by the wealthiest man in town. Brother Robert Foster had already been called upon to cast more bread upon the water than anyone else, so he needed a heavenly nudge. He got one when God spoke directly to him through His mouthpiece, and this is what He had to say: "I, the Lord God, say unto you, if Robert Foster will obey my voice, let him build a boarding house for my servant Joseph Smith, and it shall be called

The Nauvoo Mansion. And let Joseph and his seed have a place in that house forever and ever. Thus saith the Lord. Amen."

The Saints assumed Brother Foster would immediately fork over the money, because the revelation went on to say: "And again, let Robert Foster repent of all his follies and cease to do evil, and pay stock into the hands of the Twelve Apostles, but let no man buy stock in the Nauvoo Mansion unless he believes in the Book of Mormon. And each share of stock shall be no less than $50. For anything less than this cometh of evil, and shall be cursed. Thus saith the Lord your God. Amen."

Sister Foster, Robert's lovely wife, was mortified. After the revelation was formally published in the Book of Commandments, she had plenty to say to her husband of twenty years.

"What do you have to say for yourself, Robert?"

"About what?"

"About *what*? About the follies and evil you've been up to, that's what. Is it Brother Kimball's daughter? Is that it?"

"I don't know what you're talking about. Joseph wants me to pay for the mansion because he's bankrupt and I'm the only one with enough money to do it."

"Well, I certainly wish the Lord had kept whatever follies you're hiding to Himself."

24

The Whorehouse and the Steamboat

Joseph would come to regret befriending John Bennett. Unlike the rest of the Saints, Bennett claimed to be an educated man—a doctor, he'd boasted. He hadn't given the Book of Mormon more than a quick once-over, but he rose quickly through the ranks of Mormon society. He blasted past the likes of Ez, Parley, Brigham, and Sidney, who marveled at the effrontery of this ne'er-do-well who strutted around Nauvoo as if he was the mayor.

Joseph sent Bennett to the legislature to get a bill passed that would grant the city of Nauvoo the right to form its own militia. When he succeeded, Joseph was so thrilled he made Bennett second-in-command of the Nauvoo Legion, their new army.

***

Joseph had begun to take his Mohammed role seriously—perhaps too seriously. He appointed himself General of the Nauvoo Legion and commissioned Ez's sister Lorna, the town seamstress, to make him a stylish uniform. It consisted of a smart blue coat with epaulets and a large gold braid, spit-polished jackboots, and a peaked hat topped with genuine ostrich feathers. On his hip he carried a cavalry saber and two large horse pistols. He galloped around Nauvoo on Charlie, a magnificent black stallion.

"Ez," said Joseph, "do you realize I'm the highest ranking military officer in the United States? I outrank them all, even General Winfield Scott—Old Fuss and Feathers himself!"

"Joseph, people tell me you'd rather be called General than Prophet."

"Well, I am the General of the Legion."

"But don't you think that sends the wrong message?"

"You might be right. I apologize for any appearance of vanity."

Joseph was still loved by the people, but his endearing humility, which earned that love, was slipping. Outside the local courthouse he boasted, "I comprehend heaven, earth, and hell. I bring forth knowledge that covers up all the lawyers on earth!" Afterwards, Ezra pulled him aside.

"You'd be wise to show more humility."

"But I know more about the law than those lawyers. I think Shakespeare was onto something."

"What are you talking about?" Ez asked.

"Shakespeare. Henry VI. He said we ought to kill all the lawyers."

"Whatever you say, but I'd tone it down if I were you."

Every able-bodied Mormon man between the ages of eighteen and forty-five was enlisted to join the Nauvoo Legion. They marched once a week, which made folks in the neighboring towns of Warsaw and Carthage antsy. There were 2,000 Legionnaires initially, and the numbers grew each month. Members served voluntarily, as it were, and did so with God's armor.

Orson met a man from Warsaw down at the livery stable. "How come it is that you Mormons got to have an army anyway?" he asked. "That don't seem too Christ-like to me."

"We're just trying to protect ourselves, that's all."

"From what? What have we ever done to you?"

"Nothing yet, but we don't want to be caught with our britches down, like over in Missouri."

"I sure don't remember Jesus havin' no cotton-pickin' army."

"Uh-huh," said Orson, "and look what happened to him."

"Now hold it right there! That was different—Jesus went to the cross 'cause he wanted to."

"Well, maybe, but having an army would've helped."

***

The Saints had no use for "Martin Van Ruin." The Whigs, on the other hand, had extended the hand of friendship. Joseph thought they'd get more from them and instructed the Saints to vote straight Whig ticket. Well, almost straight. There was a lone Democrat on the slate to whom Joseph owed a favor. The Saints were told to vote for all the Whig candidates except one—someone who "wasn't likely to amount to anything anyway." So that is precisely what they did—they voted for all the Whigs except one, a lanky fellow by the name of Abraham Lincoln.

If Nauvoo was to be a holy city with a law-abiding citizenry it could not tolerate criminal mischief. That's why Joseph instructed the Legion to dismantle the town's whorehouse. It would not do to have ladies of the night seducing the brethren.

The whorehouse was hidden behind the Bailey's Grocery Store down off 3rd Street. Bailey's wasn't the only grocery store in town, but it had the most committed clientele. Brother Bailey was a church member of indifferent conviction. His worldliness did not affect his ability to run a profitable grocery store, of course, but his whorehouse jeopardized his ultimate goal to become a God.

Trouble started when Emma noticed certain of the men in town were the grocery store's most frequent customers. She also noticed they went in and out empty-handed, as if they'd completely forgotten what they were supposed to pick up for the missus on the way home. And as they left, they opened the door a crack, looking anxiously left and right, before stepping out onto the sidewalk, tucking in their shirts.

Emma told Rachel about this vexing observation. Rachel, however, didn't mention it to Ez until she was certain he didn't already know about it.

"Say, Ez, have you ever been to Bailey's?"

"You mean the grocery store down on 3rd?"

"Uh-huh."

"No, don't think so. At least not that I can remember."

"You sure about that?"

"Course I'm sure. Why?"

"Oh, just wondering if you've ever been inside the place, that's all."

This was a curious thing to Ez. Why, he wondered, was she asking him about a grocery store? He figured it must be a trick of some kind, so he had to be careful with what he said, because he could never understand how women think. So, he said nothing—generally the safest course to follow when dealing with Rachel. He didn't have to wait long.

"Emma is suspicious there's some hanky panky going on down there."

"Down where?"

"At Baileys."

"At a grocery store?"

"Well, she's going to have Joseph look into it."

The house of ill repute behind Bailey's Grocery Store was turning a robust profit—within mere kilometers of what had once been the Garden of Eden. Bailey knew he couldn't operate a brothel in back of the family store without his wife's knowledge. What if she snooped in the back to see how much cornmeal they had in stock? So he waited until she was in an especially good mood, and then explained the lucrative venture to her. She agreed, provided he did no shopping there (she swept the floors with her antenna up whenever he wasn't within plain sight at the counter).

It was inconceivable that one could be an exemplary Saint and run a profitable whorehouse at the same time. Therefore, Joseph excommunicated both of them on the spot and he ordered the Nauvoo Legion to destroy the brothel, post haste. Forty men marched to the grocery store (initially pretending they didn't know where it was). The store backed up to a gully, maybe fifteen feet from the edge. The men lined up to push it off the edge and into the gully. "All your might, men! On the count of three!"

Their shoulders pressed into the walls of the den of iniquity as they heaved with righteous (but ambiguous) resolve. It teetered. They gave it a final shove and it tipped over backward, crashing all the way to the bottom of the gully where it broke into splinters. The men brushed the dust from their hands as a symbolic gesture that they had successfully rid the city of sin. It was painful for some of them to give it that final push, and there was melancholy reflection among some, but they had the good judgment to hide their disappointment.

***

Governor Boggs paced back and forth in his study, an ostentatious dark paneled room nearly twice the size of the President's. Built-in shelving housed leather-bound books, his collection of pocket watches, walking sticks, the bleached skull of a longhorn steer, stacks of newspapers, and all manner of expensive knickknacks. He was in ill temper, as was often the case, striding around the room and barking out insults at unseen political foes as his secretary, a cowering man, cowered.

"I want him caught! Do you hear me!"

"Yes, sir."

"Just who in the hell does he think he is? He has embarrassed me and the entire state of Missouri!"

"Yes sir, he has, sir."

"And now I read he has the unmitigated gall to consult with Van Buren. The sheer hubris of the man! He makes us look like villains. Just look at the eastern newspapers!"

"I believe they have focused too much, sir, on the Extermination Order."

"You're goddamned right they have! They distort the facts! Smith's followers have been the aggressors all along!"

He paced more, working himself into a righteous lather at the nerve of Mormonism's Prophet.

"Just look at this!" and he shoved a copy of the New York Herald at his secretary. "This is libel! That bastard has manipulated the press, and now he has the help of Senator Clay."

"What do you recommend, sir?"

"We need to re-capture him. He is an escaped felon and a fugitive from justice. If we can put him on trial here, he'll be convicted of his crimes. He won't get away with playing the persecuted innocent in Missouri. It's galling."

"But we have no jurisdiction in Illinois."

"I know that! My God, man, do you think I am unaware of that?"

"No, sir."

"He must be caught in Illinois and brought across the border to Missouri. Then we'll have jurisdiction over the scoundrel."

***

Joseph was safe in Nauvoo, but he wasn't a fool; he knew Boggs hadn't forgotten him. He appointed twelve of the toughest men in Nauvoo to be his bodyguards and commissioned Lorna to sew white uniforms for them. She triple checked to be sure he wanted them dressed in white, mindful as she was that this would only highlight his location.

When Ez first saw them he said to Joseph, "If you're trying to prevent someone from spotting you and hauling you off to Missouri, why surround yourself with a posse of white uniforms? You stick out like a sore thumb."

"But look how sharp they look," he said. "Even Van Buren doesn't have a team of bodyguards like that."

Porter Rockwell, Joseph's greasy, longhaired friend who had visited them at the Liberty Jail, led the bodyguards, who looked like a troop of Venice gondoliers. Porter was fierce, loyal, and completely unpredictable, imposing his sense of justice with a knife, a gun, or his bare hands. His repertoire did not include diplomacy.

Meanwhile, Governor Boggs was busy with his own public relations campaign. He enlisted the newspaper publisher in the nearby town of Warsaw to excite the citizenry. Gentiles from surrounding towns were already antsy about the Mormon military power, for they had seen the Nauvoo Legion drilling. They also resented being told that they'd go to hell if they didn't join the "true" church. When someone noticed that Joseph was holding private meetings with attractive young women, some for hours at a time, his Gentile neighbors shared the news with evangelical enthusiasm.

Boggs planned the raid. Five Missourian kidnappers rowed across the Mississippi River in the middle of the night. As Joseph was leaving a private appointment, they grabbed him and shoved a rag into his mouth, holding it there so he couldn't scream. Two of them yanked him into the back of a wagon with the tailgate down and held him while the others galloped west to the river.

Joseph knew he'd be lynched if they made it across to Missouri. But the kidnappers had underestimated him—they hadn't tied his legs. He waited until the wagon hit a bump, rolled backward onto his shoulders, and kicked one man in the face. The stunned kidnapper fell backward, his jaw broken. Without hesitation, Joseph sat up and spat in the other man's eye. His captor instinctively covered his face, whereupon Joseph braced his back against the side of the wagon and kicked the man in the groin as hard as he possibly could. The man doubled over, vomiting. The Prophet grabbed the man's knife, freed his hands, and jumped from the wagon.

Porter was livid at the breech in security. He lashed out at the bodyguards who'd been on shift at the time. They'd been caught in an awkward fix because the Prophet had suggested he be left alone. Fortunately for his retinue, Joseph came to their defense—he knew Porter was so furious he might have killed them.

"Porter, I have forgiven the men, and I hope you will do likewise."

He grunted and spat. "Whatever you say, Joseph."

The Missourians appealed to the Illinois Supreme Court for the right to arrest Joseph inside the state of Illinois. The Chief Justice in Illinois at the time was Stephen A. Douglas, a man who would become famous a few years later for his spirited debates with Abraham Lincoln. Douglas was a Democrat with dreams of higher office, and wanted the Mormons' vote. He found a technicality in the warrant, ruling that Missouri could not arrest him so long as Joseph stayed within the relatively friendly confines of Illinois.

Boggs seethed.

It was about this time that Joseph bought a steamboat. The Mississippi River north of St. Louis had become a bottleneck for commerce. Boats bringing timber and other supplies in and out of the St. Louis harbor were constantly getting stuck in the mud. Before the Civil War, Robert E. Lee's Army Corp of Engineers had orders to dredge the river. The Corps owned a steamboat that served as Lee's office on the river. Once the river had been dredged, Lee no longer needed the steamboat, so he sold it to Joseph who christened it The Nauvoo.

Nauvoo had quickly become an important city (and a curiosity as well—"That's where them Mormons live," people said). The magnificent temple was well underway, sitting high above the bluff, and could be seen by steamboats up and down the Mississippi. Politicians and businessmen from St. Louis made the pilgrimage to visit Joseph and see the temple. The Nauvoo Mansion had been completed, courtesy of Brother Robert Foster's generosity. Joseph put his distinguished guests there, and in the evening he took them down to the renovated steamboat for a leisurely tour of the river.

Joseph usually wore fine clothing, but occasionally he disguised himself as a loafer or drifter. Ez was down at the dock one day when a well-appointed steamboat disembarked visitors from St. Louis. He caught the sight of Joseph. The Prophet was dressed as a farmer, and a poor one at that. He was barefoot, his britches were dirty, and he had pulled his straw hat low over his face. He loitered on the dock like a common beggar, rummaging in trashcans. Ez called out to him and Joseph put his finger to his lips, motioning for Ez to be quiet.

Joseph lurched up to a well-dressed gentleman in a black hat, gold vest, and pince-nez glasses. The man held a newspaper under one arm and clutched a valise with the other. "Where y'all from?" Joseph asked.

The man looked at him, disgusted. "I'm from St. Louis, if you must know. Now, if you'll just tell me where I might obtain some lodging . . . ."

"You here to see them Mormons, are ya?" asked Joseph.

"Yes, I have a meeting with their leader."

"Whaddya know about him?"

"Very little, but if you'll excuse me . . . ."

"What do they say about this Joe Smith fella down there in St. Louey, anyways?"

"That he commands an army, and that he's a real character."

"Do they say he's right smart?" asked Joseph.

"I suppose so. Now, if you'll excuse me . . . ."

Joseph removed his hat, stood up proud and tall, and extended a manicured hand. "Sir, I am Joseph Smith, and it is my genuine pleasure to have made your acquaintance."

"What on earth—"

"Yes, I apologize for my dress. I am wearing a disguise so that I can move freely about without causing undue commotion. If you'll follow me to my carriage we will be driven to the Nauvoo Mansion, where I hope you will see fit to dine with me."

The next day Ez asked Joseph what he'd been doing down at the dock dressed like a hobo. It was not within Ez's nature to manipulate or connive, so when he saw it in others, it was foreign to him.

"See, Ez, when you become famous, people tell you what they think you want to hear. So, from time to time, I like to know what people say about me behind my back."

25

The Kinderhook Fiasco

In April 1843, a man named Wiley had come from Kinderhook—a town not far from Nauvoo—to tell the Mormons he'd dreamed about a cache of buried treasure there. He said he'd had the identical dream about the treasure for three nights in a row. This trilogy of dreams lent credibility to his claims, because the Mormons believed genuine visions tended to come in threes. He told them he could picture in his mind's eye the exact spot where the treasure was buried, but needed help locating the general area. Wiley promised to share the treasure with any citizen of Nauvoo who helped him locate it. Some of the Saints agreed to help him. Ez, to his everlasting regret, was one of them.

"There it is!" said Wiley after they'd been looking for about an hour. "Why, I'll be damned if that ain't the exact spot I saw in all three dreams."

"You sure this here's the spot?" they asked him.

"Sure as shootin'. Look, it's even under an Indian mound! Yeah, this here's the spot all right."

They'd dug about three feet when they came upon the remains of a human skeleton. They cleared away the dirt and saw a stack of tarnished copper tablets, cut into the shape of a bell. They rested on the dead man's chest as if he had been lying in bed reading them and dozed off. They were fastened together with rusty wire at the edge, like a book.

"That's exactly what I seen in the dreams!" Wiley hollered. "I'll be a son of a sea cook. I'm gonna be rich!"

"Now hold it right there, Wiley!" said Brother Axel. "We helped you find 'em. We had ourselves a deal."

"But I'm the one who had the dreams," said Wiley. "All you did is help me dig, and I intend to pay you a fair price for the labor."

"Oh no, you don't!" said Brother Axel. "This treasure needs to be split up fair."

"Let's count 'em then," said Wiley. "Let's see, it looks like there's six of 'em. Whaddya say I take four and give y'all two. That's plenty fair."

"Hold on," said Ez. "Before we negotiate a deal we need to see how valuable these are. I'm guessing they're ancient based on the writing. Looks like hieroglyphics to me."

"Well, I'll be!" shouted Brother Axel. "The writing looks like what was on the scrolls from the mummies, only different. Maybe it's another message from Abraham."

"Why don't you let us take these to Joseph Smith," said Brother Axel. "He could translate them quick as a wink."

"Well," said Wiley, "I don't trust givin' 'em up so easy. Don't forget, it was my dream."

"Don't worry," said Brother Axel. "You can trust Joseph."

Wiley finally agreed, and the tablets were taken back to Nauvoo.

The whole town buzzed over the discovery. The earth had opened up and given the Saints her mysterious treasures—New York, Ohio, and now Illinois. This, they knew, could not have been mere coincidence.

Joseph carefully removed the copper tablets from the sack they'd been carried in, and took them inside the Nauvoo Mansion. All afternoon he studied them. The Saints loitered on the front lawn in giddy anticipation. They debated whether Adam or perhaps Noah had left the plates. Hyrum told them to shut up so Joseph could harness the spirit while he was translating.

Joseph finally opened the door and stepped to the veranda of the mansion. A breeze blew his hair. He combed it back into place with his fingers. He waited until everyone had gathered around, for Joseph knew how to seize a moment. "It will take me two more weeks to finish the translation. However, I have discovered the identity of the author who wrote these copper tablets." Joseph paused again to let the suspense build. The crowd looked at one another with foreheads raised. "The copper tablets are indeed ancient, and contain the writings of the skeleton they were buried with. He was a descendant of Ham, through the loins of Pharaoh, King of Egypt."

"So he had the cursed skin?" asked Brother Axel. He tried to hide his disappointment. Many of the Saints had hoped the tablets had been written by someone with a more impressive Biblical pedigree, perhaps someone like Moses. At least there was the satisfaction in knowing the author had been a leading man of his time, coming straight from the Pharaoh's loins as he had.

Wiley stood listening; arms folded and chin up—the smug look of a man about to become rich. Then he snickered. The others turned to look at him. He held his hand up. "Gimme a minute," he said, then put a foot in a stirrup and swung his leg around the saddle. "I'll be back in half an hour, so don't be goin' anywhere." He spurred his horse and cantered away in the direction of Kinderhook.

"What in tarnation?" said Brother Axel.

"We shouldn't be surprised by anything a Gentile does," said Brother Wilcox. "He's as loony as the rest of them."

They swapped stories they'd heard of the Pharaoh while they waited for Wiley's return. Thirty minutes later he galloped up with two other men. One was hairy and muscular and the other small and wiry. Wiley jerked his thumb at the big man. "This here's

Bridge Whitton," he said. "He's a blacksmith. And this here's Wilbur Fugate. He's a machinist." Both men grinned and tipped their hats. Neither dismounted.

Wiley said, "We hate to tell you this, but them copper plates ain't the writing of a man who come from the Pharaoh's loins. And he ain't no descendant of Ham, neither. See, we were just playin' a trick on ya. Bridge, go on and tell 'em what you done."

The big man crossed his hairy arms. "My name's Bridge Whitton, and I live over in Kinderhook. I thought I'd have some fun with ya, so I went and cut myself six copper sheets into the shape of a bell. Now, why I choose that shape I can't say, just had a fancy to do it that way I suppose. Then I called Wilbur who's good with the tools and such. We etched a bunch of strange symbols and writin' and what not onto the copper, and then we smeared acid all over 'em to get 'em all corroded and such. Then we got us a rusty piece of hoop iron and bound 'em together so they'd look like a book."

"That's when they called me," Wiley interjected with an impish grin. Ez thought about reaching out and knocking the smile off the man's face, but he didn't want to dirty his hands. "So," Wiley continued, "we went and found us a skeleton from the old cemetery and buried it, didn't we boys? We put the copper tablets on the skeleton's chest and covered it up with dirt. That's when we concocted a story that I'd been havin' all these dreams."

"So, you made it all up?" asked Brother Wilcox.

"Yep. And you fools went and believed it!" He looked at the other two who were chuckling and shaking their heads. Ez looked over just in time to see Joseph sneak back into the house.

"Now where'd Joe Smith go?" shouted Wilbur. "We wanna know how he could translate 'em so good."

"Yeah," said Wiley, "I didn't know I come direct from the Pharaoh's loins!"

Everyone turned to see Joseph, but he was gone.

"Guess he don't like bein' showed up, huh?" said Wiley, still laughing.

"That's fraud!" said Brother Axel. "And you sit there and admit it."

"Matter of fact, we do," said Wiley.

"So you're willing to admit you defrauded us?"

"Yep."

"We could have you arrested."

"Why, please do! We'd love to tell this story to a judge. Just for fun we'll make us another set of ancient tablets, won't we, boys? Fact, we'll make 'em right in front of the judge. And, we'll make sure the newspapers from St. Louey are there, too."

"You should be ashamed of yourself."

"No, that ain't true. It's Joe Smith who oughta be ashamed. He's the fraud here, not us. See, we're admitting what we did so you'd see who's *really* defraudin' you. Is it us, or is it your so-called prophet? At least we're still here. But where'd he go?"

Everyone turned around to look again, but the door was still closed, and Joseph was nowhere to be seen.

The headline in the *Quincy Whig* read: Mormon Prophet Fooled with Hoax. The Saints were divided into two camps over the fiasco. Some continued to believe the plates were ancient, while others believed Satan had been up to his dirty tricks. Neither camp blamed Joseph.

"Pretty much goes to show they wrote on gold and copper plates in ancient times. Just like with the golden plates. You ask me, it helps prove the Book of Mormon's true."

"That Wiley's a liar. Those plates are as ancient as can be. You can just tell. There's no way he made them in his shed."

"All I know is they look plenty real to me. And if it was a trick, you can bet Satan put them up to it."

"Satan'll do darned near anything to confuse people."

"Joseph didn't fall for it, either. At least not all the way. That's why he didn't finish the translation, because he knew they weren't real. I think he showed them up pretty good, you ask me."

The entire controversy was forgotten.

26

Accessory to Murder

It was a rainy night in late May 1842 when the assassin crouched below the window. He looked back at his muddy footprints in the flower garden and decided they were not distinctive; the footprints of any man's boot. Besides, they had already begun to fill with rainwater. Did the assassin feel remorse as he checked again to be sure his gunpowder was dry? Or was he beyond that—a hired, ruthless killer who felt nothing for his victim? He concluded that he felt only contempt, an emotion that allowed him to believe the man deserved to die.

Governor Boggs sat inside his warm den, reading by the light of a kerosene lamp, next to a small table where the family Bible gathered dust. Rain tapped at the windowpane. He hollered for his wife to bring him tea. She ignored him. Just once she would've liked to see if he could make his own tea. He hollered at her again.

The assassin heard it all. He stood in the mud fifteen feet from the governor, took dead aim, and fired.

***

Three days later, Porter Rockwell sat chained to a wooden bench in a house that served as the county jail. His hands and feet were manacled, and he hadn't been fed in two days. His filthy trousers smelled of urine, the result of intentionally wetting himself to protest his mistreatment. But this act of civil disobedience had backfired, for his captors now had even more cause to ignore him.

Porter had always been mangy looking. Now his greasy long hair hung over his shoulders and he hadn't shaved in three months. He was illiterate, but he'd heard the story of Samson, who wore his hair long and cowered from no one. This would have included the county sheriff, who sat just far enough from his prisoner that a kick wouldn't reach him in the event Porter wriggled free. The sheriff was a tough enough man, but both of them knew it was only the chain and manacles that kept him safe from Porter.

"Do you still deny it?"

"I told you I didn't do it!" said Porter. "But the rotten sonofabitch deserved to die."

"Are you upset he didn't?"

"Whaddya mean?"

"He didn't die. You shot him, but he's still alive."

"I didn't do anything criminal."

"You shot the Governor."

"Nah, it musta been somebody else."

"Buckshot. Your gun."

"You can't prove it."

"Your boot prints."

"No, they ain't."

"Why were you in Missouri, anyway? You live up in Nauvoo, Illinois."

"I'll go wherever I damned well please. This here's a free country."

"Do you feel free now?"

"Let me go, or I swear as God is my witness, I'll kill you!" He instinctively jerked his arms toward the Sheriff. Pain shot through his wrists.

The sheriff flinched, but leaned back in his chair to hide it. "You stole the gun from Ward. We already got a statement from him."

"He's lying. And it ain't against the law to have a gun. Look, you got yourself one. So how do I know *you* didn't shoot him?"

"Because *you* did."

"No, I didn't."

"I don't believe you."

"If I wanted him dead, he'd be dead."

Indeed, it was a miracle that Governor Boggs survived. He'd been shot through the window at point-blank range. Two lead balls had hit him in the skull, and another one struck him in the neck, just below his jaw. A fourth ball had lodged in his throat.

"Your fingers were on the trigger, Porter. We got you dead to rights."

Porter looked down at his fingers that were stained with years of dishonest labor. The dirt under his nails came not from tilling the soil like that of his countrymen, but from vice.

"The newspaper said he got killed."

"Yeah, but they were wrong," said the sheriff. "He's alive and he'll see that you hang."

"First he's gotta prove it was me."

"We've got a witness says Joe Smith offered a cash reward to anybody who'd kill him."

"That's a lie."

"Said there'd be a handsome reward."

"Whoever said it's a damned liar."

"So let me get this straight. You're offered a reward so you come down here to Missouri from Illinois. You steal a gun, and he gets shot the next day. But you had nothing to do with it."

"Guy like that's bound to have more'n one enemy. Like I say, if I want somebody dead, they're gonna be dead. And he ain't dead, at least according to you."

"Oh, he's not dead, I can promise you that. But you'll still hang for attempted murder, and your buddy, Joe Smith, is going to be arrested for hiring you. He'll hang, too."

"Bullshit!"

A warrant was made for Joseph's arrest on the charge of accessory to murder.

Joseph denied he'd put a hit out on Governor Boggs. There was no direct proof tying him to the crime, and Boggs had many enemies. The Mormons might have *wished* him dead, but there was no crime in that. All Joseph would say is that it wasn't his friend Porter who'd pulled the trigger. When asked how he knew, Joseph simply said, "Boggs is still alive, isn't he?"

Most Mormons didn't concern themselves with the Boggs shooting. So the fact that Porter languished in jail for eight months, before finally being released for lack of evidence, didn't occupy their waking thoughts. Some even speculated it had been the hand of Providence that had pulled the trigger, but Ez doubted God would stoop so low.

***

The Reverend arrived in Nauvoo shortly after the assassination attempt. He had low expectations, so he was impressed when he saw the town. The streets were tidy and the buildings were new and looked well built. The people of Nauvoo were kind and neighborly, too. They appeared to be happy, hard working, honest folks.

Rachel had forewarned her circle of friends about her father. "Now, I know the church is true as much as anyone else in town, but when my father arrives, we'd all do best to not discuss the topic of religion. Let him get settled before you go barging in about the Book of Mormon, or the mummy scrolls, or any of the rest of it. He's touchy about it."

The Reverend had long anticipated meeting Joseph, and he was pleasantly surprised when Rachel introduced them. The younger man was thoughtful, intelligent, sophisticated, and charismatic. Joseph praised The Reverend for his knowledge of the gospel and for the way he'd raised "this town's second loveliest woman."

Over the next month, The Reverend read the Book of Mormon, making copious notes in the margins and in a notebook where he made other observations about the faith and its people. "Industrious." "Hardworking." "Believe God once man." "Orderly." "Punctual." He was too proud to publically admit it, but he'd become a budding admirer. Still, the thought of actually converting to the faith, or the metaphysical concept that men could become Gods, was anathema to him.

***

A few months later, Ez was hauling stone for the masons at the construction site for the new temple. Joseph trotted up for his daily inspection. He was dressed in clean, handsome clothes. Surprisingly, this did not annoy Ez, who volunteered his labor for the temple after working full days at his wheelwright shop.

"Ez, you got a minute?"

"Sure, what's going on?"

Joseph dismounted his horse and took a few steps away; making it obvious that he wanted this to be a private conversation.

"So, whew," Joseph said and ran both hands through his hair. "I'm not sure how to say this."

"Spit it out."

"Well, see, every time I see a pretty woman, I have to pray for grace."

Ez threw the stone onto a pile and turned for another one. "Well, I suppose that's the way it is with most of us fellas."

"I know, but sometimes it's hard."

"Well, you've got a good wife in Emma."

"And I don't know what I'd do without her. But I've been giving it a lot of thought lately."

Ez crouched and hoisted another stone. "You've been giving what a lot of thought?"

"I don't know. It's just that after Parley lost his first wife to the typhoid, he married Mary Ann."

"Yeah, so what about it?"

"Well, Parley was married to his first wife for all eternity in the Kirtland temple. So when he dies he'll still be married to her up in heaven."

"Yeah, so what's the problem?"

"He loves his second wife, too. And don't forget they were also married in the temple. So, Parley will have *two* wives up in heaven."

"So?"

"Don't you see?"

"See what?"

"That Parley will be married to two women in heaven. That's what's got me to thinking so hard on the subject."

"What, the subject of having more than one wife up in heaven?"

"Uh-huh. God allows us to have more than one wife in heaven, right?"

"Well, yeah, if one of them dies and you get remarried, I suppose."

"If it's allowed in heaven, why isn't it allowed here?"

"What do you mean by 'here'?"

"In this life."

"I'm not sure I'm following you. You mean, why not have more than one wife *here*? As in *now*, when we're still alive?"

"Yes."

"Good Lord, Joseph. That isn't going to work."

"Why not?"

"Just because. It's not right."

"But what if God commanded it?"

"Don't worry. He's not going to."

"Well, Ez, actually He has."

"No he hasn't."

"Think about the Old Testament. The prophets all had multiple wives. I mean, look at Abraham and Jacob and David."

"It was different back then."

"Why was it different?"

"It just was. Those were ancient times and God treated it differently."

"But why would God have different rules for them? Why those prophets but not His current one?"

"I don't know. He just would."

"I'm not saying I'd do it without His blessing, but I've just been giving it a lot of thought lately." Joseph paused, waiting for Ez to chime in with something to fill the space, but Ez was still trying to wrap his head around the unthinkable. "I think God might want us to live the celestial law now."

"The celestial law of having more than one wife? As in now?"

"Yes, but we'd have to be careful, because some of the brethren might be tempted to abuse it."

"And by 'it,' you mean being married to more than one woman at a time?"

"Yes."

"Sorry, Joseph, but that just doesn't sound right. Sounds like plain old adultery to me."

"But that's the key, right there."

"What key?"

"It's not adultery if you're *married* to them. Adultery is if you have sexual relations with a woman who isn't your wife. See what I mean? You'd technically have to be married, or it would be a sin. It would have to be properly sanctioned."

"You're saying you'd just marry a bunch of them at once, and then it would be okay in God's eyes to have sexual relations with all of them at the same time?"

Joseph smiled. "No, not at the same time."

"That's not what I meant. I meant all together. No, I mean, you'd have sexual intercourse with one, and the next day with another one, and so on?"

"Uh-huh. But only if the Lord commanded it."

"Well, good Lord, Joseph! Get serious! There's no way God will go for that. He'd smoke out that scheming way around it quick as a whistle. He's not that stupid."

"But you agree it makes sense that Parley's going to have two women in heaven. Right?"

"Maybe. I suppose."

"So why not enjoy the same thing here on earth? That's all I'm saying."

"Go ahead and think on it all you like, Joseph. But just do me a favor—don't say anything about this in front of Rachel."

"Don't worry. Nothing will happen until I hear directly from God on it. Until then, I wouldn't even consider it. But, yeah, let's keep this confidential between us. The Gentiles wouldn't understand and . . . ." He trailed off.

"They aren't the only ones who wouldn't understand."

"Yes, but the Gentiles don't have the revealed truth. They'd just persecute us even more."

"You got that right," said Ez. "That's why you've got to quit talking about it."

"We'll only do what the Lord commands of us."

"Sure. But, listen, I best be going. Rachel's got supper on." Ez turned to gather his gloves and tools.

"One more thing," said Joseph. "We know from the ancient mummy scrolls that God Himself was once a man, just like us."

"Yeah, that's what Abraham wrote on his scroll."

"And God just kept learning and growing until He finally became a God."

"Okay, yeah."

"And once He became a God, he fathered all of us spirit children. In fact, he has millions of children, enough to populate the earth."

"Yeah, so?"

"Think about it. How long it would take to father enough children to populate an entire planet?"

"I suppose that'd take a while."

"The only way it would work is if you had a lot of wives."

Perhaps the very last thing on Ez's mind was the conundrum of how he would populate his planet once he became a God. However, he knew nothing would upset their neighbors more than if the Saints began acting like Old Testament prophets with a slew of wives. This sort of Biblical re-enactment would raise the roof, with or without God's dubious blessing.

A few days later, Parley approached Ez conspiratorially. "Ez, you got a minute?"

"Sure, Parley, what's up?"

"Say," he whispered, and looked over his shoulder, "have you by chance talked to Joseph?"

Heaven help us, Ez thought. This rumor could destroy the community, just like a small mite in the throat of a single honeybee could decimate an entire orchard.

***

Joseph had a dream (or it may have been a vision—the line between them was blurry). He saw his dead brother, Alvin, sitting next to God in the highest rung of heaven. This puzzled Joseph, because Alvin died before having been baptized into the true church. So how, he wondered, could Alvin have reached the highest rung?

Joseph prayed about this subject until his prayers were finally answered. God told him that everyone who *would* have believed in Mormonism (if the church had been around when they were alive) would be allowed into heaven as if they'd accepted it in the first place. Otherwise it wouldn't be fair. This made complete sense to him. However, even though Alvin presumably would have joined the church, he still needed to be baptized somehow, because no one was allowed into heaven without a proper baptism. This presented a quandary, for how were they supposed to baptize a dead person? There was much hand wringing over this dilemma.

Joseph came up with a practical solution: pretend a living person is a different, dead person then baptize him. This was serious business, baptizing dead people, and the Saints only wanted to do such a thing in a holy setting. But the temple's completion was several months away and there were dead souls to consider in the meantime. Therefore, they started baptizing living people in the Mississippi River on behalf of dead people.

Joseph and a righteous church member representing a dead sinner would wade out into the river. The righteous church member pretended to be someone else; like, say, Alexander the Great, or a long-lost, dead uncle. Joseph called the Saint by the dead person's name and dunked him in the river. Presumably the dead person's spirit was watching all this from the spirit world, and, if he accepted it, he would then be admitted into heaven. However, this was not compulsory: if the dead person's spirit didn't accept the baptism, then so be it.

The Saints were thrilled with this new Mormon doctrine because all their dead relatives would now be allowed to join them in heaven. Mormons immediately began collecting the names of as many dead relatives as they could. Once they'd gone through the list of old aunts and uncles, they moved to anyone who had ever lived, giving as many dead people as possible the chance to get into heaven. There was a rush to save the most celebrated people. It gave the Saints comfort (and no small amount of pride) that Christopher Columbus had now been baptized Mormon, as had George and Martha Washington.

The Reverend could barely tolerate the blasphemous notion that his Nauvoo neighbors were going to become Gods one day. But baptizing the dead was simply too bizarre. He did admit, however, it was a rather selfless enterprise, immersing oneself in the cold Mississippi River on behalf of a dead stranger. He turned a blind eye to the practice, but he made Rachel solemnly swear she would not baptize him after he died.

27

The Halo and the Noose

Zina Jacobs was a staggering beauty, and the men of Nauvoo felt compelled to repent for their thoughts when she'd walk by. When Ez heard a rumor that Joseph had quietly married her in a private ceremony above the dry goods store, he was stunned. This would have been scandalous enough if both of them hadn't already been married, but to make matters worse, her husband was doing missionary work in England.

Ez found Joseph down at the dock. "What in the hell is going on, Joseph?" he said.

"Going on with what?"

"Is it true you got secretly married to Zina Jacobs?"

"Why would you ask?"

"Did you or didn't you?"

"Listen, Ez, I know you're upset, but this is the way it will be in heaven."

"So, is that a yes?"

"Who told you anyway?"

"Parley. Course, he swore me to secrecy first."

"And you cannot tell a soul because God doesn't want anyone to know. He will reveal the commandment eventually, but for now it must remain a secret."

"Does Emma know?"

"No, and it will break her heart if you tell her, so you can't breathe a word of this until God allows me to make it public."

"And when's that going to be?"

"I don't know for sure, but probably within a year or two. Of course, that is entirely up to God."

"But she's already married! And so are you."

"And those marriages are still valid."

"Does Brother Jacobs know?"

"He's serving a mission in England."

"I know. That's why I'm asking if he knows about this."

"He can't know about this until God chooses to make the commandment public. Sister Jacobs understands that, too."

"But, this is . . . *adultery!*"

"Ez, you can't commit adultery with your own wife. That's why we had a special marriage ceremony."

"A secret one."

"I assure you that nothing happened between us before that ceremony. And it was done with a spiritual purpose."

"So it was spiritual only and you haven't, you know, gone to bed with her?"

"We are married, Ez. In fact, the marriage is probably more legitimate than other marriages because the Lord specifically commanded it."

"So, you have done it."

"Yes, but it was sanctioned by God. In fact, He *commanded* it. There are things that I'm not allowed to divulge until God allows it."

"I can't believe this. When Emma finds out, she's going to fly off the handle. And Rachel? If I did such a thing she'd have me on a skillet."

"I'm not asking you to do anything, Ez. However, there may come a time when God commands it for all the church leaders."

"Oh no you don't, Joseph. We go back a long ways, you and me, and I've followed you from here to kingdom come. But there are some things that—"

"I urge you to follow God and His Prophet. For now, that means keeping secret what God has commanded of me."

Ez set his jaw. "Let me tell you something, Joseph. The Saints trust you. They still believe you're the Prophet. In fact, you might as well be wearing a halo the way the Saints look up to you. But a halo doesn't need to drop very far to turn into a noose." He turned his back and walked away.

Ez made his way home, devastated. He knew Joseph was imperfect, but this wasn't just a crack in his integrity; it was a crevasse. Did this mean Joseph hadn't seen God? Did it mean the angel and the golden tablets were a hoax?

Ez's impression of Joseph had formed when they were children: long walks along the river bank where the catfish swayed in the current, skinny dipping in the pond, dares and double dares, treasure hunting, girls, tree huts, and Canal Street. Perhaps because of that perspective, the perspective of a childhood best buddy, Ez could not see how his oldest friend had evolved into a man. This trick of nature was only seen by Ez in bits and pieces, and always through his best-buddy filter. So he was willfully blind to what his childhood co-conspirator had become.

He passed the hardware store and crossed a makeshift bridge of planks between the hotel and the bakery. He hardly noticed the tempting smell of fresh bread. He passed the butcher shop where whole deer hung from hooks, heads down, drained of blood. The butcher waved.

Church members went about their business, smiling at him. "Good afternoon, Brother Wells," they said. Ez looked at the ground. He was self-conscious of the way he looked, aware that he held something dark inside that could be seen, like a sandwich board announcing their destruction. He saw The Reverend and almost vomited when he thought what would happen if he ever found out.

Ez would have stood like a sentinel, like the little Dutch boy with his finger in the dike until his arm became numb, if it would save the town from ruin. He tried to put it out of his mind, the way you close off unused rooms in a big house, pretending they are empty of skeletons. But he could no longer chink the cracks of his belief with blind belief.

Whispers announced something fishy was going on. Ez pretended he had no idea what his Brothers and Sisters were talking about. When Rachel said, "Ez, you'd tell me if there was any crazy talk about Joseph having relations with other women in town, wouldn't you?" he had to say, "Of course I would," and hated himself for it.

When Rachel found out about Mary Elizabeth Lightner, Ez got a tongue-lashing he would never forget.

He'd come home from the shop to find Rachel sitting at the kitchen table, patching a hole in his spare pair of trousers.

"Ez, do you know about Mary Elizabeth?"

"Who?"

"Don't you 'who' me! Mary Elizabeth Lightner, that's who!"

"You mean Brother Adam Lightner's wife?"

"Of course that's who I mean," she said, thrusting the needle into the torn knee. "Now quit stalling and tell me what's going on!"

"I don't know what you're talking about." He was relieved to be able to say it, because he really didn't know what she was talking about, but the butterflies in his stomach gave him a good idea.

"If Emma finds out it'll kill her," said Rachel.

"Finds out what?"

"She told Sister Sessions about her and the Prophet."

"Sister Patty Sessions, the midwife?"

"No, Ez, Sister Patty Sessions, the blacksmith. Of course I mean Sister Patty Sessions the midwife!"

"What did she say?"

"Well, I'm getting this second-hand from Sister Sessions, but she told me Joseph and Mary Elizabeth got secretly married."

"But she's already married," he said.

"Well, according to Sister Sessions, Joseph has this idea that he's been commanded by God to start up a new, secret form of marriage."

"That doesn't seem right."

Rachel set the trousers she was mending on her lap. "She told me Joseph called on Mary Elizabeth, who's only twenty-three years old, mind you, and told her to meet him above the dry goods store. She did, and that's when Joseph said he was commanded to marry her."

"Are you sure?"

"'Course I'm sure. So, anyway, Joseph tells Mary Elizabeth he didn't want to ask her because he knew Emma and Brother Lightner might be upset. Can you believe that?"

"That's hard to believe."

"Then he tells Mary Elizabeth that an angel came to him three separate times and commanded it. Of all the cockamamie . . . ."

"He said that?"

"Yes. So, anyway, Joseph said he told the angel he couldn't do it. But the angel wouldn't take no for an answer. Joseph told Mary Elizabeth the angel pulled out a sword and threatened his life if he didn't marry her. Can you believe that?"

"So what did she say?" asked Ez.

"I'm only getting this secondhand, but she apparently said to Joseph, 'Why didn't the angel come to me, too? And, what if Emma finds out?' Joseph told her that if she prayed real hard, she'd know he was telling the truth."

"So what happened?"

"Well, Sister Sessions told me that Mary Elizabeth started praying while Joseph was standing there. He kept asking her 'Can you feel it? Can you feel the spirit? It's here now.' Mary Elizabeth said—I'm just telling this second-hand, mind you—she said, 'I'm not sure, but I think so.' She told Sister Sessions that after praying on it, an angel came to her as a witness."

"She saw an angel, too?"

"Sister Sessions said she wasn't too specific about the angel part of it, only that it happened real fast, like a good feeling just shot right through her, so she assumed it was the angel."

"That doesn't sound like something Joseph would do," Ez said. "But maybe Joseph didn't feel like he had a choice because of the sword and all." He felt like an idiot for saying it.

"He didn't have a choice? Listen to yourself. Of course he had a choice!"

"Well, I don't want to argue about it." Ez knew there were two approaches to arguing with a woman, and neither one of them worked.

"Ez, I don't need to tell you I believe the church is true. We've sacrificed so much that I can't believe anything else. But, so help me, this is wrong. And when Emma comes home she's going to hear the rumors. You know she will. It'll kill her, Ez. Just kill her."

"Where is she?"

"She's been shopping in St. Louis. She'll be back in a week."

"You can't tell her, Rach. Not if Sister Sessions made you promise."

"She's going to find out. Sister Sessions has a mouth on her."

This was true. As the town midwife, Patty had become the hub of Nauvoo's gossip. People confided in her. But despite her soothing British accent and apparent reserve, Patty was incapable of keeping a secret. In this case, the secret she kept was so explosive, so shocking, and so indecent, that it practically *demanded* to be shared. So even though she pretended she didn't want to share it, it was the thing she wanted to do most of all.

Ez rode over to confront Patty, who was cagey at first. She told him, "I'll be honest with you, Brother Wells, I don't know if I can be honest with you." But the story spilled out like a leaky bucket. Patty said that after hearing Mary Elizabeth's story, she sought a meeting with Joseph. At first he'd denied it, but Patty had pressed him until he finally came clean. Joseph's motivation for then promptly proposing to Patty was less complicated; he needed to keep her in the loop. He figured she could either quash the rumors, or stir them up. And he wanted them quashed.

"Have you been sworn to secrecy, too?" Ez asked Patty.

"Of course."

"Then why are you telling me?"

"Because I thought you already knew."

"So you're married to Joseph, too?"

"Yes, I am. Joseph assured me that I'll be one of his celestial wives. It's been commanded by God, you know, but Joseph doesn't want it to become public just yet. When the time's right, he'll announce it."

"Did he say when that'll be?"

"All I know is it still needs to be secret."

"Has he married anyone else that you're aware of?"

"Of course not. Joseph said this will be a very select group." Ez realized Patty was quite proud at having snared the handsome Prophet.

"Does your daughter know?"

"Heavens, no! She wouldn't possibly understand."

Actually, Patty's nineteen-year-old daughter, Sylvia, *did* know the secret. But she didn't know about her mother, for she'd been sworn to secrecy, too.

Three weeks earlier, after a church dance, Joseph had pulled Sylvia aside and arranged to speak with her in private at his office the following day. She admired the Prophet, and thought him good-looking. But, of course, she had no romantic interest in him. Her heart was set on Jeremiah Patten, son of the foul-mouthed Saint-of-Saints, who had been killed in the Battle of Crooked River.

"Sylvia," Joseph said, "I am about to tell you something that is so sacred it must never be shared with anyone else."

"Okay. Am I in trouble?"

"Oh, my goodness, no. In fact, the opposite is true. God has chosen you for a very special purpose."

"Really?"

"You know that we can only go to the highest level of heaven if we are properly married."

"Yes."

"There are certain marriages that are so special that the participants are sealed together for all eternity."

"I know. Those are the special temple marriages."

"Correct. And after we die, if we've kept all the commandments, we can become Gods, too."

"I know."

"And we will live together as families in the celestial kingdom."

"Uh-huh."

"If you are married to someone worthy, someone God has specially chosen, you will be with him in the celestial kingdom."

"Oh."

"I know this is a lot to understand, and I don't want to alarm you, but God has commanded that I take on other wives to marry."

"What do you mean?"

"God has commanded, as He did in the Bible, that His prophets participate in plural marriage, meaning they marry more than one woman, and each of the women will be married to him for eternity."

"So, you mean Sister Emma will be with you forever?"

"Yes, but not just Emma. God has chosen you, too."

"Chosen me for what?"

"To also be my wife."

Sylvia was stunned. She had come to the meeting fearing she'd misbehaved, or that he would ask her to participate in a church activity, maybe teach the children in Sunday school, or lead the choir.

"I know this is hard for you to understand, Sylvia, but God has selected you to be saved as my wife. He has promised everlasting blessings for you and your family if you honor His commandment."

"This is a *commandment*?" She was trying to keep up, trying to understand the implications of what he was saying.

"Yes, it is a commandment for both of us. I was troubled at first, just like you. I asked God again and again if this is really what He wants, and He has told me that it is."

"But . . . what about Sister Emma?"

"She will also be with me in eternity."

"But does she know about . . . this?"

"No, she doesn't. God doesn't want anyone else to know. There will come a time, hopefully soon, when He will make this commandment public. But until then it must remain secret. I hope you know how damaging this would be to the church if anyone found out. They wouldn't understand."

"But, I am—"

"I understand." He reached over and put his hand over hers. "This is new to you, I know. And I know how it must be upsetting. But you will come to know that this is what the Lord wants of us."

Sylvia was a mess. She didn't sleep or eat for two days. When her mother asked if anything was wrong, she said no. Joseph called for her and she went, hoping he would tell her it had been a mistake, a cruel joke, or a test. He didn't. She couldn't talk to anyone, for Joseph was the God of the community. Everyone loved the handsome young Prophet and now he had asked to marry her. It was surreal. After it was over, and she had agreed to his proposal, she was sent home, never to speak of it.

Patty knew her daughter well and they were very close. They lived together and shared everything. She knew Sylvia's social network, her reading habits, her menstrual cycle, and even the general schedule of her bowels. So it was a wonder that she didn't notice the light within Sylvia had turned off, as if someone had flipped a switch. Perhaps this was because the switch within Patty had actually turned on. The Prophet professed his love for her and she was suddenly a woman again, and not just the mid-wife, or the breadwinner. So when Patty kept her marriage to Joseph a secret, she didn't know that her daughter was bound by the same secret, for they were both married to the same man.

When Jeremiah Patten, Sylvia's boyfriend, called on her, she told him she was not feeling well. When he called on her the next night she told him that she was no longer interested in him and they shouldn't see each other again. She was brokenhearted. He was dumbfounded.

Patty's knowledge of the secret marriages was encyclopedic. Ez was horrified. He numbly walked over to the mansion, stumbled into Joseph's office, and sat down. Later on, he would not even recall how he got there.

"Hello, Ez," Joseph said good-naturedly. "How have you been, dear friend?"

Ez said nothing.

"What is it? Is everything all right?"

"What have you done?" The question was so pleading.

"Listen, Ez, it will work out. You'll see. If we're open to God's commandments . . . ."

"*Open* to them? Have you lost your mind! My God, Joseph, what have you done?"

"When God formally reveals it, it will all make sense."

Ez got up to leave. "You're a madman."

"Ez, wait. Trust me."

"Not this time, Joseph. Not this time."

He had hoped to hear some compelling explanation, some justification that was based on sound judgment. He'd racked his brain to divine what possible justification that might be, and had come up empty. But still he had hoped. And now he stood at the brink of his innermost ledge.

Ez recollected the easy days, the days when they were kids and would float on a homemade raft in the pond behind Durfee's homestead, hour after hour without exchanging a word between them. Words had been an unnecessary burden back when the carefree days of youth sped past without the urge to reflect upon them, or try to slow them down. But those years had worn out and drifted away.

28

The Saints of the Black Veil

"Excuse me, sir, but there's a young lady here with her parents. They're from Nauvoo, Illinois, up the river. I think you'll want to hear this."

The editor of the *St. Louis Daily Union* leaned back in his swivel chair.

"Nauvoo, you say?"

"Yes, sir."

"Isn't that where the Mormons live?"

"Yes, sir. I believe so, sir."

"Very well, I'll have a word with them."

The editor placed his hands on his desk and hoisted himself up, then reached underneath his flabby belly and hitched up his trousers. The temperature was mild for March, but his shirt collar was soaked with sweat. He pulled out a handkerchief and wiped his shiny forehead, then stuffed it under his suspender. This appeared to exhaust him.

A well-dressed family sat in the small waiting room of the *Daily Union*: a mother, father and their teenage daughter. The girl dabbed at her eyes with a handkerchief. Her father tapped his foot impatiently.

"I'm sorry to keep you folks waiting," said the editor. "Step into my office." There was a shiny line of perspiration above his upper lip. "I understand you have a story to tell."

They sat. "Go on," the man said to the girl. "Tell him what happened."

"My name is Martha Brotherton and I was—"

"Let me tell it," interrupted her father. He had a pronounced British accent. "We are Mormons. We came down from Nauvoo on the steamship this morning." He paused for a moment and looked over at his daughter. "I should say we *were* Mormons until my daughter was proposed to by a married man."

"I see." This was not the riveting story he'd hoped to hear.

"Brigham Young, one of the Twelve Apostles, had the unmitigated gall to proposition my innocent daughter without a word to me. And he has done so in secret, as a man who is already married!"

All of a sudden, the story showed promise. The editor took a pencil from his shirt pocket and scribbled down the basic facts: Martha Brotherton and her parents had sailed over from England to join the church. Brigham Young, a leader of the sect, desired young Martha. He was forty-one years old and married to a homely woman named Mary Angell (those who told the story felt obliged to emphasize this shouldn't have mattered, but they mentioned it anyway).

Brigham called upon the object of his desire to meet him in the room above the dry goods store. When Martha entered the room, Brigham closed the door. He told her about the new top-secret revelation and assured her that the Prophet was in full support. Indeed, Brigham was happy to report, the Prophet would marry them that very afternoon! No one, including her parents, would know the first thing about it. Martha didn't want to marry Young, who was forty-one and already married. She was not opposed to the institution of marriage; in fact, she obsessed about it. But she had always looked forward to marrying someone she actually liked, and only after an appropriate courtship.

Brigham was eager to please the Lord as soon as possible, so he called in Joseph for backup. According to Martha, Joseph had been standing outside the door waiting to perform the ceremony. He said to her, "Just go ahead and do what Brother Brigham wants and you shall be blessed. And if you don't like it, come to me and I'll release you from the marriage, and take you on as my own wife if you'd rather."

For all its promise, the marriage proposal fell flat. Martha wouldn't agree to it on the spot. Joseph and Brigham agreed she should be allowed to consider it for a day or two. However, they reminded her that she shouldn't "risk her salvation" any longer than absolutely necessary.

Brigham and Joseph swore her to secrecy. Martha immediately went home and told her parents. They were outraged. They packed their bags and caught the first steamboat to St. Louis. They now sat before the sweating editor with their tale.

The *Daily Union* ran the story the next day. The morning edition sold out by lunchtime.

Hyrum—who knew something about the subject, having secret wives himself—gave a passionate sermon the following Sunday, railing about the report from Martha and her folks. It was outright defamation! It was criminal! Joseph stood next and condemned all the fornicators in town who were using his good name to justify their own sexual corruption. Ez hoped these spluttering denials represented a meaningful change, and weren't just a fig leaf for a former policy. But he wasn't optimistic.

Ez caught up with Joseph after the service. The Prophet was just getting into his carriage. Emma sat on the other seat, her head in her hands, openly weeping. Ez tried to get her attention, but she just waved a handkerchief in his direction without looking up.

Ez walked away from the carriage and Joseph followed him. "Dammit, Joseph, I told you this was going to happen!"

Joseph took Ez's elbow and led him a few paces farther away. "Ez," he whispered urgently, "you know I would never commit adultery."

"But you admitted it to me yourself!"

"Pipe down," he hissed. "I was *married* to those women. I would never sanction outright adultery. And I wouldn't have done it without God's blessing."

"Joseph, we've been persecuted for no good reason, but this time it will be our own undoing."

"One day we'll move west, maybe somewhere out in the Rocky Mountains where we can practice our religion in peace. I've asked Brigham to look into it. In the meantime, God will provide. If trouble finds us we'll meet it head on, because we are the Chosen People."

"Trouble *will* find us if you keep this up. Sometimes you can't keep it away. But, for God's sake, Joseph, you don't need to invite it in!"

***

Joseph invited John Bennett into the loop. He was the little man who strutted around Nauvoo in his Legion uniform like a horny peacock. Ez called him "The Honorable Brigadier General," which Bennett mistakenly took as a compliment. Bennett was thrilled with the secret marriage commandment, and didn't give a hoot if it originated with God, or not.

Bennett immediately set his sights on Nancy Rigdon, Sidney's gorgeous daughter, whose face could launch a thousand ships. The trouble was that all the men had their sights set on her, including Joseph, who could pull the trump card as the Prophet.

"I'm sorry, Brother Bennett," said Joseph, "but Nancy is an elect daughter of God and should be married to the Prophet."

"But you've already got Zina, Mary Elizabeth, and a few others. Besides, I'm still single. I should get Nancy."

"I'm afraid that's not possible. But Sister Patten is available."

"Thanks, but no thanks."

"Let me give it some thought and perhaps we can find another suitable wife for you."

Bennett yearned for Nancy, so much so that he told her ahead of time what Joseph was going to ask her, hoping this would sabotage the arrangement. So, Nancy was prepared for the pitch when it came.

"Absolutely not!" she said.

"Now, Sister Nancy," said Joseph, "there are certain things . . . ."

"You let me out of this room at once or I'll scream!"

Joseph let her go, but followed up with a private letter to her that, regrettably, became public. He wrote: "We must do whatever God requires of us, even if we don't see the reasons for it until later. God gave Solomon every desire of his heart, even things that might be considered abominable to those who don't understand the complete order of heaven. But this is sanctioned by special revelation."

Sidney wasn't in the loop (he was a bit prudish, after all). So he nearly fainted when Nancy showed him the letter. He didn't care if King Solomon was given every abominable desire of his heart or not. Joseph wasn't King Solomon, and his daughter wasn't one of Solomon's harlots.

"What in God's name have you asked my daughter!" Sidney didn't normally speak to Joseph in this tone, but nothing about this was normal.

"What are you talking about?"

"You have asked my daughter to *marry you?* What in God's name—"

"I have done no such thing." Joseph replied, quite defensively. He'd found the best defense was usually a sturdy denial, followed by commensurate outrage.

"Then what, pray tell, is *this!*" and Sidney threw the letter at him.

Joseph was rarely at a loss for words. He racked his brain for a reasonable explanation, one that would mollify the father of this girl. He silently berated himself for having foolishly written a letter in the first place. "Brother Sidney, this letter was a test. There have been rumblings of sexual impropriety in the community and I was simply testing Nancy's virtue. I am happy to report that she passed the test, as I earnestly hoped she would."

Joseph was able to hold off Emma, barely, with adamant denials. Rachel wasn't convinced, which perturbed Ez because he'd done nothing to earn her suspicion. His blood boiled when he caught Rachel smelling his clothes out of the corner of his eye, something she'd never done before.

The next day, Jeremiah Patten, the handsome son of the deceased martyr, stopped by Ez's shop.

"You got a minute, Brother Wells?"

"Sure do," said Ez. "Here have a sit," and he pulled over a stool and brushed off the dirt. Ez had taken his vow to the late Brother Patten seriously, determined to be a surrogate father to his teenage children who'd been left without a father. "Now, what can I do for you?"

"It's . . . well, it's Sylvia, Sylvia Sessions, the girl I've been dating."

"Uh-huh."

"It's just that . . . I don't know much about girls and what makes 'em tick too good."

"You're in pretty good company there, Jeremiah."

"But, see, we was thinking about maybe gettin' married and all."

"Uh-huh."

"But all of a sudden she's changed. Just like that. Says we can't see each other anymore. And, dammit all to hell, uh, sorry about my language, but dang me if I can figure out what mighta happened."

Ez had a rush of affection for this boy, who reminded him of his father, even down to his mouth. "Women are funny that way. I suspect she'll come back around. Maybe it's just her time or something. They're tricky like that."

Jeremiah walked away leaving Ez with a bad feeling in his gut. It was just an inkling, and he dismissed it. But still, there was the inkling.

Joseph excommunicated Bennett for the sin of ratting him out to Nancy ahead of time, and for other misdemeanors that were unbecoming of a Saint. Bennett was a doctor (or so he claimed), and it was rumored that he offered his paramours an abortion should they become pregnant. This, reportedly, had been a staple of his sales pitch. Joseph rounded up a few affidavits from the women accusing Bennett of agreeing to perform abortions. Now that each man had dirt on the other there was an ugly stalemate between the two.

"Ez, I need some advice here," said Joseph. "If I push Bennett too far he'll expose God's new commandment on plural marriage, and He isn't ready to have it revealed just yet."

"Why don't you let God worry about it?"

"He doesn't worry about things like that."

"Well, if God isn't worried about it, why are you?"

"But you know Bennett. He'll do everything he can to embarrass me and the church. I should have known he'd abuse it."

"You could let him back in the church on the condition that he takes back all the bad things he's said about you. Then you can end all this nonsense about plural marriage."

"It's not nonsense, and I could no sooner do that than walk straight into hell. I know you don't like it, but we're always afraid of what we don't understand. In fact, I was afraid of the new doctrine myself."

"Afraid you'd get caught, you mean."

"Wait a minute, Ez. That's not fair. You think I *wanted* to marry these women? You think I want to keep all this hidden from Emma? It's killing me inside. But until God allows me to reveal it, all I can do is keep it secret."

Joseph decided to cancel the excommunication and let Bennett back in, preferring to have his enemy inside the tent spitting out.

However, the rest of the Saints couldn't understand how Joseph could let an adulterer *and* an abortionist back into the church. So Joseph re-excommunicated him, and this time it was for good.

Bennett was so angry that he spread rumors all over Nauvoo that Church leaders had come to rank the females into three classes. First, there were the Cyprian Sister Saints. These were the women who had little virtue to begin with, those who'd sleep with just about anyone. Formal permission was not required to have sex with them. Second, there were the Saints of the Green Veil. These women were more desirable, and permission from Joseph was required to marry one of them. The third class was the Saints of the Black Veil. These were the top prize—women and girls who were reserved for Joseph in secret temple ceremonies.

Ez saw Bennett coming out of the corner of his eye. He wanted to talk to him about as much as he wanted to take Sister Benson for a second wife (Sister Benson, bless her heart, was big and bossy, and about as graceful as a sow on ice), but Bennett cornered him in the back of the wheelwright shop.

Bennett strode into the shop like Napoleon marching to Moscow. "You still believe he's the prophet *now?*"

"Uh-huh."

"Even though he's been having intercourse with married women all over town?"

"You've been doing the same thing."

"I only did it because he gave me permission. And besides, I'm not married."

"So now you're going to blame Joseph for your gallivanting around?"

"No, I'm not blaming Joseph for *my* conduct. I'm blaming him for his own. He manipulates his people just like old Tecumseh did."

"Tecumseh?"

"Yeah, the Sioux Indian chief."

"I know who Tecumseh is—I just don't know what the hell you're talking about."

"Well, Tecumseh was the chief you know, but the Indians were starting to wonder if he was in tune with the Great Spirit. There was a lot of rumbling. As it turns out, some white men were traveling through Ohio and they told him about the solar eclipse. You know what the solar eclipse is?"

"Course, I do."

"Tecumseh wasn't stupid, you see, so he called his people together and told them he was going to make the sun disappear the next day. All the Indians were amazed when, sure enough, there was the eclipse and everyone believed he was the Great Spirit's mouthpiece. And it's the same thing with Joseph. He manipulates all these gullible people through his 'revelations.'"

Ez stood over him holding a hub chisel and tenon cutter. Bennett came only to his chin. "You calling me gullible?"

"No, Ezra, not you." He backed up.

"Then get the hell out of my shop!"

Bennett pretended to stroll out, but he walked so fast his shiny boots had a hard time keeping up with him. Ez watched him cross the street to the livery stables, where some men were congregating. He marched up to them and began wagging his tongue. Ez went back to making the hub for Brother Lyman's wagon wheel. Ez hated to listen to Bennett because it was something he didn't want to hear. The signal had always been so clear, but now there was static. His unwavering belief had been replaced by the discomfort of ambiguity.

The following day Joseph took the Sunday pulpit. Rachel scanned the crowd looking for Emma, who was absent (for the first time Rachel could ever remember). Ez hoped Rachel hadn't heard the rumors about Cyprian Sister Saints.

"I am aware," Joseph began, "of murmurings about me and the subject of marriage. I will tell you there is nothing more sacred and virtuous than marriage between a man and a woman. God has restored the true church on earth and we have cornered the wrath of Satan, who will do all he can to stop the Lord's work. And how does Satan go about his mischief? He slanders God's chosen Prophet. The wretched Son of Perdition will stop at nothing. And when we listen to the demons of darkness, with their lies and blasphemies, Satan prevails. Do not let him prevail!

"Would you believe in God's chosen Prophet, or an *abortionist* who conspires with harlots and sleeps with prostitutes?" The Saints craned their necks looking for Bennett.

Sidney, who was on the dais with Joseph, flinched when Joseph said Bennett had been conspiring with harlots, because that would have included his lovely daughter, Nancy. Sidney might have up and quit the church that very moment had it not been for the timely dream of his *other* daughter. If Nancy's face could launch a thousand ships, poor Eliza's would sink them. But, at least, Eliza was impressively pious.

Eliza, Nancy's younger sister, became sick and died. Well, technically she *may* have died, but, according to Sidney, she was brought back from the grave. During her brief dead time, Eliza was shown that Bennett was a filthy liar. Sadly, Eliza took another turn for the worse and died a second time. She revived (this time for good, thank God) with a message from the afterlife that her father ought to stick with Joseph, or he'd join Bennett in hell.

Eliza's harrowing tale surprised Joseph, but he was grateful for it.

"You got lucky and dodged a bullet with Sidney," Ez told him. "It's time you ended this business, once and for all."

"Whew," Joseph said and put both hands through his hair. "That was strange, her dream and all. But I can't end it, Ez. I wish I could, but I can't."

Talk of plural marriage was pushed below the waterline, where it was muddy and the rottenness couldn't be seen. Yet, on the surface, it still looked lovely, from a distance.

And still Emma knew nothing.

29

Betrayal

"May I have a seat in his office?" The Reverend asked Joseph's secretary. He fidgeted with his gold pocket watch, the last vestige of his glory days. "We had an appointment to meet at nine, but I'm happy to wait. I've no doubt he'll be here shortly."

Judging by his office, Joseph was interested in *everything*. There was a map of the solar system, rocks, a globe of the earth, books of poetry, manuals on the subject of linguistics, walking sticks, a mosquito net, an antique musket, stacks of newspapers, a surveyor's pole, lists of potential supplies under the label "for Move West," and a menu from a restaurant in Washington, D.C.

The Reverend leaned over the desk. He looked at but didn't touch Joseph's correspondence. Next to a half-written letter to The Honorable Stephen A. Douglas, written in neat copperplate script, sat another piece of paper. It looked less formal, and was titled "Arguments for Certainty of the Atonement." And next to that was a closed ledger titled "For the Bishop's Storehouse 1842."

The winter of 1842 was a cold one. Thankfully, someone had laid a fire in the grate. The room smelled faintly of sealing wax and cologne. A copy of the Book of Mormon rested next to an elaborate feather quill. Next to that sat a well-worn Bible. A drawing of his wife, Emma Hale Smith, was propped on a bookcase surrounded by the works of Shakespeare. The drawing was a generous replication of her, The Reverend thought, for who displayed an ugly portrait?

"It's a mess, I know."

The Reverend jerked his head around, embarrassed to have been caught snooping.

"Please, have a chair," said Joseph.

"Thank you."

Joseph dropped to his chair and leaned back. He put his boots up on the desk, the look of a comfortable, confident man, without appearing arrogant in any way.

"I'll get right to the point, Joseph. I've heard the rumors."

"And that's exactly what they are."

"So you deny them?"

"Of course, I deny them, Reverend." Joseph had never proselytized to The Reverend and showed him utmost respect for his religious beliefs and title.

"What do you propose to do about them?"

"I'm not sure there is much I can do. I know you don't believe in the restoration of the gospel, Reverend, and I respect your views on it, but I believe Satan is out to destroy us. My challenge is to rise above the pettiness of my enemies. If I get into the mud with them, it would only make matters worse."

"Perhaps you should be more forceful and transparent in your denials."

"I don't know how much more transparent I can be, Reverend. I've repeatedly and forcefully denied these ugly rumors. They are vile and vicious and I swear my enemies will suffer the wrath of God and . . . ." The Reverend saw Joseph beginning to wind up, on the verge of revealing more anger than he wanted to. But he immediately relaxed and said, "But each man is entitled to his view. I trust the truth will eventually exonerate me."

The Reverend went home to think about his meeting with the Prophet. Joseph was quick on his feet, and he wasn't a fool. His deliberations over Joseph would continue; however, he would at least acquit Joseph of being an ignoramus.

Despite Joseph's affable exterior, he was afraid. Unseen hands were twisting the vice. The authorities in Missouri had issued an arrest warrant against him for accessory to murder in the attempted slaying of Governor Boggs. He knew he needed to go into hiding.

He floated on a skiff out on the Mississippi River, slipping onto shore after dark. Ez ran into him on one such excursion.

"Emma came to see me last night," said Joseph.

"And?"

"She's willing to give me the benefit of the doubt. Here, look at this letter from her." It was signed, "Yours affectionately forever, Emma."

"She's a good woman, Emma is," said Ez. "But if you keep this up, she'll find out. Please tell me you'll reconsider."

"Ez, I can't win either way. I'm doomed if I do, and I'm doomed if I don't."

"Then be doomed without dooming everyone else."

"I know how you feel about it. Believe me I do. But for now, I've got to get out of here or they'll tear apart every house in Nauvoo looking for me."

"You could turn yourself in. They can't pin that shooting on you. Maybe on Porter, but not on you."

"If I do I'm a dead man. There's no way I can stand trial in Missouri. They'll kill me if I do."

Joseph stole away to Edward Sayers house on the outskirts of Nauvoo. A month after the Prophet disappeared, Ez ran into Newel Whitney down at the livery stable. Newel told Ez that Joseph had written him a letter about how lonely he was. The letter asked Newel to bring his seventeen-year-old daughter to his hiding place to keep him company.

"That's when I learned," said Newel, "that Joseph had married her five weeks earlier."

"I'm sorry to hear that," said Ez.

"I was upset, but what was done was done, so I took my daughter to see him. He is the Prophet, after all, and at least he'll be able to provide for her."

Ez's stomach turned. He acknowledged the remote possibility that this had, indeed, been a commandment from God. But he wondered how Joseph could have asked such a thing of Newel. And how could Newel have agreed? Ez couldn't help but wonder if Newel figured that if he gave away his daughter; God might command His prophet to give Newel someone *else's* daughter. Joseph told Newel to burn the letter. Unfortunately for Joseph, the letter found its way into the public forum and became a further indictment.

Even though seventeen-year-old Sarah Ann Whitney was lovely, Joseph was still lonely. It may have been the loneliness, or perhaps it was the desire to please God, but something caused him to also marry his hostess at the hideaway, Mrs. Edward Sayers, later that month.

Meanwhile, Emma spent hours with Joseph's lawyers, trying to convince the Illinois courts not to extradite him to Missouri. Illinois agreed that Joseph could not be forcibly taken back to Missouri. But Joseph was still leery, for he knew the Missouri sheriffs would whisk him across the river if given half a chance. Just in case, he built a secret room in the basement of his Nauvoo Mansion. It had a fake door and was bricked in to resemble the original wall. Only those trained in espionage and equipped with a powerful lantern would find it.

As if it were Emma, and not Joseph, who had earned a scolding from God, Emma delivered her eighth child the day after Christmas that year, a boy, who died two days later. To describe her condition as mere grief would do an injustice to her suffering.

***

Emma emerged, somehow, from her heartache to establish the Mormon Relief Society. This was a charitable organization, run by women, who helped other families when they were down on their luck. Rachel was a member, and so was Emma's other best friend, Eliza Snow. Shortly after a meeting, Emma pulled Eliza aside.

"Eliza, can I trust you?"

"Of course you can. What on earth is the matter?"

Emma's chin quivered. She removed a handkerchief from the pocket of her dress.

"Now, now, there, Sister Emma, shhhh, it'll be all right," said Eliza and hugged her. "Whatever it is we can work it out."

"It's Joseph. I know something isn't right," she sobbed. "But he says I have nothing to worry about—that they're all lies to discredit him."

"Well, maybe it's just something you're dealing with that—"

"No, Eliza!" Emma realized her tone had been sharp. "I'm sorry to be cross with you, it's just that . . . maybe if you asked around, they might confide in you because no one will tell me a thing. They're afraid of upsetting me."

Eliza left the meetinghouse and walked down Brigham Street. She pulled her hat low to hide her tears, for she had also betrayed her friend. The next time she met with Joseph she would tell him he must announce the revelation, or end it.

Joseph walked into Ez's shop looking none the worse for wear. His hair was neatly combed and he wore a fine suit and expensive wool overcoat. There were no bags under his eyes, nor did he have the gaunt look of stress. Ez was astonished. With so much fear and negativity swirling about him, his old friend Joseph remained confident and casual. Then again, he knew Joseph was a different kind of bird.

"I think Emma may be coming around," he said.

"Coming around? *To polygamy?"*

"Uh-huh. I think she finally understands that modern prophets ought to have the same privileges as the ancient ones, provided God ordains it. And provided it isn't abused."

"Yes, of course," said Ez. "We wouldn't want to be abusing it now, I'm sure."

Joseph didn't flinch at the sarcasm. "I believe she'll ultimately trust the Lord."

"Well, I suppose that's between you and Emma. Oh, and the Lord. But I better not hear you've talked to Rachel about this."

"We're best friends. I'd never do that behind your back. And if God ever commanded it, of course I'd come to you first."

"God isn't going to command it. And if He does, you just tell Him no, because if you come to me on that, I'll clean your clock. I mean it."

"Whoa, Ez. Relax. Nobody is going to do anything to upset you."

"Good. So we're right clear on that."

"Of course."

Joseph must have been extraordinarily convincing. Either that, or Emma must have known fidelity was a lost cause, because she agreed to let him marry another woman. There was a catch, however; Emma got to select her. Ez assumed she'd pick the ugliest one in the litter and force Joseph to populate his future planet with a woman who looked like a fence post. But that isn't what happened.

There were two sets of sisters living at the Nauvoo Mansion at the time: Eliza and Emily Partridge, and Maria and Sarah Lawrence. Three of them were still teenagers. Believe it or not, Emma reluctantly allowed Joseph to marry *both* the Partridge sisters (they were the homelier pair). Of course, like any good bargain, there was the quid pro quo.

"Ez," Rachel asked that night when he came in from the shop, "did you see Emma today?" She stood over a pot of stew with a dishtowel slung over her shoulder. It smelled burnt, but with all the rumbling around town Ez knew it was best to keep his mouth shut about that. All the women in the Relief Society were on edge.

"What do you mean, 'Did I see Emma today?'"

"Did you see what she was riding around in today?"

"No, I was in the shop all day."

"Well, she was in the nicest carriage I've ever seen. And it isn't even her birthday. Now what on earth do I have to do to get a new carriage like that? Huh?" she teased.

"You don't want to know." He had no independent knowledge that Emma had traded the two Partridge sisters for a new carriage, but he could put two and two together.

"What's that supposed to mean?"

"Nothing."

"Nothing? Come on, Ez, spit it out! What's going on?"

"It's nothing to nobody, Rach. This is their business and I don't want to get involved."

A few strands of hair had fallen to her face. She swiped at them with the back of her hand and drops of soup flew from the ladle. "I don't want a new carriage, Ez. You hear me! If this is about the rumors . . . ."

"I don't know what it's about. It sounds like she got a new carriage, that's all I know. And I didn't even know that until you told me."

"You know more than you're telling me."

"And why would you say that?"

"I can just tell."

"Well it's none of our business. So let's drop it."

She slopped a ladle of soup into his bowl and it splashed onto his shirt. She stood in front of him with her small arms folded across her chest.

"What?" he asked.

"Don't you 'what' me!"

"Rachel," he scooted his chair back from the table and stood. She stepped back.

"Oh, no you don't."

"Rach, look at me."

She did.

"I love you."

"Do you swear it on your life?"

"I swear it on my life."

"Do you swear it on Thomas and Elizabeth's life, too?"

"I swear it on their lives, too."

"Would you ever do that to me?"

"No."

She collapsed into him and sobbed.

"What are you guys doing?" It was Thomas who'd come into the room.

"It's nothing, son. I was just reminding your mother how lucky I am to have her."

"Oh. So can I be out late? Me and Will we wanna go down to the river and do us some fish'—"

"Will and I want to go to the river to fish."

"I know, ma, that's what I just said. Geez, can't I say nuthin' wrong for a change?"

Thomas left and Rachel reminded Ez that seven-year-old Elizabeth was spending the evening at a friend's. He carried her into the bedroom; the ladle left dangling in the pot. She felt light in his big arms. She allowed him to undress her slowly, with only the pale early-evening light coming through the worn curtains that Rachel had sewn with leftover cloth from a dress. Her body was still firm and youthful, almost girlish. She traced the scars on his hip and stomach, and pulled his body to hers with a gentle kiss.

They woke to the sound of hammers. Ez rolled over and put his head under the pillow. He lay there and reminded himself to tighten the ropes on the bed, which sagged in the middle. Rachel brought him a cup of strong black coffee. He ran his eyes appreciatively over her body, clad in nothing but a thin housedress, and decided that Edward, his slow-minded apprentice, could open the shop that morning. Unfortunately, Elizabeth ran in.

"I just saw the Prophet! He's down where they're building the stage." This was to be the new platform for viewing military drills. Joseph would also use it for general speech making.

"That's wonderful," said Rachel. She turned to Ez and lowered her voice. "It looks like gallows for a hanging, if you ask me. But nobody asks me about these things."

"Did Aunt Lorna make his uniform? He looks like a prince!"

Rachel dressed and left for a Relief Society meeting at the mansion. When she arrived, she heard shouting coming from the upstairs living quarters. A moment later, Emily Partridge, Joseph's new nineteen-year-old bride, ran past her. The girl was holding the back of her head with one hand and her skirt with the other to keep from tripping. She was sobbing.

"What on earth . . . ?"

"It's Sister Emma! She threw a bar of soap at me!"

Rachel found Emma in an upstairs bedroom, pacing.

"Emma, what in the world is going on?"

"They've got to go, Rachel. I insist on it! I won't have them here another moment."

"Who?"

"The Partridge sisters, that's who. Both of them. This instant!"

"But, what have they—"

"I don't want to talk about it. Just leave me be. And the meeting is cancelled. I don't have the spirit with me today." She turned and walked into her bedroom and slammed the door. Rachel heard it lock.

Rachel was not a gossipy person but she couldn't ignore this latest fiasco. She'd held it in all day and the moment Ez came home she was ready to burst with it.

"You won't believe what happened today. But I can't tell you what it was."

"Okay."

"All right, I'll tell you. But you can't tell anyone else."

She told him the grisly tale and demanded to know why Emma would throw a perfectly good bar of soap at Emily Partridge. Ez said he didn't know—which was technically true—there was always the possibility that something other than Emily sleeping with Emma's husband had upset her.

The next day Joseph came by the wheelwright shop and slumped down onto an upturned bucket. His boots were so shiny that they reflected the broom leaning against the windowpane. "Ez, what am I going to do? Emma has been so cruel to the Partridge sisters. And now she's thrown them out. They're young orphan girls with nowhere else to go."

"Well, they aren't moving in with us if that's what you're getting at."

"No, I understand. I wouldn't ask that of Rachel. Besides, I don't dare talk to Rachel or you'll try to give me a whuppin'," he said with a grin.

"I won't *try* to give you a whuppin'. And this isn't funny."

"Alright, so what am I supposed to do? I can't just kick them out of the house."

"Well, it sounds like you ought to take it up with the Lord. He's supposed to be the one who got you into this mess."

"I have."

"Okay, and what does He want you to do about it?"

"God wants us to solve our own problems."

"Joseph, listen to me." He set the chisel down and stood in front of Joseph. "Stop this, please. I'm begging you. This is going to ruin lives."

Joseph ran his hands through his hair and left them there, as if his head was in a vice. He shook his head slowly from one side to the other, like there was no choice to make.

A week later, Joseph told Ez that Emma had consented to him marrying the Lawrence sisters, too.

"What? Are you *serious*? I thought Emma was fit to be tied! What've you bribed her with this time?"

"Ez, come on. I haven't bribed her with anything. And I'm only telling you this in confidence because Emma doesn't want anyone to know. I think she's embarrassed, and I want to protect her feelings."

"If you don't want to hurt her feelings then stop what you're doing."

"But it's a commandment. I've already told you that."

"Okay, marry them if you have to. Just don't have the intercourse with them."

"But, Ez, they're my wives. We are officially married in the eyes of God."

"And what does Emma say about that—the intercourse part? Or have you kept that from her, too?"

"She doesn't want to talk about it, but I know she's upset. In fact, I felt terrible the other night."

"What happened?"

"It was the wedding night with Maria, so I went to her room. When I came out, I found Emma standing by the door in tears. She'd been guarding the door so no one else would see."

Ez tried to remember the happier times. Emma had been so full of life. It seemed a lifetime ago when she'd stolen their britches while they'd been skinny-dipping in the river, or started a snowball fight, or laughed until milk came out of her nose.

Rachel made it a point to visit the widows in town, and she dragged Ez along. She usually joked about it: "Well, look at us, Ezra Wells, being good Christians and all." It was blustery, on the very edge of rain, and Rachel held her bonnet with one hand and grabbed a fistful of skirt with the other. The sky was the color of grapes about to go bad. When they passed the viewing platform Rachel asked, "Where's the noose?" Ez put his arm around her, and shook his head. Then she said, "Probably waiting for that Governor Boggs fella to come traipsin' through town, I suppose."

"We shouldn't even joke about it, Rach. There's still an arrest warrant out there."

They saw Emma out in the yard. She was bringing in the wash in advance of the storm. Ez didn't want to talk to her because it was awkward, but Rachel grabbed his arm and pulled him toward her. "Listen here, Ezra," she whispered sternly, "Emma needs us as much as any widow, so don't say it's none of our business."

"But it isn't any of our business."

"The hell it isn't," she hissed. "Now, come on!"

"Hello, Emma," Rachel called as they crossed the street and walked toward her.

"Oh, hello," Emma said and wiped a sleeve across her face.

The yard was well cared for and the forsythia was in bloom. Daffodils surrounded the house, sagging yellow trumpets that heralded the coming of spring in the year of 1843. They stood uncomfortably in the yard while Emma pretended the laundry couldn't wait. Two well-dressed children were playing in the yard, running through the dry sheets like bulls at a bullfight.

"Emma?" Rachel said.

Emma's lip quivered and her eyes filled with tears.

Ez wanted to be anywhere else. He had never been comfortable around crying women. This was between Emma and her husband, and he didn't want to get in the middle of it. Rachel put her arms around her. "Now, now, now," Rachel swayed with Emma crying in her arms. "It'll be alright. You'll see," Rachel whispered. "Shhh, shhh, shhh. There, there."

Ez looked away uncomfortably with his hands in the pockets of his trousers. He absently stared at a brassiere on the clothesline and then quickly looked in another direction. It felt wrong to be looking at Emma's underwear, especially at a time like this.

Emma pulled away from Rachel, her eyes suddenly fiery. "Ez, tell me it isn't true."

"What isn't true?" he asked even though they all knew exactly what she was talking about.

"I need to know."

"Joseph loves you, Emma. You know he does."

"Does he?"

"Of course he does."

"So why does he do this to me, Ez?" She grabbed his arm and begged. "Why?" Her fingers dug into his flesh. "If he loves me so much, why does he humiliate me like this?"

"I'm sorry, Emma. I don't know what to say."

Her voice cracked. Suddenly she was pleading. "Can't you talk to him?"

"I have talked to him. He believes it's the Lord's will."

"Oh, come on, Ez. You don't believe that, do you?"

"I don't know what to believe."

"But you haven't taken other wives," she said. Then she suddenly pulled away. "Or have you? Don't tell me you have, Ez." She turned to Rachel. "Has he?"

"No, I haven't," he said sadly.

Emma said nothing. None of them did. She stared, lost in thought, with her arms across her chest, hugging herself. She unwrapped herself and straightened, then looked down at her hands. They were rough now, but they had once been soft and beautiful.

"Where would I go?" she finally asked. "I'd have nothing."

"You'll stay with the Saints," said Rachel, "because we love you and this is where you belong."

The breeze picked up and sent the dry leaves scooting along the ground like they were running from some unseen trouble, clashing and scratching against each other in their frenzy to make haste across the yard. The shutters rattled, and the rain began to fall.

30

The Revelation

Jeremiah Patten was flabbergasted. He had replayed the events of the past two weeks, trying to decipher what offense he'd been guilty of to cause his first love to reject him so suddenly, and without explanation. Perhaps he'd been too forward, so at the church dance that night he resolved not to hover.

Jeremiah was a handsome lad of Irish decent, with reddish curls and blue eyes. He was unusually tall—tending to hunch forward because he was self-conscious of his height. He'd fallen irretrievably in love with Sylvia and her blond hair and dimples. She'd fallen for him too, and they'd talked about marriage, but suddenly she'd lost interest.

He dressed for the dance in the only buttoned-up shirt he owned, for his family was poor and the small bureau he shared with his brothers had room for only a few things. He walked to the cultural hall where the Saturday night dances were held, jumping over puddles of muddy water with elegant ease reserved for the young. His stockings were wet by the time he arrived and there was the squish with each step. He shook himself off like an Irish setter after a bath, and opened the door.

The room was decorated with bunting, and chairs had been set around the perimeter. Sylvia and her friends had clustered around a punch bowel next to a thin flower arrangement. Members of the Relief Society flattened their dresses and touched their hair.

The music started and the dancing began, at first tentatively, and then with enthusiasm. Jeremiah danced with a number of girls, and only said hello to Sylvia, who'd been reluctant to meet his gaze.

Jeremiah noticed the Prophet escorting Sylvia by the elbow out into the corridor, away from the crowd. What, he wondered, had Sylvia done to attract the attention of the Prophet? Her mother normally wouldn't have bothered going to the dance, but she'd primped for nearly an hour. She, too, noticed Joseph taking her daughter aside.

And so did Emma.

The three of them, Jeremiah, Patty, and Emma, from different locations in the dance hall, watched as Joseph backed Sylvia up to the wall. He stood slightly closer to her than would ordinarily be expected, except for intimates. Sylvia's head was down and she didn't look up at him. There was awkwardness between them. It wasn't a "scene," and it didn't attract the attention of the others who were dancing and clapping, but it appeared to be more than casual chitchat.

Jeremiah didn't know what to make of it. But Patty's heart sank, and so did Emma's.

Patty wrote her journal in code. That evening's entry read:

> *T'was a dismal day. My heart was full bc of seal to J, but now fear affection not reciprocated as I had hoped. My heart is heavy too bc events re S, who has become morose for reasons not clear. J may have discussed events? I hope and pray to God not. Shall I discuss with S? Do I mention to J? Not sure how to proceed. And yet my love for gospel is strong.*

Emma left the dance early, and when Joseph returned home an hour later he slipped quietly into their bedroom. He assumed she was asleep in bed, where she'd taken refuge because of the loss of another infant, and the humiliation over her husband's exploits. But a kerosene lamp burned on the nightstand. Emma stood in her nightdress next to the bureau with her back to the door. She did not turn around when Joseph opened the door.

"I thought you would be sleeping."

She did not respond. He took a few steps toward her. He knew she was in pain and wanted to comfort her. She turned and slapped him in the face.

"How *could* you?"

Joseph was stunned. He put his hand to his face.

"How could you do this to me?" She had no fear of him—he had never raised a hand to her—but this secretive plural courtship was worse than if he'd repeatedly slugged her in the gut.

"Emma, I don't love these other women. I'm just doing it because of the commandment. None of those women hold a candle to you."

"Do you have any idea what it's like?" she hissed. "Do you have any idea how humiliated I am? To walk around town and not know which girl you're going to bed with? Not know who you 'visit?' I can't do this anymore. Even the servants pity me. The only reason I went to the dance tonight was to support the Relief Society. I see the way you flirt with the other women. Are they your secret wives, too?"

"No, Emma. You know the ones I've married. You selected them."

"I saw the way you were talking to Patty Session's daughter. Surely you were not discussing the scriptures."

"No, I was counseling her."

"Counseling her."

"Emma, look at me."

She did, looking up at his face as if seeing him for the first time. His cheek was red where she'd slapped him. He was thirty-seven, but looked ten years younger. At thirty-eight, she looked ten years older. This struck her as outrageously unfair, for while she'd gained weight and looked matronly, he was still attractive and youthful looking.

"You're the only one I love, Emma."

She smiled bitterly. "Whatever you say."

***

God, at long last, finally saw fit to dictate His plural marriage commandment. And He did so, word for word. Joseph hailed it as the most important revelation he had ever received. He put it snugly into the Holy Mormon Scripture where it belonged, alongside equally important directives such as loving thy neighbor as thyself. God emphasized this was not mere advice, or a simple rule of thumb. It was an absolute prerequisite for admittance to heaven.

Ez was skeptical, especially when he read God's prologue, which appeared to mimic Joseph's rationalization. The Almighty began as follows: "Verily, thus saith the Lord unto you, Joseph Smith, that because you want to know why I, the Lord, justified Abraham, Isaac, and Jacob, and also Moses, David and Solomon, as touching on the doctrine of having many wives and concubines, I will answer you. So prepare your heart to obey the instructions that I am about to give you. For behold, if ye abide not in this new covenant, ye are damned; for no one can reject plural marriage and be permitted to enter into heaven."

So there it was, straight from the lips of the Almighty. If you wanted to go to heaven, this was something you must do. However, lest the brethren become giddy at the prospect of marrying any pretty young thing they wanted, God made it quite clear that Joseph would be the gatekeeper. "And verily I say unto you, that all marriages must be entered into and sealed by the Holy Spirit, by the only one I have appointed for this purpose. And I have appointed my servant, Joseph Smith, to hold this power, and only him. Thus saith your Lord."

Then God laid out the basic rules. "If any man marries a woman under the law of the priesthood, and desires to marry another, he is justified; he cannot commit adultery, for he cannot commit adultery with that which belongs to him. And if he has ten women given unto him, he cannot commit adultery, for they belong to him; therefore he is justified. But if one of the women, after she is married, shall be with another man then she has committed adultery."

This provision stuck in the Sisters' craw. When Ez asked Joseph about Zina Jacobs (whose husband was serving a mission abroad), Joseph patiently explained to him that his marriage to her was allowed because her marriage to Henry hadn't been performed with the holy priesthood. So, fortunately for her, this technicality erased her sin of adultery, per se. This was no small comfort to Zina.

Emma, who already felt like a beaten dog, was furious over God's final comments. The Almighty had publically called her out, telling her in no uncertain terms that she was walking on thin ice. "And I command my handmaiden, Emma Smith, that if she will not abide by this commandment, she shall be destroyed; for I am the Lord. And verily I say unto Emma that she must forgive my servant, Joseph, of any transgressions, for he has obeyed my commandment. Thus saith the Lord thy God."

Later that day, Brigham was discussing the new commandment with several men in town, some of whom were rather randy. They sat on overturned barrels at the hardware store, a place they knew their wives would not frequent. Each of them felt obliged to publically emphasize their focus on salvation, making it clear that they hadn't given much thought to the cravings of their loins.

Joseph opened the door and a few bells jingled to let the shop employees know someone had entered. He sat down with the other men.

"Did Emma read it?" asked Brigham.

"Yes, then she threw it in the fireplace."

"She burned God's revelation?"

"Yes, but it was only a copy."

Brigham didn't much like Emma. She'd tried to poison the new commandment from the get-go. "I don't mean to intrude Joseph, but you need to lay down the law with her." Brigham, in his haste, had presumably forgotten that God had already done so, publicly and emphatically.

Joseph held up his hand. "You leave Emma out of this. I'll have her in the hereafter if I have to go to hell to fetch her!"

By that time, there were nearly 15,000 Mormons. They had come from Canada, Ohio, and the slums of England, all places where marriage to one person at a time was the norm. The vast majority of them had no idea what had taken place in the room above the dry goods store, and presumably would've been horrified to know. Some had heard rumors, but dismissed them because the Prophet had been strident in his denials. Others assumed Joseph *had* been telling the truth and hadn't begun serial marrying until permission had been formally granted. They didn't know that Joseph had jumped the gun.

Ez would've freely admitted that he had impure thoughts about Brother Lyman's eighteen-year-old daughter, who looked like Venus. Of course he would. He figured he could've populated an entire town on his new planet with her alone. But it seemed to him that was the one thing that would've probably *kept* him from the highest rung of heaven. Rachel saw it the same way.

"Oh, no you don't, Ez," she said as soon as word hit the street. "Don't even *think* about it. And don't give me all that 'salvation' baloney, either."

"I wasn't even thinking about it, Rach. So don't go get a bee in your bonnet."

These were tough times for Ez and other members of the church, who believed in their hearts this commandment hadn't come from the same source as the Book of Mormon. Ez began to have serious doubts, doubts that twisted in his brain like a giant corkscrew, causing atrophy in his otherwise strong belief. He didn't doubt that Joseph had been chosen—there had been too many miracles to tell him otherwise—but perhaps he'd fallen since then.

Ez was joined in doubt by William Law (Joseph's second in command) and Robert Foster. Law and Foster were members of the Twelve Apostles and they were appalled. Joseph's conduct was more than mere doctrinal sloughing.

"Ez," said Joseph, "many of the Saints are concerned that you aren't following the word of God."

"Let them think on it all they please."

"They've asked me, 'Why isn't Brother Ezra Wells following the new revelation?' What am I supposed to tell them? If you won't follow it, it doesn't look good."

"I can't say I never would, but I've prayed on it. Both Rachel and I have. And so far the Lord hasn't answered our prayers."

"Maybe you need to pray more sincerely."

"I can't believe God wants me to go sleeping around with a bunch of other women. And if He does, why, He ought to tell me so."

"But He has—through the sacred revelation I received. That's the way God works. He speaks to His children through His appointed Prophet."

"You're saying He doesn't have the time to tell me directly? About something this big?"

"That isn't the Lord's way."

"But I thought you said that if we pray sincerely God will answer us."

"He will."

"Well, Joseph, I hate to tell you this, but He hasn't."

"Maybe it's because you haven't been following the commandments."

"That's a bunch of malarkey, Joseph, and you know it! For Pete's sake, look at all I've done. Me and Rachel both."

"You say you're following all the commandments, but how can you say that when you aren't following the most important one of all?"

"So you're saying God won't answer my prayers on this deal until after I start doing it? Because that doesn't make a lick of sense to me. No sense at all."

"All I'm saying is the Lord has commanded it and if you choose to ignore Him, He won't answer your prayers. It's as simple as that. Be faithful and you'll get the confirmation you need."

"So, you're saying that if I start having intercourse with other women, *then* He'll tell me if I should have done it to begin with? Come on, that can't be the way it's supposed to work."

"It is, provided you go about it righteously."

Ez knew he wasn't a scholar, but this was nonsensical. Some of the brethren wanted to believe, just like they wanted to believe there was a pot of gold at the end of the rainbow. The women were a different story altogether, and especially the younger ones, who faced the ugly prospect of being forced into marriages with self-proclaimed holy men who were twice their age and had hair coming out of their ears and new-found energy to populate future planets, one unpleasant coupling at a time.

***

Eliza Snow, Emma's trusted friend, found herself in the medical clinic with a bruised tailbone two weeks later.

"You ask me, I think she had it coming, I really do," said Rachel. "And I'm not the only one."

"I refuse to get in the middle of it," said Ez, "and I suggest you do the same."

"I'm sorry, but I say 'Good for Emma!' And if God damns me to hell for saying it, then so be it."

The scuffle was partially related to living conditions. Eliza also lived at the Nauvoo Mansion, on the second floor in Room #10, a few doors down from Joseph and Emma's bedroom. Two weeks after the revelation, Emma walked out of her room at the most unfortunate time. Joseph had been in Eliza's room and both he and Eliza came out of her room at the same time that Emma came out of hers. Joseph didn't know Emma was watching when he gave Eliza a goodnight kiss.

Emma went berserk. The cook had just put a pot to boil when he heard the scream of a woman scorned from upstairs. The cook ran from the kitchen in time to see Emma chase Eliza down the upstairs hallway with a broomstick, whacking her left and right. A sconce on the wall was knocked off by the swinging broom and crashed to the floor, sending dried candle wax off the balcony to the floor below. Eliza ran for the staircase, ducking blows while desperately trying to explain that it "wasn't what it looked like."

Just as Eliza reached the top of the stairs, Emma gave her a shove, causing Eliza to tumble down, grateful that the carpet runner had recently been installed. Emma was not yet satisfied, for the betrayal stung, and she chased Eliza down, taking two stairs at a time. Eliza lay on the lower landing with a bruised tailbone. Emma grabbed a fistful of her hair and dragged her to the threshold, and then threw her out.

The cook ducked behind the parlor door to watch. Guests at the mansion were curled up in the parlor on scattered armchairs covered in worn velour. They didn't look away, but they pretended not to see. Soon, half the town pledged they'd seen it. Joseph, who had lost the battle over the Partridge sisters, insisted that Emma apologize to Eliza, because she'd only been doing what the Lord had commanded. And surely that shouldn't have resulted in a bruised tailbone that took three weeks to heal.

Ez also felt betrayed when his sister, Lorna, told him Joseph proposed to her. "What did you say?" Ez tried not to show any anger because Lorna was not a church member and he didn't want her to believe he was having his doubts.

"I told him no," said Lorna. "What do you think I am? I thought he was joking at first. He asked me not to tell you, but I couldn't care less what he thinks."

Joseph was in his office with the door closed when Ez barged past the secretary before he could be stopped and threw open the door. Joseph was huddled in conversation with a few of the apostles. Joseph dismissed them with a slight wag of his chin. They left and closed the door.

"Dammit, Joseph!" he said and banged his fist on the desk, tipping over a candle. "I told you not to discuss this with my family!"

"Ez, calm down. I haven't said a word to Rachel."

"I'm not talking about Rachel. I'm talking about Lorna!"

"It's true that I described the revelation to her, just as I counsel all the Saints from time to time."

"She's not even a member! And don't give me that malarkey that you were just counseling her. You asked her to marry you! What in the hell do you think she is? For God's sake, Joseph. She's my sister!"

"Now just hold on. I didn't ask her to marry me. All I said was *if* she ever got around to it, I'd be willing to marry her so she could reach the highest kingdom. That's all I said."

"Dammit, Joseph!"

"Ez, tell me what is so wrong about preaching the gospel to those who haven't yet joined the church?"

"Go ahead and preach the gospel all you like, but don't talk to my family about plural marriage, dammit! That isn't the gospel."

"You know me, Ez. We go back a long ways. I realize you're still searching for confirmation that other brethren have received through prayer."

"Through prayer and a whole lot of ants in their pants."

"Ez, that's not true. They are following the commandment because they asked the Lord and He answered their prayers."

"I've damned near worn out my knees on the subject. You think Parley is more in tune with God than I am? Or Brigham? Or how about Heber? Don't you think it might have just a tiny bit to do with the fact that Heber's drooling over Brother Widscomb's teenage daughter?"

"Ez," said Joseph, "we shouldn't judge what's in Heber's heart."

"Amen! So don't judge what's in mine!" He slammed the door behind him as he left.

Joseph caught up with him a few minutes later at the shop. Ez was still upset and didn't want to talk about it. Joseph sat on a dirty sawhorse next to the table where Ez was sanding a spoke. He didn't look up.

"Hey, Ez, I'm sorry."

Ez grunted.

"And I swear I'll never bother you about this again. You deserve better than that. You should follow what's in your heart."

"Thank you."

Joseph put his hands on his knees and stood to leave. He brushed sawdust from the seat of his trousers and stopped at the door.

"One more thing," he paused like he wasn't sure if this was the time or place. "If you ever change your mind, and I'm not saying you need to, but if you do, I'll make sure . . . ."

"No, Joseph. Even if I wasn't already married, I wouldn't want a woman who didn't want me. And that might be the difference between us. But I'll not judge you, either."

31
Kidnapped

It was the summer of 1843, and people said they heard the yelling two counties away. They said it sounded like someone on the rack.

"What in the bloody hell is going on down at the Lucky John?"

"Got some fella locked up in there, sounds like, and he don't like it a bit."

"They say it's that Joe Smith fella from over in Nauvoo."

And indeed it was. He'd been kidnapped and was being held in the Lucky John Tavern in the neighboring town of Dixon, Illinois. Missouri law enforcement got wind that Joseph would be there on a preaching tour, so they decided to take another shot at nabbing him and hauling him back to the Show Me state, to be tried on the charges of treason and accessory to murder.

Joseph had been preaching from a soapbox in the middle of the town square when suddenly the Missouri sheriff and constable pulled guns on him, gagged him with a dirty handkerchief, and put a bag over his head.

It was only mid-day, but the men at the Lucky John were already drinking to all the luck they weren't having. They sat at the bar, belching and spitting, and lamenting their horrible lot in life, when the tavern doors burst open and two men dragged in a third man with a burlap sack over his head. The hooded man's hands were tied behind his back. He tried to yell but he'd been gagged, so what came out sounded like someone who was trying to talk underwater. He kicked and arched at the waist like a spring, occasionally striking his captors with a shoulder, or landing a beautifully polished boot on a shin. The men at the bar ordered another drink.

His captors pulled Joseph up a narrow wooden staircase to an upstairs room, where they threw him in and locked the door. The constable stood guard outside the door while the sheriff rode hard into Missouri for backup.

Joseph felt his way along the side of the room until he bumped his head on a sconce that had been nailed to the wall. The candle fell to the floor but the sconce held firm. He was able to hook a piece of the burlap hood onto the lip of the wax catcher and wiggle out of it.

It took some time for his eyes to adjust to the dark. The only light came from a dormer window at the far end of the room. It was shuttered closed, but sunlight streamed through the cracks of the shutters. He made his way over to the window and placed his face against the latch of the shutter. It was tight, but he pulled up as hard as he could until the bandanna slid down to his chin. He pulled on the latch with his teeth and opened the shutters inward.

Joseph banged his forehead onto the window frame and it swung open. He stuck his head out the window and began yelling. And that's when the townsfolk said, "What in the bloody hell is going on down at the Lucky John?"

Joseph's bodyguard, who'd been outmuscled by the kidnappers, galloped for Nauvoo shouting, "*The Prophet's been kidnapped! The Prophet's been kidnapped!*"

There happened to be a lawyer in Dixon that day campaigning for Congress. He agreed to defend Joseph for free if Joseph would tell the Saints in Nauvoo to vote for him. Joseph would have promised anything if he'd help him, even take him on as another wife if necessary. The lawyer secured a trial date with Judge Stephen A. Douglas, who granted Joseph a speedy trial.

The Nauvoo Legion galloped to the rescue. They lay in wait at the outskirts of Dixon, hiding in the bushes along the dirt road leading to the town where Judge Douglas held court. They pounced when the sheriff and his deputy led their captive past. When Joseph saw the cavalry coming to his rescue he grinned. "I'm not going to Missouri this time!" he announced. "These are my boys!"

The Legion outnumbered the sheriff and deputy by about fifty to one; the tables turned and they were taken prisoner instead.

"Go easy on them, boys," said Joseph. "They were only doing their job."

The Nauvoo brass band hastily assembled at the outskirts of the city and played The Star Spangled Banner to herald Joseph's triumphant return.

The banquet room at the Nauvoo Mansion was readied for that evening. No expense was spared. The tables were set with fine porcelain and silver-plated stemware, and draped with white linen tablecloths. When all the guests had been seated, Joseph and Emma descended the staircase looking resplendent (well, Emma not so much, what with the bags under her eyes, but her dress was lovely). The audience stood and clapped. They sat at a table for eight at the front of the room, beneath a large painting of a scene from the Revolutionary War.

Joining Joseph and Emma at the head table were William Law and his gorgeous wife, Jane, Eliza Snow (sitting two seats away from Emma, but still too close), Sidney, and the Missouri sheriff and his dim-witted deputy. These latter two had been invited (ordered, really) to stay for the celebratory dinner. They didn't look happy about it.

Joseph tapped his wine glass with a spoon and stood.

"Brothers and Sisters," he said, "I would like to extend an especially warm welcome to the sheriff here and his fine deputy who have been kind enough to join us all the way from Missouri." Some snickered while others politely clapped and then, realizing it'd been a sarcastic joke, quickly put their hands in their laps. Joseph looked down at his Missouri guests. "I want you to know there are no hard feelings, gentlemen. You are free to leave as soon as you enjoy the meal."

The following day, the euphoria of the triumphant evening having passed and the lamb chops fully digested, Joseph spoke to his people. His honored Missouri guests had returned to their like-minded Gentiles with tales of debauchery, for while in Nauvoo, they heard rumors of Joseph's new commandment. They were slightly embarrassed because their prisoner had escaped, and then had the unmitigated gall to feed them the fatted lamb before letting them go. As such, they felt obliged to embellish the numbers and ferocity of the Nauvoo Legion.

The Legion had just completed their morning drills in the open town square. They sat with the citizenry now gathered to hear the Prophet speak. A few shirtless boys in dirty dungarees sat in the crotch of a gnarled apple tree that provided a small ring of shade. They could feel the excitement. Their mothers waved for them to come down, but they pretended not to see. It was hot and the women wore sunbonnets tied below the chin, and cooled themselves with accordion fans. They swatted at the infestation of mosquitoes, congregated as they were near the marshy banks of the Mississippi River.

Joseph climbed the wooden scaffold and strode over to the middle of the new outdoor stage, resplendent in the uniform of Commander of the Nauvoo Legion. He removed his hat and tossed it to the side of the platform. The crowd roared. This was Joseph, handsome and confident, at the very pinnacle of his life.

"They will not leave us in peace," Joseph shouted with his slight whistle. "They will not allow us to worship our God, a worship that encompasses the full truth in this, the Last Days."

"We continue to turn the other cheek, and for what? To be kidnapped! To be bound and gagged! No, it is enough. Today I have filed a petition with the United States Congress, requesting that Nauvoo be granted statehood. I have asked that the leaders of this country declare us to be an independent sovereign state from this time forth!

"The time has come when forbearance is no longer a virtue. If I am ever taken unlawfully again, you are at liberty to let loose blood and thunder! I will shed the last drop of blood in my veins before I will bear this unhallowed persecution any longer. I will see my enemies in hell!" His face was red and spittle flew. "If mobs come for me again, dung your gardens with them!"

Congress flatly rejected the petition for statehood. Indeed, within the halls of power in Washington, D.C. there were only a few officials who actually read it. Joseph had attached a handwritten note to the petition. It read: "I prophesy in the name of the Lord Jesus Christ, that if Congress will not grant our petition for statehood, they shall be broken up as a government and God shall damn them, and there shall be nothing left of them, not even a grease spot!"

Regrettably, this ominous threat did not produce the hand wringing in Washington D.C. that Joseph had hoped for.

The denial of statehood was the beginning of the end. The American government was so corrupt that Joseph was forced to take matters into his own hands. He handpicked his fifty closest friends and associates to be on a council. Like so many things in Joseph's life, this council was to be top-secret. All fifty of the members were called "Princes" and it was to be, from that time forth, the highest court on earth, dwarfing the United States Supreme Court because the Almighty Himself had sanctioned it. They called themselves the Secret Council of Fifty.

They met in the upstairs room of the church. Joseph sat on an ornately upholstered chair in the middle of the room. The fifty Princes sat in a large circle surrounding him.

The first order of business was historic. One by one they went around the circle and solemnly voted by raising their hands. And when all the votes had been counted there were exactly fifty votes in favor, and none opposed.

Joseph had been voted King of the Kingdom.

32

Ewe on the Altar

Helen Mar Kimball was only fifteen years old. She claimed to love God, but her concept of Deity was framed by the four walls of her home and the isolated community where she lived. Her house in Nauvoo was located on a street called Temple, her sister was named Faith, her friend was named Chastity, and her father told her that one day he would become a God.

Helen was an ordinary looking girl, tall and gangly. She liked boys, and had whispered with her friends about how babies were made. But still she had no desire to actually do this sort of thing. Indeed, she felt sorry for her mother when she heard the noises at night through the thin wall she shared with her parents and six brothers. She'd bury her head under the pillow and hum hymns she'd learned in church.

One day she came home from school when her father asked to speak to her. This was unusual, for she had never spoken to her father, alone, about anything before.

"Shall we take a walk?" he asked.

Helen looked at her mother to see what this might mean. Her mother turned her head away. "Of course, Father," she said. "Where shall we go?"

"Oh, I thought perhaps we might walk to the candy shop and back," he said. And then to her mother he asked, "Would you like us to pick up something from the store, Mother?" She shook her head without turning around. "Very well, then," he said. "I suppose it's just the candy store."

They sat on a bench under a large red maple. Helen later wrote in her journal of the conversation:

> *Without any preliminaries, my father asked me if I would believe him if he told me that it was right for a married man to take other wives. My first impulse was anger. To mention such a thing to me I thought altogether unworthy of my father. I replied emphatically, "NO I WOULDN'T!"*

Helen's father explained to her that the principle of polygamy had been re-established on the earth. Helen neither knew, nor particularly cared, that it may have once been established. She looked away. This was a terribly upsetting conversation to be having with her father, who told her that Joseph Smith had married Sarah Ann Whitney. Sarah Ann was Helen's best friend. How on earth could she not have known such a horrendous thing?

> *This had a similar effect of an earthquake's sudden shock. I was astonished beyond measure. My heart broke for my friend.*

When her father told her that he had also taken another wife, Helen nearly vomited. Then he dropped the bombshell: Joseph Smith wanted to marry her, too. She looked at her father feeling completely disconnected from reality. She took a few steps away from the bench and her father who still sat there, his hands on his knees, a look of willing sorrow.

> *Having a great desire to be connected with the Prophet, my father offered me to him. My father had but one Ewe Lamb, but willingly laid her upon the altar. How cruel this seemed to my mother whose heartstrings were already stretched until they were ready to snap*

asunder, for her husband had already taken Sarah Noon to wife and thought she had made sufficient sacrifice. But the Lord required more.

Helen's innocence never stood a chance.

Several of the apostles were nearly apoplectic. What in the world was Joseph doing? William Law, second in command of the church, was dumbfounded. This new doctrine they called The Principle was anathema to him.

He began forming a coalition of the unwilling.

Ez believed the eager polygamists would be doomed, which salved his jealousy. He would also privately acknowledge that he felt nobler for his discipline. However, he finally relented to the pressure a few months later, but it came from the most unlikely source: Rachel.

A few months earlier she had said, "For the record, I'm not saying the commandment came from the Devil. Who knows, maybe Joseph really did get a revelation to care for the single sisters and widows." And a few days after that she'd said: "I just wish the revelation had emphasized that the true purpose of the commandment should be to care for the widows and homeless, because that's what it should have said. I'm not the prophet, mind you, but that's what it should have said. And that's all I'm going to say on the subject."

A week later she was cooking dinner, a sad dish of beef and something else that Ez couldn't identify. He was scrubbing the grease from his hands in the bucket just outside the door.

"Poor Dorthea Hyde, bless her heart. Can you hear me out there?"

"Yes, something about poor somebody and blessing their heart," Ez said as he came back inside, wiping his hands on his trousers.

"As I was saying, poor Dorthea Hyde with those four youngsters and no husband to help."

Ez knew the wheels were turning. He didn't mind, but as long as they were in motion he preferred they turned in a different direction, perhaps in the direction of the widow Dalton, who was still young and beautiful, or Nancy Rigdon. He could have catalogued every feature of Nancy's face, and made a tortured inventory of every curve of her body. But he didn't, or at least he didn't do it very often.

There was no further talk about it, and Ez assumed the wheels had ground to a halt. It was late one evening when Ez returned from work. The children were already asleep. He sat at the foot of the bed and heaved his right ankle up over his left knee to remove his boot, then dropped it to the floor. It missed the rug and landed with a thud.

"Hush," said Rachel and looked at the sleeping children.

He sat contemplating his labors, absentmindedly scratching the bottom of his foot. Rachel was already in bed. The sleeping cap she wore would hang off her head like a white earmuff by morning; she tossed and turned at night as if she had fleas.

"Ez, I've been praying hard over this new revelation that's got everybody so up in arms."

"Oh." Ez kept scratching his foot and tried to look noncommittal, in case this was a trick, or a test.

"I believe God has finally answered my prayers."

"Humph."

"I believe there are some circumstances where plural marriage is appropriate."

"You do?"

"I think we should accept the commandment."

"You *do*?" Now he was doubly careful so as not to fall into a trap. "Are you sure?"

"Yes, I think I'm sure. I know it will be hard, because there would be four more children to feed."

"Four more children?" He knew what she was getting at, and he realized with unimaginable regret that Rachel had not been inspired to force Nancy Rigdon upon him.

"Well, of course. We can't just take Dorthea in and not her children."

"Dorthea? You mean Dorthea Hyde?"

"No, Ez, I mean Dorthea Finkelstein. Of course I mean Dorthea Hyde! Who else would I mean? She's one of my dearest friends. She's been through so much, and she's suffered so. That's why God has inspired me to accept the commandment on the condition that you marry Dorthea, because she needs the most help. Besides, all these other marriages with these pretty young things are distasteful. I don't believe for a minute that's what God had in mind."

"Maybe we should talk to Joseph first," he said. "He might know someone who needs even more help."

"No, Ez. I'm pretty sure God wants it to be Dorthea. In fact, I'm set on it."

"Maybe I ought to pray on it, too, just to be sure God is giving us both the same message."

"Oh, I'm sure He will, but I suppose you need to be in full support. I'd just be very surprised if God chose someone else, and especially a young unmarried woman."

"You're probably right, but God works in mysterious ways."

"Not that mysterious. God made it quite clear to me that He'd only allow Dorthea. So I didn't press Him further."

"But, maybe we should—"

"Ez, you know I haven't been too supportive of this commandment before now, but when I prayed about it God showed me the real purpose of it. Seems Dorthea already has children of her own, I was told through my prayers that this marriage would be for support only."

"What's that supposed to mean?"

"God doesn't want you to have intercourse with her."

No, this was definitely not what Ez had envisioned. He wanted to be a good Christian, of course he did, but he was being told to marry and support a large woman with childbearing hips and a passel of kids, without the benefits the other brethren were receiving. It seemed unfair.

"Have you talked to Dorthea?"

"No," said Rachel, "because I didn't want to interfere too much in this."

"I can see that."

"So you should talk to Joseph and tell him that's what God wants. If Joseph doesn't agree, or has someone else in mind, you just have him talk to me."

Ez eventually made his way over to Joseph's place, but without the urgency if it had been, say, Nancy who needed the support. He knew Dorthea was a generous person, both in body and spirit, but she was prone to prying, wheedling, and gossiping. She did all this in a benevolent way, of course, for she was a good Christian woman. Her lot in life had been to spend it in secondhand clothes, marry a vengeful tyrant of a man, and give birth to his children before he died, leaving her a young widow.

"Joseph, you got a minute?"

"Sure, Ez. What did I do this time?"

"It's about the new commandment."

"Listen, Ez, I know how you feel about it, and I'm not going to force you to—"

"I've decided it's time I take on another wife."

"Seriously? Why, that's wonderful! You must have prayed about it and received confirmation from the Lord."

"Not really."

"Then . . . ."

"I've decided to take on the widow Hyde."

"Sister Dorthea Hyde?"

"Yes."

"Well, that's very charitable of you, Ez. That embodies the true spirit of the commandment and God will bless you for it. But I didn't know you took a fancy to Dorth—"

"I don't. It's Rachel that wants me to."

"*Rachel?*"

"Yes, and she's the one who received an answer to her prayers on this here deal, not me."

"I know this is an extra burden on you, Ez, taking on poor Sister Hyde and her children. I have no doubt the Lord will bless you."

"Well, I suppose we'll just get along the best we can. At least I'll have Rachel's support."

"Rachel's a good woman and she only needed time to see the truth in this. She'll be blessed, too, for sharing her husband."

"Well, see, that's the thing. She doesn't want me to sleep with Sister Hyde."

"But you'll be married."

"I don't want to upset Rachel. It's not worth it."

"That is certainly up to you, Ez. But as the priesthood holder in your home, I believe you should decide whether or not you are intimate with your new wife."

"It sounds like Rachel has a pretty good idea what God wants."

"Well, taking on Sister Hyde is profoundly generous, Ez. I can't thank you enough for supporting me here. This will send a message to other brethren who may still be sitting on the fence."

"Well, that's not why I did it."

"Your motivation is pure and God will reward you. Now that you have demonstrated your willingness to obey His commandments, God might grant you every desire of your heart, just like he promised the ancient prophets. Now, I happen to know that Brother Widscomb's daughter might be a good—"

"No, Joseph. I'm not angling for another wife, no matter how pretty she is. Rachel would never accept it and I'll have enough trouble as it is managing things from now on."

This turned out to be an understatement. Ez had never understood how women think. The more he tried to keep Rachel (and now Dorthea) happy, the deeper the hole he dug. For example, about a month after he'd added a room to the back of the house for Dorthea and her children, Rachel told him Dorthea was lonely and he should pay more attention to her. So he did. But no sooner did he pay some attention to Dorthea (which is what he thought he was supposed to do), then Rachel got sore. So he stopped paying attention to Dorthea, and Dorthea got sore. So he paid attention to neither of them, with predictable results.

When Rachel told him he should comfort poor Dorthea, who was lonely and insecure, she meant that he should go lie with her. This confused him, because he thought that was the one thing Rachel did *not* want him to do. So he said he would, but must have said it too quickly. The next morning Rachel hardly even looked at him. And when he said the breakfast Dorthea had prepared was tasty, Rachel said she'd been foolish because she hadn't made enough (even though it seemed like there was plenty of it to Ez), and she also said it was too salty. When Dorthea said she hardly used any salt, Rachel turned on Ez and said, "Ezra doesn't like it this salty, do you Ezra?" He said he liked some salt, but not too much.

Dorthea had never paid much attention to her hair and the way she dressed. But soon she was putting her hair up fancy and sewing new dresses. Ez didn't notice, but Rachel did. Ez did, however, smell the perfume. Rachel must have also smelled it because she started dousing in it, too. It smelled like a florist shop in their little house. Ez could hardly breathe but he didn't dare say anything. He felt like the laurel bush in their back yard, the one the dueling dogs kept pissing on to better mark its territory.

After a few months of this, Dorthea began to show. Rachel was furious. "So now Dorthea is *pregnant*? And just when did you plan to tell me this little secret?"

"I didn't know until you just told me," he said. "Dorthea is *pregnant*?"

"You're darned right she is, and she's strutting around here like a peacock. She ought to have more grace."

"I don't think she's acting any different."

"So now you're going to defend everything she does?"

"She's not doing anything, Rach. I promise."

"Well, it surely appears that *you've* done plenty."

"Rachel, I didn't even *want* to marry her. It was your idea."

"So now you are going to blame *me* that you've gone and made Dorthea pregnant? Please, Ezra, at least spare me that."

"No, it's just that, yes, it was your idea. And you told me to go lie with her so I did. What did you expect would happen?"

"Well, I certainly didn't expect her to try to drive me from my own home, I'll tell you that!"

"Nobody's driving you anywhere, Rach. I don't want you to be upset. If you've changed your mind and don't want me to lie with her anymore I won't."

"Well, it's a little late for that, now isn't it?"

When Dorthea had the miscarriage, Ez was sad for her. Rachel pretended to be sad too, and Ez supposed somewhere in her heart she was.

Dorthea wanted to have another baby. Ez privately hoped for a virgin birth. She tried to entice Ez to sleep with her and he didn't know what to do. When he asked Rachel if she'd be upset, she said,

"Now, Ezra darling, what on earth would possibly lead you to believe I would be upset if you and Dorthea spent the night together?"

"So you really don't mind?" he asked. She looked at him like he'd come directly from the moon, then turned and stormed out.

Ez reminded Rachel that he loved her as often as he could, because it was the gospel truth. And he helpfully reminded her that it'd been God's idea anyway, because he didn't want her to feel bad for having proposed it in the first place.

"You men are all the same," she said. "You're all anxious to follow Joseph and your precious Principle come hell or high water. But I had hoped you were different, Ez."

"But, Rach," he protested, "you were the one who proposed this! Remember? And you said you had prayed about it and God told you it was the right thing to do. I didn't even want to. I still don't."

"Don't blame God for this, Ez."

"I'm not blaming anyone for this. I'm just saying you wanted to do it because God told you to."

"I only suggested it because that's what I *thought* God wanted. And I thought Dorthea would be more appreciative, instead of trying to take over the whole house."

"I don't think she's done that, Rach. I think she's tried to stay out of your way. She knows you're upset about some things."

"So now she's been telling you how I feel, has she?"

For the life of him, Ez didn't know how Joseph did it.

33

Candidate for President

The Reverend was outraged. So it was true after all, he thought. Joseph and his cohorts really *were* marrying other women. And Joseph had denied it to his face! Had it not been so despicable he might have laughed at the hubris of it. But now his own son-in-law had gone and done the same thing.

"You have disgraced my daughter!"

"Actually," said Ez, "it was her idea."

"How dare you! How dare you insinuate that my daughter asked you to marry another woman, right under her nose! At least have the decency not to blame this debauchery on her. My God!"

"Ask her." Ez was too tired to engage the old man, the one who now claimed to care so much about the daughter he'd disowned. He knew The Reverend was right; this was all wrong. It was confusing, complicated, odd, and wrong. How could he defend it with a straight face, and especially to someone who didn't believe Joseph had ever been called of God? Ez didn't even have the energy to try.

The Reverend sought refuge with William Law's Coalition of the Unwilling. Law was thirty-three years old, five years younger than Joseph. He had come from Canada, climbing quickly up the ranks of Nauvoo's society until he'd become one of Joseph's closest confidants. Law was earnest and handsome, and his wife, Jane, was the most beautiful woman in all of Illinois.

Law was a true believer, but Joseph's brushes with the Missourians troubled him.

"I don't understand," he said. "Just turn yourself in, and let the truth set you free. We believe in the administration of the law."

"I couldn't possibly get a fair hearing on these charges. They'll try to pin the Boggs assassination on me. You know that. I'd already be a dead man if I didn't control the courts here in Nauvoo."

"But can't you see? That's what's got them up in arms—you mixing church and state. They're calling it a theocracy. They say 'Let him run his church all he wants,' but you control the judges, and you both write and enforce the laws. And you have a private army—the Legion—which just reinforces their fears that we'll do whatever we want, regardless of the law."

"Well, we will. I'm not going to follow the law when it's wrong. Not when it prevents us from worshipping how we please."

"But you've heard them. They say 'worship all you want, but with one wife at a time, and quit thumbing your noses at the law.' Can't you see why they're upset?"

"They can be upset all they want, but God's kingdom isn't compartmentalized, William. This distinction between church and state is for man, not God."

Law was more conflicted than most. He still believed that Joseph was God's chosen prophet. Chauncey Higbee was in the same boat. They surrendered their conviction gradually, like the tiny slivers of wood with each revolution of the screw. Thoroughly disillusioned men like Robert Foster, on the other hand, were quick to pounce.

The Coalition met in secret, for every man who belonged stood to pay a terrible price for their apostasy. "And what's this heresy about Joseph appointing himself King?" Foster said.

"Some would call it blasphemous," said Higbee."

"Some? Now, don't get me wrong on this, I'm as faithful as the next member. But my God, 'King of the Kingdom?'"

"I heard he refers to himself as 'a God to this generation,'" said The Reverend, the eager gadfly of Nauvoo who buzzed with evangelical giddiness.

"I think you may have misheard that."

"Not according to William. He was there and heard it with his own two ears. Didn't you, William?"

William Law had been loyal. Even during dismal days when Joseph appeared to be spinning wildly out of control, William defended him. However, there were times that William did not, simply could not, toe the line.

The Saints had no use for a government that stuck its nose into their private affairs. They needed their own space, where two-faced politicians and their laws couldn't reach them. Ever since Lewis and Clark's expedition forty years earlier, there had been a tug to move west, like the genetic hard-wired beacons of homing pigeons, whales, butterflies, and swallows. If they could find an isolated place out west where they were left alone, they could manage their own affairs with only God's laws to contend with. Whether this new isolated settlement would be utopian depended upon one's gender and perspective.

Joseph paced back and forth. Lists of possible western settlements were scratched on random pieces of paper on his desk, with pros and cons listed for each. On top of one sheet he'd written "Rocky Mountains." Below it, in the Pro column, he'd scribbled, "Left alone," "Privacy," "Free," and "Jim Bridger notes." In the Con column he'd written "Arid," "Indians," and "Water?" Lists of supplies went on for pages.

He and Brigham had bandied about a move to what is now Texas, but the place had been a powder keg after the Battle of the Alamo, and they wanted nothing to do with crossfire from lawless banditos who didn't speak English. They had also discussed following the Oregon

Trail to the northwest, but too many Missourians had already moved there, and they had no more stomach for *them*.

Joseph's next petition to the United States Congress was rather immodest. It arrived, as all petitions did, not on the President's desk, or near the Speaker of the House's gavel, but in a clerk's office. This clerk had heard stories about Joseph Smith and his Mormons, but had no experience with them, having only been on the job a few months.

He sat in a musty office in the basement of the Congressional office building. The office was decorated with faded paint and smelled of mildew. The room had once been a utility room, and looked it. The cramped desk was almost crowded out by old furniture, stacks of wobbly chairs, and buckets of paint. Pipes crisscrossed the low ceiling at head height; fortunately, the clerk was not a tall man.

"Holy Moses, Myron!" he exclaimed. "Look at this!"

"What is it?"

"It's a petition from Lt. General Joseph Smith of the Nauvoo Legion."

"Who's he? We don't have a General named Smith. Do we?"

"Not that I know of."

"So what does it say?"

"Well, if I'm reading it correctly, this fella wants Congress to appoint him General in the U.S. Army, and he wants them to do it 'posthaste.'"

"Well, that's not going to happen. Is he a West Pointer?"

"Beats me. But he wants 100,000 troops under his command to patrol the western U.S."

"Is he *crazy*? The army doesn't even have that many soldiers. Not by a long shot. My guess is there are only about 15,000 troops in the entire army."

"What should I do with it?" The clerk was new on the job, and hadn't received this sort of petition before.

"Give it to Jim, on Senator Clay's staff. Let him worry about it."

The staffer named Jim sent it up the chain where others marveled and chuckled at it. But, alas, no one in power saw fit to bring it to a House vote. There were some loyalists in Nauvoo who were disappointed by the rejection. But others thought this wasn't something the Prophet ought to be doing anyway, traipsing around the desert hunting Indians and Mexicans, instead of staying put to work on sermons for the flock.

Because no one in power took his request seriously, Joseph decided to run for President himself. It was early in 1844, when he threw his hat into the ring. He stood before a crowd of supporters, all of whom were eager to meld church and state into one gigantic Mormon caliphate, and proclaimed, "When I look at the Eastern newspapers and see how popular I am, I am afraid I shall be President!"

This was bluster, and so was mention in those same Eastern papers that there were between 100,000 and 200,000 Mormons, all of whom would vote for Joseph. They wondered who'd spread such a rumor because there were only about 15,000 Saints at the time. But then William Law saw a letter Joseph had written to Senator Henry Clay wherein he claimed there were about 200,000 Mormons.

"Joseph," he'd said, "you can't say that. Two hundred thousand of us? It's not even remotely true."

"I haven't counted, but don't worry. This is the sort of bamboozling you do in politics. Everyone knows that."

The Saints, who were unfamiliar with political bamboozling, felt better after hearing there were so many of them. The church *must* have been true if there was such a mad rush to join. They relied on the faith of others to shore up their own. But even the most cynical would acknowledge this bandwagon mentality was common to all political movements: everyone wants to back a winner.

Many of the Saints thought Joseph would win, that God had foreordained it. Maybe it really *had* been foreordained; maybe everything that had happened was a harbinger of things to come. Seeing God and Jesus (to say nothing of all the angels) would ordinarily be the high-water mark of one's life, but if it was his destiny to become President, Joseph would do it, for God and country.

The unintended effect of Joseph's candidacy was to make the Mormons political orphans. If Joseph ran as an independent, and if all the Mormons were going to vote for him, the two major political parties had no reason to curry their favor. This political miscalculation would come back to haunt them.

Joseph instructed the Twelve Apostles to stop spreading the gospel of Jesus and start spreading the gospel of Joseph instead. He asked Ez to be a part of his campaign staff. Ez had misgivings.

"Joseph, that isn't me. I don't want to go around talking politics to a bunch of strangers. I wouldn't even know what to say."

"Just tell them what I'd stand for."

"Well for Pete's sake, Joseph, I don't even know what that is."

"I believe in a Theo-democracy."

"A what?"

"A Theo-democracy."

"See what I mean? I don't even know what the devil that means."

"That's where God shares the power with the people."

"So who has more, God or the people?"

"It depends. As they become more righteous, God gradually allows the people to make their own decisions. If they're wicked, He'll have to step in and make the decisions for them."

"Who decides if the people are righteous enough?"

"As the president, I suppose I would."

"I hate to tell you this, but that won't go over too well."

"Sometimes the truth hurts. People will come to see that God only wants what's best for them."

"No, they won't. You're dreaming."

"Listen, Ez, God can make anything happen. I'll take Illinois easily, and I might take a few other states as well. If God wants it to happen, then it will."

"Whatever you say. What's your position on Negroes? You just know that'll come up."

"I think Negroes ought to be freed. We can reimburse the slaveholders with money from the federal government."

"But that isn't what you've said before."

"We shouldn't have slavery, Ez. I know I've said and written things differently in the past. But God loves all His children, even Negroes."

"But what about the mummy scrolls? God made it pretty clear they're cursed."

"It's true God put the dark skin curse on them, but that doesn't mean He doesn't love them."

"Okay, so what else would I tell them?"

"Tell them we should turn most of our jails into schools. Jails should only be for the most hardened criminals. Lesser criminals ought to be put to work building roads and bridges. Oh, and tell them I think we ought to bring Texas into the Union, too."

Joseph was awfully busy those days. He was running for President of the United States while still serving as the mayor of Nauvoo and judge of the municipal court. He owned the largest store in Illinois, and one of the largest hotels, too. He was in charge of the church, and controlled all its money. He was the General of the Nauvoo Legion, and he was the King. At only thirty-nine years old, he was thinly spread.

The scales groaned with the weight of those cumulative responsibilities, but it was the weight of nearly forty wives that would break an ordinary scale to pieces. The arithmetic is debatable; maybe he had a few more than forty, or perhaps a few less. With so many in the mix, and so many secrets, there was bound to be room for calculable error.

He had four wives named Sarah. He had three more wives named Nancy, and two each of Fannys, Marys, Olives, Marias, and Elizas. But there was only one Sophia, Lucinda, Prescinda, Clarissa, Louisa, Zina, Patty, Delcena, Sally, Elvira, Martha, Ruth, Desdemona, Emily, Almera, Lucy, Helen, Flora, Rhoda, Melissa, Hannah, Elizabeth, Vienna, Cordelia, Sylvia, Jane, and Phoebe.

And, of course, there was only one Emma.

34

The Printing Press

It was Joseph's play for a second wife named Jane that cost him the most. The voluptuous wife of William Law was not someone to be trifled with.

It was early evening, not yet dark, as Joseph made his way over to William and Jane Laws' home. The North Star was the only star visible in the sky. That star, which should have led him to his own home, led him to trouble instead.

Joseph knew that William was at a city council meeting that evening and wouldn't be home for a while. His wife was a loyal church member, but like most women, she opposed polygamy. Some said Joseph's proposal to Jane was made to spite her husband for openly challenging him on The Principle. Others theorized it was simply a challenge to see if he could pull it off. His apologists claimed it didn't even happen, and if it did, it was only meant to save Jane's soul.

But it may have cost him his own.

Jane was dressed conservatively in a housedress and slippers. She had taken down her long blond hair for the evening's mandatory one hundred brush strokes, something she did every night without fail, because she believed it would give luster to her hair. She was on brush stroke forty-nine when there was a knock at the door. It wasn't so late to worry her, and there was little crime in fair Nauvoo. She opened the door.

"Brother Joseph. What a surprise. I'm afraid William isn't in."

"I have come to see you, Sister Law. May I come in for a moment?"

"Certainly."

She had a pit in her stomach. Joseph got right down to business in the hurried way marriage proposals were extended around town those days, always with an eye on the door.

"Brother Joseph," she said, "this is quite inappropriate."

"But it is commanded of us."

"I have not received the same witness that you have. Now, if you will excuse me, William will be home shortly."

"He's at the city council meeting and won't be home for at least another hour."

"I must ask you to leave." Her blond hair, fifty-one brush strokes from full vitality, tumbled over her shoulders seductively. Her skin was like porcelain—she was one of the few women in the community who wore make-up, so people thought her eyes were larger than they actually were. William counseled her against the deadly sin of vanity, but he did so half-heartedly, because to look at Jane was a rare blessing.

Joseph's back was to the door with a hand on the knob, as if he was preparing to flee. "Sister Law, please consider my request. You will be sealed for eternity to God's Prophet. I only ask for half of your love. You are at liberty to keep the other half for your husband."

The arrogance of the man, she thought. "I choose to keep it all for him, thank you. Now, if you will excuse me."

It was dark by the time Joseph left. The sky throbbed with stars. Which one was Kolob, he wondered? Was God watching him now from His orb? Would he be rewarded for his commitment to The Principle? Or would he be punished? He continued walking the quiet streets, contemplating what he would tell Emma to explain his late arrival. There was only the sound of crickets. He passed the small cottage on Hyde Street where Zina lived. Her husband was still in England preaching the gospel. But, wait; *he* was her husband, too. He checked his pocket watch. Yes, he had time to pay her a visit, but he mustn't tarry.

The next evening he visited Sister Foster at her home, which was the second largest house in Nauvoo (Brother Foster had previously paid for the largest one, but Joseph lived there). Brother Foster was away on business and not expected home until the following day. Sister Foster (unlike Jane Law) was conflicted. She believed Joseph was the Prophet and wanted to be sealed to him in heaven. This was not meant as a snub to her husband, but Joseph was so undeniably handsome and charming that he was hard to say no to. So she didn't grab a pot, or butcher knife, when he made the pitch.

She sat in a wingback chair upholstered in red plush and Joseph sat across from her on the sofa. The fire cast a romantic glow to the room. It was a perfect setting for a wedding proposal (except for the portraits of severe-looking relatives who looked down their Calvinistic noses with disapproval).

"This is something that I must pray about."

"I certainly agree," said Joseph. "Let's pray together."

"But maybe I ought to do so with my husband. Perhaps we can discuss this further in a few weeks when—"

The door opened. Robert had come home early to surprise his wife. He was clutching a bouquet of flowers. He stood stock still. His face was a jigsaw puzzle of emotion, but the corners, sides, and most of the middle were filled in with betrayal.

"It is time you left," he said to Joseph while staring at his wife, trying to decipher the words she had been speaking.

"I was just on my way. Sister Foster and I were just chatting." He left before Robert could inquire into the subject of their chat, as if he needed to.

Robert dropped the flowers on the table and stood over his wife. "What was that about?"

"Nothing."

"*Nothing?* How dare you insult me with *'nothing.'* You are my wife!"

"We were just . . . talking."

He stomped his foot and the china in the hutch next to the fireplace trembled. He stood contemplating it for a moment. It had been a wedding gift from his wife's mother, and was her most prized possession. Without preamble, he reached up and pulled the massive oak shelves to the floor, where they smashed to bits. Broken china, glass splinters, and candles scattered across the hardwood. Sister Foster was in shock, for her husband was a peaceful man and knew how much it meant to her.

The loaded pistol he kept on the top shelf of the cabinet lay on the floor. They stared at its shiny, malevolent blackness, each thinking it impossible that it might actually be used against the other. He reached down and picked it up.

"Robert, please. I have been faithful to you. I swear it!"

He stopped and looked down at her. The look in his eyes alternated between vacant and agonized.

"Robert, please, come sit by me."

He slowly raised the pistol to the side of his head.

"No!" she sobbed. "Please, don't!"

He cocked it.

"Please! I beg you!"

The only sound was the tick of the grandfather clock. Neither dared to breath.

Robert's hand quivered. How had it come to this, he wondered? How had the restored church of Jesus Christ, for which he had sacrificed so much, come to this? Would all those sacrifices be nullified by a twitch of his index finger? Would he burn in hell if he blew his head off? He lowered the pistol and looked it over. He was deliberate in his inspection.

"No," he said, not taking his eyes off the gun. "Not me." He walked over and placed the gun to her head. He was not angry. He was profoundly sad, as if he were reluctantly obliged to take dramatic action.

"Oh my God, please, Robert!" Her head was down, nearly to her knees, bracing for the blow.

One, two, three, four ticks of the clock.

"Then you will tell me what he wanted, or as God is my witness, we will both face Him together." His tone was measured, calm, and resolute.

She told him the truth. He dropped the gun to the floor and put both hands to his face. There was the sharp intake of breath before the sob, and then his shoulders shook. He crumpled to the sofa. His hands never left his face. He smelled the metal of the barrel on his hands and tasted the salty tears with his tongue. His once well-nourished faith in Joseph and the Church was a rotting carcass lying at his feet.

No longer would Law and Foster protect Joseph from himself. This was a momentous leap of faith for Law. Despite it all, he still believed Joseph had once been touched by God. He was now convinced, however, that Joseph had fallen.

Joseph lashed back at their public criticism by excommunicating them. And because their wives had accused him of all the cockamamie lies, Joseph excommunicated them, too.

"This is ridiculous!" said William. "You can't excommunicate us without a proper tribunal."

"I have already done so."

"I solemnly swear to you, Joseph, I will expose this entire ugliness for the entire world to see if you don't renounce it. Do you hear me?"

"No one will believe you."

"You've appointed yourself King! You've taken countless wives, and you thumb your nose at the law! My God, Joseph, is there no end to your blasphemy?"

Joseph called an emergency meeting of the apostles who were still with him. "My life is more in danger from some little dough-head in this city than from all my enemies abroad. I can live as Caesar might have lived, were it not for the right hand of Brutus. We have a Judas in our midst!"

Law and Foster believed it was repugnant not to belong to a church, so they started a new one in the heart of Nauvoo. It was called the *True* Church of Jesus Christ (not to be confused with the Church of Jesus Christ, which, presumably, was false). The church doctrines were identical, excepting only Joseph's teachings regarding polygamy. Indeed, Law and Foster's Truer Church acknowledged the role Joseph played in retrieving the golden tablets, and all the rest.

And they did something else. They bought a printing press.

The *Nauvoo Expositor*, Law and Foster's newspaper, would only print one issue; Joseph would see to that. But one issue was all it took. Several hundred copies were printed to give its readers the inside scoop on what Joseph had been up to. It exposed his philandering, his casual contempt for the law, and his confirmation as King by the Princes of the Secret Council of Fifty.

Joseph branded his female accusers unrepentant whores and liars. This aggressive defense only played well for so long, and to a shrinking audience, for objective jurors assumed they couldn't *all* be whores and liars.

Joseph had his backers. The Principle had been closely regulated so the majority of the Saints didn't know just how pervasive it was. The insiders, the merry band of marriers, didn't wish to backtrack. In fact, Brigham was so dead set on the new rules that at the next church service he called Apostle Higbee (an opponent of The Principle) "a bald faced liar with a strong case of venereal disease from a prostitute." He said Law and Foster's group was nothing but a gang of adulterers. This, his opponents thought, was richly ironic.

Joseph ordered the Nauvoo City Council to order the town's Marshall to order the Legion to destroy the printing press (such was the order of command). The council obliged by voting unanimously that the newspaper was a public nuisance. The Order stated: "You are hereby commanded to destroy the printing press from whence issues the *Nauvoo Expositor*, and scatter the type-face of said printing establishment into the street, and burn all the libelous handbills found in said establishment."

Ez was one of vandals who destroyed the press. He couldn't make himself read the *Expositor.* He couldn't stand to see in print what he knew his oldest friend had done.

They assembled in the late afternoon of June 10, 1844 with torches, hammers, and clubs. Joseph did not participate; he needed plausible deniability. He assured his soldiers that they were authorized by God in this holy undertaking because Law and Foster had violated his constitutional rights by printing libelous things about him. They attacked the paper's offices with righteous fury, burning every copy of the villainous newspaper they could find.

All hell broke loose. Newspaper editors from surrounding towns were thrilled with Joseph's miscalculation. The *Warsaw Signal* shouted: "War and extermination is inevitable! Citizens ARISE, ONE and ALL!!! Can you stand by, and suffer such INFERNAL DEVILS?! Will you sit by while these miscreants ROB men of their property and RIGHTS, without avenging them? We have no time for comment, for every man will make his own. LET IT BE MADE WITH POWDER AND BALL!!!"

The Coalition of the Unwilling demanded this outrage be punished. They rode to the nearby town of Carthage to obtain an arrest warrant and stir the pot. Nauvoo's municipal court ignored the warrant, so a legal skirmish ensued over who could do what to whom.

Joseph sought the help of Illinois Governor Thomas Ford, an uninspiring man who had neither the backbone nor the political savvy to navigate this crisis. He was never meant to be the governor in the first place, unless one believed in fate, because he'd been elected only when the front-runner died unexpectedly at the eleventh hour. He was the wrong man at the helm with civil war about to erupt in Hancock County. But he could see which way the wind was blowing. He knew the Mormons were fast becoming unpopular, "nay odious, to the great body of the people," he impolitely said.

Ford temporarily moved the governor's office to the neighboring town of Carthage to reign in the unrest. But the newspapers, whose editors were in a lynching mood, only upped their font size: "To our friends at a distance, we say come!" they screeched. "We are too weak in the county without aid. Come! You will be doing God and your country service in aiding us to rid the earth of a most daring wretch!"

Meanwhile, in Nauvoo, the Legion drilled every morning at 8:00 a.m. sharp. From the journal of one Mormon Legionnaire: *"We are ready at a moment's notice to lose our lives, or lay them in jeopardy in defense of our rights."* And from the *St. Louis Daily Union*: "At Nauvoo, a bayonet bristles at every assailable point! Boats are not permitted to tarry, nor strangers permitted to land!"

Every newspaper in every neighboring town whipped its citizenry into a frenzy of bloodlust and righteous indignation at the gall of the "despicable Mormons and their nefarious leader, that Ol' Joe Smith!" Every town assembled its militia.

Ford urged Joseph and his friends who'd destroyed the printing press to turn themselves over to the constable at Carthage and await trial there. He promised Joseph they would be safe and well protected from the wolves. This promise had barely a whiff of reliability.

35

Like a Lamb to the Slaughter

Rachel was frantic. Governor Ford had demanded that anyone connected with destroying the printing press turn themselves over to the law immediately, or he would order the state militia to go fetch them. The town felt like a time bomb with a fuse lit.

"Ez," she begged, "What were you *thinking*?"

"I don't know what I was thinking."

"Do you realize how serious this is?"

Thomas came into the room. He had grown like a spring weed. "What's the matter, Pa? I heard they were lookin' for ya." He walked over to the shelf and took down his rifle.

"Just where do you think you're going with that gun?" asked Rachel.

"I'm gonna sit outside in case they come for Pa."

"Not with that gun, you're not. We're in enough trouble as it is. Ez, tell him."

"She's right, son. I'm going to need a man around the house until I come home. So go on now, put it away."

"But Pa—"

"You heard me, son."

"If *who* takes you?" Dorthea had come in from the back room where she usually stayed when Rachel was in the house.

"It's none of your affair, Dorthea," said Rachel.

"Is the law looking for you, Ezra?"

"I said it's none of your affair. Now, if you'll excuse us, we were having a private conversation."

"She's entitled to know what's going on," said Ez.

Dorthea came over and put her hand on his arm. "So what is it?"

Rachel said, "The children are making a fuss in the other room, Dorthea. They need your attention so we can have a moment's peace. Ez and I can discuss this privately."

"Dorthea," he said, ignoring Rachel, "I helped destroy the printing press, and the sheriff may come looking for me."

Dorthea was uncharacteristically speechless. After a moment, she recovered her natural equilibrium. "What on earth will we do? What about the children?"

"We can take care of this," said Rachel, "without having to worry about you and your croupy children. If you wish to help, you can keep the children quiet long enough for us to think."

"Rachel, that will be enough," he said. Turning to Dorthea, he said, "I'll be fine. It's really Joseph they're after."

"Yeah, Sister Hyde," said twelve-year-old Thomas. "My pa and ma can fix it without you interruptin' all the time."

"Thomas," said Ez sternly, "Sister Hyde lives with us and you will speak to her with respect. Do I make myself clear?"

"Yes, Pa." Thomas would have accepted Dorthea if his mother had, but he was just a boy and could feel the tension in the house like a spring wound tight. He didn't understand what his father was doing with a second woman anyway. He'd heard that men needed to marry more than one woman to go to heaven. He pictured hordes of mostly old, decrepit people elbowing their way through the Pearly Gates and didn't think heaven was worth it.

He tried not to cry, hiding his face in his father's shoulder. But his shaking body betrayed him.

"It's the Prophet's fault!"

"Now, Thomas, we shouldn't blame him," said Rachel without enough conviction to complete a proper defense.

Ez didn't correct him. Perhaps the boy was right. He could have told Thomas that one day he would see that life was not so simple. He could have told him that some people did bad things so often that over time they lost their power to shock. But he didn't.

"I'm going over to Joseph's. Keep an eye out," said Ez.

"But, Ez, you—"

The sound of hooves stopped Rachel cold, as if the enemy might pass by if only they kept still. The horses continued past.

It was nine p.m. when Ez found Joseph. He had gone to ground in the secret basement under the Nauvoo Mansion. Hyrum was there with him and so was Willard Richards, Joseph's plump scribe. He was pale and shiny, and perspiration dripped from his fleshy jowls. He'd been eager to live The Principle, but now he wondered whether it had been worth it to take young Myra Stenson to the Quincy Hotel like he did.

"What're we going to do?" Willard pled. He was clean-shaven but had a shiny mustache of sweat.

Joseph sat on a rusted can of wheat with his head down. He was quiet. Ez didn't know if he was praying, or what.

Willard paced back and forth across the small dungeon like a condemned man waiting for the noose. "We've got to *do* something!" he said.

"Willard!" said Hyrum, "shut your mouth before I go and shut it for you! Can't you see we're trying to think?"

"It's just if we get caught—"

"I said shut it, dammit!"

"I don't trust Ford," said Joseph. His head was still down and his elbows rested on his knees. Chairs scraped the floor above them. A baby cried.

"Me neither," said Willard.

"It's me they want," said Joseph. "They don't give a lick about you, Willard, so let me think."

Hyrum grabbed the lantern off the nail. The room was in shadows. He squatted next to his brother. "We could run for it, just you and me!"

"And the others?" asked Joseph.

Hyrum looked up at Ez and Willard in the shadows. There was a flicker of shame. "You said so yourself, Joseph—it's the Smiths they want. These others can scatter on up to Chicago or off to St. Louey until the dust settles."

"And where would we go?" His voice was flat, without hope in it.

"We'll go out west. We can leave tonight. Right now. Just gather some provisions and—"

"Provisions?" asked Joseph. "Provisions for how long? For the rest of our lives?"

"You leave," said Ez, "and they'll turn out every house looking for you."

Suddenly Joseph perked up. "No, Ez, I think Hyrum might be right. Willard, go fetch Porter. Tell him to ready a boat. No one can know, so don't tell a soul. Now get!"

"Joseph," said Ez. "Think this through. Where would you go? Out west? What in the hell does that mean? You'd just leave and never come back?"

"If I don't, I'm a dead man."

"And if you do? Then what? How are you going to survive out in the wilderness for the rest of your life? And what about the Saints?"

"The Saints will be protected. I'll pray for them. Besides, they'll be safer without me."

"And me?" asked Ez.

"It's me they want. All you've got to do is disappear for a few months and they'll give up."

Porter Rockwell showed up thirty minutes later looking like a drowned rat. It was raining hard, an ominous late June thunderstorm. Porter had languished for the preceding eight months in a Missouri jail for the attempted murder of Governor Boggs, but had been released for lack of evidence.

"Willard here says you was lookin' for me. I come soon as I could git the boots on."

"Get a skiff and meet Hyrum and me down at the river in an hour."

"I don't mean to argue with ya, Joseph," said Porter. "But I been down there some earlier and she's overflowin' the banks—what with the rain and all. And it's gonna be muddier'n hell. Just so long as you know it."

"I need you to row Hyrum and me across the Mississippi tonight. But, Porter, no one can know. Listen to me good, Porter; no one can know. Do you understand?"

Porter grunted.

"And what about Emma?" asked Ez.

"I'll tell her. Can you round up some provisions for us?"

"And the Saints?"

"I'm doing this for the Saints, Ez. Don't you understand?"

An hour later, Ez was down at the river in a wagon from his shop. The wagon was loaded with as many provisions as he could get from the bishop's storehouse. Brother Webster was at the store when he'd hustled in.

"Give me a wagon load of supplies and make it quick!" he'd said. "I need them now!"

"What in tarnation's gotten into *you*, Brother Wells? You can't just march in here like the Prophet, demanding whatever you want. That ain't how it works, and you know it!"

"Just do it," he said with a set jaw. Brother Webster knew he meant business, especially when Ez pulled out his pistol.

"What in the—! Have you lost your mind?"

"*Now!*"

Brother Webster had a round belly and narrow shoulders that sloped down from the neck at an alarming angle to a wide waist, all of which made him look like a children's top. He spun around the storehouse with one eye on the pile of flour and coffee bags and the other on Ez, who, he assumed, had completely lost his mind.

"Wait 'til the Prophet hears about this!" Webster said with as much bravery as he dared, which wasn't much, because he hardly slowed down long enough to say it.

The wagon strained under the weight. The load caused the axle to bend in the center, which made the wheels bow out at the bottom, as if the wagon was knock-kneed.

"Thanks, Brother Webster," Ez said as he shook the reins and pulled away into the dark downpour. "Put this on Joseph's account," he hollered over his shoulder into the rain.

When he was far enough away that Brother Webster knew Ez's wet pistol couldn't possibly shoot him, he waited a few more moments to be doubly sure, then screeched, "I'm tellin' Joseph! This here is theft!" Ez waved his pistol in the air without turning around. "And you pulled a gun on a brother in the Church!" Brother Webster yelled. "I'll see to it you're excommunicated for this!"

There was hardly anyone out on account of the rain. But along the way, Ez encountered Caleb Stone, the young man who'd been lined up to be shot in the pig sty a few years earlier.

"Where you goin', Brother Wells?"

"It's Joseph. He and Hyrum are down at the river. They're fixing to row across to Iowa to escape and I am taking them some supplies."

"They're going to leave?" he asked.

"I'm afraid so. Want to go with me to help unload this stuff?"

"Uh, I'd love to, Brother Wells. But I best be getting home. It's late."

Ez didn't blame Caleb for passing on another of Joseph's death-defying adventures. Ez continued on through the deserted streets, for everyone else was hunkered down in their homes hoping Joseph had a plan for them. When he got to the river, he saw it had spilled over the banks and water ran all the way to the steamboat's maintenance shack. The shack was halfway under water and filled with mud. A gray cluster of people huddled under cover from the rain. They disappeared into the trees on the riverbank until they saw it was Ez, and then came out like phantoms appearing from nowhere.

Emma was there, too. Her umbrella listed to the side as if she didn't care that it no longer covered her head. She was soaked and her cotton bonnet sagged down the sides of her head like the ears of a sad hound dog. There was something gone from her face that could not be put right again. She didn't say a word.

"Help me unload this, dammit!" Ez hissed when Joseph and Hyrum crawled into the rowboat. They got out and helped load the rowboat with enough supplies to last a week or two—but not until the Second Coming. The small craft looked ready to sink from the weight; the water came nearly to the brim of the sidewall. Ez pushed while Porter rowed against the wind. The water was icy cold and Ez's trousers stuck to his thighs. Finally they were free of the mud and Ez gave a final shove before wading back to the shore. He took Emma's arm and they walked through the muck to the wagon.

"Why is he doing this?" It was barely a whisper.

"He thinks it's for the best," said Ez.

"The best? The best for whom?"

Ez didn't reply.

"What am I supposed to tell my children? And what about the Saints? Should we just tell them he left us like a coward to fend for ourselves?" Ez had no answer. "It's wrong, Ez. It's wrong and you know it."

Ez was quiet as the wagon fought the mushy road.

"Has it all been a pack of lies?" she asked.

He didn't dare take his eyes off the ruts, for they'd get stuck if they didn't keep moving. So they sat, side by side, saying nothing. Not because there was nothing to say, but perhaps because there was too much.

"You'll stay with us tonight," he finally said. "Your children will be safe with Eliza." The mention of Eliza's name was boneheaded, but Emma didn't flinch; she looked straight ahead into the driving rain as they made their way up the muddy hill from the river and into the city.

Ez's sleeping arrangement was delicate. It was a subject he dreaded because he couldn't win. So he left it up to his wives. Initially they were civil, even generous. "No, it's all right if he stays with you two nights a week," Rachel had said. But the tone of this generosity had deteriorated into: "I think Ez should spend every night with me. Now, if it's your birthday or something we can consider it on a case-by-case basis." Ez went where he was told and didn't keep track, secure in the knowledge that track *was* being kept. At any rate, this was a Rachel night.

Rachel and Emma stayed up talking most of the night. Ez didn't know what time she crawled into bed, but it was still dark out. He could feel her resting on an elbow looking at him, that well-known intuition of being watched, even though his eyes were closed. She touched him softly at first, rubbing his arm and then his chest. He was naked on account of the muggy night and heat from the fireplace. She knew he would never have swum in the murky water of polygamy if she hadn't proposed it, unlike some of the other men in town who'd jumped in with a squealing cannonball. And now he would pay a price for it.

Emma was still at the kitchen table when the sun came up. The rain had leaked through the roof and the ceiling hung in the corner like a sack of wet mud, dripping steadily into a bucket on the floor. Emma nudged the lantern across the uneven tabletop to make some noise as soon as Ez stirred. In front of her was a letter she had written to Joseph.

"Ez," she whispered, "I need to get this to Joseph!"

"He'll be in Iowa by now."

"But Porter said Joseph and Hyrum were going to wait on the other side of the river. If Porter goes quickly he can still find them."

"I don't even know where Porter is. If I know him, he's probably in some hole somewhere. But I'll try and rustle him up if you really want me to."

"Please, Ez, I'm begging you."

It was early, and the streets were empty. Steam rose from the ground. Ez found Porter sleeping under the rowboat and hauled him back to the house, grumpy and sore as ever.

Emma jumped up from the table. "Porter, can you row back across and give this letter to Joseph? Please? It's important, really it is."

"Took me half the night, Sister Emma. Course I was up against that goddamned wind, if you'll excuse the crude language." His boots were untied and the tongues lolled out of them.

"So will you help me?"

"Don't mean to pry now, Sister Emma," Porter said while scratching his backside without any shame, "but what's so damned important in your letter there, anyways?"

"Joseph needs to come back. The sheriff will be here first thing this morning. Please, Porter, if he doesn't come back we'll be ruined. He can't just leave us like this."

Porter's mouth twitched under his long, filthy beard. He looked at Ez who nodded.

"You know," Porter opened the door and spit chew, "the Prophet's a stubborn cuss on these things. I can't force him to do nuthin' he don't wanna do." He picked up the letter with his stained fingers and shoved it into his grimy britches.

"I'm going with you," said Ez.

Emma looked wretched. "But . . . you're coming back, right?"

"Course he's coming back." It was Rachel, standing behind them, sleepy-eyed. Her red hair was wild and thick. She wore Ez's shirt and it hung to her knees. She also wore a fierce look—a look that said she'd always believed in him more than the golden tablets.

"I'm sorry, Rachel," said Emma. "I didn't mean anything by it."

"I know you didn't."

Rachel made oatmeal while Ez dressed. Porter wolfed it down, wiped his fingers in the bowl, and then licked them clean.

"Where are you going, Ezra?" It was Dorthea.

"This is between Emma and Ez," said Rachel. "You can go back to bed."

"Why can't I know what is going on?"

"Because it's personal between them, and the three of us don't need any more help deciding what to do."

"Ezra, are you in danger?"

"No, Dorthea. Thanks for your concern, but Rachel is right; this is a personal matter. Please don't worry. I'll be back in an hour to explain everything."

"I'll make some of those biscuits and gravy you like so much," she said.

"I've already made him his favorite oatmeal, Dorthea, so I don't think Ez will be hungry. Will you, Ez?"

The trip across the Mississippi was quiet. Porter didn't say much, so Ez was left alone with his thoughts. He recalled the first time he met Joseph. They had shared a small desk in the one room schoolhouse in Palmyra. He remembered the musty smell of Mrs. Wentworth, the teacher, and the scrape of chalk on the board. He remembered their days of adventure, staring at the magic stone for any whiff of buried treasure, long walks to school, Joseph's easy grin, hookers on Canal Street, and the smell of Joseph's mother's rhubarb pie which the boys inhaled in the time it took her to bring it from the brick oven to the table.

He remembered the time Jess Clawson peed his pants and Joseph stopped the teasing with a diversion to race the boys to the Hathaway River for a swim, and the look of relief on Jess's face when Joseph, the most popular boy in school, had said, "Hey, it ain't that bad, Jess. You got us out early and that old bag Wentworth didn't even know you'd done it on purpose!" And the time they'd had the notion to spoil the grapes to make their own wine, which tasted like spoiled grapes, but they pretended they could "feel it kickin' in." And there was the time they'd put hard-boiled eggs under Hinckley's setting hen and then laughed so hard it felt like they'd done fifty sit-ups. There was the rope swing, and the time they watched Mr. Durfee's horse birth a colt, and the time they accidently started a fire in the barn melting an old harness into a slingshot.

And, of course, there was all that adventure looking for arrowheads, Indian pottery, and finding the golden tablets. Yes, the golden tablets, the discovery of which changed their lives forever and ultimately led, one small shard of shared history after another, to this moment.

It was late morning by the time Ez and Porter finally made it across the Mississippi. Porter stuck two dirty fingers in his mouth and whistled when they approached the shore on the other side. Joseph and Hyrum appeared from behind a large river birch surrounded by the pile of supplies. Hyrum waded into the river and pulled them to shore.

"What is it?" asked Joseph. "Have they come for me?"

"Not yet," said Ez. "But they will. You know they will."

"Here," Porter said as he dug Emma's letter from his pocket. "Sister Emma said to give it to ya. Said it was important."

Joseph walked up the bank and sat on the pile of burlap sacks. He opened the letter and read it slowly. When he finished, he sat with no expression, staring at nothing. A whistle from a steamboat sounded in the distance.

"What are you going to do, Joseph?" Ez finally asked. "Time's wasting."

"If I go back I'll be butchered."

"And if you don't?"

"History will brand me a coward. My enemies will see to that."

"Emma's not your enemy, Joseph," said Ez. "If the shepherd deserts his flock, who will keep the wolves away?"

"We'll fight it in court," said Hyrum. "Governor Ford said he'll make sure we get a fair trial."

"Ford can't guarantee anything," said Joseph. "He's like Pontius Pilate. He'll wash his hands of me and mark his place in history alongside Boggs."

Ez walked over and put his hand on his best friend's shoulder. Joseph looked up at him. "Ez," he said, "What should I do?"

There wasn't much King left in him.

"I'm going back," Ez said, "and I think you should come with me. But it seems to me you ought to follow the Lord on this one. If He's not speaking, you ought to follow your heart. And I think your heart's telling you not to leave the Saints like this."

Joseph slowly stood and nodded at Hyrum. "Then I'll go back, like a lamb to the slaughter."

36

June 27, 1844

They started off at dusk for the fifteen-mile ride to Carthage to turn themselves in: Joseph, Hyrum, Willard, John Taylor, and Ez. The small town of Carthage, Illinois, was the county seat but had fewer than one thousand citizens. Its meager industry had been lost to its neighbor, Nauvoo, the thriving Mormon town on the Mississippi River.

The Carthage town square was bordered by a courthouse, jail, general store, and the Hamilton Hotel, where Governor Ford had set up shop. Never before, or since, had Carthage been so historically relevant. The square was packed with three hundred local militiamen, plus rag-tag militias from neighboring towns. Altogether nearly seven hundred irate citizens jammed the square to riot against Joseph Smith and his followers, determined to put an end to Mormon lawlessness, once and for all.

They milled about playing cards and drinking cheap whiskey. They all shared one common sentiment: "Death to the Prophet!" However, despite their bravado, they were afraid the Nauvoo Legion might attack *them*.

"What if the Legion shows up?"

"I heard there's three thousand of 'em!"

"We need us more men! The Mormons'll try and kill us all."

It was nearly midnight when the five Mormons rode into Carthage. "He's here!" a militiaman shouted. "By damn, he went and turned himself in!" They crowded the road, eager to see the Devil incarnate with their own eyes. They held their muskets and bayonets, hooting and jeering at the riders, straining to see their faces in the flickering light of lanterns and bonfires. The mob looked behind Joseph and the others, expecting to see the cannons, soldiers, and the dreaded Nauvoo Legion. But there was nothing.

They rode through the crowd directly to the Hamilton Hotel. They dismounted; their horses were confiscated; and they were escorted the two and a half blocks to the jail. The jailer led them to an upstairs bedroom that would serve as their cell. It was a plain room with virtually no furniture, only a single bed and thin mattress, three chairs, and a small writing desk. Two windows overlooked the square where the militia congregated. There were no bars on the windows—nothing to prevent the prisoners from jumping to the ground fifteen feet below them. Nothing but the bayonets.

None of them slept well that night.

The next morning they were taken across the town square to the courthouse, a stage-set affair from the Wild West. The five prisoners were pushed through the throng of armed men who crammed the square. They were struck, prodded, and spat upon as the scrum pressed forward. One ugly face after another thrust itself before them to insult or spit on them. Ez's legs wobbled, but he stared straight ahead and forced himself to keep walking.

Sitting in the courtroom that day for the preliminary hearing were William Law, The Reverend, and others who had once been quite fond of Joseph. They testified against him with grim enthusiasm. Law believed Joseph had been the Prophet, but was on the threshold of destroying all that was good with the Mormon faith. He felt justified in doing what he could to stop him with the clear conscience of a true believer. The Reverend's testimony was especially vitriolic, emphasizing Joseph's claim that he would be God one day. This testimony was apropos of nothing relevant to the proceeding, but

The Reverend was determined to put Joseph's blasphemy on record. Both men believed they were doing God's bidding.

The hearing was a sham. Bail for the charge of inciting a riot was set at an impossibly high sum (this was a formality: a warrant had been sworn out charging Joseph and his brother Hyrum for treason, a crime for which bail could not be set in any event). The prisoners were then shoved back through the throng of angry, drunk militiamen to their cell on the other side of the square.

Governor Ford arrived at the jail to meet with the Prophet. Joseph was taken downstairs for the meeting. An hour later, the others heard him clomping back up the wooden staircase to their cell. Ez tried to decipher if it was the clomping of a man in good spirits, or bad, and it sounded like bad. But what could really be told from the sound of clomping? The jailer let Joseph back into the cell and locked the sturdy wooden door.

Joseph fell to the bed. The others were anxious to know what the Governor had said, but Joseph said nothing.

"Well, spit it out!" said Hyrum. "What'd he say?"

Joseph sat up. "He said he's going to Nauvoo tomorrow to address the Saints. He's worried they'll march here to Carthage and start a riot. He wants to calm them down before they do. I begged him to let me go with him, because I would tell the Saints to let the law take its course, and he agreed. He gave me his word that he wouldn't leave without me. As long as the Governor's here, we'll be safe. The mob won't try anything with him around." Joseph paused. "If he breaks his promise and leaves without me," he said, "they'll kill us."

It was dark and hot that night in jail. But that isn't what kept them up. And it wasn't the noise of the militia they could hear outside the open window; their tin pots clinking as they talked around their campfires. It was their cold fear.

The state militia was there to protect them from the mobs. At least that's what Governor Ford had said. But the prisoners knew otherwise. They could hear voices over the crackling pop of the fires and the snoring down below. The voices said things like "fraud" and "golden bible" and "lynchin'." Ez walked over to the window and looked down. He couldn't make out faces, only the cigars, the glowing intensifying with each inhale, like fireflies. One of them said, "Look, there's one of 'em now!" and he raised his arms to the window like he was holding a musket, stumbling drunk, and said *"Bang!"* He roared with vulgar laughter. "Don't you worry, Old Joe, we won't let 'em getcha! Will we boys?" and he laughed again.

Eventually the men outside drifted off and it was quiet except for the occasional pop from their fires or one of them snoring, farting, or rustling up to relieve himself. Joseph took the mattress off the bed and laid it on the floor next to Ez.

"You awake?" he whispered.

"Can't sleep."

"Me neither."

They lay on their backs looking up at the ceiling. Willard was mumbling something and Ez didn't care to listen, those being Willard's private thoughts.

"Do you think we went too far?" asked Joseph.

Ez didn't answer for a while. "Why did you do it?"

"I only did what the Lord commanded."

"All this time I've supported you, Joseph. I've never talked behind your back about any of this, not even once. But now it's just us—just you and me. So I'll say it. You ask me if we went too far. No, *we* didn't go too far, but you did. And you blame it on God."

"All the ancient prophets did it. I was no different."

"Come on, Joseph, that's hogwash. And so what if they did? You were looking for an excuse, and now look what's happened."

"But God requires that of His chosen people, and His Prophet."

"Shut up! That's enough. Not now. I shouldn't have to die because you wanted all those girls."

Joseph was silent. "Then it will be God's will. I will die tomorrow or I will live to complete my mission."

"*You* will live or *you* will die. Listen to yourself. What about me? And how about Emma? Or Willard over there, who might be dragged out of this goddamned cell and lynched tomorrow? Have you thought about him? What have *we* done to deserve this? All you talk about is what God wants for *you*, or how *you're* being picked on." Ez didn't care if Joseph was the King of the Kingdom, or not. Not when he was lying in that cell waiting to be shot.

"I'm sorry, Ez." It was barely a whisper. "You're right; I got too big for my britches, and now look what I've done. I tried to follow God's lead, I really did. I've hurt a lot of people. Okay? You don't think I know that?"

"Our lives aren't over, Joseph. Not yet."

"It feels like it."

"Ford will demand we get a fair trial. He knows the Saints will riot if we don't go home in one piece."

"God willing," Joseph said and was quiet again. Finally he said, "I've hurt the people closest to me. And for what? So I could be a big wheel? Look at me now—some big wheel, huh?" His voice whistled from his chipped tooth when he said "wheel."

"Think of all we've been through," said Ez. "We're barely thirty-nine years old. We have our whole lives ahead of us."

Joseph leaned up on his elbow to face Ez, who couldn't see his face in the dark. "If we get out of this alive, I'm going to make it right. I swear it on my life."

Ez did not respond.

"Do you believe me?"

"Yeah."

"Because it's the truth, so help me God."

The next day dawned hot and muggy. Visitors came and went, but they were searched each time. A daring Mormon convert visited and was searched, but they didn't check his boots. As soon as he was inside the cell, he slipped a small, single barrel pistol from his boot.

"It's only a single shooter," he said "but it'll knock the brains outta the scum."

"Let me have it," Hyrum said, and took it.

About noon, Brother Wheelock faced the heckling, surly crowd and was admitted to the cell. Wheelock was not searched, even though he wore a baggy coat. Did the jailer simply forget, or did the hand of Providence cover his eyes? They wondered, for inside the coat, hidden within the lining, was a loaded pepperbox pistol.

"Got me this six-shooter. Here, you can have it," Brother Wheelock said and handed it over to the Prophet. It was shiny and black, and seemed to draw all the light in the cell to it. Joseph took it with a steady hand. "God bless you, Brother."

Willard, his bulk difficult to lose in a crowd, was allowed to leave long enough to send his family a message. When he returned he was completely out of breath. His huge frame wheezed and he was drenched in sweat.

"Joseph!"

"What is it?"

"I just found out . . . ." He tried to catch his breath with each syllable, for he had run for the jail and up the stairs.

"Spit it out!" yelled Hyrum.

"Let him catch his breath," Joseph said patiently.

"It's the governor."

"What about him?"

"He . . . left . . . for Nauvoo . . . about an hour ago."

Joseph collapsed to the bed. They knew the mob would now do whatever evil it wanted with the Governor out of town. Hyrum screamed that Ford would burn in hell for the betrayal. Joseph scribbled an order for the Nauvoo Legion to come save them at any cost, even if it meant breaking down the jail, or firing into the militia. He gave the note to Brother Wheelock who was still wearing the baggy coat.

"Ride as hard as you can to Nauvoo! Tell them it's an emergency! Hurry! And God speed, Brother."

A few minutes later, the captain of the militia climbed the stairs with three of his men. He ordered all visitors from the room at the point of a bayonet. All that remained in the cell were Joseph, Hyrum, Willard, John, and Ez.

It was precisely four o'clock in the afternoon.

"I don't want to die!" Willard sobbed. "I heard them out the window! One of the companies left and I heard them say they'd be back in an hour to finish us off!"

"We must trust in the Lord," said Joseph. "We have no other choice."

"But you're the Prophet! Can't you do something? We can't just sit here and let them kill us!"

"Get a hold of yourself!" Hyrum yelled at Willard.

Willard wiped his eyes with his sleeve. He wanted to be brave, but they were going to die and they all knew it. They heard a pair of boots on the stairs. There was the jiggling of keys and the jailer opened the door. He held a bottle of wine, and two pipes of tobacco.

"Here, go on and take yourselves some comfort. I figure it's the least I could do for ya."

The bottle was passed around. They listened hard, hoping to hear the Legion's approach to rescue them, but knowing it couldn't possibly arrive for at least three more hours. In the meantime, they smoked the pipe and tried to think of anything else but the mob outside their cage.

"If I am to be a martyr for the kingdom, I will do it willingly," Joseph said as he turned the loaded pistol around and around in his hands, "like a lamb to the slaughter."

"The Legion will come," Hyrum said, but without conviction.

And then they heard it, the faint sound and quiver of the earth's rumble—the sound of horses pounding toward them. Two hundred of the mob, their faces painted black with wet gunpowder, thundered toward them. They were trapped with nowhere to run.

Ez ran to the window to jump, but there were at least twenty of them standing in the yard, directly below the window, with their muskets pointing up. The late day sun glinted off the silver bayonets attached to the end of their long muzzles. Ez was petrified that if the lead balls missed, those very bayonets would be shoved into him at close range. He practically doubled over at the thought.

The prisoners said nothing. There was no praise to God for making them martyrs, nor pleas for mercy. The only sounds were the bestial screams of the mob. There was no need for Joseph to call upon his power as a Seer to know what appalling evil force was at the door. He stood next to the bed, checking his pistol. Hyrum, who was standing in the middle of the room, was doing the same with his single shooter. Ez found two hickory canes under the bed and gave one of them to Willard who took it, then bent over and retched.

The prisoners heard them explode through the door down below and screamed incoherently at the jailer who was trying to restore order. There was a loud stampede of boots running up the wood staircase. John dropped to his knees in the corner, pleading hysterically for God's mercy. Willard dropped the cane and tried to hide under the bed.

"God, please help us!" Joseph shouted. They rushed to the door and tried to brace it as the first musket ball ripped through. Then another. Willard was now standing on one side of the door and John and Ez were on the other. Joseph was behind Ez, while Hyrum stood in the middle of the room, pointing his pistol at the barricaded door.

A lead ball thudded into Hyrum's face. Blood sprayed from his nose, splattering his white shirt. He stumbled backward, but didn't topple. Three more muskets fired at once through the splintered door. The balls hit him in the chest.

Hyrum fell over, dead.

The mob crowded the landing at the top of the stairs. The noise of gunshots and screaming was like the sound of bloody hell. There was heavy smoke, which made it difficult to see. The smell of gunpowder and fear was overpowering.

The mob finally shoved the splintered door open about a foot, even though the remaining prisoners were pushing against it as best they could. Ez and Willard stood at opposite sides of the door, frantically chopping down at the intruding muskets with the hickory canes. The tips of the bayonets and the fire at the end of their muzzles were now a few feet inside the room.

Joseph pointed his six-shooter over Ez's shoulder through the wedged open door and began firing at point blank into the logjam of murderers crowding the doorway.

"Goddamn! I've been shot!" one of them shouted and fell backward toward the stairs.

Joseph unloaded his pistol into the crowd, and when it was empty he knelt over Hyrum who lay on the floor in a pond of blood. He stood and ran toward the open window. A lead ball thudded into his back just as he was about to jump into the thicket of bayonets below.

"I got him!" one of them shouted from the doorway. "I got Joe!"

Ez felt time slow down. He watched Joseph fall forward, toward the window. The half-inch lead ball had struck him squarely in the back, ripping open his white linen shirt. Blood spurted from the wound as if someone had thrown a cup of wine at his back. The militiamen down below were yelling that they'd finally got him, that they'd finally got Joe Smith.

History would record the events occurring in a matter of seconds, but those seconds would produce oaths of revenge for decades. The mob had now burst through the door and watched it, too. Joseph clung to the windowsill for one, two, three precious seconds. The colonel down below yelled, "Shoot him! Goddammit! Shoot him!" but no one did.

Joseph's fingers lost their grip, and he dropped to the ground.

The mob ran from the cell, tracking Hyrum's blood down the stairs. The air was still smoky and smelled of gunpowder. John had been shot five times, and he stumbled around the room in shock. His wounds were not fatal; one ball hit him in the chest, miraculously, on his pocket watch that saved his life. The clock was stopped forevermore at sixteen minutes after five o'clock. Willard and Ez were only grazed.

Ez looked out the window. All of a sudden, he wasn't afraid of anything. He didn't care that he was standing directly in front of the window with the mob below. They could have easily shot him, but they already had their man. Joseph was crumpled on the ground below the window. He was still alive, moaning and trying to crawl away.

"Joseph!" Ez yelled down to him. The mob looked up at him and then back down at Joseph. One of them grabbed Joseph by the arm and dragged him through the dirt, propping him up against a stone water well about fifteen feet away.

"Joseph!" Ez yelled again. His eyes were open and he slowly rolled his head to look up at the window. The colonel ordered four of his men to line up no more than ten feet from Joseph.

"Don't!" Ez screamed.

"On your ready!" shouted the colonel.

"Joseph! Look at me!" And he did. He stared up at Ez with an expression of, of what, Ez wondered from that day forward. Was it love? Was it hope? Or was it a sardonic resolve that these men were only fulfilling a preordained plan?

"Aim!"

"Joseph! Here I am! Look at me!" Ez wanted Joseph to see the face of someone who loved him more than any other man.

"Fire!"

There was a cracking sound. Joseph shuddered as the musket balls tore through his chest and then his head dropped.

The mob and militia stood in silence for a moment. Perhaps they realized in that awful moment that they had killed God's chosen Prophet, or maybe they thought they had finally rid the earth of an evil imposter. They looked around in fear, and ran.

Ez turned to John, who lay on the bed, the flesh of his thigh ripped open to expose the bone. Willard had the shell-shocked look of a sergeant stumbling back from the battlefield. He looked at Ez, who nodded slowly. It was June 27, 1844. The rest of their lives would be measured by this one day, and they knew it.

Ez crouched next to Hyrum and combed the hair from his face with his fingers. The puddle of blood was dark, nearly black, and cooling like drying candle wax. Hyrum still held the pistol in his dead hand. Ez pulled it from his grasp and threw it against the wall. He walked out through the splintered doorway, stepping over two of the men that Joseph had shot. One was clearly dead and the other was still writhing in that fragile space between life and death. His gunpowder-blackened face looked like a demon from hell.

It was quiet downstairs, the jailer having fled. Ez stumbled outside. He made his way to Joseph and knelt next to him in the dirt. He pulled his friend into his arms and rocked him. Ez opened his eyes to see a few strangers standing nearby, gawking at the scene. "Get out of here!" he yelled unkindly, for they had done nothing wrong. He picked Joseph up in his huge arms, carried him back into the jail, and laid him on the braided rug in the jailer's room. He climbed the stairs, again stepping over the dying man, and picked up Hyrum. He carried him down the stairs and laid him next to his brother. It was so quiet. He dropped to his knees and put his forehead to his best friend's chest.

"Why, God? Oh, dear God, why?"

EPILOGUE

Thousands of Mormons lined the dirt road as the bodies of their prophet and his brother wound their way to the Nauvoo Mansion in the back of a wagon. The doctor stripped and cleaned the bodies, then stuffed cotton balls into the gunshot wounds and stitched them back together. Impressions were then taken for their death masks. They dressed the two martyrs in white and placed them into velvet-covered caskets. The word "martyr" was affixed to the two men from that time forth, a term that incensed The Reverend, for it implied they'd gone to the grave gracefully, and not in a gun battle. It was easy for The Reverend to argue semantics; a gang of murderous outlaws hadn't been shooting at *him*.

The caskets were carried to the mansion's salon and placed against the west facing windows, which overlooked the Mississippi River, Joseph's favorite view. Fifteen thousand mourners filed past the open caskets to pay their last respects. Some wept hysterically, while others were left to melancholy reflection on the man who was greater than any man they had ever known. There were still others who figured, with sober regret, that Joseph might have had it coming.

Rachel clung to Ez. This was the second time she had nearly lost him. She was heartbroken for Emma, and tried to comfort her, but Emma would not be comforted. She had worn the look of a disappointed woman for too long. Now her husband had been taken from her, and this, for the final time. She was bitter, about many things, but especially The Principle. When she was asked a few years later where the doctrine of plural marriage had come from, she responded, "Straight from hell!" For the remainder of her long life, she did all she could to erase Joseph's involvement in it. Indeed, she inexplicably insisted Joseph had never taken any other wives. It was a curious thing to insist, but an understandable one.

There were fifteen thousand stories of Joseph, for each person claimed to know him. He was a man of the people, and it was difficult to overstate his relevance. He was the most important figure in their lives and became even more important after his death. Nearly everyone had left something behind to follow him: a family, a job, a homeland. He was the earthly hero of the Saints. And now he was dead.

Joseph's death was national news. The *New York Herald* shouted in its headline, "Thus Ends Mormonism!" Its pronouncement that "the death of the modern Mahomet will seal the fate of Mormonism," was premature, for it underestimated the power of martyrdom. The legendary newspaper editor, Horace Greely, understood this when he wrote, "The blood of Joseph Smith, spilled by murderous hands, will be like the fabled dragon's teeth sown broadcast, that everywhere sprang up armed men."

Governor Ford understood it, too. His eulogy was written with overstated cynicism:

> Thus fell Joe Smith, the most successful impostor in modern times. His natural gifts were obscured by his lusts, and his love of power. The Christian world which has heretofore regarded Mormonism with silent contempt may yet see its uprising.
>
> An eloquent orator may be able to attract crowds by the thousands who are ever ready to hear the sounding brass and tinkling cymbal, and may succeed in breathing new life into Mormonism and make the name of the martyred Joseph

> ring as loud as the mighty name of Christ itself. And in that sad event, I will be the humble governor of an obscure state who would otherwise be forgotten in a few years, but would be dragged down to posterity with an immortal name, like Pontius Pilate, hitched to the memory of a miserable imposter.

Enemies of the church hoped the Mormons would retaliate and kill Governor Ford, whom the Saints believed just *had* to be involved. Indeed, the Saints salivated for that revenge, but they knew that trying to settle the score by assassination or force of arms would empower the neighboring militias to descend upon Nauvoo with self-righteous justification. Besides, they were without a leader—most of the apostles had been sent away to campaign for Joseph Smith For President. So they held their fire and prayed to God that He would be their Avenger.

There was the question of what to do with Joseph's body. "You know," Brother Huntington said, "they won't leave the Prophet alone. They'll come for his body and make a mockery of it. As God is my witness, they'll stop at nothing."

"I heard rumors they tried to cut his head off there in Carthage and Brother Ezra Wells is the only thing that stopped them."

So they hatched a plan. As soon as the last mourner left, they hid the bodies in the mansion, filled the caskets with sandbags, and put them into the back of a wagon. Several thousand grieving Saints followed behind on the slow walk to the Nauvoo City Cemetery.

Just after midnight, a group of secret pallbearers sneaked out the back door of the mansion with the corpses in tow. They crossed Water Street under the cover of darkness and dug temporary graves by lantern light. Once the holes were dug, they lowered the caskets inside. They threw stones and rubbish on top of the freshly dug graves to hide them.

Several midnights later, Emma had the coffins dug up again. This time they were hauled about a block away, to the two-story log home where Joseph and Emma first lived upon their arrival in Nauvoo. There was a small shack next to the log home. The men lifted the shack, dug two graves, re-buried the caskets, and replaced the shack where it had been, on top of the graves. No one was the wiser. Nearly eighty years later, they were moved once more, some twenty feet farther up the hill because of the potential for flooding. Joseph and Hyrum were finally allowed to rest in peace.

Factions within the church splintered off following Joseph's death. The anti-polygamist crowd left first. There was a political battle for the remaining Saints, but Brigham Young eventually prevailed, taking the majority of Joseph's followers with him. When their enemies saw the church had not disintegrated after Joseph's murder, and that polygamy was alive and well within their fair state, they renewed their persecution until, finally, the Mormons agreed to leave Illinois for good two years later.

Some said Joseph's death was serendipitous. The church was reeling and would have imploded if Joseph hadn't been murdered when he was. Would the church have survived? Would Brigham Young have been allowed to show his greatness if the musket balls of Carthage had missed their target? These questions are academic—who can say what might have been?

The Mormon pioneers' trek westward from Nauvoo to the Salt Lake Valley remains one of the most impressive and courageous epics in American history.

None of Joseph's children made the trip west. His parents and none of his siblings did either. And neither did Emma. She was remarried, to a non-Mormon, and operated the Nauvoo Mansion as a hotel. By that time Nauvoo had become a ghost town. The temple was nearly burned to the ground by an arsonist, leaving only the limestone walls standing. Shortly thereafter, a tornado ripped through the deserted town and finished it off. Those who saw God's mysterious hand in everything from the miraculous to the mundane insisted the tornado was the finger of God tracing the funnel's route, because He didn't want His holy temple desecrated by unworthy Gentiles.

Ezra began to write his history at the ripe old age of eighty-three, upon the urging of his daughter, Elizabeth. "Dad," she'd told him, "you're one of the last people who actually knew the Prophet. You should write it all down, for posterity."

Ez wondered what the statute of limitations was for disclosing the secrets of a dead person. Or was there a statute at all? He knew this was an ambitious project for a man of any age. But he had much to say, so he picked up a pen in his hand that looked like the root of an old grapevine, and began.

June 19, 1889.

Elizabeth has been kind enough to take me in. She worries about me and says I shouldn't be alone since I lost Rachel a few years ago to pneumonia. I think it makes her feel better. Rachel's death was the most difficult challenge of my life. I lie awake at night wondering where she is. Is she really in heaven? Does it really exist? I believe so, but it seems so far away. I would have spent every waking hour since she died climbing to her on these wobbly legs of mine, one rung at a time, but there is no ladder tall enough. So, I figure my time is better spent writing my story.

I now sit on Elizabeth's porch overlooking the valley. The sun is almost down. It's low enough now that I can look at it without hurting my eyes. I can only see the top half of the sun, resting on the jagged edge of the Oquirrh Mountain range. In the daylight hours, the range looks two-dimensional, as if someone painted it on a giant piece of canvas. But when the sun gets low in the sky, the shadows reveal peaks and hills stretching far out to the west like rows of purple waves. Now I can only see the last sliver of it hanging up there over the border of Nevada. Now it dips into the mountain. And now it's gone.

Those mountains guard the west side of the Great Salt Lake Valley, here in Utah. From far away they look so grand and magnificent. But I've hiked damned near all of them and up close they look different to me; they're mostly just ordinary dirt and rocks. It seems that's the way it so often is; when you get up close, the view is sometimes less magnificent—you see flaws that you didn't see from far away. Other times the closer you get the opposite happens, the more magical things appear to be.

I've lived in the Salt Lake Valley forty years now, and this is where I'll die. It was hard enough getting here and there's nowhere else I'd rather be. I came over in 1847 in a wagon train, along with the first wave of Mormon pioneers. Well, actually I walked. I was strong back then, big and strong. And I was driven by what I believed was the truth. I still am. But I'm eighty-three years old now and the sun is setting on me, too.

Last week I took the streetcar downtown to the Tabernacle to listen to our famous choir. The Tabernacle sits next to the Salt Lake Temple that is almost completed after nearly forty years of construction. The final spire is finished and I'm told there are plans to put a large golden statue of Angel Moroni on top.

The Tabernacle that evening was filled to capacity. Midway through the performance, the choir sang one of Mormonism's favorite hymns honoring Joseph. Their voices thundered as one:

Praise to the man who communed with Jehovah!
Jesus anointed that Prophet and Seer
Blessed to open the last dispensation
Kings shall extol him, and nations revere
Hail to the Prophet, ascended to heaven!
Traitors and tyrants now fight him in vain
Mingling with Gods, he can plan for his brethren

Death cannot conquer the hero again

My mind drifted to all the fun Joseph and I once had, and all the miracles, sorrows, persecutions, and joy. I looked around the crowd. No one there had ever met him; few were even alive when he was shot. Yet there were tears in their eyes as they reflected on the polished memory of their martyred hero.

Praise to his memory, he died as a martyr
Honored and blest be his ever-great name
Long shall his blood, which was shed by assassins
Plead unto heaven while the earth lauds his fame

I wish they had known the real man, the man who was imperfect and full of life, and not the Prophet they demand him to be. I wish they had known the uneducated lad who rose to such heights, the one with the grand vision and the optimism of eternity.

Great is his glory and endless his priesthood
Ever and ever the keys he will hold
Faithful and true he will enter his kingdom
Crowned in the midst of the prophets of old
Hail to the prophet, ascended to heaven!
Traitors and tyrants now fight him in vain
Mingling with Gods he can plan for his brethren
Death cannot conquer the hero again

I wanted to stand up and shout: "I knew him! He was my best friend! He was brave, but he was afraid. He was strong, but he was weak. He was kind, but he had a temper. He was loyal and loving, but he could be cold and calculating. He was self-centered, but he was selfless, too. Honor him, and honor what he did, but please, do not worship him." Those in the audience would have probably written me off as some old lunatic.

We finally made our peace with plural marriage: Rachel, Dorthea, and me. But plural marriage continues to hang around our necks like an iron yoke. We are petitioning for statehood here in the Utah Territory, and the federal government tells us they'll let us in if we abandon polygamy. It will come to a head soon enough, but probably fifty years too late for some people, including Emma and others who were driven away because of it.

Dorthea passed away nearly twenty years ago, and when she did, Rachel wept along with me. Dorthea was a good woman who was only following Joseph's counsel. Same with me. When Brigham Young told me I should take on another wife, I refused. I figured I didn't need to keep proving I could face God's crucible.

Joseph was murdered in the prime of his life and will always be remembered that way. He has been idolized and worshipped, reviled and condemned, to the point that his personality has practically disappeared. His followers have scraped off the rough edges, polishing them to an impossible sheen. He has been cast in bronze in the town square, for every famous man should have a statue. Joseph stands tall, regal, young, and handsome. He holds a Book of Mormon. His hair and coat are perfect, and his countenance is devoid of blemish, or sin. For that is the Joseph to be remembered. And it may be that legacy which haunts the likes of Governors Lilburn Boggs and Thomas Ford, neither of whom have their own statue, or fame, beyond their persecution of Joseph Smith. Therefore, perhaps it is a reasonable booby prize that Ford be given the last word on Joseph:

> It must not be supposed that the pretended Prophet practiced the tricks of a common impostor. He was full of levity, even to boyish romping. He dressed like a dandy, and at times, drank like a sailor and swore like a pirate. He could, as occasion required, be exceedingly meek in his deportment, and then again as rough and boisterous as a highway robber, always being

> able to deftly satisfy his audience. At times he could put on the air of a penitent sinner, as if feeling the deepest humiliation for his sins. At such times he would call for the prayers of the brethren on his behalf, with a wild and fearful earnestness.
>
> He was a full six feet high, strongly built, and uncommonly well muscled. He was indebted for his influence over an ignorant people to the superiority of his physical vigor, his charm, his great cunning, and his surprising intellect.
>
> His followers were divided into the leaders and the led. The first division had nothing to lose by deserting the known religions, and carved out a new one of their own. They were mostly infidels, who, holding all other religions in derision, believed that they had as good a right as Mahomet to create one for themselves, and impose it upon the labor of their dupes. Those of the second division were the credulous men and women whose easy belief and admiring natures are always the victims of novelty.
>
> Some of the Mormons were abandoned rogues, who had taken shelter in Nauvoo as a convenient place for the headquarters of their villainy, while others were good, honest, industrious people, who were the sincere victims of an artful delusion. Such as these were more the proper objects of pity than persecution. With them, their religious belief was a kind of insanity, and certainly no greater calamity can befall a human being, than to have a mind so constituted as to be made the sincere dupe of a religious impostor.

Millions of people now reject that indictment of the Prophet, honest believers who have searched their souls for confirmation that Joseph was, indeed, the man who communed with Jehovah.

Author's Note

Many biographers have chronicled Joseph Smith's life, the majority of whom are members of the Mormon Church, and seem reluctant to reflect upon his shortcomings. Devout Mormons consider Joseph Smith to be the most righteous man who ever lived on earth, next only to Jesus Christ. For that reason, they may take offense at my portrayal of him. I hope not, for such is not my intent.

I was born and raised a Mormon. I was indoctrinated into the faith of my parents from the day I was born. I did not choose to become a Mormon any more than my parents made that choice for themselves. My ancestral line of Mormonism began with my great-great-great-grandfather who knew Joseph Smith, and made the arduous pioneer trek across the plains to Utah after Joseph was murdered.

Growing up in Utah, I was untroubled by incredible tales of angels and golden tablets. To the extent there may have been whispered misgivings about the authenticity of Joseph's revelations (many of which are nearly comical to the non-believer), no one spoke of them openly. To do so would have been religious heresy. Everyone I knew believed, so I assumed it was the truth.

After graduating high school, I went on a two-year Mormon mission along with the rest of my friends. At the time, I knew nothing of Joseph's mummy scrolls, his peep stones, or Zelf. I assumed the earth was 6,000 years old and Darwin was a kook. It wasn't until I reached my late twenties that I peeked into Joseph's unvarnished history. When I did, I discovered what I believe to be a profound, consistent, and methodical effort by the church to misrepresent his history and the origin of Mormonism. The Joseph that emerged from my study was unfamiliar to me. He was still immensely talented and charming, but also incorrigibly flawed.

When I left the church, my parents were heartbroken. I didn't talk about it much because I didn't want to disappoint them, but my faithlessness was evident. My mom often said to me, "Honey, the embers of faith still burn inside you. I know they do." She was partially correct—the embers still burn deep down, but they are the embers of cultural angst, not of belief.

I still find Joseph to be an extraordinary figure. Handsome, charismatic, warm, and brilliant, Joseph was larger than life to his people. It is not hyperbolic to say he may be the most iconic figure in American history that hardly anyone knows about. Joseph was murdered when he was only thirty-nine years old, and yet he accumulated a remarkable resume in his shortened life. With limited formal education he wrote the Book of Mormon when he was twenty-three. A little more than ten years later he had become the mayor of Nauvoo, the second largest city in Illinois, rivaling the size of Chicago at the time. He was also Nauvoo's municipal court judge, architect, and the leading merchant. Joseph was the General of the Nauvoo Legion, an army of his own making, which boasted nearly 4,000 soldiers (in comparison, the entire United States Army had approximately 15,000 at the time). He was also the trustee of the Mormon Church, his sole creation, which had nearly twenty thousand members at the time of his assassination. He was a candidate for President of the United States. He was the husband to over forty women. And he had himself anointed King of the Kingdom.

People loved Joseph. I can only imagine how warm and charismatic he must have been to persuade nearly twenty thousand people to follow him through hardship and ridicule, and millions more to worship his name after he died. But Joseph's legacy is complicated. The church he started with just two members in upstate New York is now a multi-billion dollar corporate enterprise, with over fifteen million members, that does mostly good in the world.

Modern Mormons cringe at the mention of Joseph's polygamy, a practice they are associated with to this day. Utah obtained statehood about fifty years after Joseph's death, but only on the condition that the Mormons renounce polygamy. Splinter groups of fundamentalist Mormons continue to practice polygamy today, claiming the main branch of the church sold out to modernity, an act that would have caused Joseph Smith to roll over in his grave. Polygamy is the ugliest smudge on Joseph's legacy, but the stickier corners of Mormonism are many.

Other religions have begun to retreat from their staunch literalistic claims involving miraculous stories of angels and visions. This they presumably do in view of the steady advance of science that makes those claims, and those who make them, look foolish. However, the Mormon Church has actually reasserted its belief in Joseph's supernatural claims. They do so at their own peril in my opinion, because it seems difficult to imagine such claims can long survive the scrutiny of science and a concession to logic. The recent Prophet of the Mormon Church stated: "If the First Vision did not occur, then we are involved in a great sham. It is just that simple."

And therein lies the rub.

My challenge in writing this book was to relate Joseph's story without the sugar coat of blind faith, and to do it in such a way that the reader would not dismiss it as a farce. Joseph's claims are so incredible that those who know nothing of Mormonism's colorful origin may struggle to believe this tale is really Mormonism's story. Many devout Mormons will scoff at my portrayal of Joseph and retreat to the comfort of their own favorite histories.

Joseph wasn't the first talented and charismatic man to claim the status of Prophet, and he won't be the last. Those who see Joseph as a true prophet of God are determined to see only the good in him, and those who see him as a narcissistic opportunist are determined to see only the bad. But Joseph Smith was a complex man who lived a remarkable life. Even his foes must begrudgingly acknowledge his originality, intellect, charisma, and imagination. Joseph, and Joseph alone, was the architect of the most popular religion ever born on American soil.

Warren Driggs is an attorney who lives with his family in Salt Lake City. He is the author of *A Tortoise in the Road* and *Old Scratch*. He can be contacted through his website at www.warrendriggs.com.

70439953R00246

Made in the USA
San Bernardino, CA
01 March 2018